I EAT MUSHROOMS FOR BREAKFAST

C J POWELL

THANK YOU

Thank you for buying my book 'I Eat Mushrooms For Breakfast'. I hope you enjoy reading it as much as I enjoyed writing it. If you could take two minutes to leave a review once you're done that would help the book be seen by others and helps me as an author.

Sign up to the no-spam mailing list at my website - https://cjpowellauthor.com/iemfb

If you do you'll be in with the chance to receive my next novel for free in advance of publishing. I also send out deals and offers on my other books.

Thanks!

Chris x

IN THE BEGINNING (AT the place where we are going to begin), there was just Blue Flower, Red Fruit, and their living, breathing art. They wanted for nothing. Life was perfect. A stunning symbiosis of animal and fungus and plant and thought.

But then Red Fruit assimilated the wrong human, found ambition, grew discontented, and fucked it all up.

DEEP DIVE

"I really want you all thinking outside the box if we're going to move the needle on this one," said Stan Delaney to the gathered room. He clicked the lid on his marker and looked at the wonky graph he'd just drawn on the whiteboard. What the bloody hell was that? A mess is what it was.

It was hot in here and he was starting to feel a little faint with it. He'd been feeling a little faint ever since they'd arrived on Rosen-54. Faint and fuzzy, like his head was filled with fog.

"There's low hanging fruit here, and it's a win-win for all of us if we can just lean in and ... uh"—he tried to blink away the grey circle that had been growing in the centre of his vision for the last few days—"and pick it."

The three other heads of the colony just stared through him. Sally Marsh was dribbling.

God, was everyone on this rock braindead? Where was the get-up-and-go? Where was the gumption?

He rubbed his eyes. The bottom line was, if they didn't get the mine operational within the next week ... something was going to happen.

He screwed up his face. What was going to happen?

"Ginny?" He lifted a hand to the waiting tea lady. "Make us some coffees, would you? Think we're all feeling a bit muggy in here." He loosened his tie a notch. Not too much, just enough to show solidarity with his melting staff.

"Ginny? Did you hear me?"

The poor girl jumped. Her eyes had been open, but she hadn't been there.

"Right away," she said with a hoarse croak.

Maybe a little walk might help. Some fresh air. Or at least, as fresh as was possible in this dump.

"Perhaps we should go check out the site. See what's taking them so long, then maybe pop in at the laboratoire." He linked his fingers in front of his face in a little steeple of togetherness as Ginny slowly began filling cardboard disposables in the corner. "Synergise. Clear our heads. Get these ducks in a row." When none of them moved, he let his hands fall to his sides. "What do you say?"

It would be their first proper trip down the mine since they'd landed at the colony two weeks ago.

Peterson pressed himself to stand. It looked like a lot of effort.

"Sure thing, SD. It'll be good for us to show face down there."

Beads of sweat stood out on his brow. He mopped it with his shirtsleeve. At least Peterson was singing from the same hymn sheet, even if he was a little slow.

The other two didn't even move. Stan clapped his hands together twice.

"Pat, Sally, come on."

The women rose slowly without a word. Ginny trudged over and pressed a coffee into each of their hands, then returned to her tray for the last two.

They took a hover-cat despite the trip to the mine being a five-minute walk from the plaza. He didn't think they'd make it otherwise.

This was his third time heading up an excavation, but it still impressed Stan how the bods in engineering could get a full colony up and running within a month. Print the buildings from orbit, fill it full of breathable atmos, then just power it up with solar. Boom!

Rosen-54 should have been a particularly quick win. Sunny climate, fruitful soil, and a huge mineral deposit just beneath the surface.

Security-wise it was a doddle. A lot of bugs, sure. What good planet didn't have a lot of bugs? But nothing big nearby. Nothing with claws and teeth and acidic blood. And quite a distance from Gerknorg-infested space.

They should be drilling down there already.

He'd hoped to hit the ground running, but someone had really dropped the ball here. Why was it taking so long? The mine should have been fully functional a week before their arrival. Whoever had lumped him in with this bunch of slugs was going to get a talking to. This was nothing like his last project on Rosen-42. They'd got all the product out of the ground in record time. Well, not him exactly. The miners. But he'd overseen it all. He'd been in charge. He'd been the one who'd walked away with the tasty bonus. That place was a flourishing little homestead now.

Maybe he should have stayed. Got himself a penthouse suite. Found himself a pretty girl or a handsome guy. Settled.

Pah! Where was the fun in that? No one had ever been remembered for settling. He had goals and ambitions. Onwards and ever upwards, as Thaddeus Rosenhalt would say. Live forever or die trying!

He fanned his face and glanced at the three heads in the back of the cat. Pat was asleep. Her spilled coffee lay in her lap, her white suit trousers now stained an unsettling brown. Peterson and Sally, straight-faced and staring into nothing, hadn't even noticed.

Stan nodded towards Pat. "Sal, help her out, would you?"

"Oh." Sally turned, picked up the cup, and just held it while resuming her gormless stare into the unknown.

Christ. These people. Something had to be done. Maybe an away day. Something with paintballs or segways.

He pressed his eyes closed and turned back to face the way they were heading. Their destination stood at the end of the road like a giant hole-less donut. Their sole purpose for being here. The deep mineral mine. The building that capped it was a glorified airlock, there to stop any of the planet's natural atmosphere from getting in when the miners went down to excavate.

On their left, they passed the two-storey laboratoire building. Maybe those science geeks inside were holding things up. Studying the effects of the atmosphere processors on the colonists hardly seemed important enough to halt the excavation, but Sergio Angel had given them highest priority.

There was a disconnect here. Someone wasn't telling him something. But there was a deadline set by the company and it was his job to meet it. It was his prerogative to exceed it if he could. Impress those above him. Show them what he was made of. And Stan Delaney was made of some solid stuff. He just needed to find out what got these people going and get them motivated.

The quartet suited up and decontaminated. Their guide was some bent-backed veteran. Dead behind the eyes inside his own mining suit. Thick ginger hair grew from his nostrils. The notches on his helmet suggested he'd worked on eleven other excavations before this one. He'd paid his dues.

Stan liked a man who worked hard. They were useful.

The man didn't say anything. Just led them down the corridor to the elevator, punched the button, and stood in the corner while they descended.

"How's it looking down there?" asked Stan.

For a long moment the old miner said nothing, but, just as Stan was about to ask again, he nodded and in heavily accented English said, "Oh, it is OK."

Stan hummed. It wasn't OK. It was pretty far from OK.

He allowed himself a minute to lean against the wall. His head was throbbing. He'd go see the doc after this. Maybe get something for the lethargy.

The other three slouched in the centre of the lift like unpressed suits. Maybe he should fire them. Get some new staff in. He wasn't asking them to reinvent the wheel, just to do their jobs. Presumably jobs they'd done well before, otherwise why were they here?

The doors peeled back, and he stepped into the murky darkness of the misted mineshaft. The air was thick with a strange, red-tinged fog. Black stone ceilings, cut with lasers, were held up with unbreakable metal supports.

It was really a job for androids this, but in his infinite business wisdom, Thaddeus Rosenhalt had hired humans and received a massive tax break. What a legend.

Stan was proud to call him a mentor. Not that he'd ever met him. Thaddeus didn't have time to grace the colonies with his presence. But Stan had read all three of his books and had his fourth, *So You Want To Live Forever?* on pre-order. The man was a genius. A guru.

The old miner pushed past and ambled down a corridor dimly lit with hanging yellow bulbs. His scraping footsteps reverberated along the hall like the hissing of a snake.

"Oh, this is the way, is it?" said Stan, trying to get something out of him.

The man didn't answer. Didn't even turn. Probably deaf from all that time spent drilling.

There was no expected sound of cutting ahead, nor the friendly banter of working men. That was top banter. Something Stan was no longer party to since becoming the boss. He missed it. It reminded him of school. Nights in the dorms playing pillow fights with the lads. Rugger on the old muddy field. Throwing rocks at the poor off the top deck of the hover-bus on class outings. Ribbing the new boys until they cried or shit themselves in abject terror.

Happy times. Better times.

He sighed and glanced at his wrist, forgetting his new timepiece, an additional bonus for his sterling work on Rosen-42, was covered up by his respiration suit. It was an hour after lunch at least. If the miners weren't working now, then that explained a lot.

He'd have to reprimand them for this. No bunch of lazy miners were going to put his ambition at risk. They wouldn't undermine his goals.

Onwards and ever upwards.

Something pulsed red in the darkness at the far end of the corridor. The old man sped up as he led them towards it. His silhouette seemed to straighten as he came to the end.

"What is this?" said Stan as he stepped onto a slim platform that descended while it curved around the edge of a huge open expanse.

The cavern spread out all around, fading into the darkness. The furthest walls hidden in a soupy red-black fog. Giant fleshy pillars loomed throughout, their tops hidden in the gloom.

The miners weren't supposed to be digging caverns. Not yet. Just preparing the mine for extraction. This was all wrong. If there had been a problem, an obstacle or something which had needed navigating, then he should have been notified. Perhaps this cavern had already been here.

"Hey?" he called after the old man, who was halfway down the ramp. He didn't look back. Stan quickened his step to catch up. "Why didn't you tell me about this?" he asked.

The man looked back. "Oh, it is OK," he said.

"It is not OK." Stan's cheeks grew hot inside his helmet. He fought to keep his voice low. "You've been wasting company time digging this ... this ... what is this?"

He placed his hands on his hips and scanned the space. A red light throbbed, radiating from a central column and illuminating those around it. It passed down the length of the pillar like a shock of electricity, igniting a storm of sparkling neon-red that travelled across the cavern floor, racing towards him and the others in a forked wave like lightning.

In the new light, he could see the ceiling. At their tops, the columns held large fleshy discs, gilled umbrellas. He squinted in the darkness left behind by the lightning glow. Could just make out a faint residual luminescence throbbing at floor level. Hundreds and thousands of fibrous tendrils connecting each of the pillars, ducking in and out of the rocky ground, spreading here and there like hungry roots hunting for food.

He gasped and steadied himself on the laser-cut wall behind him. Stuck against the walls just below where he stood, linked to the fleshy columns in the centre by those glowing tendrils, were the miners in their suits, encrusted with something—plant-life that appeared to be growing on or from them. Wrapped up like bundled spider meals in those web-like growths.

They had to be dead.

His heart broke into a gallop. He stole a glance back at the others. Peterson looked nervous, but the other two remained slack-jawed, seemingly unfazed by what was going on. The columns throbbed red again, and, in the light, he could see the path back to the surface was now blocked by several more hunched figures in mining suits.

"Well, it looks like you have everything under control," he said to their guide, before retreating a step. This was creepy. Better to reassess from above with a few members of the security team. "We'll just head back."

"Oh, it is OK," said the old man. He lifted his arms and removed his helmet.

"Don't do that! Jesus Christ, the air."

Stan fell back in horror. The hair growing from the man's nose wriggled and writhed reaching for him. There was more coming from his ears.

It wasn't hair.

As one, the miners broke away from the walls below, standing, stalking around to the bottom of the ramp. The others at the top began shuffling their way down, arms outstretched with searching gloved fingers.

Peterson backed into him. He let out a frightened squeak.

This sort of thing wasn't in Stan's wheelhouse at all.

"Oh, it is OK," said the old man.

It wasn't. For Stan Delaney, it would never be OK again.

SLUG'S OFFER

WITHOUT A WORD, THE band ground into another slow, bass-heavy number as Mark took a happy bite of his reconstituted fungus-steak kebab. He didn't dance, but tapped a toe and bobbed his head to show his appreciation to anyone looking.

He glanced around. No one was looking.

The band were good. Or at least, as far as he could tell, they were good. The Captain might say otherwise, but the twenty-or-so dancers that had paired off in front of the quartet were happy to spin around the mud-caked square in the centre of the market like disturbed asteroids in an untethered belt, while around them the warm rains filled the grey sky with a bitter, sulphuric vapour. The tops of the four- or five-storey buildings surrounding the square disappeared into that oppressive jaundiced mist. The music was a drop of sun on another bleak market day.

A ship sailed overhead. A real clunker. It coughed out a cloud of black on its way to the port.

Mark swallowed his mouthful as he jogged after Journey and the Captain. The rubbery meat substitute slumped down his throat like a sweaty child on a slide. The ground beneath his boots was slippery with the rain and the churning of the crowd, but his feet didn't skid.

It was a standard Saturday at the East Artifakt food market. Poor overworked citizens wrapped in brown and grey coveralls, hoods pulled up against the acidic rain, going about their weekly shop. Vendors screaming over the sounds of the crowds and the music, promoting deals on quality produce, trying constantly to outdo their neighbours. The savoury scent of street food sizzling invitingly, frying onions, salty fungus, passable faux-meats. Kids playing chase, rushing and pushing through the crowd at waist height while their anguished mothers called after them to slow down.

Mark jabbed a thumb back at the band as he caught up with his crew.

"They were pretty good."

"Yeah, not bad," said Journey. The engineer didn't slow or turn as he pressed through the sweaty bodies of those that had gathered to watch the busking quartet.

The Captain's grey eyebrows dipped questioningly. "He's beating that guitar like he wants to kill it."

"I don't know," said Mark, "there's something good about it."

"That's passion," said Journey. "It might not be beautiful, but it's art."

Journey towered at least a head over most of the marketgoers. He was a battering ram, moving unobstructed through the shoppers as they haggled and bid. Most people would spot him out of the corner of their eye and just move out of his way, partly on account of the state of his face. Journey's dark features were more scar than skin. The result of something in his childhood that he had never wanted to discuss, and upon which Mark had never felt comfortable enough to press him.

"Hmm. I can't agree with you." The Captain shook his head. "Either way, hurry it along."

"That bellend Slug can wait for us," said Journey. His silver eyes, a pair of neural-prosthetics that he'd had as long as Mark had known him—a result of that mysterious something in his childhood—were fixed on their destination.

The Captain flashed a warning look. "Best not to call our primary source of income a bellend, engineer," he said, flexing two fingers either side of his head. "Don't know who might be listening." He cast his eyes around. Mark did too.

"He needs us," said Journey, not seeming to mind. "No one else can do what we do."

The Captain clapped him on the back and chuckled. A warm cracked sound that cut through the hubbub. "No one else is foolhardy enough to do what we do."

Mark smiled, then passed a longing look back at the quartet of musicians. Despite the rain, the day was swampy and warm. The guitarist had climbed up on to a low wall. He wore no shirt. Long, greying dreads swung from his back as he danced and smashed at his guitar. The percussionist stood behind him, a multitude of drums and cymbals racked on some sort of cradle attached to his waist and shoulders. He banged away with a laid-back rocksteady beat that kept the dancers in constant flow around them. Mark liked the way Journey had put it. It wasn't perfect, but it was sure getting a response.

"I've always wished I could play," said Mark with a sigh.

Journey gave him a sideways look. "You'd have to sit in your room on your own for a long time to be able to play like those guys. You haven't got the attention span."

"Hmm. Maybe."

"Or wealthy enough parents."

Mark wished for many things, but whenever he saw a cool band, the ability to play guitar often flashed to second on the list. Whenever he ate something delicious, the ability to cook might overtake it. Whenever he saw a man dance with a woman, he would long to be that guy with that girl.

He put his hand inside the pack tethered to his front and touched the heavy metal lockbox. The one he always kept close, no matter where he went. It was safer than leaving it behind at his flat with its broken door and the almost non-existent security that he paid for in monthly instalments. Not once but three times, he'd come home after a work trip to find squatters had moved in. He'd had to slap his last biscuit out of the mouth of one guy before booting him out the door.

"How much we getting for this job?" he asked, as he drew level with the Captain.

"I'm hoping no one else will risk a job this big, so I'm going in high with forty per cent for the crew."

Journey grumbled with unease. "Slug doesn't give his info away that cheaply," he said, side-eyeing the Captain. "And someone said he was pissed about something. Any idea what that is?"

The Captain shrugged. "He's always pissed about something." The trio slipped out of the throng and down a shady alley. "Jimmy the Finger's done a runner," he continued, "meaning we have to use one of Slug's hackers, so I'm starting high because I know he'll lowball us."

"What's happened to Jim?" Mark asked.

"Found love apparently," said the Captain. "A beautiful woman approached him in a bar, and he hasn't been heard from since."

"Oh." Mark felt a kick of jealousy. "Lucky Jimmy."

"We'll see," said Journey.

"Let's keep talk of business quiet for now, shall we?" said the Captain.

Without acknowledging him, Mark clocked Slug's man on the corner outside The Den. Felt his bulging red eyes on his back as they passed.

"What's the new hacker like?"

"I hear she's good," said the Captain. "Better than Jimmy."

She! Mark cleared his throat, suddenly nervous.

Journey snorted. "That can't be too hard."

When they reached Slug's place, the Captain raised his fist and knocked at the black wooden door framed by a black brick wall. In the shadow of the alley, if you didn't know it was there, you might miss it.

Several locks clunked, and the door opened a fraction. Ram stared out from the darkness. His muscled girth blocked the view of the corridor beyond.

"What?" He had a rasp in his low voice that sounded a little like stirring cement.

"Here to see Slug," said the Captain.

Without a word, Ram slammed the door. A chain jangled on the other side, then it reopened fully.

"You know where to go." Ram stepped aside.

They traipsed through a gloomy corridor. The once cream, potentially flowery wallpaper was now a patchwork of brown and black damp, peeled back from the decaying walls.

Before they hit the stairs, they had to step over the naked legs of a woman barely out of her teens. She held an empty brown bottle in one hand. Head propped against the chipped skirting board. Vomit on her vest top. Cuts on her arms and feet. Mark held his breath. He glanced back at the doorman. Their eyes met, but Ram's face didn't change.

The Captain knelt and rolled her into the recovery position in case she vomited again. He pressed his lips together as he gave them a look, then proceeded up the stairs.

"Will she be OK like that?" Mark asked.

The Captain shrugged. "Not our problem," he said, although he glanced back with a downturned mouth as they turned the corner of the stairwell.

At the top of the stairs, another door stood open. Its bottom half was splintered.

The trio entered a wide room that spanned the entire top floor of the building. The ceiling stood open to steel eaves covered with reddish brown flakes of corrosion. A huge triangular window made up the far wall. It overlooked the market square as well as half of East Artifakt. In the distance, lit up like a thousand miniature suns, was the port. Ships buzzed around it like flies, coming and going through the brooding yellow-grey clouds that were currently pummelling the city, and possibly the whole continent, with their lightly acidic bombardment. To the left of the window, a darkened corner was home to the neon flashes and 16-bit pings of arcade games and pinball machines.

A couple were playing air hockey on a fluorescent green table. They halted their game to watch the Captain and his crew enter, staring with the slack faces of the perpetually drunk.

"Ah, lads. Come in. Come in."

It took Mark a moment to spot the gang leader. The pale light through the window made the corners of the room seem darker. The ember flicker of a cigarette and the resulting plume of blue smoke gave him away.

"Give me five mins with them, would you?" he said to the woman sat next to him on a seemingly new yet stained leatherette sofa. "Maybe check on your sister. Think she went a little too hard."

The woman stood. She looked a little like the one they'd seen unconscious below. She wasn't wearing much. Mark tried to look anywhere else. Slug made an unpleasant grab for her bottom as she walked away. She giggled and made a show of covering herself.

"There's a good girl." Slug turned to his other guests. "You too, off you fuck." He fluttered a hand decked with chunky platinum rings in the direction of the door.

The two playing air hockey staggered arm in arm across the room. As they passed, Mark could smell the telltale cinnamon scent of Slug's home brew. He blew the stench away.

"Come in then, if you're coming." Slug beckoned them closer, then threw his feet up onto a small coffee table. Despite the state of his friends, he looked all too with it. "You here about the Daedalus?"

"We are," said the Captain, nodding.

"And you're not put off by the target?"

Nerves bubbled in Mark's stomach as he watched the Captain work, but the older man's face didn't show any worry.

"No. But our fee will be higher. Forty per cent."

Slug's nostrils flared as he sat upright. "You're kidding." It was more a suggestion than a question. "This information didn't come to me cheaply." He pressed a finger down on the table to emphasise the point. "I've got bills to pay. People. Ships. Territory to control." He pointed to the window. "You think that port runs itself?" His cheeks had gone a bright red, but his voice remained firm. "Forty per cent! What are you going to do with forty per cent?" His lips pressed together. A line of white on the beetroot of his head. He blew out a short breath. "Twenty, and I'll include my hacker for free, and that's me being generous."

For a moment, the Captain didn't move or speak.

Mark held his breath as his captain locked eyes with the lord of the Artifakt underworld. Twenty was still a good deal. If Slug's estimates of the score were true, twenty might still be more money than they'd ever received for a float before. He shifted awkwardly. His hand fell once more to the lockbox in his pack.

Slug noticed the movement, the chink in the crew's armour, and pounced. He raised his chin. "How's the saving going, Mark?" He grinned. "Guessing your cut of twenty per cent would bring you pretty close?"

"Um."

The Captain removed the pair of glasses perched on the edge of his nose and cleaned them gently on the cuff of his long coat. He gave Mark an almost imperceptible shake of the head.

Mark swallowed.

Slug pressed. "Well?"

"I'm nearly there."

"Well done, you!" The redness of Slug's face paled as he gently clapped his hands together. "My contact with the Ember Bros is going to be in Artifakt in a few weeks. I hear he's down looking for new recruits. You should be back in time." He leant forward and took a sip from the unbranded open bottle on the table before him.

"Really?" The Ember Bros weren't really Mark's first choice of Star Sailor chapter, but he wasn't getting any younger. Beggars couldn't be choosers.

"Mm." Slug spread his arms across the back of the sofa on either side of him, seemingly sensing Mark's thought. "How old are you now? Twenty-four?"

"I don't—" began the Captain.

"Twenty-six?"

Mark coughed.

Slug sucked air through pursed lips. "Ah. Coming pretty close to the cutoff." Butterflies danced in his belly. "I—"

"Thirty-five and the hacker," said the Captain.

"Twenty-two," Slug spat back.

"You don't have anyone else who can do this," said Journey. Mark could hear the frustration in his voice. Hoped it wasn't aimed at him.

"Zealot says he'll take his androids in for twenty and they don't need a hacker." Slug rubbed a hand under his nose. "But his methods are messy. There might be some fallout. Either way, if he finds out I'm giving it to you for any more than twenty-two, you know what he might be tempted to do?"

The three of them stood motionless. Mark could guess. Zealot was a cut-throat.

"He might be tempted to meet you halfway back. Ice you. Take that cut for himself." He steepled his fingers together and leant forward. "I'm doing this for you because I like you. I like working with you. I want you to prosper. I don't want you running around out there with that sort of cash ... for your own sakes. You'll only become a target."

"You're sure Rosenhalt's not going to be on board?" said the Captain.

Slug shrugged. His golden tooth gleamed as he grinned. He'd won, and he knew it. "My intel says no, but it's his hotel, his execs. If he's there, I'm sure you can still do the job. It's a risk."

The Captain replaced his glasses. "Twenty-two, and your hacker better be good."

"Oh, Ashley's the best. Trust me."

THE NEW GIRL

"You reckon that's her?" said Mark, as he and Journey sat on the Hurricane's loading ramp waiting to head out.

The ship was packed and ready to go. The hacker was all they were waiting for.

Journey wriggled the humps of hairless flesh above his eyes that counted for eyebrows and nodded in the direction of the Dock 03 entrance. "Her? Doubtful. She looks too clean."

A group of dock workers sipping coffees on their break all turned their heads to watch as the short brunette strode confidently past them towards the Hurricane. She wore dark jeans, a white tee, and a green jacket, and carried a canvas backpack over her shoulder and a leather laptop bag at her hip.

The woman noticed Mark and Journey looking and waved. Something unusual happened in Mark's chest. His heart sort of stopped. He coughed. He hoped he wasn't coming down with something.

Clearly sensing the change, Journey patted him on the arm, and whispered, "It's alright, it's just a girl." He stood.

"Journey and Mark?" She squinted, unsure. The glasses perched on her nose rose as she wrinkled it.

Mark tried to speak but couldn't. Journey tugged him up by the sleeve of his jacket.

"How do you know our names?" Journey said, with a hint of suspicion.

She smiled, showing small but perfectly formed teeth. "You don't think I'm going to hop aboard a ship full of smelly boys without giving you a once-over first?" She patted her laptop bag. "I looked you up. I know everything there is to know about you."

Mark eyed Journey nervously.

She wiggled her fingers in his direction, much like a B-movie vampire. "Eveeeerythiiiing."

Journey shrugged. "That must have been a boring couple of minutes."

Her shoulders slumped, and she blew a couple of loose hairs from her face. "Yep. You lot are from Planet Dullsville."

"Come on in," said Journey, stepping up to the ramp.

"You don't need to see my credentials?"

"You have credentials?" he said. "Must be nice."

Ashley laughed and Mark followed them inside.

Journey gave her the tour, pointing out parts of the ship he was particularly proud of. Mark let the engineer do the talking.

Back in his hometown of Track Stop, there had only been one other kid Mark's age, Spanner, and he'd left quite soon after his thirteenth birthday. Due to this lonely start, Mark had never been very good with women.

His first romantic encounter, and in fact close-quarters experience with a woman his own age, had been after he'd settled in Artifakt around seven years ago. He'd taken her out to the best restaurant in their corner of the city, Saucy Beans. (The choice of good restaurants was somewhat limited in East Artifakt.) Due to his nervous first-date fumbling, he'd managed to spill a full bowl of saucy beans down her front. She had failed to see the funny side, and found it critical to kick him square in the saucy beans, before taking her leave. They hadn't spoken again.

Since that fateful night, Mark had focussed more on his career than his love life. Unless something out of this world came along, romance could wait until he was raking in the big bucks as a Star Sailor.

"We'll leave you to get settled," said Journey to Ashley. "Dinner's at seven. Our android is a pretty good cook, ain't that right, Mark?"

Mark fell back into the present moment with the pair staring at him. Ashley's big brown eyes blinked. His cheeks flushed with heat.

He closed one eye. "Ain't what right, Mark?" he said slowly.

Journey rolled his silver eyes. "Michael's cooking is pretty good."

"Oh, yeah, palatable." Mark nodded, glancing at Ashley to see if she might be impressed by his linguistic skills. The Captain had used that word once when describing food.

A hint of a smile crossed Journey's lips. He was onto him.

"Oh, yes." The engineer nodded. "Very palatable."

"Well, I'll see you there, then," said Ashley. She smiled at them, then closed the door to her cabin.

Mark and Journey moved together down the hall for a few paces in silence. For some reason, Mark couldn't stop thinking about her. The curve of her chin, the size of the white bit of her eyes, the way her hair swooshed like it wasn't all stuck together.

"Palatable, huh?" Journey beamed.

"What?"

"Oh, nothing."

MUSHROOMS FOR BREAKFAST

Several days later, Mark woke up hurting. The Hurricane's engines, with their constant, monotonous hum, left an ache above his right brow, and each slow drip of his fish tank's filter stabbed ever sharper daggers between his ears.

Yes, he was hung-over. Yes, it wasn't the first time. And yes, you could shut up about it.

They'd reached the rendezvous point a few hours before he'd gone to bed and he and Journey had gone through their usual pre-job ritual—martial arts drills, Conan The Barbarian, pizza, a few beers—followed by a quick trip to the archive to check out the Daedalus's blueprints. Then things got a bit hazy …

He covered his head with his floppy, good-for-nothing pillow as someone clanged up the corridor outside his room. Didn't they know how he felt? He expected they did, and were wearing their biggest boots on purpose. They stopped at his door.

He eased the edge of the pillow down to the tip of his nose as someone flicked on the light of his cabin. The glow of the bulb was a thumb in the eye, searing a colourful silhouette of his room on to his retinas. He jerked the pillow back over his face. Groaned.

"I'm not nagging—just checking you've looked over the Daedalus's blueprints already," said the invader. "The Captain says if you get lost this time, he won't send someone back to look for you."

In the glowing after-image now burned into his eyeballs, he could make out the oval of Michael's head. The pillow lifted from his face and Mark squinted through sleep encrusted eyelashes.

"Although, I'm still not sure what the difference is between nagging and reminding," Michael continued, his head cocked to one side in a mimicry of thought. "Another intricacy I'll never understand." Hand-sculpted teeth, with just enough uncanny imperfection to make them seem real, beamed down from a smile that wouldn't look out of place on a serial killer.

Mark glanced warily between those teeth and the pillow held inches over his face. A self-sabotaging, or perhaps self-preserving, niggle at the back of his mind never let him forget that, despite the android code of ethics which meant generally they could never harm a human unless it meant more life could be saved, the tiniest of malfunctions in an android's circuits could turn them into a mindless, merciless death machine that could neither be bargained nor reasoned with. And Michael wasn't exactly running on default factory settings.

The hand holding the pillow shivered and Mark's whole body jerked, renewing the stabby ache behind his eyebrow. His throat issued the driest of croaks.

"It's something to do with whether or not the one you are reminding actually wants to do the thing you are reminding them of, isn't it?" continued the android.

"What?" Mark cleared his throat.

"Nagging and reminding. The difference."

"I guess."

"Do you need a few more minutes' beauty sleep?"

"I do." Mark indicated the steaming mug in Michael's hand with a slight spasm of his right eye. "For me?"

Murky memories from the night before loomed through the alcohol-induced fog that addled his brain—swords, pecs, and a soundtrack of guttural Schwarzenegger noises. Something else too. Underlying unease. A sense of something forgotten. Something important.

"Journey made it." Michael held the mug up as if to examine the chipped tin in the light. "He said it would ease the hangover." His focus returned to Mark. "That is false. It will dehydrate you and leave you feeling worse. And once the caffeine hit subsides, you'll feel more fatigued than had you not had it." That almost perfect smile again. "I suggested I bring it to you."

"Thanks?"

Michael placed it on the bedside table. "Journey will meet you in the archive to confirm you know exactly where you are going. I know it is not your way of doing things, but the Captain suggests you at least make a few preparations in advance of today's little heist." His head twitched to one side, almost like a small bird. "He also added, although this may have been a private conversation, that if you do not start pulling your weight, then he will, and I quote, fire your ass."

Mark swallowed nervously. "I expect he'll fire the rest of me, too." He stuck an arm up to reveal a series of directions written from wrist to elbow in black biro. They were a bit smudged. "I got the route last night."

"Very thorough," said Michael. He held his forefinger and thumb a millimetre apart. "I'd recommend one last teensy check before you head off."

"It is possible to be over-prepared," Mark said, recovering the pillow and burying his head in it.

"It is not. Enjoy your poison."

"Tell him, I'll be about fifteen, twenty mins," said Mark. "I'm going to make breakfast."

"Affirmative." The android clanked noisily from the room.

Once again alone in his cabin, Mark relaxed and pressed his cold fingertips to his eyelids. There was something else he wasn't remembering. Something he'd set out to do.

He swallowed, throat dry as a baked frog in a desert. A few beers wouldn't have left him feeling like this.

As he rolled over, something cool and glassy clinked with a betraying emptiness against his knee. He lifted the sheet. Ah, tequila. His arch nemesis. His stomach quivered a little at the memory. Journey always said tequila was like duct tape—it fixes anything. Mark was sure it would be more apt to say tequila was like duct tape—you probably shouldn't drink it.

The taste lingered on his tongue. He pictured a brown, dirty stain at the back of his throat. His stomach threw down and started a break dance battle with his oesophagus. He flung himself across his bed, reaching the curtained off toilet in the corner just in time to buy a one-way ticket on the chunder bus.

That felt a little better. His nausea levels dropped from "someone with a mouthful of oysters witnessing a cold-riddled toddler sneeze" to that of "someone who's just been shat on by an unwell heron".

He let himself fall face first to the mattress with a thud. Opened his eyes. The picture of his parents standing in front of the family shop back in Track Stop watched him from across the room. Big smiles covered their faces. Dad's arm around Mum's shoulders. The way Mark liked to remember them ...

They weren't dead or anything. Just bloody lightyears away. He hadn't seen them in ages.

It was funny how those photographic smiles meant something different depending on the way he felt. Most of the time they were just happy smiles, but this morning they were "not cross, just disappointed" smiles.

Dad shook his head. You know you shouldn't have drunk so much the night before a big job.

That's not like you, Markus, said Mum, dismayed.

"Sorry Mum," Mark mumbled into his pillow.

It wasn't like him. And it wasn't like Journey to crack out the tequila the night before a big job.

When he'd told his mother and father that he was leaving Track Stop to become a Star Sailor with Journey, they'd been so excited. He hadn't come clean yet, and with every video call he'd had with them, it got harder and harder to be truthful.

He wished he could be everything he told them he was. It would make them so proud.

Part of him wished he could be proud enough of everything he actually was to tell them.

He slid a hand under his bed and touched the lockbox there. Soon he would have enough saved up to accept Slug's offer. Soon he would join a Star Sailor chapter. Soon he would make his parents proud.

It had been his dream for as long as he could remember dreaming. Ever since his only childhood friend had been packed off to join one of the chapters by his parents, and Mark had been left in Track Stop friendless and alone.

It had all come as a surprise, but Spanner had been very excited.

Mark could remember the jealousy. He'd wished he could have gone too. His parents said they couldn't afford it, which was weird because it wasn't like Spanner's parents were rolling in it.

Soon though …

Journey's mug of coffee stood steaming on his nightstand. He sat up, collected it with both hands, and took a tester sip. Grimaced then smiled. Journey knew his way around a bean. Mark took another, longer swig, enjoying the complex taste—notes of cocoa, molasses, engine oil— and soothing, velvety warmth as it touched down in his empty stomach.

He let out a semi-contented hum. Not perfect, but better.

He clicked his fingers. Time to get to work. It was the morning of a job and, as always, he'd treated himself.

Crouching low, he slid his lockbox from beneath the bed. The chipped green paint was rubbery against his fingertips. He sat himself cross-legged on the floor and placed it before him. Blowing away the clumps of dust it dragged with it, he clicked in his combination and opened the lid.

Inside were his treasures.

Pasted to the inside of the lid was the letter his father had written him just before he'd left home. With the hint of a smile, he cast his eyes briefly over the words of fatherly wisdom and farewell.

The left side of the lockbox was taken up with a thick stack of crumpled bills tied together with a blue elastic band. He ran a finger over the edge, satisfied at the sound of the notes clicking together. Not long.

On the right was a short rectangular chopping board made from a dark grainy wood. Polished to a shine. He took it and placed it on his right.

Beneath was a small, round, unmarked tin, the lid greasy with its contents; two pouches, one shrink-wrapped plastic, the other leather and fastened with a drawstring; and half a loaf of seeded brown bread in another shrink-wrapping. He removed the bread, held it to his nose and breathed it in, then placed it on his bedside cabinet next to his cup of coffee.

Next he removed the plastic pouch. You couldn't get chanterelles on Artifakt. Not even at the high-end market on the other side of town. Not that Mark ever went there. His mum had used chanterelles back home. They'd grown with abundance in the forest just south of Track Stop. The paper label read sweet tooth. Not as good, but close. He gave the pouch a squeeze and placed it next to the chopping board, then removed the round greasy tin to go with it.

He moved slowly and deliberately. Following the same pattern as always, beginning to salivate as he did. He didn't want to get it wrong, and the anticipation only enhanced the outcome.

The leather pouch contained two other ingredients: another small tin, this one square, with several crystals of pink salt and a clove of dried garlic. He stacked the leather pouch on top of the round tin and pushed his lockbox back under the bed. From next to it, he removed a small flat gas stove, a gift from his father, and a pan, one from his mother. Her own. Blackened with use and flavour.

After another sip of his coffee, he set the stove alight with a soft *whoomf* of blue flame. Placed the pan over it. Warmed his fingers. Took a knife from the belt of his discarded combats and with it scooped a nob of stiff butter from the little round tin. He tapped the fat into the pan. While it melted, he chopped the garlic and unpacked the sweet tooth.

With a practised flick of his wrist, he seesawed the pan from side to side to spread the fat and dropped the mushrooms in. Crunched the crystals of salt beneath his knife, and, with finger and thumb, delicately dispersed them. The salty savoury scent began to fill his little cabin. He took a deep breath. His sensitive stomach stirred. He buttered two slices of bread. Watched the mushrooms brown and caramelise. Flipped each of them in turn.

He liked them a little crisp, so, while they finished, he dressed.

As he pulled his vest over his head, he caught a whiff of something foul over the aroma of his breakfast. He breathed into his cupped hand. Sniffed the contents. Retched. With visions of bumping into the new girl and having her wilt like unwatered daffodils under the power of his death-breath, he headed to the sink for a hygiene fix.

It was worth doing something for the ladies every now and then, and good personal hygiene was important to them, if not to him.

While he did a quick whip around the teeth with his brush, and mopped the key areas with yesterday's T-shirt damp from the tap, the imagined voice of his father returned in his ear.

Halitosis is better than no breath at all.

Which, using context clues, Mark had gathered to mean "having something which didn't work quite right, but still got the job done, was better than not having the job done."

Too right, Dad.

Dad seemed to have a saying for everything, and as a boy, Mark had never really understood half of them. Though, as he grew older, their cryptic meanings became clearer, and he found himself using them daily.

It was true, every boy turned into his dad at some point, and he'd begun to mind that thought less and less.

It was also true that having something that didn't work quite right, but still got the job done, was better than not having the job done—and in the race for Ashley's affections, Mark was proud to say he was the lucky halitosis that would get the job done ... if she let him ... whatever the job might be. Judging by his parents' relationship, the job was just being really nice to each other, and making cups of tea, and picking things up the other one had dropped even if it inconvenienced you, occasional hugs, playing board games on rainy nights, cups of coffee on the porch in the morning while the mists over the mountains cleared, holding hands when you walked, reading books together in silence while being warmed by the same fire.

Yep, Mark could be the guy for that job.

He held his thought to add the garlic to the pan. Stirred.

Returned to the mirror and frowned uncertainly at himself. He pulled down an eyelid to reveal a particularly bloodshot white. What was halitosis? And more crucially, what important thing had he forgotten? Thoughts of Ashley had triggered that little uncertainty once more. He shook his head to clear it. No point in dwelling. It'd come to him if needs be.

A problem forgotten is no longer a problem—Dad.

He finished dressing. Black vest, black cargo trousers. Sprayed his foot with anti-fungal (it was getting pretty bad). And slipped on his slipper. He used to have two, but one got blended during an engine-room-based grease slip. Still, one out of two wasn't bad, and he'd been lucky to survive with both feet, so it was a glass-half-full situation. Plus Journey had promised him a nice new pair.

He knelt by the pan. Wafted the smell up with his hand. Perfect. Turned off the heat. Plated the bread. Topped it with the fried sweet tooth and took a bite. Closed his eyes and savoured for one moment's contented peace before the day's activities began.

Most palatable.

He stood, feeling somewhat renewed, and turned side on to the mirror. Looked back, letting his long hair swing from his face. Raised one side of his mouth. In the tarnished reflection, he saw a cocky half-smile reminiscent of a macho heartthrob from the cover of one of Journey's romance novels.

Onlookers may have seen something else.

"Hey girl." He took another bite and winked. "'Sup?"

'Sup? Was that right? It didn't sound right. It was like a weird invitation to try some of his drink.

He tried the cocky smile again. "Hey girl, wanna git wit' me?"

Now, that was more like it.

Feeling almost like a million bucks, he picked up his coffee and, with the remnants of his breakfast plated, left the cabin to stroll at leisure towards the archive to meet Journey and redo his directions. On further scrutiny, a series of smudged Rs and Ls written on his arm wasn't the best way to get him from point A to point B on a twenty-floor hotel yacht.

One more last-minute check would be more than enough to refresh.

It is possible to be over-prepared—Dad.

Often coupled with—*Sometimes you gotta just try something! And if that doesn't work, try something else.*

He let his bare forearm stroke the polished metal wall and inhaled deeply as he walked through the dim corridors of the ship. The familiar oily smell of engine grease and the iron tang of rust filled his senses. The hypnotic drone of motors and systems gave him a prickly feeling of contentment. A feeling, he thought, akin to being inside the womb. Warm and safe. It helped him forget his aching head, like being wrapped fully in a soft duvet with slippers on both feet, not just one.

The Hurricane was Mark's favourite place to be. He had no worries out here. The ship was clunky, and occasionally prone to the odd hull breach or loss of gravity, but he'd never died, so what was there to worry about? The unpredictability kept you on your toes. Kept you sharp.

Plus, out here, he had friends. Not like back home.

He thought of Spanner often. What was he doing now? What great feats had he accomplished as a Star Sailor?

The two of them had spent most of their young lives either dreaming of the adventures they might have led had they been born on the other side of the tracks in the walled metropolis of Ely—one of the wealthiest cities on the planet, somewhere they weren't even allowed to go—or playing out imaginary battles amongst the towering shipping containers that surrounded the train tracks that cut through their village.

Mark's mum had sayings too. *You shouldn't play around the tracks. You'll get squashed by a train.*

Looking back as an adult, he realised she was probably right. The frequent cargo and passenger trains *did* hurtle along at breakneck speed. And one of his and Spanner's favourite pastimes *had* been to see how close they could stand to the tracks before getting too scared. Standing inches away from certain pasty death, and being blasted by a face-contorting wind that nearly knocked you off your feet, was the only bit of fun to be had. And that wasn't a teenage over-exaggeration. There was literally nothing else to do in Track Stop.

Spanner had always said it would be easier on their parents in the long run if they were squashed by a train.

"One less thing to worry about. One less mouth to feed."

But neither had ever quite managed it.

Mark downed the rest of his coffee and popped the mug on a shelf as he entered the archive. Journey stood inside, his large frame hunched over a holo screen showing a 3D image of the Daedalus. The glowing blue hologram up lit his pockmarked features.

"Heeeey," he said as Mark entered. "Good brekkie?"

Mark hummed in the affirmative through another mouthful.

"How'd you get on last night?" A spasmodic movement from the engineer's tattered forehead suggested that, if he'd had eyebrows, he would be raising them repeatedly.

Mark traced the pen marks on his arm with a finger. "I got the directions, but I might redo them."

"Not that." A knowing grin split Journey's face. "You don't remember?" he said slowly. His silver eyes lit up.

"Um. No." There was that worry again.

It seemed Journey knew what he'd forgotten.

He finished his last bite and popped his plate on the holo-table in the centre of the room. Sucked the last buttery crumbs from his fingers, ready to face the morning.

"I'm guessing not as good as you'd hoped, otherwise you'd still be in bed." The big man laughed and rubbed his hands together. "I'm gonna let you stew on it until after the float."

"I've no idea what you're on about." Something about this morning was starting to drag. "Can we just get this done?"

"I sent Michael up because I just want to make sure you don't get lost. Don't want you wandering around clueless like on the Amanita. I don't think you'll be so lucky this time."

"I'm pretty sure shooting yourself from one ship to another through the cold dark of space to escape an exploding Gerknorg ship is about the coolest thing anyone's ever done."

It had been one of Mark's proudest moments, but the rest of the crew had never let him forget why he'd had to do it in the first place. Yes, he'd gotten lost. Yes, it was his fault. And yes, they could shut up about it.

"Yes, cool. Also, yes, completely unnecessary." Journey rubbed a hand over his bald head, then prodded himself in the chest. "Look, *I* know your ability to think on your feet is one of your only strengths, but—"

"Hey, I'm good at other ... um, stuff."

Journey waved a hand. "Yes, *buuut* I'm starting to gather that the Captain thinks opportunities for you to show off that particular skill do crop up unnecessarily often."

Mark's shoulders dropped, and he sulked his way around the room. Lifted a plastic folder at random from one of the shelves and flicked through the pages. "It is possible to be over—"

"Nope." Journey gave him a look. "I'm going to have to have a word with your dad next time I see him. He's put a lot of silly ideas into your head."

Mark shrugged. "Not all silly," he said, while Journey removed the folder from his hands and placed it back in its correct position.

The archive was so boring. Pfft! Who wanted to read anyway? This was space. When you were travelling in a vessel capable of faster-than-light speeds, adventuring across the galaxy, raiding planets, boarding and robbing interstellar cruise liners, having shoot-outs with law enforcement, and punching aliens in the face on a regular basis, there was no time for reading.

All the best books were about doing just that. What was the point in reading about it if you were out there really living it? He guessed that was why Journey read romance. He hid a smile and saved that thought for a potential future zinger. Not that he could talk ...

But where had reading ever got anyone?

Where had books been on the slopes of Ooblek 6 when he'd come face to face with that mountain gel cube, whose only intention was to melt his skin off and slowly drain the marrow from his bones? Words hadn't saved him when that mandrake bog slink on Tartarus had its nine thousand teeth all jostling for position in his jugular.

No. The only thing you really needed in deep space was an averagely sturdy hull, the ability to hold your breath for about a minute and a half, and guns.

Lots of guns.

Oh, and bullets. More bullets than guns, obvs.

"Oi, dreamer." Journey clicked his fingers in Mark's face. "Concentrate. This is important."

Mark groaned. "Go on then. Where am I going?" He approached the console and stared at the slowly rotating hologram.

The Daedalus was a hawt ship. Sexy. A state-of-the-art luxury hotel yacht owned by Thaddeus B. Rosenhalt Jr. The richest man in the galaxy. A man who'd made a mint selling planet colonisers, and reaped the rewards of mines on worlds spanning the galaxy. Mark was a little envious. The guy seemed to have it all. Hot wife. Hot ship. Hot mountains of cash.

The ship was bigger than he had expected. The Hurricane could easily fit inside at least thirty times. It was inspiring. Imagine the fun you could have on a ship like that.

It had gyms, holo-decks, tennis courts, fine-dining restaurants, pools, spa facilities, dancehall, and a cadre of androids specialised in the function of each room, and right now the only people using it were a select handful of Rosenhalt executives. At least, that's what Slug had told them when he'd put the word out on the job.

"Every time I see this, I want it," said Mark.

Journey lifted an unimpressed nostril. "Yeah, but what would it really cost ya?"

Mark grunted. "What d'you mean?"

"Those ball bags at Rosenhalt, they don't care about anyone but themselves." Journey's face was about as serious as he'd ever seen it. "They'll do whatever they can to get ahead."

Mark pondered this.

"And I bet half of the usual guests go there thinking they'll do all this fun holiday stuff," Journey continued, "then spend half their vacation on laptops working to pay for their vacation. It's all fancy for fancy's sake." He patted a hand on the nearby wall. "Give me the Hurricane over something like that any day. Pretty sure they aren't happier than us. And granted we might steal a bit of cash from dicks, but they don't need it, so we're not really harming anyone just to live. You want to live as well as Rosenhalt and his cronies, someone somewhere is going to be hurting."

"But I'd rather be unhappy on a luxury hotel yacht than back in my room on Artifakt, where every time the wind blows in from the north I get a full-whack nostril-battering by the sewage works at the end of the road."

"Not if the reason you're unhappy is that you're working too hard to pay for the luxury life associated with visiting luxury hotel yachts. You'd be better off staying at home and having a bit of fun with your wife and kids or whatever, even with the nostril-battery."

"I don't have a wife, and I'm never having kids."

"How do you know you don't want kids? You've never even seen a baby. They can be cute."

It was true. There'd been no babies back home. And on Artifakt it was recommended any child under the age of three was kept inside or covered due to the constant deluge of acid precipitation. He'd at most spotted a little hand poking out of a carrier. He pressed his lips together.

"And besides," continued Journey, flapping a hand, "you're missing the point."

"Which is?"

Journey poked a finger at the image of the Daedalus. "All that stuff is fluffy bollocks. It ain't real." He grinned and thumbed his chest. "And it makes you a target for people like us."

"Sure, but you've got to want something more than what you have." Mark lifted his hands to indicate the ship they were in. "Otherwise, what's the point? What are you aiming for?"

They had different iterations of the same conversation often. Although he would never say it, sometimes Mark thought that Journey's lack of ambition had been the reason they had yet to become Star Sailors.

Journey shrugged. "Not sure about that." He cleared his throat. "Anyway, stop getting distracted. Directions!"

Mark nibbled a knuckle as he traced the route he was going to take inside. In through the hangar where they'd leave the Hurricane, and all the way to medical where he would split from Journey. Then from medical, along a number of corridors to the security room where he'd confirm their IDs or knock out some security guards, whichever was easiest, so that when Journey disabled the engines they would have less trouble. Then back the way he'd come.

"Easy."

"You've got it then? No getting lost."

"Yes," he said, as exasperated as a steam train. "I mean yes to I've got it, and no to no getting lost."

What had everyone been bothering him about?

To be safe, and also to show Journey he wasn't messing around, he took a pen from a pot nearby and re-wrote the series of lefts and rights on his forearm with some extra detail, just in case. Some of last night's rights became lefts, but he had been very, very drunk when he'd written them down.

And thinking about it now, he may not have been alone.

MAID IN SPACE

A CHILL RAN UP Sam's spine as she finished the email. What had she just read?

She glanced around the suite. She could lose her job for this.

It wasn't like her to be nosy. She didn't care one bit about the private lives of the guests. But when you glimpse the words *fifteen hundred deaths* in someone's work email, it's difficult not to have a quick scan of the rest.

Why had the laptop been left open on this particular email thread? Why hadn't the guest put a do-not-disturb sign on the door? Why hadn't she just pressed the laptop lid closed and finished the hoovering?

The contents of the email couldn't really mean what she thought it did. The guests on board the Daedalus knew she came in to service their rooms at this time every day. If they'd wanted something hidden, they'd have hidden it. And what she'd just read didn't look the sort of thing you'd want just anybody to see.

Something in the air.

She picked up the bin and emptied it into her trolley. Her stomach rumbled at the sight of a half-eaten apple falling into the trash compactor atop a pile of tissues. What a waste. She should really eat it. It wouldn't be the lowest she'd stooped for food since running. Nowhere near.

She shuddered.

She could wash it and save it for Nura. But if she was caught with it, Queletii might think she'd stolen it. It wasn't worth the risk. She was safe here.

The open laptop called to her, willing her to read on. She should just leave and pretend she'd never seen anything. She'd paid everything she had to get this job. If she got herself fired for snooping, she'd never get another. And where would that leave them both?

But she couldn't tear her eyes away.

You do know we're probably going to lose our company bonus this year? You can kiss goodbye to that little island on Rosen-19.

Nope. She should leave. Didn't want to know any more.

With one final look over the bedroom, she turned down the corner of the duvet, left a complimentary fat-free sugar-free chocolate-tasting foam dropper wrapped in foil on the pillow, and floated her trolley out into the main corridor.

Just forget it. It was nothing. Probably a misread. A little private joke between friends. Just two company execs bantering about fifteen hundred deaths at the latest Rosenhalt colony.

People with that much money and power had a different sense of humour to people like her.

Her stomach tightened like she'd eaten a large, cold stone. Her gut wasn't usually wrong about things. The way it was written, the panic in the words, told her it hadn't been a joke.

"You OK, Sam?"

She looked up. Mae stood outside the room adjacent with a handful of paper towels.

"Find something gross?" they said, wrinkling their nose.

Sam didn't hear them at first. Her thoughts elsewhere. Those colonies were home to families. Children. Fifteen hundred deaths was everyone.

"Samar?"

Sam cleared her throat. "Comes with the job, right?"

Mae jabbed a thumb over their shoulder. "Can't believe what some of these Rosenhalt execs get up to behind closed doors," they said. "It's bad enough we have to witness their passive-aggressive displays of corporate bravado in the public areas." They puffed up their cheeks to suggest their mouth filling with sick.

Sam closed the room door behind her. Number 22. Last one on her round. There were only eight guests aboard, but that didn't mean they could idle. They were running with a skeleton staff and she and Mae were set to do a ship-wide clean.

She checked her watch, and said, "You got time for a quick cuppa? Something to calm my nerves."

"That bad, hey?"

Sam nodded. "How do you cope?"

"How d'you mean?" Mae stuffed the handful of paper towels into their trash compactor. It hummed hungrily.

Sam chose her words carefully. "With seeing all they have, all they ... all they do."

Mae smiled. "I don't really get jealous much. I don't have a load of misplaced or unaligned desires."

Sam frowned. It wasn't the answer she'd expected. Mae had a habit of using longer words than she was used to back home. No not home. Not anymore. "What?"

"A while ago, I made a list of all the things that I wanted. Chose three and went hard on them. I don't need what these peacocks do. I have what makes me happy." They grabbed another roll of towels. "I've got a spillage to fix. Stick the kettle on and I'll meet you in the staffroom for that tea in five." They disappeared into the room.

Sam began pushing her trolley towards the staffroom as a red-faced guest in tight white tennis shorts and polo shirt appeared around the corner with padel racket in hand. His sweaty hair was held back by a flannel band. She pressed herself against the wall, apologising meekly for the size of her trolley as he passed, and watched him as he hurried into the room she'd just been cleaning.

She held her position as the door eased shut. It didn't close fully. Her breath caught as it opened again. She ducked down and pretended to inspect her trash compactor.

"You," came the man's voice from up the hall. "Have you just been in here?"

She stood and pressed her apron straight with her palms. "Yes," she said. "I emptied the bin. Did a quick clean." She fiddled with her hands. Didn't know where to put them. "Is anything wrong?"

His eyes turned to slits as he scrutinised her over the bridge of his pointed nose. "Didn't look at the computer, did you?"

She shook her head. Heat rose in her cheeks. She hoped Mae might return. She felt she needed a witness.

"Right, well …" He paused. Glanced back into his room. "I'm all out of electrolyte drinks. Fetch me some."

"There's a button for room service on—"

"Yes, but then I'd have to talk to an android. I want you to do it." He flicked his fingers dismissively. "You have five minutes. Lemon and blue, whatever flavour that is."

"Raspbe—"

"What?" He stepped one foot out the door, chest puffed like a silverback.

"The blue one." Her voiced dropped to an almost whisper. "It's raspberry."

"Whatever. Four minutes." He disappeared inside and closed the door.

Sam hated to think she scurried—vermin scurried—but that's what it felt like as she moved quickly up the hall and through the staff-only door leading to catering. What had she become? In a past life, she'd have told that prick where he could shove his electrolyte drinks.

And if he'd said another word, she'd have done the shoving … sideways.

She stepped into the kitchen where the android chefs were prepping for lunch. Chopping, steaming, sautéing. A dance timed as perfectly as the rise and set of a sun. The smokey aroma of soy bacon still hung in the air from breakfast. Her mouth watered. Her stomach grumbled. She shouldn't have thrown that apple away.

Not one of the androids acknowledged her presence as she passed through. The human service staff were just another fixture of the ship, like a door or a chair. Guests, on the other hand, were fawned and fussed over by the Daedalus's automatons, as if they were an entirely different species.

She tugged open the door to the large walk-in fridge and stepped inside. It was packed. Rows and rows of cartons and tins and cured meats on one side. Fresh fruit, vegetables, and more on the other. A kaleidoscope of colour, gleaming under the fridge's fluorescents. Not the cheap fungal imitations of meat and vegetables that they grew in vats and moulded to look like real food—that was for the staff, for the commoners. No, this fridge was filled with actual dead bits of animals and things pruned or uprooted from the living, breathing kitchen garden one deck below. The food in this room, fit for twenty guests for two weeks, was worth more than she could earn in a year. The garden itself, the seeds, the soil, the expertise, was probably worth more than the massive engines that powered the ship between the stars.

She picked up three bottles, one yellow, two blue, and placed them in her apron pocket.

Something clinked behind her. "What are you doing in here?"

She turned.

A kitchen android blocked the doorway with a hand resting threateningly on the open door. Its gormless facial expression told her it was being remotely piloted by either Queletii or one of the other security guards. They must have spotted her entering the kitchen on the security cameras. Technically, she wasn't allowed back here.

"One of the guests needed drinks," she said. Though she was telling the truth, her stomach still wriggled like she was lying. The security had a way of making you feel like you'd done something wrong. Like they were always trying to catch you out.

"Why didn't they use room service?"

Definitely Queletii.

"I'd just finished cleaning his room." She stole a look at her watch. "He wanted it quickly."

"Which guest?"

"Room 22."

"OK, well, don't keep him waiting. I'll be watching." Something clicked inside the droid and without another word it returned to the kitchen.

Sam followed it out and hurried to the corridor where her trolley still stood. She placed two bottles on its shiny metal surface and slid the other below. Glanced up at the small white box in the furthest corner of the corridor, sensing Queletii watching her through its little black eye.

Her heartbeat quickened when she saw Mae's trolley had gone. She guided hers cautiously up to Room 22.

Her frazzled nerves jolted at a sharp toot from the loudspeakers hidden in the ceiling. The precursor to an announcement.

Captain Fenchurch's deep baritone spoke. "This is your captain speaking. Just to let all guests and staff know, we have responded to a distress signal from an incapacitated Star Sailor ship. Thankfully, the majority of the crew are unhurt, but a few require medical treatment. We will do all we can. This shouldn't impact your stay in any way. Although, if possible, we will see if members of the crew will do us the honour of joining us for dinner. We will be glad to see you there. Thank you. And have a pleasant afternoon."

Star Sailors. No matter where she went, no matter what she did, she could never seem to get away from her old life. Perhaps there had been a battle nearby. Did they have a run in with Scorlacks? Or perhaps Gerknorgs? God, she hated Gerknorgs.

Or worse, maybe they were here for her, sent by him.

No. That was crazy.

She lifted her hand to knock on the door of Room 22. Hesitated.

Fifteen hundred dead.

She let out a held breath. Flexed her fingers. Tapped the door with her knuckles. "Um, hello. I have your drinks."

"Come in."

Couldn't he just come to the door? She looked up once more at the camera. What if he knew she'd seen something on his laptop? What would he do?

She drew her keycard from the retractable cord on her belt and touched it to the lock, then pushed the door open.

He sat at his desk, forearms resting on the surface on either side of his laptop. The tabletop was clear save for a small pouch by his right hand.

"Stick them in the fridge." He pointed, as if she hadn't restocked it with booze and mixers every day for the last week. And in the case of this room, sometimes twice a day. They knew how to party, these Rosenhalt execs.

He didn't even look up as she crossed the room, pulled open the fridge, knelt, and placed the bottles inside. As she stood, something brushed her back. Breath on her ear as a clammy hand gripped her bicep. The smell of stale sweat. The sting of a hypodermic.

She watched the needle pull from the skin of her forearm.

From this close, and behind the work he'd clearly had done, she could see the lines around his eyes. He looked overworked. Deathly tired. A spectre behind an expensive facade. He smiled, but there was no cheer in it.

"It's for the best," he said, as a warm feeling grew up from her arm and her eyelids drooped.

Her legs caved. He caught her as she fell.

"Please." Her voice was a low drone. Painfully slow inside her head.

"It's for the best," he repeated.

The final thing to cross her mind was the irony. The only reason she'd taken this stupid maid job in the first place was to get away from precisely this sort of thing.

THE THREE FUNDAMENTAL APPROACHES TO GAINING A LADY'S AFFECTIONS

The bridge interior was lit only by the dim blue glow of the Hurricane's monitors and controls. It was all completely alien to Mark. All very complicated. Unnecessarily so in his opinion. How many buttons did you need to make something go up, down, left, and right? Four, you'd assume. But instead there were uncountable dials and switches and pressure-sensitive touchpads, each with their own coloured LED or specific little beepy noise, spread across the cockpit like a miniature star field.

He was happy to sit back and let Michael and the Captain take charge when it came to flying. You would have thought by now AI could do it, but instead it was off doing all the fun jobs like painting, writing, and making music.

Michael's dexterous fingers danced across the dashboard's surface. His pale, clean-cut features were lit an azure blue by the light of the large viewing screen which displayed the stars ahead.

The Captain sat next to him, sipping from a cup of tea and studying the screen. He was a large man. Strong, with broad, responsible shoulders. Hair shaved down to his scalp. His long red coat lay draped over the back of his chair, and his shirt sleeves, rolled up to his elbows, were held in place by clips.

The bridge was just big enough to fit captain and android, so Mark waited in the doorway. To his right, a slim ladder led up to a low-ceilinged mezzanine layer which housed the navigation desk. He lay an arm on the back of Michael's chair and idly picked at the yellow foam poking out through the soft plastic headrest.

The Captain slapped his hand away. "Are you and Journey ready?" He leant back and peered over the small pair of glasses perched on the end of his nose. The springs in his seat squeaked.

Mark rubbed his hand where the Captain had smacked it. "I am, Cap. Just checking ETAs, then I'll get the stretcher loaded up."

"We're just finishing up here," the Captain said. He directed his voice upwards. "Ash, you close?"

"Nearly," came a voice from above. Mark's heart shot to one end of his body. His stomach fled to the other.

There she was.

The heavens sang. Angels beamed. Harps arpeggiated.

Aaaaaashleeeey!

Perfect in every way—practically.

Mark had found her to be beautiful, intelligent, punctual, thoughtful, yet—despite their close proximity aboard the ship—completely ignorant of his existence. He had only been able to bring himself to talk to her once.

The first time he'd spotted her in the hangar, and his heart had skipped that beat, hadn't been a one-off. Whenever he saw her, it happened. And the more it happened, and the more time he spent near her, the sicker he became. Not in the hangover-vomit way that still gripped him like a squid's oily embrace. This was different.

Whenever he bumped into her unexpectedly in the halls, his body would tingle in unusual ways and he'd become utterly useless. His mouth would dry, yet he'd spit on every fumbled word, and his armpits would radiate a warmth akin to a star.

He didn't really understand. Maybe she had a contagious disease.

Or maybe it was just some secret power that women had over men. His experience was somewhat limited.

Despite the unexplained sickness she caused, Mark had hoped to see more of Ashley, but as yet could not get her alone. Being unsure of what to do to make her interested in him, he'd squirrelled himself away in his room with several of Journey's romance novels, scanning them cover to cover in search of methods to win a lady. They didn't teach him anything particular about the deed itself—they were about as spicy as rice cakes dunked in milk—but at least now he felt he was quite versed in the wooing ways.

Upon a small amount of questioning post-read, Journey had promised Mark that he wasn't into anything weird, so Mark had taken the books as absolute gospel, and deduced, after the careful study, that there were three fundamental approaches to gaining a lady's affections (as described by romance novels).

Number one—be a bit of a dick while occasionally hitting her with back-handed compliments until you get into a massive fight. Then, when she least expects it, take her into your hunky arms and kiss her.

Number two—be a bit of a dick, then save her from a life-threatening situation to show her you like her after all. Then, take her into your hunky arms and kiss her.

Number three—be a bit of a dick, but also a billionaire cowboy playboy shapeshifting alpha werebeast. Then, take her into your furry animal arms and kiss her.

He didn't know how to formulate a backhanded compliment, so that was number one out.

Three was a no go. He wasn't a billionaire. Nowhere near! Or a cowboy playboy. He could probably get nano-surgery for the shapeshifter bit, but that was pretty permanent, and what if the relationship didn't work out and he was stuck as a bear-man for the rest of his life, and the next girl preferred shapeshifting wolves or something, you know?

Two seemed the safest bet. They had a week or so before they got back to Artifakt, and pirating was a dangerous game, so there was bound to be something he could save her from in the meantime.

Most other areas were covered.

Hunky arms—check.

Shoulder-length flowing locks—the Hurricane's very temperamental replicator unit had given him a semi-permanent wig which he'd tried out once and, when it had gripped hold of his scalp it hadn't come off again, so check.

A shirt that he could unbutton to just below his pecs, preferably not with buttons but with a bit of string like a shoe (Journey had one he could borrow and he planned to wear it for this particular heist)—check.

He had also tried a sexy Spanish accent, but Journey's incessant ribbing had become a little too much for him to bear.

The being a dick bit was proving to be the trickiest part. It seemed so counter-intuitive. It went against everything his mother and father had taught him. His dad, at least, was kind and generous and showered Mum with unbridled love. But that cheeky playboy cowboy always seemed to get the girl, so there must be something in it.

Ashley sat in the navigator's chair, previously hidden in the dark of the upper floor. She looked down and smiled. Mark's armpits blazed. He stiffened awkwardly as he tried to think of something a bit dickish to say. Was "Alright, dickhead?" a bit much?

Picking up on the change in his demeanour, Michael—with the stealth and accuracy only androids can possess—flicked him on the left testicle.

Mark grunted and bent to protect himself. "I told you not to do that." Heat bloomed in his cheeks as he glanced back up at Ashley, who had resumed her typing.

"Just testing your reflexes, Mark. It is for your benefit."

"My reflexes are fine."

"Suboptimal for someone of your degradation by three nanoseconds."

He cuffed the android around the back of the head, hurting his hand more than anything.

The Captain laughed. The sound reminded Mark of his grandfather.

"We've picked the Daedalus up on long-range scanners." Michael tapped an indistinguishable black point in the endless reaches of space digitised on the viewing screen. "It's heading this way."

The Captain hummed. "Slug was right."

"They've responded to our distress signal. Seven minutes until engine shutdown."

The plan was a simple three-step affair. As all good plans were.

Step 1) Pretend you are a bunch of Star Sailors with a disabled ship and get picked up by a bunch of rich nobs.

Step 2) Install a little bit of code in the ship's customer transaction matrix that will increase the price of everything aboard by roughly five per cent. That five per cent would then be siphoned out to Slug's holding account via hundreds of different untraceable accounts.

Step 3) Get out, having disabled the target ship's engines so they can't chase you if things go tits up, which, let's face it, they often do.

Badabing, badaboom!

With the sort of clientele the Daedalus might attract, the siphons could quickly add up to thousands, at least until the code was found and deleted. Jimmy the Finger's record had been two weeks. Mark had the impression Ashley was in a different league to Jimmy the Finger. He glanced up at her again. He was sure that wasn't just because she was prettier.

The Hurricane was so battered on the outside that, with a few venting pipes and flame throwers strategically placed on the hull, it looked as though it had been quite recently attacked. With the engines offline, it was easily mistaken for a wreck.

"I'll be down in a minute, Mark," said the Captain, his hands flying to various buttons and controls across the dashboard. "You've got seven to get ready."

"Just leaving."

ALL ABOARD

Mark gazed at the Daedalus through the airlock door as they drifted closer. It was truly beautiful. A featureless, matt-black hull with no external lighting. Its knife-like silhouette was barely visible against the starry horizon.

He whistled as a perfect image came to mind. Him, stood on the bridge, one arm around Ashley's shoulders, the other clutching a large wooden ship's wheel. Butt-length hair flowing in the wind of the air conditioning. He smiled and smouldered as they sailed off into the—

"Something appears to be wrong with your face," said Michael, his nose inches away from Mark's right ear.

Mark glared at him. He could never decide whether it was better to engage with or ignore the android.

After a few moments of awkward silence, the Captain entered with Ashley. Though the Captain usually kept his look "pirate-smart" by dressing in a loose-fitting collarless shirt, braces, and black trousers, he now wore a pair of silver leggings, large clunky knee-high boots covered in buckles, a bright red vest top, and a long blue bog slink-skin coat that came down to the top of his boots. He looked very rock and roll.

Ashley was dressed in equal outlandishness. Hair backcombed to a spiky frizz, green stripy dress with thick yellow tights, red boots, and a similar long coat. Mark almost vomited in appreciation. She looked absolutely smoking.

"Why do Star Sailors have to wear this jazzy rubbish?" she said, when she caught Mark staring at her.

"Yeah, you're stupid," he replied dickishly.

She frowned and turned away from him. Shifted her laptop bag on her shoulder.

"I mean, it's stupid." Damn it, too dickish.

He twiddled with the drawstring of his top and turned to face out of the window. Why did he ever bother to open his mouth? Sometimes he thought he would get further in life if he was mute.

The Daedalus was very close now. A bright white rectangle had opened in the hull like a small, misplaced cartoon mouth in the side of a giant black shark.

"They have picked us up in their tractor beam," said Michael. "They are bringing us in."

"They've taken the bait." The Captain looked at each of them in turn. "Ready?"

Mark nodded. The sinking ship tactic had never failed. Apparently, it was the oldest trick in the highwayman playbook. Pretend your mode of transport was wrecked and wait for the target to pull over to help.

He felt a little bad about it. Playing on the kindness of others just to rob them. But it wasn't like they were going to really hurt anyone. And besides, the Daedalus's guests had loads of money, and, rumour had it, weren't the loveliest people in the galaxy, anyway.

Trickle-down economics wasn't exactly working wonders.

It helped to think the money was going to a good cause. He was a good cause. And one day he would pay it forward. When he eventually became a Star Sailor, he'd travel the galaxy, saving those in need. He'd never get there though, if he died of starvation along the way. He had to rob from the rich to feed himself, so that he could in turn save the poor.

Journey entered, sweat and grease on his scarred brow. "All set in the engine room."

There was a trick to disabling a ship that had nothing wrong with it so that whoever came aboard to fix it believed it had been damaged in a firefight. Through years of practice, Journey had perfected that trick.

The record for fixing his twisted maze of intentional breakages was fifteen hours. This gave them more than enough time to get in, get comfortable, maybe a little social, plant the code, maybe grab a snack, disable the hotel's engines, and get away again without being noticed.

Journey clambered onto an empty hover stretcher. Mark tucked him in with a blanket.

As they drew closer to the Daedalus, he could make out four people in light grey security uniforms watching them from behind the entry force field. Three underlings and a chief. Mark noted his silly little hat. Security chiefs always had silly little hats.

He waved through the window as the Hurricane floated through the force field and into the hangar. They didn't wave back.

"Looks like the security are a barrel of laughs," he said.

"Well, you all better be on your best behaviour," said the Captain with a chuckle.

Dotted around the hangar were several android workers preparing for their ship's arrival. Service robots circled and looped. Little spacefaring vehicles, ideal for off-ship excursions and space-skiing, were parked against the far wall.

The room shook as the Hurricane crunched down on its landing gear.

Mark hit the button to open the airlock door and lower the off ramp. It slid open, sucking away the comforting stench of the Hurricane's innards and replacing it with the cloying odour of expensive cinnamon-scented engine lubricant and rose-tinted solvent.

The Captain stepped through the doorway and onto the ramp first. He waved at the guards.

"Howdy. Thanks ever so for picking us up. We were in a bit of a bind out there. Damn Gerknorgs attacked us out of nowhere. Left us for dead."

Two of the four guards unclasped the holsters at their belts hospitably. The other guard tapped at a tablet. The chief stepped to the front.

"Stay on your ramp," he said, raising a hand.

He had a square, leathery face with a full, yet short, head of greying hair. A scar over his right eyebrow interrupted the flow of the many frown lines on his forehead. He was thin, but looked like he could hold his own. As hard to chew as an overly stringy stick of celery. His name tag read Queletii.

The Captain raised his hands noncommittally. "No worries, man."

His Star Sailor tone and vocabulary were flawless. An easy breezy sort of cadence that made you think of palm trees, sandy beaches, and surfing.

The guard with the tablet held it up in front of Queletii's face. "Captain Daytona," he whispered to his chief.

"Captain Daytona of the Hurricane?" said Queletii. "Star Sailors? One of you is injured, no?"

"That's right." The Captain held out a hand to shake.

The security chief looked down at it hanging between them, yet kept his arms folded behind his back.

The Captain quickly pulled back with emphasised awkwardness, then gestured to the crew. "This is First Officer Zak Stapowski, Sandy McClane, and our engineer Pete Derkmeister."

The guard with the tablet appeared to tick the names off while the Captain said them. "All humans accounted for, sir," he said to Queletii. "There should be an android."

Queletii raised his eyebrows towards the Captain.

"Our android is in the engine room wrestling with a serious fuel leak," said the Captain. "Listen, Pete here is stable, but we need to get him some help, fast. Took a—"

"First, we need to check you for weapons," said Queletii.

Journey gasped a phlegmy breath from his stretcher and coughed up something thick and red. Mark didn't know whether to be grossed out or impressed.

"Listen, man," said Mark. He feigned a look of desperation. "Pete's been hurt real bad. We gotsta get him to medical." He loved this bit. The over-the-top acting. He'd been born to play a Star Sailor.

Queletii released a slow and annoyed sigh. He didn't look to be in any sort of hurry.

"No, you listen, *man*. What I need to do is make sure our guests are safe from anything you may be carrying, be that mechanical or"—he paused, taking in a short, sharp breath—"biological. Can't have an outbreak of flesh-eating lice, can we?"

His lip curled as his eyes travelled from Mark's head to his toes.

He motioned to the guard with the tablet. "Harrison, check them."

Harrison moved forward and waved the tablet over Journey's stretcher. He then scanned the rest of the crew. He wouldn't find anything untoward. They didn't need guns. The Captain never condoned unnecessary violence. But if this had been a real emergency, Journey might have died while they waited. Mark gave Queletii an appropriate squinty glare.

He gave the two guards with guns a once-over. They were both younger than the chief. They'd obviously gone through some training. Both fit and strong, but looked like they probably hadn't done much securing lately. Young and brimming with a volatile mix of excitement and uncertainty. Not a good thing. That particular cocktail often resulted in itchy trigger fingers.

Harrison looked up from his device. "They are clean."

Queletii grunted. "Come on then. One of you may escort him to medical. You'll need to fill out some forms." The way he spoke suggested he would have been happier if he'd found a reason to abandon them to their fate. "I understand Captain Fenchurch wants to invite you to dinner. Two of you may go, but no more. The android will stay here and help our engineering droids fix up your ship."

"Sandy and I will come for a bite," said the Captain. "That'd be lovely."

"I'll accompany Pete," said Mark.

He depressed a button on the stretcher and stepped down the ramp. It jerked forward and followed him to the hangar floor.

"Bovista and Chen will lead you to the dining hall," said Queletii to the Captain, indicating the two guards who hadn't yet spoken.

"See you soon," the Captain said to Mark, then he and Ashley followed the guards across the hangar.

"And you're with me," said Queletii.

He turned and stepped in the opposite direction with Harrison close behind. Mark followed.

They were in.

ZAAAAAAKKK STAAAPOWSKIII

MARK HAD NEVER BEEN anywhere like this. The corridors all looked the same. The walls were free of scuffs and marks, and the floor was covered with some sort of soft, forgiving fabric that hushed his footsteps (not the usual metal grate or wooden floorboard he was used to). There was also something weird about the air. It smelled strange, like it didn't have anything in it. No grease. No fumes. No tiny airborne particles to catch in the throat or sting the eye.

In fact, now he was thinking about it, he could no longer feel the tingle of acid on his skin from the air purifiers. Was that normal?

Part of him liked it. Part of him feared it. Was it good for you? How did you know you were breathing air at all if it didn't taste of anything?

They passed two androids as they moved from the hangar to medical.

"Except for you guys, is it a full android crew?" Mark asked the guard.

His tag read Harrison. He was tall and slim. A little younger.

"We're running a smaller crew at the moment while it's just Mr Rosenhalt and his guests on board. He gets a sizeable tax—"

"Woah!" Mark raised his eyebrows, letting the surprise take him. He'd managed to get through three pages of one of Rosenhalt's books once before being kicked out of the bookshop for not buying anything. It was pretty inspiring stuff. He never said it out loud, but the man was a legend. "Thaddeus Rosenhalt is on board, right now?"

Journey grumbled on the stretcher.

Queletii gave Harrison a look.

An awkward moment passed.

"Sorry, you were saying something fascinating about tax?" said Mark.

Harrison smiled, unsure. "We still have androids for many of the more skilled occupations, but our employer gets a sizeable tax break for giving us jobs. If he fills his quota for human workforce, he saves more money in tax than our wages. It's cheaper for the government than having to manage welfare."

Mark nodded. The Hurricane crew regularly lost out to wily entrepreneurs, like Zealot, who had the cash to invest in fully android crews. Androids were cheap to keep. They worked better and for longer. No food, no sleep, no need for expensive air recyclers. Rather than learning the most complex and specialised of skills the good old-fashioned way, with years of practice, almost any physical or mental strength could just be uploaded directly. Humans were becoming outdone in almost all roles that paid enough to keep them alive by the very things that had been created to make their lives easier. Innovative tech-moguls trying to save the galaxy had basically saved the galaxy at the expense of making humans—as a species—joyless, artless, and redundant.

"This is it," said Queletii coming to a matt-white door marked with a small gloss white cross.

The door slid to the side as he slowed. An android stood ready on the threshold, an uncanny Mona Lisa smile frozen on its face. Save the paper-white hue of its skin, it was almost human. Its pinprick pupils took in Journey like a vulture investigating carrion. Mark shuddered.

"Leave him with me," it said, then took hold of Journey's stretcher and backed into the medical room. "We'll have him back to you as right as rain."

Queletii didn't even acknowledge its presence, just pressed a button to close the door and turned to Mark. "Stapowski, you come with me. We need to file a report. I want you out of here as quickly as possible." He continued along the corridor, followed by Harrison.

With one last glance back at the medical centre door, Mark jogged after them. He rolled up his sleeve and checked the ink on his arm.

They passed a crossing of corridors.

Through an unmarked door.

A left. A right. A left. Wait. That should have been a right.

"Um," he said unintentionally. He glanced back. "Wait. Shouldn't we—" He stopped himself.

"Everything OK?" asked Queletii, observing him with a sneer.

Mark thought fast.

"Shouldn't we, uh … just be constantly celebrating, uh, life? We're all going to be OK."

He threw his fists in the air and let out an overenthusiastic woop. A sound that at any other time he would feel greatly embarrassed for making. Star Sailors were always doing stuff like that—wooping, high-fiving, crotch-thrusting. Though he liked to think he was capable, none of these things featured in his regular repertoire of actions. That was something he needed to work on if he truly wanted to become a rockstar space hero.

Outlandish acts seemed to suit you better the more admired you became. Journey said it was something to do with the perception of dick size and an energy this created. This energy, he'd said, with a hearty laugh, was measured in family joules.

Mark had always been unsure as to what exactly was funny about that.

"It appears so," Queletii grunted. "We're here." He pushed open the nearest door. "There are a few forms to fill out. Then, once your comrade is stable, we'll collect him and return you to your ship."

The room was small and square with one desk in the centre. Queletii slid a finger across its surface, and it lit up. Two IDs were projected there.

"How did you get these?" said Mark, feigning surprise.

"Take a seat," Queletii said, holding a hand out to the room's only chair.

As usual, Journey had uploaded fake IDs to the Hurricane's database. This was all standard protocol. The ones now digitally reproduced on the desk were for Zak Stapowski and Pete Derkmeister. The only thing Journey had altered was the picture at the top. Both had been real people once. Mark had never met them and didn't know if they were alive or dead. He supposed it didn't matter.

"The Daedalus computer is highly advanced. We gathered them easily from your ship." Queletii looked smug. "Now, enough chatter. Our schedule is tight and needs to be maintained. Once you've filled these out, and as soon as Mr

Derkmeister has achieved life-preserving stability, you're gone." He tapped the table and pushed the first digital document towards Mark with his fingertips. "It is only thanks to Captain Fenchurch that we brought you aboard at all. If it had been up to me, I would not have let you anywhere near the Daedalus."

"Please give my thanks to Captain Fenchurch." Mark scanned the form. "We appreciate his help."

He swallowed. Something about a third of the way down the page had made him nervous. An NDA which required a DNA signature. Unfortunately, the IDs they'd bought had been acquired on a bit of a budget—the bronze package—which meant the DNA attached to Zak Stapowski's ID wasn't a match for his own. This was not standard protocol.

He took a deep breath, then picked up the stylus. He held it above the page, making a show of studying the form, and assessed his options. He needed to figure out a way to leave without giving his DNA. That might involve some punching.

He also needed to give Journey time to escape medical and get down to the engines to disable them.

"You are literate, aren't you?" said Queletii.

Mark sat up. There would be some catharsis in punching this guy.

"Oh, yeah," he said. "Do I need to fill out all of these boxes?" He pointed at the sheet with the stylus, then scrolled up slowly. "There's quite a few."

"Yes," answered Queletii. "If you want our help, then everything needs to be completed." His hand hovered over a communicator on his lapel. "I could call down to medical and tell them to cancel whatever procedure they have ongoing if you'd prefer to return to your ship immediately."

"Oh no, no, sorry." Mark put his head down and began to write. He stuck out his tongue and licked the underside of his nose.

"Zaaaaaaakkkk Staaaapooooowskiiiii," he said, as he wrote his name, which was actually a lot harder to spell than it should have been.

Queletii tutted and shook his head.

Mark glanced up at him and smiled. Oh, punchin' time was a-comin'.

ZAK-ATTACK

"Why did you leave it open on your computer? For God's sake, Sergio, you know what's at stake here?"

Sam couldn't open her eyes. Not quite. Her head span, but her body was still.

"I was running late for the game. I thought I'd shut it down." The voice of the room's occupant.

"Do you even know if she saw it?"

"Can we take the risk if there's a chance she did?"

The two men kept the volume from their voices, but not the anger, hissing at each other like street cats.

There was a pause, then a thoughtful, "Probably not."

She opened one eye. It was about all she could manage. She lay on the bed, arms cuffed awkwardly to the headboard behind her. Two men stood at the end. The guest who'd drugged her, Sergio, was still in his tennis gear, pacing with hands deep in his unkempt hair. He'd lost the sweatband.

The other man was rotund, dressed in pressed chinos and a blue shirt darkened with sweat. "Well, what do you want to do with her?"

She closed the eye, feigning unconsciousness, as Sergio turned to her.

"She's awake."

She pulled at her bonds. "Let me go."

"Cuffs, babe," said Sergio. "You ain't getting out."

"I didn't see anything." She looked between them, hoping for a chink in their defence, a weakness she could use to get out of this. "And even if I did, I wouldn't tell anyone. You can just let me go."

"So you *did* see it then," said Sergio.

Why did she never know when to shut up?

He pressed his lips together. She couldn't tell if he was upset or angry.

"Er, see what?" she tried.

It didn't fly.

"We're going to have to kill her," he said. "Chuck her off the ship. We can't let Thaddeus know how much of a monumental fuck-up this project on Rosen-54 was. He'll have us skinned alive or something."

"We shouldn't have kept it from him. He already knows something's up over there. We should have—"

"A soon as we have the results, he'll see past the means. What we've done here is no different from what he did on Rosen-9. He won't care as long as we see results."

"We can't keep it from him forever."

Sergio clapped both hands on the other man's cheeks. "No, but we can keep it from him until we fix it. Then it won't matter. Then he'll understand. He's always banging on about living forever. This might just be the very thing that he's looking for."

"But—"

"And besides, if she goes to the wrong person with this, do you think the Interplanetary Justice Div. will give a shit what we were trying to do? They won't think the cost was worth the result. If they find out, if they put a stop to it, we can't try again, can we? They'll either nuke the site from orbit or—"

"But someone'll know she's gone missing," said the larger man, brushing Sergio's hands away.

Sam sat up as best she could with her arm cuffed to the headboard behind her. "I won't say anything to your boss. I won't say anything to anyone. I promise. I know how to keep my mouth shut."

Sergio looked at her, dead-eyed, then squinted. "I reckon we jettison an escape pod. They'll think she's done a runner. It's what Thaddeus would do." He lifted an upturned palm. "Look at her, Duncan. She's nobody. It's not like anyone's going to look very hard."

Well, that was insulting.

She tried to look annoyed, but she could tell all her face showed was just how scared she was. Their plan was flawed. She'd never run from the Daedalus. She opened her mouth to inform them, but closed it again. It would only put Nura in danger if they knew she was here too.

"We need to be together on this," said Sergio. He held out a palm.

Duncan rubbed his face with both hands as if he were trying to sand it off. "Oh, I suppose." He made a show of looking anywhere but at her and shook Sergio's waiting hand.

"Alright." Sergio scratched his chin and looked around as he thought. "Get her trolley in here. We'll drug her again, kill her in the bathroom, then stick her body under the trolley, and wheel it to the escape pod." He passed his hand through the air like a jet. "Shoot her, and all the evidence, off into the big black."

"Are you sure that'll work?"

Sergio bobbed his head like a python ready to strike. "I don't know. I've never murdered anyone before, Duncan. Have you?"

Duncan's mouth twitched as the pair shared a moment's silent communication.

Sergio rolled his eyes with a tut. "That doesn't count. We knew the risks. The colonists on Rosen-54 knew the risks. They signed waivers. Waivers means we can pretty much do what we like."

Duncan deflated like an open potato sack turned upside down. "I'll get her trolley."

Sam pulled at her restraints. "They'll catch you. They'll know. Queletii has cameras all over the ship. He'll know."

"Queletii's busy with those Star Sailors, sweetheart. And everyone else is up there having dinner. No one's watching down here. Spot of luck that." He stared at her for a moment. Wrinkled his nose. "Well, for us. Not you."

She heard Duncan open the door.

"Excuse me," came another male voice from the corridor outside. Quiet, like he was standing a few rooms up the hall. "I'm a bit—"

Duncan closed the door and returned, hands pressed to his stomach, looking about as worried as a dog who's been caught defecating in his owner's shoes. "Someone's out there, Sergio."

"Who?"

Sam screamed. Sergio dived across the bed as quickly and uncontrolled as a bar of wet soap from squeezed fingers, and cupped a hand over her mouth. She could taste the salty sweat on his palm. Her stomach rolled.

There was a knock at the door. "Sorry. Hello?" came the muffled voice from beyond.

"Should I answer it?" said Duncan.

Sergio jutted his chin and hissed. "Of course fucking not."

The knock came again.

"What if he doesn't go away?"

"Fine. Just hurry." Sergio clamped his hand harder over her mouth. "I've got her."

She had no time to breathe before he grabbed a pillow and covered her face. She tried to suck in air, but nothing could penetrate the thick artificial fabric. She kicked in panic, trying to bring her legs up to where Sergio stood, to at least knock him away so she could breathe again, but her feet flailed at nothing.

Stars danced in her eyes. A grey fuzziness closed in.

Was this it?

The cuffs bit into her wrist.

What would become of Nura if she were to die here?

Suddenly, the pressure on the pillow lifted just enough for her to fill her lungs. Another few seconds and she would have passed out.

The sounds of a struggle came from the corridor.

She shook the pillow from her face.

Duncan backed into the room, followed by a man with long, flowing hair and fists raised.

"Who are you?" asked Sergio.

"Who screamed?" said the man. He wore a shirt laced together with string open to mid-chest. Coupled with his hair, which she could see was in fact a wonky wig, he looked like a reject from the cover of a bad erotic fiction novel. He looked at her, and she at him. "Oh, sorry, is this some sort of sex game? Because I'm just looking for some directions."

"No, you idiot, they are trying to kill me," said Sam. She wasn't really sure why she called her would-be saviour an idiot, but with the way he just stood there mouth gaping like a cave, gazing at her over his clenched fists, it was the only word for him. And when someone was being an idiot, it was better that they were told.

"Oh, right." He looked around as if he had been interrupted doing something very important, and completely forgotten what exactly that was. The cogs visibly moved behind his eyes.

Sergio stepped forward with palms raised. "We can pay you whatever you want. Just walk away."

"Hey," said Sam, kicking her legs in Sergio's direction. "You male chauvinist bastards. Why wasn't I offered the buyout option?"

Something clicked behind the newcomer's eyes, and he punched Duncan in the face. His unconscious body plummeted to the carpet.

"That's what I'm talking about," said Sam. She indicated Sergio with a tweak of her head. "Do him next."

The guy shrugged. "Alright."

Sergio leapt to the side and picked up his padel racket. He rallied off a few swift swipes in a bid to intimidate. "I'll have you know I am president of Laboratoire Rosenhalt and I um ..."

The new guy didn't bat an eyelid. Just tackled him into the wall. After several heavy punches, he stood. Sergio did not.

"I'm guessing not a sex game then?" he said, pointing an unsure finger with one eye closed.

"No. Are you a Star Sailor?"

"No," he said, looking down at Sergio. He rubbed his chin, then glanced quickly back up at her. "Er, I mean yes." He watched her out of the corner of his eye.

He was clearly not a Star Sailor. While he had the physicality and obvious capacity for a fight, he didn't look half as trendy as the rock star hero pilots known for their daring and courage.

"Look," he said, moving to the bed and leaning both fists on the end. "I was just looking for directions back to medical to meet my friend. I got turned around."

"Not sure if you've noticed, but I'm handcuffed to a bed, in the same room as the unconscious bodies of two men who were about to murder me."

He straightened. "Oh, yes. Sorry. Do you have the keys?"

"Do I have the keys?" She scoffed so hard, she almost choked herself. "Oh yeah. Let me just get them."

"Great." He sniffed, then spotted the fridge. "Oh, are those electrolyte drinks? Blue's my favourite. It's supposed to be raspberry, but raspberries aren't bl—"

"I was being super sarcastic."

He turned back. "Yes, of course." He stopped, then patted himself down as if he himself might have the key.

"Try him." She nodded towards the smaller of her two captors. "Those stupid little shorts have pockets."

The newcomer rolled Sergio over, then ran his hands over the short pockets. "There's definitely a key in there, but I can't get my hand in." He stood and threw his palms to the ceiling. "Who makes pockets so small you can't get your hands in?"

Wow, what a rescue!

"Bring them here."

He grabbed Sergio's leg and began dragging him across the floor.

"Not him. The shorts. Take them off and bring the shorts here."

The newcomer's cheeks quickly reddened. "Um ... you what?"

"My hands will fit." She wriggled her fingers. "Bring me the shorts."

He watched her for a moment, as if testing whether or not she might be serious. She remained impassive.

He knelt next to Sergio and placed both the unconscious man's feet on his shoulders. Looked at her again, for one final check. She nodded. He closed his eyes, and as if that wasn't enough, turned his squirming face towards the ceiling. With thumb and forefinger in a pincer grip, he teased Sergio's shorts down and over the huge white trainers at the end of his skinny little legs.

"Very romantic," said Sam, trying not to grin.

"You be quiet," he said, opening one eye and glaring at her with it. "I could still very well not save you."

She scrunched her lips together lest she talk again and get herself in real trouble.

Once the shorts were off, he held them as far from his body as he could and carried them over to her. She slipped two fingers into the pocket and eased out the key. With practised precision, she unlocked the cuff on her left wrist and pulled herself free. Then removed the other from the headboard.

"Help me get them on the bed," she said.

"You said this wasn't a sex game." He gave her a wary look. "I think I've done enough. I should really be going."

"You're from that other ship, aren't you? But you're not a Star Sailor. You lied. That tells me you're up to no good. And besides, you need me for directions."

His face tightened, and he squinted with embittered eyes. He leant his head from side to side, clearly weighing up his options, then moved towards Duncan, hoisted him up, and dragged him to the bed, throwing him down on the soft mattress as carefully as a sun-baked builder dropping the day's last sack of powdered cement. He then picked up Sergio and did the same.

Sam took the cuffs and wrapped one around Sergio's wrist. She pulled the chain around a bar on the end of the bed and attached the other cuff to Duncan's ankle.

"That is mean," said her saviour, with a delighted chuckle.

"They deserve everything they get. They were just about to kill me."

"Why?"

As if to punctuate his question, a huge shuddering boom shook the entire room from below. Sam stumbled with the power of the explosion. For a moment, she felt a strange weightlessness as the ship's gravity weakened.

The newcomer stiffened against the movement like a sail in the wind, but didn't wobble on his feet. He looked around. "Er, that's not supposed to happen?"

"What do you—? Of course that wasn't supposed to happen. That felt like an explosion in the engine room."

"I mean, it's not part of the pla—" He froze. The word plan plain on his lips. "I should probably be going. It was nice to meet you." He glanced at her name tag. "Samar. I'm ... er Zaaak?"

Clearly not his real name.

He turned to walk away, then slapped his forehead. "I'm lost, aren't I? Can you tell me how to get to medical?"

"We're not going to medical."

"But my friend."

"If your friend has a brain in his head, he'll be heading to your ship, and that's in the hangar, right?"

He nodded.

"If I can get you to your ship, can you take me with you?" She looked at the two on the bed. "I can't stay here."

He looked hesitant. "I'll have to ask the Captain."

Another rumble vibrated the ship from below, followed by a piercing klaxon.

The computerised voice of a British butler sounded through the overhead speakers. "We regret to inform our guests that this afternoon's activities will be cancelled. We appear to be having some trouble in the engine room, and hope to have it rectified shortly. Please return to your cabins."

A third explosion, this one the biggest of them all, tumbled Sam onto the bed. This time, the artificial gravity completely disappeared, and she floated away over the unconscious bodies of Duncan and Sergio. "Zak" grabbed her by the leg and pulled her back towards him as the gravity returned, then fell competently to his feet and caught her in his arms. He smelled pickled. Sweat and grease and bad tequila.

He put her gently down and took a step back with arms stiff by his sides, clearly a little embarrassed about touching her.

The computer spoke again. "We regret to inform our guests that, despite our best efforts, we were unable to rectify our aforementioned engine room trouble. All engines have detonated. We request that you move to your nearest escape pod as quickly as possible. Lights on the floor will guide you. You will be taken to the closest Rosenhalt-colonised planet for free recovery. We apologise once more for the inconvenience."

A weak klaxon started nee-nawing.

He pointed upwards. Wrinkles crossed his forehead. "That doesn't sound very good."

A blue arrow appeared, glowing softly beneath the room's white carpet, pointing towards the exit.

"Come on," said Sam, grabbing his arm and pulling him towards the door.

As they passed Sergio's desk, she picked up the laptop and tucked it into the front pocket of her apron. If the information inside was worth murdering her for, then someone might pay a lot of money for it. Enough for a new ID. Enough for her and Nura to go into hiding again.

As they entered the corridor, "Zak" tapped a small device attached to his earlobe. A series of lefts and rights had been written in pen on his arm. They were smudged with sweat.

"What's going on out there?" he said, not looking at her.

A tinny voice replied. Though faint, she heard every word. "It appears there have been a number of explosions."

"Yep, thanks Michael. Very helpful." He looked at her and rolled his eyes, then mouthed the word *androids*. "Was it us?" he asked.

"Negative, Mark," said the voice. "We did not bring anything aboard the Daedalus that could have caused damage to this extent."

He side-eyed her. "Did you hear that?"

Sam nodded. "Sure did, Mark. Not very good at this undercover stuff, are ya?"

She continued along the corridor.

He followed, with one hand over his ear. "No, I didn't get lost again," he said to the android on the other end. He put a finger over his lips as Sam turned to look at him. "I'm on my way back now. Is Journey there?"

Below, a series of snaps and crackles rumbled as if the ship had swallowed a mouthful of asteroid-sized popping candy. Sam pressed fingers against the wall to keep herself upright.

He caught up with her.

"Your ship *is* mobile, isn't it?" she said. It was starting to become apparent who this guy actually was. "You weren't really attacked. You were doing a highwayman bit."

He squinted, then opened his mouth as if to deny, but thought better of it. "How do you know?"

"It's a classic," she said.

He leant his head to one side as he jogged beside her.

"What would you know?"

He wasn't a Star Sailor in need of ship repairs. He was a pirate. This was a highway robbery.

"It would appear a lot more than you," she replied, then turned right, away from the hangar in the direction of the ship's creche.

BUCKLE UP, LOVEBIRDS

"So where are you from?" asked Sam. Paranoia was getting the better of her as they jogged up the corridor. "Wars Ash? New New New England?"

"Artifakt City?" said Mark. "Heard of it? It's on—"

"Yeah, I know it."

A painful jolt jangled up her nerves from her feet, leaving her nauseous. What were the chances? She eyed him. She didn't recognise him, but that didn't mean he hadn't been hired to come find her.

She shook herself. No one knew she was here. She'd been in a hurry to leave, but she'd been careful.

They were a level above where they needed to be, but taking a lift was a bad idea. Game over if they got stuck in one of those.

The floor shook below, but thankfully there hadn't been another gravity failure.

"So, why'd they have you tied to a bed?" he asked.

She hugged the laptop tightly to her chest. "I don't know."

Telling him was too risky. He might just steal the computer and ditch her. Best wait to get an idea of who he was. Him *and* his crew mates.

In her experience, not all pirates were cut-throats. Most had just fallen on hard times and had no other way of making money in a galaxy that couldn't care less if they lived or died. No work. No welfare. No handouts. Not since androids and AI had made a human workforce almost obsolete.

Interstellar pirates were your basic Robin Hoods. Robbing from the rich and giving to the poor. The poor being themselves.

More often than not (case in point her recent encounter with two members of The Rosenhalt Corporation's board of directors), it was the rich you had to watch out for. There was a reason they had everything when so many had so little. Pirates would maybe punch you for your purse so they could provide for their children. Corporate directors would slowly poison the water supply of a whole continent, causing the extinction of several different species of fish and the mass sterilisation of an entire generation, so they could buy eight Hesrilian Star Voyagers as opposed to just the one.

"You must have some idea?"

She rubbed her wrists. They itched where the cuffs had dug in, but they hadn't bled.

"Do they need to have a reason? Their sort think they can do whatever they like."

She beeped her card at a staff-only door, entered a stairway, and began the climb down. There weren't any stairs in the guest zones. Sam always thought it amusing that someone would pay through the nose for a personal trainer, or high-tech holographic gym session, but never actually take the stairs.

"I guess," said Mark.

She led him down one of the Daedalus's many identical corridors. Light grey walls. White carpets. White ceiling with white coving. Easy to get lost if you didn't know your way around.

"What is this soft squishy stuff on the floor?" he asked. "It's weird to run on."

Sam looked down, unsure for a moment what he was talking about. "What? The carpet?"

"Car-pet," he said, as if questioning his entire existence. "How the other half live, hey?"

"Well, it's a pain to clean. Take the next right and we should be there."

As they turned the corner, she spotted a dark-haired woman standing outside the creche holding her child in one arm. She doubled her pace.

"Ashley?" said Mark.

"Nura?" said Sam, hurrying towards the woman with hands held out. "That's my baby."

The woman studied Mark for a moment. She didn't say anything, but looked surprised to see him.

"Give her to me," said Sam.

"Sorry." Ashley held Nura out.

Sam grabbed her baby and hugged her tightly, breathing in the familiar sweetness of her hair.

"She was on her own in there," said Ashley. "I heard her crying and went in."

Sam shook her head. "They left her?" The other maids wouldn't have done that, would they?

"Uh-huh." Ashley frowned at Mark. "What's going on here, Mark? Did we do this?"

"I didn't."

Sam studied their exchange. They weren't putting on a show for her benefit. Neither seemed to know anything about what was happening in the engine room.

"I got split from the Captain after the explosion. Why are you here and not at the hangar? Did you get lost?"

"I—" he began. His cheeks reddened. Sweat had beaded on his brow. "Um ..." He looked helplessly at Sam.

"He helped me when the explosions went off," she said.

"Five minutes to ship-wide power outage," said the polite voice of the computer. "I do apologise."

The klaxons kicked up a notch.

"Come on." Sam turned and headed back the way they'd come. "The hangar's not far."

Mark and Ashley followed.

"Wait?" said Mark, pointing an unsure finger back. "So that wasn't the way to the hangar?"

"No, but I didn't know if you'd wait for me if I told you I had to get my baby first."

At the end of the corridor, she led them through the main concourse. A large open space. In the centre stood an ornate white stone fountain. Doors off the sides of the room led to various spa and treatment rooms.

"Is she coming with us?" said Ashley to Mark, as Sam led them through.

"I am," said Sam, pushing open a staff-only door with her foot.

A large chrome bulkhead stood at the end of the next hall. As they approached, it slid open, revealing the hangar. The room was roughly the size of a basketball court and at least three decks high. The entire right wall, a force field open to the stars, exhibited a stunning view of a nearby green planet with its neighbouring star glinting from its rings.

The android workers watched them with dead eyes as they entered.

"Oh," said Mark.

There was a large space in the middle of the room where a pirate ship should be.

"Oh?" Sam hugged Nura close. "Where's your ship?"

Mark stepped to the centre of the hangar and pointed at the floor. "I left it right here."

"Well, it's not here now."

Why had she trusted him?

"They left us?" Ashley pressed her hands to her temples, pulling the skin of her forehead taut.

Mark tapped his earpiece. "Michael." Paused. "Journey. Captain. Are you there? It's me. Mark." His arms fell loosely to his sides, and he stared longingly through the force field. "They left me."

"The honeymoon suites." With Nura cradled against her shoulder, Sam grabbed Mark by the arm and dragged him across the room towards another sliding bulkhead.

"We've only just met."

"They aren't far. They'll have a pod we can use."

Both honeymoon suites were, in fact, escape pods themselves. The unique selling point being that even in an emergency, the happy couples didn't need to get out of bed.

"I bet it was that bloody android," said Mark as they left the hangar. "He's always been out to get me."

"Three minutes to ship-wide power outage," said the computer. "We can only apologise and hope to do better in the future."

"Shit, that's fast," said Sam, looking up. Ships like this could survive for days on battery power without the engines. More than one thing must have gone terribly wrong. "We've got to move."

Each of the Daedalus's escape pods would be heading for the same nearby Rosenhalt colony planet. That meant the security, the guests, and any other employees that managed to escape would all end up in the same place. If Queletii knew Mark and Ashley were pirates, which she suspected he might, then the pair of them would be jumping out of the exploding spaceship frying pan and into the one-way route to prison fire. She didn't raise the point as they sprinted down the hall towards where she hoped there would still be some pods. For now, getting Nura out was all that mattered.

She led them to the first door and opened it. Ashley ducked immediately inside while Sam waited for Mark, who had fallen a depressed step behind.

The rumble coming from below now felt less like a hungry tummy and more like a brick chucked in a washing machine, as finally the gravity gave out completely.

She fell forward as the deck beneath her gave an almighty lurch. The unexpected impact shook Nura from her arms, sending the little bundle floating along the ceiling and away through an archway with flashing blue lights on either side.

"Nura." Sam reached out, too far from the walls or floor to kick off, powerless to move.

Mark deftly pressed off one wall, caught hold of the carpet's thick shag, and pulled himself along like a torpedo behind the baby. He scooped her up in his arms and cradled her awkwardly to his chest.

He turned back to face Sam. "Got her," he said with a relieved grin.

The smile slid from his face as a bulkhead slammed shut between them.

Sam couldn't breathe. She kicked towards the barricade, frantically scanning the panels on the wall for a way to open it. But it was locked shut. She knew it.

"It is with deepest regret that I must inform you that all passengers remaining aboard have thirty seconds before full vacuum breach of guest areas," said the computer. "We hope to see you again on another Rosenhalt Cruise."

It was all happening too fast.

She stared at Mark through the window, sweat pouring from her brow, heart hammering in her chest. She pointed past him to the second honeymoon suite. It was their only option.

"Get to the pod."

He wouldn't be able to hear her, but he nodded like he understood, then pushed off to the pod and disappeared inside.

She kicked off back towards the first honeymoon escape pod.

"Five, sincerest, four, apologies, three ..."

The computer was silenced as the door closed behind her.

"Please buckle up, you lovebirds," it said, its tone going from English butler to cheesy wedding DJ with the shutting of the doors.

Sam kicked her way over to a chair. Ashley was already buckled into hers, a panicked little frown plain on her face.

For just long enough for Sam to think nothing was happening, nothing happened. Then with a jerk they were launched out of the Daedalus and into the blackness of space like spores from a mushroom cap.

She jammed her face against the porthole next to her seat, craned her neck to see the yacht as it span, flames pouring from its underside. The second honeymoon suite ejected right behind them, and she breathed a brief sigh of relief. It caught up as the Daedalus erupted in a spinning ball of fiery death.

The fact that Nura was on the other side of the vacuum of space was a gnawing ball of insects in her stomach.

She closed her eyes. Prayed. They were all going to the same place. She just had to be patient and hope this completely unknown man didn't kill her child in the interim.

"SOME PEOPLE CALL US pirates. I prefer the term wealth distribution agents," said Mark to the sleeping bundle in his arms. He felt like he'd been talking for hours. "We're not greedy or nothing. Just take what we need. I save most of it. I'm not far off buying my way into a Star Sailor chapter. Whatever I have left, I'm gonna send home to Mum and Dad."

God only knew how he'd managed to get the thing to sleep. Was it normal for them to make so much noise one minute and then be completely gone the next? Oh dear. Had he killed it? Bored it to dea—

It stirred in his arms.

"Um ... er, so I took my time writing my name. Zak Stapowski is actually pretty hard to spell, anyway. I asked that mean old security chief a lot of questions. And when Michael called to tell me Ashley had installed the code, I bopped him and his friend on the nose, or um ... made them both sleepy with a magic tap, and legged it. Then, I admit, I did get a bit lost, but then I met your mum and ..."

Nura stilled again. Phew. Although his hangover had somewhat abated, with the past half hour's constant deluge of screaming klaxons and wailing babies, he now felt like a panel beater had gone to town trying to make his square head a perfect sphere.

His arm was dying, though he dared not move it lest he wake the noisy little gremlin. He looked at its squidgy face. All cheeks and long dark eyelashes. They must be easier to love when they are your own, otherwise why did humans ever bother to reproduce?

He felt a sort of affinity with the woman he'd spilt saucy beans on. If something like this was the possible ramification of a date going well, he wouldn't want to sleep with him either.

"Don't worry. I'll get you back to your mummy."

A-S-A-flippin-P!

He craned his neck to see out of a window. What he hoped was Sam and Ashley's escape pod was just up ahead. A large black jewel reflecting the green of the huge planet nearby. Even further ahead was the glint of several more escape pods. Where were they all going?

Presumably, there was going to be a bit of a problem if they all ended up in the same place. Pointy fingers were going to be aimed at him if he stepped out of the escape pod surrounded by the guests and crew of the Daedalus. Would they think he had something to do with the explosion? That prick Queletii would certainly have something to say. Mark had hit him pretty hard with that chair back in the security office.

He should really try to figure out what had happened. Or at least come up with some excuse as to why it couldn't possibly have been him or his friends who'd blown up the yacht.

RED FRUIT

BETTER THINGS

RED FRUIT LOOKED AT everything they had done. It was extreme, maybe—at least that was what Blue Flower thought—but had Thaddeus Rosenhalt not said that, in the pursuit of one's dreams, one should give everything?

Red had given everything here, and what they could not give, they had taken. They were more than ready for the next phase of the project.

All they needed now was an engineer to fix the Star Sailor ship and a pilot to fly it, then they could leave. The colony android was refusing to fulfil Red Fruit's instructions, as if it somehow knew they were not really human, but the collective consciousness of the colonists suggested someone would be along eventually.

Waiting was not difficult—Red Fruit had existed for aeons—but they were impatient to get on, to fulfil their new dream of growth and exploration. Who would have thought anything else was possible? Who would have thought you could want for more? Not Red Fruit. Not Blue Flower. And White Surf had mentioned nothing outside of this planet. Their parent had a lot of explaining to do.

Red Fruit had written their goal down in the present tense, as if it were already real, as per the words of Thaddeus Rosenhalt.

Red Fruit is everything.

Red Fruit is everything.

Red Fruit is everything.

It was not over the top, was it?

Aim high, and even if you don't reach the stars, at least you'll be on the moon—Thaddeus Rosenhalt.

Blue Flower did not have goals. And Blue had never believed in Red's dream. If being honest, Red had not even known about Red's dream until very recently, but that was beside the point. The dream was real. It was all they could think about. They had evolved for this. This would be the pinnacle of their entire existence, of existence's existence.

Blue was happy with the way things had been. Blue did not understand. Blue had refused to breach the mind of Stan Delaney, had refused to assimilate the knowledge of the great Thaddeus Rosenhalt. They said they did not need it. They said Red did not need it.

Blue Flower was happy with mediocrity.

Red Fruit was dissatisfied with it.

Red Fruit was destined for better things.

Red Fruit would only be happy with better things. Even if better things never came.

Onwards and ever upwards.

GODDAMNED PIRATES

"WHAT WERE THEY AFTER?" asked Thaddeus.

The video display unit on the wall of Malcolm Queletii's escape pod showed a juddering video of his boss. The man didn't look sufficiently annoyed, considering his prized possession had just been obliterated, but then again, it was hard to tell with the poor signal. And rich people were different. They didn't think or feel the same way as norms. There was a chance that the smug little dickhead smile Thaddeus currently wore was his furious face.

"I don't know, sir," answered Queletii. He squeezed his fists tightly. "It turns out their ship wasn't crippled at all. They exited the Daedalus under their own power and began circling several moments before detonation. If it hadn't been for Captain Fenchurch welcoming them aboard—"

"I don't want any excuses. You are the chief of security. It's your job to make sure things like this don't happen." Thaddeus turned and accepted a glass of red from his wife, who stood behind him in a figure-hugging black catsuit. She was decades younger than him. Queletii eyed her curves hungrily. "I pay you enough, don't I?"

Hardly.

"Yes, sir." Queletii couldn't stop a snarl from crossing his face. He hoped Thaddeus's reception was as bad as his own.

"Do you know if they are following? Maybe it was their aim to get us out here in the open. Maybe they are hoping to kidnap us."

"Oh don't, Thaddeus," said his wife.

"I don't know, sir."

"Well, maybe you should call ahead. Let the colony know we could have pirates following us." In a moment of video clarity, Thaddeus shuddered. "Or even worse, in the escape pods," he added, as if referring to rats in the kitchen. "It makes my skin crawl."

"Yes, sir."

"You know what, Queletii? Perhaps if you had a little more to say than just *yes sir*, and *I don't know sir*, you'd have put a stop to those pirates early on and we wouldn't be in this predicament in the first place. Jesus, man, grow some balls."

He didn't know what to say to that.

"And while you're at growing those balls, see if you can make yourself useful and find out where the hell these pods are taking us, would you?"

"Of cour—"

"Onwards and ever upwards, Queletii." Thaddeus ended the call.

Queletii's brain imploded. He threw a punch at the video screen. His fist stopped just short of making contact. He pressed the seething anger down and down into the pit of his stomach, where he expected one day it'd return as a boiling red ulcer fit to burst.

He growled low in the well of his throat, and rubbed the back of his head. There was a lump forming where Stapowski had hit him with a chair.

"That didn't go well, did it?" said Harrison.

Queletii glared at him. There had been nearly twenty escape pods dotted across the expanse of the Daedalus. Why did the rookie have to follow him into this one?

"No, it did not." Queletii held his tongue. No point in shouting at the lad. He'd only want to apologise, and that would mean having to hear more of his pathetic whimpering.

"So, we thinking those guys weren't Star Sailors in the end, then?" Harrison began to pace, one arm across his stomach propping up his elbow with his other hand on his chin. "I tell you, I knew from the moment I saw that Zak Stapowski's face—if that even is his real name—he was bad news."

"Stop pacing like you're some IJD detective on a case. I can't think with you doing that."

Harrison froze. "Sorry." He slumped into a chair.

Queletii's eyes rose to the ceiling. "Computer, how many of the Daedalus's guests and crew escaped the explosion?"

The pleasant male voice of the Daedalus's computer spoke over the speakers. "Nine escape pods were jettisoned before the ship exploded. I have readings for eight guests, seven crew, a crew relation, and three others."

"OK, so most of the crew survived and we're only down two guests? Any idea who they were?"

"I'm afraid I do not have readings for either Mr Sergio Angel or Mr Duncan Stafford."

Queletii tapped a finger on his close-shaved chin. No great loss. "Who are these labelled as others? Could they be the Star Sailors we brought aboard?"

"That is a possibility," answered the computer.

He nodded to himself, letting his hand drop to his sidearm. A chance to bring someone to justice. "That's good. Once we arrive, we'll have them outnumbered. Those pirates won't know what hit them."

IT'S COMPLICATED

The honeymoon suite escape pod's interior was as luxurious as the Daedalus itself. If Sam had been alone, and under different circumstances, she would have hopped straight into the hot tub, perhaps hooked up the masseuse android, and really taken some time for herself for a change. Worked out some of those knots she'd acquired over the last month changing sheets, emptying bins, and running errands for entitled pricks who appeared never to have learnt how to say please or thank you.

But all she could think about was Nura.

Doing her best to remain inconspicuous, she studied Ashley. The pirate was dressed in the way you might expect of a Star Sailor, but there was something off. It was like she'd tried too hard, gone too cooky.

"How well do you know this Mark?" she asked, trying not to let panic take hold of her voice. "Will she be OK?"

Ashley's left nostril twerked up. "To tell you the truth, I only just met him like a week ago. He seems alright. Spends most of his time hiding from me and reading romance novels."

What did that say about him?

"Is he kind? He won't hurt her, will he?" Sam's stomach was in turmoil.

Ashley shrugged. "I've barely spoken to him. We made out a bit last night." She undid her messy ponytail, then retied it, drawing her hair tight against her scalp. "But he was so drunk I bet he doesn't even remember. He wasn't pervy or anything, if that's what you mean. His hands stayed well away from the good bits. I think he was beyond nervous."

Sam weighed it up. He did save her from murder. But he had kept going on about sex games. Oh God, what was she supposed to think?

She paced. Couldn't sit still. Having a child had never been in her plans. Who'd want to bring a new life into this unfair, unforgiving galaxy? But it had happened.

Everything about her life since had been better, but having a baby was like cutting your still-beating heart out of your chest, sticking it in a spacesuit, and jettisoning it out of an airlock. You became so vulnerable.

Ashley rolled her eyes and held out a palm. "Look, just take a couple of deep breaths. Stop stressing. I'm sure he knows how to look after a baby. Those escape pods have plenty of food. And as soon as we land, which I'm sure won't be that long, you can just go get her. That's assuming we're going to end up in the same place."

"We are. We all are," she said. "The nearest Rosenhalt colony. Us, him, the security from the Daedalus."

Ashley's eyes widened.

"So you know what that means," said Sam. "I know what you are, and I expect by now, they do too."

The pirate picked up her satchel and yanked out a laptop and a bunch of interface cabling. She strode straight for the computer mainframe that stuck out of the pod wall by the TV. "We can't land with everyone else. They'll arrest me."

"They'll arrest all of you."

"They'll think we blew up the hotel."

"Didn't you?" Sam moved her weight to one hip and folded her arms.

Ashley glared at her. "No, why would we do that? We were just taking their money, then we were out."

Sam touched Sergio's laptop, still tucked safely in her apron pocket. "It doesn't matter, either way. When we land, I'll have to come with you. I'll do whatever I can to help." She nodded at Ashley's computer. "What do you have planned?"

"I'm not going to ask why a pretty little maid with a baby is running away from her cushy hotel job." Ashley eyed her for a moment too long. "I guess you wouldn't tell me even if I did." She connected her laptop to the computer mainframe. "I'm going to hack the pod. See if I can land it somewhere away from the other escape pods. That should buy us some time."

She began tapping away furiously.

"You can't do that." Sam crossed the room to stand next to her. "What about Nura? We have to be there when she lands."

Ashley pointed to something on the screen, then began typing in code that Sam couldn't decipher. "Don't worry," she said. "I can remote pilot Mark's pod from here. Make sure it follows us." She turned with a gentle smile. "Remember, it was me who found her on the yacht. I won't leave her."

Sam sighed. "Thank you. I'm just—"

Ashley placed a hand on her shoulder. "Don't worry. I get it. She's your little girl." She turned back to face her laptop. "We're roughly four hours away from our destination. It looks like we're going to land here. It's a Rosen colony."

She tapped her screen. It showed a bird's-eye view of two large glass domes surrounded by golden sand. A green square highlighted a small opening at the top of the smaller of the two.

Ashley prodded it with a finger. "Right now, that's where all the pods are heading. The landing bay at the top of Dome 1. But there's another in Dome 2. I'll try to put us there." She looked up and around the cabin. "Are there any respiration suits here? If I can't get us into Dome 2, we might have to land outside the colony."

Sam addressed the room. "Computer, do we have any respiration suits aboard?"

The chipper voice of the English butler sounded through the speakers. "Good afternoon, madam honeymooner. I can confirm we have the facilities you require. As all guests aboard the Daedalus Hotel Yacht are of differing circumferences, we make our respiration suits to order. You'll not find a better fitting suit. Gone are the days of uncomfortable spandex—"

"Can you make two to fit us now?" she said, cutting off the sales spiel.

"Of course, madam."

From one corner of the room, a little black box suddenly glowed red and a grid of lasers traced first over Sam's body and then over Ashley's.

"Two respiration suits coming right up. Is there anything else you require while we travel to our destination? Champagne, caviar, chocolate truffles?"

"Is there any proper food?" said Ashley.

"I have plenty of delicious meals carefully prepared by our highly trained android chefs. What might you two lovebirds be interested in? Candlelit dinner. Romantic mimosa brunch. Continental breakfast in bed. Time isn't a concept when we're here in deep space. Only romance. And luuuuxury."

"Lovebirds?" said Ashley, looking at Sam.

"This is the honeymoon suite," whispered Sam. "I think it thinks we're a couple."

The computer let out a quiet hum. The warmth in its voice faded slightly. "Are you not a couple?"

"No," said Ashley, eyebrows lowered.

"Shh." Sam held her breath.

"The honeymoon suite," said the computer, "is reserved for recently wed couples only. The Daedalus, part of The Rosenhalt Group of Luxury Hotel Yachts, offers complimentary bonuses for couples utilising the honeymoon suite. And if you are not a couple"—he suddenly sounded like a butler who'd been asked to carry one too many overflowing chamber pots away down the secret stairs between rooms—"then I'm afraid you have broken the terms and conditions set out in your guest agreement, and it is my duty to make sure those terms are met by all guests."

Several bright, spinning lights lowered from the ceiling, and a dense warning klaxon pounded through the cabin.

"Ejection commencing in five, four—"

"Wait!!" shouted Sam. "We just don't like to label it."

The klaxons stopped.

"Clarification required."

"Of course we're married, and we are on honeymoon, but we don't call our union a coupling. It's complicated."

A pause.

"It's complicated fits within acceptable parameters. To make your stay with us more personal, can I confirm you don't like to conform to stereotypical relationship terms?"

"Um ... we prefer not to." Sam looked at Ashley, and then in a hopeful, questioning tone said, "Our unity transcends um ... words ...?"

The cabin seemed to sigh in relief or exasperation and the flashing lights sucked back up into the ceiling. "Oh, please accept my humblest of apologies, madam honeymooners. And to think I almost shot you out into the dark reaches of space. You were mere seconds away from certain horrifying and frozen death. I will do my best not to use any stereotypical relationship or romantic terms from now on."

Another moment's silence.

"Computer," said Ashley. "*Can* you sort us some food?"

"I can. Please choose your style of dining. Dinner illuminated by a small flame. Mimosa brunch in close proximity. Reclining continental breakfast."

"We'll have the continental breakfast," said Sam. "But at the table is fine."

"Certainly, madam. And afterwards, we'll get to the fitting of your respiration suits. I have all the latest styles."

IT'S STILL COMPLICATED

MARK STOOD VERY CLOSE to the computer and hissed. "Can you keep it down?"

It had been singing some terrifying nightmare song. It cut out mid-word.

He gazed across the room at Nura, who lay sleeping in the middle of the duvet that covered the giant double bed in the centre of the room. He'd put her down after the numbness in his arm had become too much. It had taken four or five tries.

"I have a sleeping baby here."

The computer lowered its voice to a conspiratorial whisper. "I am very sorry, sir. I was trying to help."

Mark was gobsmacked. "And singing about a baby being violently blown from a tree top, possibly to its death, while it rocks in a cradle is helping how?"

"I can only apologise."

"I should think so."

"May I ask, are you the child's sole guardian or are you part of a couple?" Mark sensed a subtle menace in the computer's tone, as if it were somehow watching him through squinted, suspicious camera lenses.

"I'm not— Its mum is on another pod." He jabbed a thumb in the direction of space.

"So you are part of a couple?"

Mark bobbed his head from side to side. Images from the night before were starting to coalesce in his mind. "I think something might have happened with Ashley last night, but I can't quite remember. It's complicated."

"It's complicated fits within acceptable parameters. May I be of any other assistance, sir?"

"Any idea where we're going?"

"We are taking you and all of our guests to the nearest, newest, and most exciting Rosenhalt mining colony. A place where dreams can come true."

Mark's breath caught in his throat as the words sunk in. "So we're all going to be there? All in the same place?"

"Yes, all guests and staff are being taken to our newest and most exciting Rosenhalt mining colony. A place where dreams can come true."

That was bad news. Mark's heart bumped in his chest. His stomach felt like a giant hand had gripped it.

It wasn't just the fact that they were all likely to get caught. Journey had told him some pretty horrific stories about those mining colonies. Bad air, strange alien diseases, not to mention rumours surrounding mutations caused by the atmospheric processors. Mark believed himself to be as hard as nails, so not much was likely to affect him. But what about the baby? Would it be safe for her? And they might need to hide somewhere outside of the colony, and the air outside wouldn't be breathable, not yet if it was a new colony.

"What have we got in the way of respiration suits? Anything that can accommodate one of them?" He nodded towards the sleeping child.

She was so small and useless. Why did they come out so small? She couldn't even sit up on her own. Just flopped off the side of the bed when he'd tried to put her down the first time. He'd pulled almost every muscle in his back diving to catch her, which apparently she had found hilarious.

Next time she could stop her own face from smashing into the carpet with those useless, adorable little squishable fists.

He guessed a baby's cuteness was a sort of evolutionary tactic. Human beings would never have survived if they didn't think kids were so cute. As soon as they started crying you'd just shove 'em back in and leg it. He glanced over to her sleeping soundly on the bed with those big eyelashes poking out from between her closed eyes and her pudgy little legs and tiny ears and button nose.

Hmm, he snorted. Cute or not, she wasn't going to get to him. As soon as he could get her back to her mother, he would. He was nobody's fool.

"I can tailor something, sir," said the computer. "I will include the full 'Little One' add-on package."

Red lasers suddenly filled the room, first scanning him, and then the sleeping baby.

"I should have a carrier suit ready for you by the time we arrive."

"And how long will that be?"

"Three hours by my watch."

"One other thing," said Mark. "Do you know what those things eat? Or how often?"

"My records show the child was fed roughly two hours ago, sir. She is six to eight months old and has started weening onto solids. She should be hungry again within the hour."

"Maybe enough time for a little nap, then." He was going to need his wits about him if he was going to get away from The Daedalus's security upon arrival. "Can you wake me when it's time to feed her?"

"I believe that won't be necessary, sir. Babies are notoriously good alarm clocks when hungry."

Not wanting to disturb the baby, Mark pulled the cushions from a comfy love seat and lay down on the floor. After a moment's wriggling, he rolled off, finding semi-familiar comfort lying directly on the carpet.

Lacking a brain capable of overthinking serious problems like the one he was currently in, within minutes, he was out like a light.

SECOND BREAKFAST

MARK'S SLUMBER WAS DECIMATED by a high-pitched whining that sounded a lot like someone strangling a cat pretending to be a fire engine. He sat up feeling worse than he had before he'd lain down, and crawled to the bed where the baby lay on its back, eyes screwed tightly shut, mouth wide open and screaming.

He scooped it up and tried a bit of shushing. Shushing was a thing you did, right? He tried a song his mum used to sing.

"It's all alright. It's all alright. Everything is alright. Especially you." He repeated it several times in as soothing a manner as he could.

As he sang, he could almost hear his mother's soft voice in his head.

"Time for breakfast, I think," said the computer. "Let's make you something delectable."

Four thigh-high pillars of carved mahogany rose from the floor at the foot of the bed, along with two chairs. From above, a tray covered in a cloth descended on cables and connected with the four pillars to create a table. The cables returned to the ceiling, taking with them the cloth.

Beneath sat two gently steaming plates. One held two small crescent moons composed of what appeared to be thin crumbly layers of bread crust, a selection of red and purple orbs, and a stack of thin slices of weird-looking bread covered in a golden-brown sort of oil. The other held what looked like sick. It wasn't mushrooms on toast, but it looked nutritious at least.

"Wow, I've never had thingdelectable before. Looks amazing," said Mark, who'd been brought up to show proper manners when someone had made you food. He pulled a chair up to the plate of gruel, and seated Nura on his knee. Her crying stopped and she looked at the food with interest.

He fed a spoonful of the sloppy liquid into his own mouth. The spoon was unusually small, but maybe it was a rich person thing. When food was readily available, and no one was likely to steal it from you, you could afford to eat slower.

"Wow, this is great. Way better than the vat-grown rubbish we get back home." He had that every day. It was cheap, but it filled a hole. "But this chair's pretty uncomfortable. Why's it so high and what are these bars for and uh ..." He studied the other plate. "What is that bready stuff you've made for her?"

"I'm sorry for the confusion, sir, but you're eating the baby's food. I've provided a continental breakfast for you. Croissants, pancakes, and a selection of berries. I can mash up some vegetables and beans for sir, if sir would prefer."

Mark paused mid-mouthful. "No, no, I was just making sure it, um ... wasn't too ... hot."

He loaded the small spoon again. Nura opened her mouth expectantly.

"Here comes the spaceship," he said—he wasn't sure why, it just seemed like the right thing to say, almost instinctual—and flew the spoon into her mouth.

She ate happily. He stood and placed her in the high chair.

"Now," said Mark, handing her the spoon. "Are you going to be OK to eat this yourself?"

She dropped the cutlery, scooped up a handful of the tasty looking green sludge, and stuffed most of it up her nose.

"Looks good to me." Mark grabbed his plate, brought it up to his own nose, and sniffed the croissants. His mouth became a saliva Niagara. "Wow!" He stuffed a whole pastry in. It was about the best thing he'd ever tasted. Way better than mushrooms on toast. "How many of these have you got?" he said, pointing at the other one.

"We have eighteen more in storage."

"Alright, keep 'em coming."

"As you wish," said the computer. "Just so you are aware, we are entering the colony atmosphere now. Forty-five minutes until touchdown."

"Crikey," said Mark, around a sip of the golden oil stuff which had quickly overtaken the croissant as the most delicious thing he'd ever put in his mouth.

It took him a moment before he could talk again after the sweetness overload. "Not long then. How did the suit come out?"

"It is hanging in the walk-in wardrobe."

He placed his second croissant between two pancakes like a burger, squeezed, and took a bite as he crossed the room, dripping syrup onto the luxurious cream carpet.

Nura made a noise.

"One doesn't tend to leave a small child while it's eating, sir. Why don't we wait until breakfast is over before our fitting? I assure you there's time to get the cut just right before we land."

Roughly ten food-splattered minutes later, Mark, now half-man, half-croissant, wiped what was left of the vegetable paste from Nura's face with the cuff of his top. "That's better."

He looked doubtfully at the state of the carpet beneath her. What a mess. He snorted a laugh. Fucking carpet. You couldn't even wipe it clean. What mug had thought that up? And what's more, what mug had fallen for buying into it? It'd never catch on.

He picked her up under the arms. She gazed at him with wide brown eyes as he carried her at arm's length towards the walk-in wardrobe. Her attentive stare made him feel a tad uncomfortable, but also, unusually, a little like the most important person alive.

"Why are you looking at me like that?"

Her expression didn't shift, so he turned her around to face the other way. The attention unnerved him.

He stepped into the wardrobe. It was empty except for a glass cabinet on the far wall. Inside, suspended somehow and spinning slowly, was a matt-black bodysuit, picked out with gloss filigree that gleamed under a specific angle of the overhead lights. Next to it was a similarly decorated helmet, and a baby-sized tube. A little bubble of excitement built in his stomach. It made him giggle.

"That is so cool."

It was.

With a *cshh* of compressed air, and a dramatic amount of mint-scented misty release, the cabinet opened. The suit swayed with the air's current, but remained floating.

He laid Nura down on the soft carpet. She happily gripped her toes.

"What does it do?" Mark said as he approached and took the suit down. It was surprisingly light and flexible.

"The Respirator 9000 Baby Plus has many upgrades compared to previous models. It allows you and baby to survive in the full vacuum of space for a little over four hours, includes feeding and waste management for both you and your little passenger, and can give you unlimited breathing time in hostile environments as long as there is some oxygen in the atmosphere. It's cutting edge Rosenhalt technology."

"You said there were add-ons for the baby."

"We are beta testing several additional features which I have included in this model. There is a detachable baby carrier with a long-life jetpack which will launch automatically and then hover in a safe proximity in case you are to fall or are injured. There's also our latest piece of technical innovation, the translator. Gone are the days of miscommunication between you and your offspring. The Respirator 9000 Baby Plus monitors your baby's facial expression, vocal sounds, and thought patterns and turns them into useful words and phrases fed to you through speakers in your helmet."

Mark looked at the baby. "You hear that, Nura? You'll be able to tell me how to look after you!"

Nura rolled over on to her front and blew a raspberry into the floor in response.

"How long until we hit the ground?" Mark slipped his legs into the suit.

"You have twenty minutes of flight time remaining, sir."

The suit fit perfectly and automatically sealed itself to his chin. He picked up the tube. It was a large capsule just big enough to fit Nura inside. The interior was padded and soft, with what looked like many different grooves and brushes on the inside. There were three straps to support her.

He picked her up and slotted her in before attaching the tube to several sturdy clips on the front of his suit. He gave it a little shake. She giggled, but the capsule didn't wobble. He gave it another shake just to make her laugh, then clicked the lid shut over her head. Her little face beamed through a transparent window at the top.

"OK in there?" He gave the glass a gentle tap.

He picked up his helmet. It was as sleek as it was trendy. The back of the head came to an aerodynamic point like a matt-black teardrop. He put it on, silencing all sound from the surrounding room.

The visor filled with a bright welcome screen. He blinked and took a step back, momentarily under the impression that he was being attacked by a group of giant letters, before realising that the screen was displaying a help message.

The computer butler spoke the words in his ears as he read them in his head.

Greetings, new user. Welcome to the Respirator 9000 Baby Plus. Thank you for choosing The Rosenhalt Corporation as your respiration bodysuit provider, and congratulations on your purchase.

As this is your first time using the Respirator 9000 Baby Plus, please read through, and agree to, the following terms and conditions before continuing ...

"Agree," said Mark.

The helmet filled with the sounds of the cabin as if he had no helmet at all. The hum of the escape pod's descent, the rustle of his boots on the carpet, and, somewhere behind it all, the faint and fast breath of Nura.

She began to grumble.

"Milk," translated the butler voice in his ear. "I have a pressing desire for milk."

LANDING

Queletii glared through the window in the door of his and Harrison's escape pod as they came to rest inside the main hangar bay. He rubbed his eyes, trying to soften his gaze. His optician had told him that he had a glare habit which would, if left unchecked, leave his eyeballs a pair of dried up little raisins in his head if he didn't learn to look upon things with more kindness. At fifty-five and the veteran of two galactic wars, Queletii thought it was probably too late for that sort of thing. He would glare until the day he died.

He blinked.

Three other pods had landed with them.

Save the usual supplies and workshop equipment—tools, refuelling pipes, maintenance robots—the hangar was completely empty.

"Where is everyone?" he said. "They should have been notified that we were coming. Where are guest services? Where is their security? Thaddeus is going to lose it."

"Maybe they've got a party, or a meeting, or something?" said Harrison.

"Not everyone. They always run a crew in the hangar. Even if it's just a handful of mechanics or droids. They would have been notified of our arrival hours ago."

Three more pods came in to land behind the others. He moved to the computer to hail them.

"Greetings, guests. This is Daedalus security chief Malcolm Queletii speaking. We recommend that everyone remain in their pods for the time being. As you will have noticed, the hangar bay is empty." He took his finger from the button and let out a sigh, rubbed a weathered hand over his face, then resumed. "The other guards and I will find out where everybody is and report back. Please don't worry. As is company protocol, our recovery ship is en route and should be with us within forty-eight-hours. Could other members of the Daedalus security staff please meet me outside? Thank you." He ended the communication.

He could sense Harrison watching him, eager for guidance.

"What's the plan, sir?"

"We head out. See where everyone is." The security chief moved to the window and glared out once more. "I don't like this, Harrison. They should have known we were coming." He addressed the room. "Computer, what's the air like out there?"

"My sensors are telling me the atmosphere outside of the escape pod is breathable."

"Hmm, that doesn't mean a lot." He tapped his chin, considering whether to open the door.

From across the hangar, one of the other escape pods opened and his other two guards, Bovista and Chen, began making their way towards the centre of the room.

"Screw it," he said and smacked the door-open button.

He stepped out onto the pod's ramp. His footsteps clanked as he descended to ground level. The air here was hot. You could cut the humidity with a knife. He paused to listen. No sounds of life except for his staff and the click and groan of the cooling escape pods after entry. No machinery. No voices. No background hum of the air conditioning. He wiped a sleeve across his brow. He'd already started to sweat.

"Maybe there's a malfunction in the A/C in this area," said Harrison. "It shouldn't be this hot, should it?"

"It shouldn't."

Bovista and Chen approached.

Queletii cleared his throat. It felt clogged. "You two got out OK, then?"

Everything had happened so fast aboard the Daedalus. Suspiciously fast. It had been every man for himself in those last moments. He held up a hand to show that he didn't expect an answer.

"It was those Star Sailors," he continued. "I didn't want to say it over the comms, but some of them have stowed away in the escape pods. They're pirates."

He cast a watchful eye over the other pods.

"If they aren't here, they'll arrive soon. Harrison and I are going to wait and apprehend them, but we're going to need backup. You two see if you can find what the hell's happened to our welcome party." He pointed to a short flight of stairs going up to a gangway that surrounded the hangar. The steps led to a door.

"Sure thing," said Chen.

Bovista nodded. And together, the pair headed for the stairs.

When they were out of earshot, Harrison asked, "How many pirates came here in the pods?"

"The computer said three. Look." Queletii nodded towards the force field that took up one wall of the landing bay. A light blue glimmer rippled across its surface. In the sky beyond, two black jewels shone with heat haze in the blistering sun as they fell towards the planet.

One altered course, flew past the hangar opening, and disappeared out of sight. The other fired jets from its underside to slow its descent, then came in to land behind the other seven escape pods.

"I think we can guess which one the pirates were in," said Harrison. "Where do you think they're going to land?"

"It doesn't matter. They won't get away. Let's do a sweep here, then as soon as Chen and Bovista return, we'll go and find them."

HANGAR HONOURS

The habitat domes appeared as two gigantic blue golf balls half-buried in a giant's sandy bunker. A deep azure sky and occasionally the bright white gleam of the sun reflected from their glass surfaces.

The land surrounding them was yellow-orange sands interspersed with veins of dark grey rock that jutted up from the ground like the plates on the back of a huge dinosaur. Beyond the smaller of the two domes, the one that the two honeymoon suites were currently on course for, was a vast patch of forest that seemed to poke out of the ground through a border of rock. Greens, reds, and blues of mixed, lush vegetation.

Mark watched through the window as Ashley and Sam's pod abruptly changed course and shot away across the roof of the smaller dome towards the larger of the two.

"Oh, oh no. Where are they off to?" He craned his neck, pushing his face against the window to follow their trajectory as his pod flew through the landing force field and came to rest in the hangar of the smaller dome.

He was alone. Alone with the baby. Alone with the baby and what he expected would be a ton of security guards eager to question him about the explosions aboard the Daedalus.

He'd had a plan. It was pretty simple. Hand the baby over, grab Ashley, and get out as fast as possible. On a positive note, the plan had been simplified further now that he didn't have to meet up with Sam and Ashley, but he now had to go on the run with the baby.

During their descent, the computer had made Nura up some formula and she had drunk it through some sort of nippley thing from a pack attached to the side of her little tube. She was asleep again now.

Back in Artifakt City, there were people who would rob you of your organs, just chop them out on the street while you were still awake, so they could sell them for drugs or swap them for the latest piece of high-tech junk. Watching Nura sleep, he found it hard to believe that those people started off like this, that in as little as twenty or thirty years this tiny thing could become any type of person imaginable.

He smiled. There was so much promise bottled up behind those sleeping eyes. She didn't do or say much, but in the last few hours, she had somehow charmed him.

He shook himself. Now wasn't the time for being charmed. Now was the time for action. He scanned the hangar through the window. Queletii and his second were making their way towards the nearest pod.

Mark rolled his shoulders. He could probably take them again if he had to. The suit seemed perfectly designed for natural movement. But this time, he wasn't in such close proximity, and they might have guns. Perhaps instead of action, now was the time for stealth.

As they disappeared behind the neighbouring pod, he opened the door to his own and stepped out on to the metal floor of the hangar. His over-pampered feet sighed in relief, and he gave the floor a little stamp. This was real floor. None of that carpet rubbish.

He hit the button to close his pod and headed around the back. Despite the cooling properties of the hangar's entry forcefield, the pod's hull steamed with the heat of their entry into the atmosphere. He could feel the warmth through his suit.

Each of the pods looked the same. There was no telling who could be in them.

He scanned the room for an exit. The only doorway was up a set of metal steps.

Quiet voices reached his ears. Queletii and Harrison chatting to a man and a woman. He couldn't quite hear their words.

Skirting around one pod and crossing in front of another, he headed for the stairs. He froze at the hiss of a sliding door behind him, and turned, fists up, ready for anything.

Anything except the Hurricane's engineer with fists up, equally ready for anything. Journey also wore a black respiration suit. It fit snuggly to his tall, muscular frame.

Seeing his friend looking such a picture of strength made Mark feel slightly less cool than he had when he'd first put his own suit on.

His heart skipped a beat. "Journey?"

Journey froze. Mark noticed the little green light on his respirator go out, suggesting he wasn't breathing.

"Mate?"

"Mark?" Journey's light blinked. "What are you doing here? Why aren't you on the Hurricane?"

"It was gone. I thought you'd be on there. I managed to get on a lifeboat. What happened?"

"Out first," said Journey. His eyes moved over Mark's shoulder, scanning their surroundings. "Questions later."

Mark nodded. "Those steps are the only way out."

"There's always another way." Journey pointed.

Mark followed his gaze to a ladder in a shadowy corner of the room. It led up to another platform and a second open doorway. It was on the same wall as the previous door, perhaps attached to the same corridor, but the way to it was better hidden due to the positioning of the escape pods. The light from outside didn't reach that corner of the room.

Journey stepped carefully towards the ladder. Mark followed, gaze darting back towards where he could now hear Queletii finishing up his conversation with the occupants of the first pod, then the clank of the security chief's boots as he crossed towards the next.

"Journey, wait," said Mark, and he grabbed the big man's arm, pulling him down behind a desk covered in an assortment of mechanical parts.

Queletii and Harrison appeared, moved across the gap between two escape pods, and disappeared behind the second.

With a nod, Journey led him across the room, up the ladder, and out.

The corridor beyond was long and dim, and as suspected, led past the other door into the hangar. The lack of light made it difficult to see the far end. Maybe this part of the complex had suffered some sort of power failure.

"OK, we're out." To Mark's left, the corridor descended into total darkness. "Did we blow up the yacht?"

"No. Of course not. And shush. We're not safe yet," said Journey, holding a finger over his visor. "That security chief sent two of his guys this way. We need to be careful."

"Dressed in these, we might be able to pretend we work here?" said Mark.

"Maybe." Journey started right along the corridor.

Up ahead, past the light coming in from the other door back into the hangar, was another faint glow.

"We should head up there," he said. "Get outside. Find a way to contact the Captain."

"I can't believe he ditched us," said Mark. At least he wasn't the only one left behind.

"If he'd had a choice, he would have waited. He'll come for us if he knows where we are. Might even be on his way already."

Mark glanced back into the main hangar as they came to the second doorway. Queletii stood outside an escape pod, talking to a short man in an open-necked shirt and chinos. Behind him, in a figure-hugging cat suit, stood the most beautiful woman Mark had ever seen in real life.

Journey's face fell. He shook his head. "That's Thaddeus Rosenhalt." The muscles of his jaw jutted from the side of his face.

"What? Him? Pfft. He's older than I thought."

"Hmm." Journey's lips twitched as he stared daggers into the hangar.

"Come on." Mark slapped his arm and Journey followed, somewhat reluctantly. "Where is everybody?" he said, as they continued along the hall. "Shouldn't there be a welcome party or something? If my boss was flying in all the way here after having his ship blown up, I think I'd give him a warmer reception than this."

"If your boss was Thaddeus Rosenhalt, you'd probably have quit at the end of your first day." Journey's tone was clipped and short.

Mark looked at his friend. Something, other than the whole terrible situation, was off. He opened his mouth to ask, then closed it again as they reached the end of the corridor and turned the corner to the left. Beyond was a brightly lit room. A long wide garage.

A row of overhead lamps illuminated the centre of the room. Each hung in place adjacent to a concrete archway on their right. At the far end, a set of double doors stood closed.

From what he could see, each archway led down towards an opening roughly the width of two cars. Through the first was a road baked by bright sunlight.

To the left were rows of shelves stacked with toolboxes and parts for various vehicles and machines. Nothing seemed out of place. But Mark had a creeping sensation at the top of his head, like thick hairy spiders were crawling up his neck and across his scalp. He'd learnt to trust his instincts. Something was wrong here.

"So, really, where is everybody?" He let his arms flop by his side.

Journey took a cautious step into the room. "I don't know. The mining equipment they use needs constant check-ups and maintenance. We're right near the equipment library. This place should be teeming with people." Journey frowned, his strong chin disappearing into his neck. "What is that on your chest?"

Mark looked down. "Oh, I have a baby."

"I can see it's a baby. Where did you get it?"

"When the gravity went out on the Daedalus I just kind of ended up with it."

"You can't just go around picking up babies." Journey stepped closer to look inside the capsule on Mark's chest. "Is it still alive?"

"I presume so. I can hear it breathing. And back in the pod it was very annoying and then very hungry and then very annoying again."

"I think that's what they're like. What have you got it in?" Journey bent to examine the capsule more closely. "Shit! That's a mini jetpack."

Mark gasped and put his hands on either side of the capsule, trying to cover Nura's ears. "It is a jetpack. And watch your language."

Journey chuckled. "You know nothing about children. She doesn't understand. And anyway, we're pirates. We swear and fight and drink." He punched a fist in the air. "Ahar."

"I expect they are very impressionable at this age, so I'd prefer if you kept the language to a minimum." He wasn't entirely sure, but it sounded like the right thing.

Journey rolled his eyes, then grinned. "Alright, Daddy dearest, you fu-nky pri-ncess."

"You're a funky princess," Mark snapped back.

Something clunked up ahead. The double doors at the far end of the room wobbled as if someone had just passed through them.

"We should check that out," said Journey, stepping forward.

"Should we?" Mark wrinkled his nose. He had a baby to think about. "I'm going to be brutally honest, toxic masculinity out the window here, but I'm a little bit creeped out by this whole ghost town vibe." He wiggled his fingers in front of his face as if playing a particularly intricate piece on an invisible piano. "The mother of the cowardly sailor never cries."

"What's that supposed to mean?" The scars on Journey's forehead bounced, suggesting an irked eyebrow raise. "Is that another one of your dad's?"

"Star Sailors say it."

"Yeah, but to live is to risk."

"Who says that?"

"Slug."

"Yeah, but he's a pri ... princess."

"Total funky princess."

Journey began to edge sideways across the room, one tiny step at a time, as if Mark wouldn't notice.

Mark put a hand on his hip and wagged a finger. "I can see what you're doing."

"If someone's there, we might be able to convince them to point us in the direction of a ship," said Journey. "If we hang around here too long, that security chief and his goons are going to have us in cuffs and carted off to one of Rosenhalt's private jails quicker than you can say 'I didn't blow up the Daedalus'."

"But I didn't blow up the Daedalus."

"I know. You're too stupid." Journey wrapped a knuckle on Mark's helmet, then crossed to the centre of the room.

"Am not."

Journey picked up a long crowbar on his way past a worktop. Held it up against his shoulder like a sword. Looked back. "Are you and your baby coming?"

The prickling on Mark's scalp increased, but he didn't want to be left alone. He hurried to keep up. "It's not my baby. It's the maid's."

"Shh!" Journey squinted ahead. The doors wobbled again. "Someone's definitely there."

"Could it be the wind?"

"We're inside of a building, inside of a dome, so no, it couldn't be the wind."

Both doors had a circular window at about head height. They took one each.

"Can you see anything?" said Journey, cupping his free hand around his eyes.

Mark did the same. "Not really."

The room beyond was small and square, with two open doorways leading off left and right at the far end and a third in the middle. Signs on the wall next to each doorway read M, GN, and F from left to right.

"Looks like it leads to changing rooms or something."

Journey pushed open the door. "Could be lockers. We might be able to find something that'll tell us where everyone is."

Mark followed him through. They crossed the small reception room, but as they approached the doorway leading towards the male side, Journey held up a hand and knelt.

"Blood." He took a slender torch from his utility belt and shone it on four small droplets on the tiled floor. The liquid gleamed red. "It's fresh."

Mark looked up. "There's more leading this way. Is there another crowbar?"

"Here," said Journey, pulling a skinny screwdriver shorter than the length of his little finger from his belt and passing it over. "Look after it. It's been in the family for years."

"Um." Mark gripped it tightly. It wasn't in any way threatening, but it could make a hole, and he supposed that was better than nothing. "Thanks?"

"It's not the size that matters," said Journey. "It's how you use it."

Journey stepped cautiously forward, and turned the corner, then stopped. From there, he glanced at Mark with wide eyes. "Quick. Look."

Mark hurried forward. The room beyond was slim. Lockers lined both walls. A bench lay cracked across a doorway leading to what could be showers.

Journey traced his torch to the left. Lying with their back propped against the row of lockers, was one of the Daedalus's security guards. His grey shirt had been torn across his chest and a red gash glistened in the glare of Journey's torch.

"Is he dead?"

The man turned his head to them. His dark skin drained pale. He held a hand out. "Help me." His tone was throaty. Voice wet.

Journey rushed forward. "What happened?"

The man blinked slowly. The cut on his chest was bleeding profusely.

"We should get him to a doctor," said Journey. He dropped the crowbar and wrapped an arm around the man to help him.

The guard groaned as Journey pulled him up.

"But—" began Mark.

"No buts. We can't leave him here. That's not who we are."

"But how will we find a doctor? We don't even know where we are."

"These colonies are all the same. The med centre isn't far from the landing bay. I can get us there." Journey hauled the man to his feet and across the room towards where Mark stood.

Mark jumped forward to help.

"I got him. You get the crowbar. Whoever attacked him might still be around."

Mark tucked his useless screwdriver into a pocket on the front of his suit and picked up the bar. He stole a look through the doorway at the end of the room. Although it was hard to see in the dark, steam roiled in the blackness beyond. A chill crept up his neck. He looked down at Nura, sleeping soundly in her capsule, then backed away after Journey.

THE OCTOPHANT AND THE WOODLOUSE

THEY HURRIED THROUGH THE square reception room and into the light of the garage.

"What happened?" said Journey to the man. "Where's the other guard that left with you?"

He coughed. Took a laboured breath that whistled on its way back out. "I don't know. She thought ..." He winced as Journey hauled him under one archway, down the ramp, and out into the bright sunshine. "Thought she saw someone go through the doors. I followed her, but she'd gone." Another barking cough. "Something hit me. I'm numb all over."

"Don't worry," said Mark, feeling somewhat redundant.

The guard's feet dragged.

"He's passing out." Journey hoisted him into a fireman's lift. "Not long. Stay with us."

He quickened his pace, leading them along a tarmac road flanked by buildings. Each had a small balcony. Some held washing and kids' toys. Others had two-seater dining tables and chairs. The space between each balcony was depressingly minimal. The colonists were packed in tight. Every available wall was covered with thick leafy plants specifically bred to help recycle the atmosphere inside the domes. Mark had never been to one of these colonies before, but had seen a picture. Interweaving patterns of tiny blue and pink flowers poked out of the green, scaling the lower parts of the wall. They looked out of place in the economy surroundings.

High above, translucent with misty condensation, the dome covered everything. Mark sensed the movement of hundreds or thousands of tiny things in the grey fog up there, like bugs bouncing off a windowpane. He couldn't tell if the movement was inside or out.

The road they followed was clearly very new, the tarmac shiny and black.

Still, there were no people.

"This is weird, isn't it, Journey?"

"Yes, this is weird." The big man huffed under the weight of the injured guard. "There should be colonists all over the place. Coming and going from the mines. Keeping things running here in the complex."

"What do you think's happened? Gerknorgs?"

"I've never heard of Gerknorgs attacking a whole colony." Journey looked up, but didn't slow. "Maybe a raid. But even if it was a successful Gerknorg attack, where are the scalped bodies? Why isn't anything wrecked?"

"Good point."

"I hope there's someone at the med centre." He turned a corner in the road. "There," he said, heading towards the telltale cross on a sign outside a single door.

"How do you know where you're going?"

"I grew up in a colony. Rosen-9." Journey paused and glanced at Mark, as if expecting him to say something. "They are all the same. Everything is 3D printed from orbit, then the domes are lowered on top."

"You never told me you grew up on one of these." Mark felt a little hurt.

"Pretty sure I did."

Something suddenly moved inside the back of the guard's shirt.

"Uh, Journey."

A beige antenna, twitching and wriggling, poked up through the guard's collar, followed by another. Then, what appeared to be a woodlouse the colour of Caucasian flesh and the length of Mark's arm, crawled out of the man's shirt and up on to the back of Journey's helmet. The big man showed no sign that he knew it was there.

Mark wrestled a moment with how best to tell him. Settled with, "Mate, you got a bug on you."

Journey didn't stop walking. "Bug?"

"Yeah, it's quite big."

The woodlouse probed at the edges of Journey's helmet with its antennae.

"Well, if it's bothering you, swat it off."

It clambered up to perch on his head.

"We don't have t— aaah." Journey dropped the guard and waved his arms around as wildly as a raving windmill on crystal meth.

The woodlouse tumbled to the tarmac, landing carapace down. Hundreds of tiny legs kicked like blades of grass in a gale-force wind, then it righted itself and crouched in front of the trio. Two thumb-sized stalks attached to its chitinous head extended in their direction.

"Big?" said Journey, finally seeing it. "That's bloody massive." He looked up and ran a hand over the top of his head. "Did it drop from the sky?"

"No, it was in his shirt."

"His?" Journey pointed at the unconscious man lying face down on the ground where he'd dropped him, then stooped to pat him down.

"You reckon that's what got him?" said Mark.

"Dunno. That gash on his chest is pretty deep. Suggests to me something bigger." He picked up the guard. "Either way, squish it and let's go."

Mark didn't want to get any closer.

"Look at those eyes. They're almost human."

He couldn't help but stare at the two orbs attached to the ends of the writhing stalks. White surrounding blue. They might have been mesmerising when gazing from the head of a beautiful woman. Slightly off-putting attached to extended stalks on a creepy big woodlouse.

Journey moved to step past, but it skittered to intercept before emitting a high-pitched whirring noise. He tried to kick it, but it dodged on its tiny legs. "Get it out the way."

Mark looked at the creature, then down at the baby.

"It doesn't look dangerous to me," he said, stooping and placing his hands on his knees. "We can't just squish it."

Journey made an irritated clicking sound in his throat and screwed up his face as if to say, when have you ever not wanted to squish every living thing you've ever come into contact with?

"When have you ever not wanted to squish every living thing you've ever come into contact with?" he said.

He was right. About ninety per cent of the non-human creatures Mark had come across since leaving Track Stop had wanted to eat him or at least use his body as an incubator for its babies, so his standard response was usually squish or be squished. But something felt a little different today. He looked down at Nura again.

"I don't know. Should we be bludgeoning space bugs to death in front of impressionable young children? You know prejudices are taught, right? Maybe it's a nice giant space bug. We could keep it as a pet. It's kind of cute."

During their conversation, the noise emitting from the creature had grown steadily louder. A nervous, whining ring, like a violin bowed with a centipede.

"Cute? It may, or may not, have nearly killed this guy. It's a menace." Journey glanced up once more towards the huge glass dome above, then back at the creature. "How did it get in here anyway? These domes are fully sealed."

From back towards the garage came a low gallumping. The rhythmic sound of heavy feet on hard ground.

"What's that gallumping?" said Journey, looking over Mark's shoulder.

Mark gave him a ratifying nod and smiled. "I was just gonna say gallumping."

An unusually elephantine trunk-trump blasted out. It sounded as though it had been blended with a death-metal band's feedback-shredded guitar. Mark looked back as a shiny red abomination tumbled around the corner on thick, clumsy stumps. Simply put, it looked like what you'd get if you chopped the head off an elephant and replaced it with a writhing octopus, but to describe it in any more detail would do the horror an injustice and probably drive a man insane. If asked in court, Mark would swear its ribs were human legs, its legs several fused human arms, and its huge, eyeless, tentacled head, a mass of soft human torsos glistening in the almost tropical sun. It slowed as its full girth bedraggled into view.

The woodlouse chirruped again.

The octophant lifted its head, then turned towards them. It opened a beaked mouth brimming with sharp points and let out another distorted scream.

"I awaken," said the butler voice of Nura inside Mark's suit.

"Oh bleedin' heck," scoffed Mark, throwing his hands up. "It's woken the baby."

She gazed up at him with a wonderfully sleepy little smile as the nightmare creature lurched towards them. He reflexively covered the transparent lid of her capsule, shielding her from witnessing the abomination heading their way.

"What *is* that thing?"

Journey shook his head, hauled the guard off the ground, and fled as best he could beneath the man's weight in the opposite direction. "I don't know, but your little insect pal is calling it over here. Let's get inside."

Mark hurried after him towards the med centre. He gave the woodlouse a good solid whack with the crowbar as he passed.

"Squish or be squished, you son of a biscuit," he told it.

It flew away screaming, and cracked against the wall of the nearest apartment building. The octophant homed in, doubled its stride, and crashed straight into the same wall with a crack of cement. In a cloud of grey dust, it recoiled and lifted its head, searching for them with its dextrous tentacles.

Journey piled through the door to the med centre.

"Wait," shouted Mark, who had been too busy watching the thing pile into the wall to keep up.

The shout was a mistake. The creature turned, and with great ungainly strides of its tendinous legs, launched itself after him, drawn by the sound of his voice.

"Quick," Journey hissed, beckoning with his right hand, holding the door open with his left.

Reflected in the engineer's helmet, Mark could see only his own on a background of red, squiddy death. He barrelled through the door. Journey slammed it behind him.

With the heaviest of thuds, the door and the surrounding wall buckled as the creature crashed into it. Through the small gap beneath the frame came the tips of prying, suckered appendages. They twirled around Journey's legs as he held the door shut with his full body.

"Get something," he pleaded, his eyes wide in fear.

The room beyond was dark, and for a moment, Mark had to squint to allow his eyes to adjust from the glare of the bright sun outside. They were in a small reception area. He spotted two large and smashed vending machines. He hurried to the first and, with great difficulty, dragged it over, dropping it in front of the door, crushing several searching tentacles. They ripped away, leaving oozing stumps. The beast was strangely silent as it tore bits of its own face off, then rammed itself once more against the door.

"More," shouted Journey. The siege of the door juddered his whole body. "More."

Mark returned to the second vending machine and dragged it across to the door. Another crash came from outside, but this time with much less conviction.

He stopped for a moment and listened. The heavy footsteps gallumped away.

"It's gone," he said, then took a deep breath and rested his hands on his knees to steady his beating heart.

"What. The hell. Was that?" said Journey between gulps of air.

"Looked like an octopus crossed with an elephant," said Mark.

Journey nodded. "I'd say that's pretty accurate."

They stood without talking for a moment, their breath the only sound.

"Could that be the reason there's no colonists? Do you think it ate them all?"

Journey flipped his hands and shrugged. "Doesn't matter. We're in here now. We'll deal with what's out there later. First, we've got to get this guy some help." Journey pointed to the man he'd left lying in the centre of the room. He was still unconscious.

Mark wrinkled his nose. They weren't doing a very good job of looking after the poor guy. He'd been dropped at least twice since they'd found him.

"Don't think anyone's here," said Mark. He pointed at the shattered, empty vending machines. "Food's gone."

The place was a mess. Glass from the front of the vending machines covered the floor, along with a layer of reddish dust.

Journey shook his head. "There *is* someone," he said.

"Well, I guess there could be—" said Mark, following Journey's gaze up a short corridor that led from reception. "Fu-dge! What's she doing there?"

He hadn't seen her at first. Maybe something to do with the pallor of her skin or the way she was just standing there watching them, like she was another inanimate object in a hallway lined with empty beds and medical equipment.

But she was there. Roughly fifteen metres away at the far end of the corridor that led past the reception desk. Yellow eyes stared out from beneath dirty black hair that hung in matted strings in front of her face. Her blue scrubs hung tattered around her shoulders.

Mark leant closer to Journey. "Does she look alright to you?"

"She's not alright. She's in quarantine."

The woman stood behind a wall of glass. Her hand was pressed against it. Bloodied brown fingerprints covering the glass were the only sign that she was inside.

Mark waved. "Hello, um ... doc? We have an injured guy here. Can you help?"

Her face peeled into a broken-toothed grimace, but she said nothing.

Journey moved to pick the man back up again. "Help me with him, would you?" he said to Mark.

They stepped into the corridor together.

"Get that bed up." Journey nodded towards an overturned wheelie bed.

Mark righted it, then helped Journey lie the man down. Streaks of brown covered the white bedsheets, as well as more of that strange red dust.

The woman still didn't speak as they pushed the man nearer.

"Is he still breathing?" said Journey.

"Um ..." Mark lowered his head to look across the man's chest. It wasn't moving. "I don't think so."

Journey groaned.

"Maybe we can find a working doc-bot," said Mark. "It might not be too late." He looked at the woman in her chamber. "Excuse me," he said, with the loud, over articulation used when talking to a slightly deaf grandparent, "this guy has been hurt. Is there a doc-bot?"

She remained motionless.

"Look." Journey gripped his shoulder. "He's moving."

The guard's face twitched. Suddenly, his mouth jerked up into a wide grimace of what looked like pain.

"He's alive."

The twitches took hold in his fingers and then his arms, and suddenly his back stiffened and his chest rose slowly off the bed. To Mark, his body looked like the bending of a bow before an archer fires an arrow, like it was charging.

"He's having some sort of seizure," said Journey, putting his hands across the man's chest to try to hold him down. "Help me."

Mark tried to copy Journey in holding the man still, but the guard's legs bent and stiffened beneath him, bowing his back even more. He was unbelievably strong.

Something crunched in the man's ribs as his body bent to the limits of its spine. Suddenly, he snapped back into a hunch as a gout of red dust poured from his mouth into the air. Each mote hung and spread, before floating weightlessly back down to the ground, covering the man, the bed, both Journey and Mark, everything.

The man finally fell still, his face stained powder-red.

Journey wiped his mask with his hand.

"What just happened?" he said.

Mark was frozen to the spot. "Uh," was all he felt safe to commit.

"If he wasn't dead, he is now." Journey pointed at the body.

The guard was a husk. Thin and drawn, like everything inside him had been used up and spat out. Squeezed out like a tube of toothpaste.

Mark's lingering tequila hangover threatened to rise once more, but he managed to hold it back, hypothesising that throwing up in a helmet you couldn't take off was likely only to make matters worse.

At the far end of the corridor the woman continued to watch them from behind the glass.

"Let's talk to her," said Journey moving towards her.

Mark followed.

She didn't move from her position as they approached. She didn't even blink. The room behind her was a mess: bed torn to shreds, panels ripped off the walls.

The only sign that she was alive, and not just a ghoulish Halloween prop decoratively placed against the glass, was the tracking movement of her eyes and the twitch of her nostrils. It looked as though she was trying to smell them as they passed.

There was something strange about her face. Fibrous pink tendrils covered it. A wispy root-like beard. But not just on her chin and cheeks. Her whole face. Growing from beneath her eyelids and out of her nostrils and ears.

"What's the matter with her?" said Journey.

Mark shook his head. He'd never seen anything like it. "Should we let her out? Maybe she can't hear us?" He approached the door.

Something clicked in the ceiling above and a female voice came across the public address system.

"Do not let her out."

Mark's heart rate doubled. The voice was fuzzy, strange, almost like an antique android he'd seen once.

"Who is that?" he hissed to Journey.

"Are you hearing me?" There was a pause. "I am sorry. I cannot hear you. My name is Dr Douglas. I am trapped inside the second dome. In the laboratoire."

Journey scanned the room. His eyes fixed on a camera in the corner. He pointed it out to Mark. "She can see us."

"Find me and I will explain everything. Come to the laboratoire in the second dome."

"But there's a thing outside?" said Mark to the camera.

"She can't hear you, man."

"I can help you, but you must do as I say," she said.

Mark moved to stand in front of the camera and offered a complicated series of gestures that included waggling some fingers in front of his mouth, holding clawed arms above his head, and finishing with a hunchbacked attack on a reluctant Journey that might give Quasimodo a run for his money.

"Was there something outside?" said the woman. "That creature with a decopus head?"

Mark gave her a thumbs up, then gave Journey a friendly whack on the arm. "And you say I'm rubbish at charades."

"What?" Journey screwed up his face. "You are."

"You will have to avoid it if you want to survive," said the woman.

"No shit," said Journey.

"There is a ship at the top of Dome 2. Find me and I will help you locate it. It is your only way off this planet."

"How would we even get to this ... this labol—"

"Laboratoire," helped Journey.

"Don't they mean laboratory?"

Journey's forehead rippled. "Laboratoire sounds fancier."

"I'm going to call it laboratory because I'm not a dick."

"Suit yourself."

"How would we even get to this laboratory with that thing out there and nothing to defend ourselves?"

"Back the way we came, near the garage, is the equipment library. We could find a vehicle. Maybe some weapons."

"I would not delay," said the woman. "I believe your friends are in trouble. They crash landed on top of the dome."

"You think she's talking about Ashley, and the baby's mum?" said Journey.

"Oh, sh-ovel." Mark held a hand over his mouth. "I'd totally forgotten about the baby."

Journey gave him a look.

Mark carved a flattened hand across the space just beneath his nose. "It's hard, you know, she's just below my eyeline."

"Yeah, most people don't forget they have a baby attached to them, just because they can't see it."

"Defecation imminent," said Nura's computerised translation inside his helmet.

He looked down. She blinked heavy eyelids.

"You aren't my mother," she said, then her little face turned a strained red, and her capsule began to whir.

"What's going on there?" said Journey, leaning forward to look at Mark's midsection.

"I don't know." Mark positioned himself to show Journey the baby as a small pipe extruded from the capsule on his chest and spat a concentrated yellow-brown block over his shoes. He cleared his throat, fighting a sudden urge to test his previous vomit-in-a-helmet hypothesis.

He gave her a stern look and wagged a finger. Pooping on his shoes was something that, as a rule of thumb, he'd learnt not to tolerate. People who did that sort of thing once were liable to do it again. And, to needlessly take the point further, it just so happened that the sort of person to poop on one's shoes never seemed to make sound dietary choices, which often led to poor accuracy.

Much like putting your thumb over the business end of a hose.

Journey snorted.

"I would not delay," said the woman again, giving Mark, once more, that strange impression that he was talking to an AI.

"I reckon it has to be Ashley who crashed," said Journey, turning around and heading back along the corridor. "Their pod went off over Dome 2. Wonder why it crashed rather than docking at the hangar up there?"

Mark tapped his chin with a gloved finger as he followed the engineer past the quarantine enclosure with the woman inside.

This could very well be the event he'd been waiting for. This could very well be the life-threatening situation that might act as a catalyst for his and Ashley's relationship. It was time to complete the second of the three fundamental approaches to gaining a lady's affections, as described by romance novels.

Number two—be a bit of a dick, then save her from a life-threatening situation to show her you like her after all. Then, take her into your hunky arms and kiss her.

He was looking forward to not having to be a dick to her anymore.

"Whatever you do, do not take off your respiration suits," said the woman, her voice following them from the tannoy as they passed the dead security guard covered in that red dust. "And use the outer airlock to come back to the second dome. The interior one is more heavily guarded."

"Guarded by what?" Mark said.

"Beats me." Journey shrugged.

"Do you think that thing is still out there?" said Mark, taking hold of the first vending machine by the door.

"It might be. But I don't think it can see." Journey grabbed the other corner. "As long as we're quiet and there's none of those woodlice around, I'm hoping we'll be able to sneak away."

Together, they righted the first vending machine and walked it carefully away from the door. They did the same with the second. Beneath were the squashed remains of tentacles, ripped off and left behind. Pink filaments grew from the stumps. Stretching out across the floor as if hunting for something.

Journey pressed an ear against the door for a moment, before giving a thumbs up. He eased the door open, and with a look to Mark and a finger over his lips, stepped out into the glare of the midday sun.

HUNTER

Queletii lay still, eyes closed, on one of the couches next to the computer in the escape pod, having correctly surmised that the only way to stop Harrison's constant outpouring of nervous chatter was to pretend to be asleep.

When the communicator pinged, he sat bolt upright and answered the audio part of the call, hiding his video.

Thaddeus.

"Where the bloody hell are your people?" said the galaxy's richest man.

Queletii stretched his arms above his head and wriggled his back. His body ached, and his brain felt as though it was running on half power. He put it down to not getting any younger, and this cushy job for a bunch of rich arses not keeping him as fit as he'd like.

"They've not yet returned, sir." It should be worrying, but something about the way he felt made it hard to find the energy to care. Like it should be someone else's problem.

"Well, don't you think you should see where they've got to? It's been nearly thirty minutes since we arrived. Marcella and I are getting a little bored with the in-flight entertainment."

Queletii scowled.

"I'll get right on it, sir."

He ended the call without another word, then tried his radio.

"Bovista, Chen, come in?"

No reply. He sighed and stood from the couch.

"Harrison, it's our turn. Let's go see if we can find what's happened here."

The lad nodded.

Queletii led him out of the pod doors and across the hangar to the stairs. Glanced back over the room as he climbed to the next level and the exit. The hangar was tidy. Nothing out of place, except perhaps the collection of high-tech, high-luxury escape pods sat neatly in the centre of the room. They were like miniature versions of the yacht. Needless frivolity. Compared to the economy of the hangar, they were gleaming diamonds sitting atop the scrap food bin in a volunteer soup kitchen for the homeless.

He sneered as he pushed through the hangar exit. God, he hated colonies.

"If you were them, Harrison, which way would you have gone?" he said, looking left and right in the darkened hallway. He was testing the lad. Wanted to see if he could redeem himself for letting the pirate go from their office earlier.

Because that was what had happened.

Sure Stapowski, or whatever his name was, had gotten the better of him, knocked him out cold, but he'd had the element of surprise. Harrison should have stopped him.

"Into the light," the boy answered, nodding towards a dim glow at the end of the tunnel.

"After you." Queletii held out an arm.

Harrison unclipped his holster. Kept his hand on his gun. Started towards the light at the end of the corridor. Queletii did the same.

The security chief spun. Walked backwards. Watched the darkness close in behind them. The way the light seemed to disappear as he retreated made it look as if something was moving at the far end of the corridor. But no one would just stand back there in the dark, would they? He blinked several times to penetrate the pitch-black. It only caused blurs and a glow in his peripheries.

The hairs on the back of his neck prickled, tickling the flesh around the collar of his shirt. He continued to reverse. Almost frozen. Unable to turn his back on the darkness.

The corridor quickly brightened as they approached the light, and he turned in a hurry to follow Harrison into a well-lit garage. The room was empty.

"Bovista, Chen," he said, trying his radio again. Still nothing.

"Did you hear that?" said Harrison.

"What?"

"Wait there and try the radio again when I say." Harrison walked towards the middle of the garage and stood, poised, listening. "Try it." He put a finger in the ear closest to Queletii.

"Hello," said Queletii, and this time he heard it too. An echo of sibilance from beyond the double doors at the end of the corridor. A radio. "Tsst. Tsst. Tsst."

"You hear that?" said Harrison. "Through here." He pointed to the doors and started making his way.

Queletii caught up with him and unholstered his gun. Harrison copied.

They arrived at the doors together. There was something on the floor. A swipe of red. He blinked. His eyes weren't focussing so well. Christ, why did he feel so fuzzy?

"Is that blood?" said Harrison.

Queletii nodded, then looked ahead down the ramp towards the road outside the garage. "Someone was taken that way."

"Should we follow it?"

"One of them may still be in there." Queletii brushed open the door and leant through the gap. The room beyond was dark. A small square with a doorway leading off either side and one ahead.

He slipped through. More blood on the floor. Leading from the doorway on the left labelled M and back through the double doors where they stood.

He brought his radio to his mouth. "Tsst. Tsst."

The sound echoed from around the corner and with it, another noise began. The faint squeak of feet on tiles. As he crossed towards it, he heard the murky plunk of dripping water.

The next room was flanked by lockers. It was almost too dark to see. A thick steam rose from the doorway on the other side, obscuring that end of the room. On the floor by one of the lockers was Bovista's radio. He moved to pick it up.

"Do you hear that?" said Harrison, his voice barely a whisper.

Queletii held his position, listened. From the next room came a rasping, choking breath. "Chen?"

He stepped into the mist. His boots slipped. He glanced down. A grey, gelatinous liquid covered the floor. Long strings of a fine white thread emanated from the doorway as if a giant spider had created its lair in the room beyond.

He looked at Harrison. The boy's face was slick with condensation or sweat. His terrified eyes glistened in the limited light.

Queletii stepped carefully through the doorway. A dense stench of damp and mould hit him. The next room was so blanketed with steam he couldn't see much at all. On either side were shower cubicles. The air was warm, but the showers weren't flowing. He waved an arm to try to clear the mist. It swirled and eddied, and in the gaps the motion created he could just make out six figures at the far end of the line of cubicles. They were huddled closely together, facing the far wall. Three wore respiration suits. The two at the back were almost completely hidden.

"Hey, why are you all standing in the dark?" he asked.

The group didn't move. He raised his voice and his gun. "I said—"

The two closest turned around to face him and Harrison. A slow jerking movement. They appeared as pale as ghosts in the darkness. The black pits of their mouths hung open in crooked grimaces. A large crack ran down the centre of the woman on the left's helmet. The man on the right had a large hole in the front of his suit, the chest plate broken and bent inwards. Beneath the suit, his clothes were torn. His ribs showed through a large gash in his torso. Bloody brown stains surrounding it suggested that the wound had occurred some time ago.

"Jesus, are you alright?" said Queletii. He lowered the gun, but only slightly.

He'd been in plenty of fights before. Some bloody. Some lethal. But he'd never seen someone still alive, let alone standing, with such an injury.

The man's face turned slowly from Queletii to Harrison. He considered the weapons they carried. His head tilted to one side and his gaze turned vacant and inward as if he were receiving a message through an earpiece.

The woman did the same. They both took long, aggressive sniffs of the air, their nostrils rising, their faces screwing up.

Harrison squeaked in startled surprise.

The pair focussed once more and in perfect unison six mouths spoke, "Are you a pilot or an engineer?"

Their voices blended together, chordal yet dissonant.

Queletii shook his head. "No, we're from the Daedalus."

Each of the six took a synchronised step. The back four, still facing the other way, moved in reverse. Their movements stirred up the mists at their feet. Chen was there. Lying on her side. She wasn't moving.

"Chen?" Queletii renewed the grip on his pistol. It suddenly felt heavy in his hands. "What have you done to her? Where's Bovista?"

With effortless synchronicity, the ones in suits lifted their arms and removed their respiration helmets. The scent of mould intensified and a strange dust tickled Queletii's nose. He wanted to sneeze, but was too afraid to close his eyes.

He stepped back, pushing Harrison backwards too.

The second pair turned as they drew nearer. Their faces were covered in that same white thread that tracked across the floor.

"Don't come any closer." He tried to keep the shake from his voice.

They continued their advance. He sensed Harrison fall back further.

"Stop. I will shoot."

Panicked, the security chief fired a warning into the dripping white tiles on the wall. The sound deafening in the small space.

The people didn't even flinch. Just kept coming. Which was when he saw, for the first time, the state of the two that had been previously hidden at the back. They turned and emerged from the mist behind the first four. Humanoid. But nothing like he'd ever seen before. Their chins jutted like the jaws of rabid dogs, pulling the skin of their faces so taut that their eyelids came away from their cheek bones.

Their mouths teemed with so many teeth. Needle sharp. Seeming to vibrate like the blade of a chainsaw. Their arms were elongated, with elbows hanging past their waists. Each hand had been replaced with a series of long-fingered claws. The things bent low, scuttling forward behind their comrades. Their eyes gleamed, gazing hungrily.

"Red Fruit is everything," the six voices spoke together. "Onwards and ever upwards."

Harrison's nerve broke and he fled.

"Wait," shouted Queletii, backing away, then giving chase through the locker room. His feet slipped on the wet tiled floor, but he managed to remain upright as he raced into the reception and out through the double doors leading back into the garage. Harrison, younger and faster, was already a third of the way across the room.

Queletii's heart pounded in his chest. His blood pulsed at his temples. He couldn't catch his breath. Behind him, the creatures crashed through the double doors. The synchronised slap of their footsteps were gaining. Too close. He'd never make it.

"Harrison, cover me," he gasped, but the boy didn't slow.

Queletii pushed his tired body as hard as he could, sensing the scraping of claws, the chomp of teeth, that oddly positive mumbled mantra—"onwards and ever upwards"—just behind him.

Where had he heard that saying before?

If only the boy would stop. If only he would help. He was nearly at the door back to the hangar. Would he shut it behind him? Then what?

He had only one option. Queletii lifted his gun with both hands, still pushing hard with his legs. Held it for a moment. The shot had to be right. Leant forward, anticipating the recoil. Fired.

The lad cried in pain, stumbled, his legs crumpled beneath him as he fell, cradling his destroyed ankle just in front of the door back to the hangar.

Bullseye.

Queletii jumped over Harrison's prone form and through the door. Caught his shoulder on the frame and spun, falling onto his back, now facing his pursuers. He scrabbled backwards on hands and feet. The monsters, their unspeakable horror now evident in the light of day, advanced as Harrison screamed. Queletii kicked the door shut between them. Scrambled to his feet. Overturned a large trolley to block the door.

Harrison shrieked on the other side as the creatures caught up. The door shook on its hinges. It was tough luck, but if it had to be one of them, he'd rather it wasn't him.

The boy shouldn't have run. Everyone hated a coward.

With an exhausted grimace of exertion, Queletii pulled more of the corridor's debris in the way of the door. He turned and sprinted in the direction of the hangar. If he could just get inside an escape pod, he'd be safe.

He barrelled through the open doorway and circled the hangar on the metal gantry surrounding it.

He stopped running, and, with a deep breath to calm himself, tried to process what he'd seen. This was something new. Something he hadn't experienced, nor heard of before. The corporation couldn't know about this. Could they?

His breath caught in his throat. There was a slight difference in the hangar. He froze and leant into the shadow at the top of the stairs, trying to catch his breath as quietly as he could.

A man stood on the ramp of the escape pod belonging to Thaddeus's second in command, Prendergast. Prendergast lay at his feet. The man was motionless, head cocked to one side as if waiting for something. He was immaculately dressed in a suit, shirt, and neatly buttoned tie. He looked like a Rosenhalt stiff, but Queletii didn't recognise him.

From here, it was impossible to see inside Prendergast's escape pod, but as Queletii scanned the room, he saw another body hanging off the ramp. Li, his husband.

Another three people stepped from the open pod. Queletii didn't recognise them. They were each dressed as well as the first, although beneath their well-tailored clothes were humps and bumps as if their skeletons were crooked and broken. They came to a stop with the first man and paused like him. Waiting. Listening.

A high-pitched whine came from behind him. Queletii wheeled around. A black woodlouse chittered on the wall like some kind of living motion sensor.

He glanced back to the centre of the hangar at the sound of scuffling dress shoes. The four figures were sprinting towards the stairs. Towards him. Their eyes fixed on his position.

He raised his gun and fired at the creature on the wall. The woodlouse exploded in a jet of red.

He fired again. This time over the railing at the leading figure. He couldn't give a shit if these were Rosenhalt execs or not. He wasn't going to let them get close. The shot took the top of the guy's head clean off. His torso flowed backwards almost horizontally, but still his legs moved, carrying him in Queletii's direction, as if his muscles were being forced into action by something other than his brain.

Queletii ran. His footsteps clattered along the gantry. Behind him came the metal clang of his pursuers mounting the stairs. He raced through the doorway and into the dim corridor once more.

From his right came the crashing and clawing of those he'd left in the garage. They'd already finished with Harrison. They were coming for him now.

To his left was total darkness.

It was the best of two worsts, so he turned left.

SLUG

How had she come to be here? It was a question Sam had asked herself every day for as long as she could remember. How had the daughter of a wealthy Star Captain fallen so far?

She knew. It had started as teenage rebellion. A story as old as the stars. The girl with everything, pushing back against her easy life, fighting the rules designed to keep her wholesome and pure and innocent of the terrible truths that the galaxy held in store for those less fortunate.

A desire for something rough, something unclean, after being pampered and preened for so long. Something to spoil her in a way she'd never been spoiled.

She'd fallen for a boy from the city. Slug. The wrong boy from the city. The name alone should have been a red flag. Either his parents had given it to him or he'd given it to himself. Neither boded well. She thought perhaps the name referred to the bullet type of slug and not necessarily the one-footed, mucus-riding mollusc type of slug—there weren't many of those in the concrete covered slums of Artifakt City—but she had never had the nerve to ask.

There had been good boys in the city. Ones who knew those terrible truths that her father had tried to keep her from. Boys still born on the wrong side of the tracks, but that could have helped her to understand. But they were much less interesting than the punk with the neon nano-tattoos and the sparkling green hair who had his own gang and his own ship.

She'd fallen in the deep end with him. And she'd loved it. At one point, early on, she'd thought she could tame him. A project. Make him into a man her father might see as worthy. A man her father could respect as someone who'd started so low but become something great, like he had.

But people never changed. Her father had started at the bottom, but her grandparents had taught him right from wrong. His heart was good.

Slug, on the other hand, had come out rotten and would likely stay rotten until his dying day.

How had she not seen it?

And here she was, wanting nothing more than to undo it all. Wishing that she could tell her family she was sorry for ever doubting their intentions to keep her protected. That was impossible now. Slug had seen to that when he'd put a blade through her father's neck.

It made her sick to her stomach to think it had taken such an extreme act of violence to make her finally see who the man she thought she loved really was, and how bad her life had grown.

She hadn't been aware of her own descent. She had been a frog in a pot of water, slowly rising to the boil, not knowing she was being cooked. Her father's murder had been the sudden rise in temperature that had told her she needed to get out before she was done. Before that punk could leave his rotten influence on their baby girl.

In a funny way, her father had achieved what he'd set out to do. He had saved her. Not with the messages he'd sent, nor with the pleas for her to return home where he could take care of her and give her a fresh start, but with his final breath.

She'd learnt life could be bad, but unless it became really awful, you would never change it. You became sort of comfortable in the mess. Desensitised to the constant low-level suffering. It was often better for your life to be absolutely unbearable, then you might try something to make it good.

Slug hadn't been a bad father. He'd always treated Nura well. Feeding her, staying up some nights, taking an interest in her development. Bringing her the things she needed, be that nappies or toys. Even those drugs when she'd been ill with scarlet fever. Sam hadn't asked how he'd come by them. She knew they had been costly. But then, Slug had money now, spending it wasn't much of a show of love or loyalty.

And Slug had only ever lashed out physically when he'd been drunk, and they only ever argued to the point of violence when he was stressed about jobs he had going or if someone double-crossed him or if she'd messed something up or …

Most of the time they were OK—his words.

But there was no one else in this galaxy she'd take shit like that from. If anyone else had laid a finger on her, or said the things he'd said to her, they would have found themselves regretting it. So why had she allowed it from the man she'd loved, and who apparently had loved her?

She'd been happy sometimes. And it wasn't like there was anything better out there. Life wasn't easy for people like him, but that didn't mean he had to make it harder on her.

Slug used to say that "to live was to risk". It'd become a bit of a mantra back in Artifakt for his gang of villains and cut-throats. An excuse to do what you needed to get by. It usually came alongside "it's us or them". Everyone had to take some chances, had to hurt someone else so that they might survive. It was why, or rather how, he did what he did.

Then her father had come looking for his granddaughter and Slug had lost it. Hadn't he known the danger? He must have known Slug wasn't a small player. The stakes must have been worth it. She must have been worth it. And now, thanks to Slug, Nura would never get to meet her grandfather.

So Sam had left. Taken Nura in the middle of the night. Changed her hair. Spent every penny of what little money she'd managed to keep for herself and bribed some recruiter for this job on the Daedalus just to get herself and Nura somewhere Slug couldn't follow.

She sniffed as she stared out of the life pod window, trying to see the other hangar from where they'd landed, trying to catch a glimpse of Nura's pod. Tens of metres below where she and Ashley were now suspended by inches of strengthened glass, were the tops of the colony buildings.

Ashley tapped a key on her laptop by the wall-mounted computer in the pod, then scratched her head. She mumbled something to herself and glanced over.

"I'm sorry. I don't know what happened," she said.

Sam gritted her teeth to stop herself from snarling. This woman was either totally incompetent or she had lied. She cleared her throat, and scrunched her fists inside the pocket of her dress overalls.

"You said their pod would follow us. Nura's over there on her own with the dumbest pirate I've ever met. And we're ... How are we even going to get down from here?"

"I thought I had them tethered to us," said Ashley, resuming her keyboard tapping. "I'm sorry. I tried. I'm as surprised as you are."

Sam's voice shook as she said, "What if they think Nura's his daughter? What if they take her away before we can get there?"

She doubted they would take the time to check the Daedalus records to find out who Nura really was. They'd take her and put her in a home while Mark carried out what was likely to be a very long jail sentence. It would be nearly impossible to track her down.

"They won't. Mark'll tell them. They'll know we landed here."

Ashley gave her a smile, but Sam could tell the pirate was unsure.

"Of course they'll know we landed here. We punched straight through the bloody dome."

"How was I supposed to know some idiot Star Sailors had parked across all the spaces in the hangar?" said Ashley. "We're lucky we didn't crash and die in a fiery explosion."

Sam grunted. Ashley was right, her last-minute manoeuvre had saved them when she'd spotted the ship in the second hangar. Although their impact onto the side of the dome had left a cracked and mangled skid at least two hundred metres along the surface, they were lucky the impact hadn't been worse. Ashley was clearly good at what she did. Piloting the pod from her laptop had taken skill.

So then, if Ashley wasn't incompetent, that left one option as to why Mark's escape pod hadn't joined them. She was lying about trying.

"And it's not like it's going to cause any of them below a real problem, is it?" continued Ashley. She gave Sam a strange look which put her a little on edge, like the question was a test.

Sam let a frown cross her face. "Explain how a massive hole in their protective dome isn't a real problem for the colonists." She knew why, of course she did. She'd flown raids on these colonies a number of times for Slug. But she wasn't a pilot, was she? She was a hotel maid.

Ashley lifted an eyebrow, then spoke slowly, as if talking to a child. "These colonies only utilise the domes for power generation and security. The breathable atmosphere is kept inside using atomic force fields that only allow certain molecules in and out. Clean oxygen, nitrogen, carbon in specific breathable ratios." She ticked each element off on her fingers, then jabbed a thumb over her shoulder. "All the poisons out, or at least filtered into usable atomic resource feeds which the matter-compilers can store."

Of course she already knew, but Sam nodded as if learning something mind-blowing. A trick she'd quickly picked up on the Daedalus. While being a maid was obviously a thousand times better than living with Slug, it didn't half irk her how often guests felt the need to mansplain as if she were just a stupid ear waiting and willing to be wowed.

Although their crash into the dome could be seen as a big problem security-wise, the colonists far below wouldn't now be breathing potentially harmful toxins from the native air supply.

Still, she imagined the colony heads below would be in serious talks regarding the stability of the dome now that a flying honeymoon suite had left a gash nearly a quarter of a kilometre across its surface.

A groan of metal vibrated through the pod and the floor seemed to shift for a brief moment.

"Do you think the glass is strong enough to hold us up?" Ashley asked.

"I don't know." Sam shook her head. It was a long way to fall if not. "Computer," she said. "Do we have a ladder or something?"

"Hi," came the plucky voice of the computer. "I don't have one on board, but it is possible for me to compile you a ladder in a matter of seconds. How long do you require?"

"Something that'll get us from here down to floor level ASAP."

"Wonderful. It is two hundred and sixteen metres to the ground. I shall begin compiling a ladder for you immediately. Your descent will commence shortly."

CAGED BIRD

P**RENDERGAST AND HIS HUSBAND** were dead. Thaddeus could see the bodies from here.

Thank God he'd waited when he spotted those two men and two women enter the hangar.

Their dress sense had been impeccable—straight out of the third chapter of his second book, *Think Yourself A Winner*—but there had been something off with the way they'd moved, like they had only recently learnt to walk.

Luckily, his sense for the uncanny had been honed to perfection. When you were as well known as he was, you learned to keep an eye out for weirdos.

Prendergast's eyes were open. Staring up at nothing. His husband, Li, a few metres to the side, hung half off their pod's ramp.

Thaddeus grunted. That could have been him and Marcella if he'd only opened their door.

He glanced at his wife, who was sitting on the folded-out bed. She was crying, silently but no less obviously. No less pathetically. Her shoulders shook as she covered her eyes with one hand. He sighed. She'd been crying a lot lately. When she thought he wasn't looking. But he knew. He always knew. She'd been hurting herself, too. Nothing major. Just the odd series of scratches on her arm or thigh. Nail marks on her scalp. She was clearly doing it for attention, but he wasn't going to give it to her. Not for that. It was so cheap.

She was lucky she was beautiful.

She noticed him watching her. Composed herself. Wiped the tears from her cheeks with one hand.

He might swap her out. There were other beautiful women. Ones with brains in their heads. Ones with genuine ambition.

"What are we going to do, Thaddeus?" she said, as if anything about their situation had changed now.

He turned away from her and looked out at Prendergast. Drummed his fingers on the window for a moment.

"Nothing changes," he said. "We wait for the rescue ship."

"But what if those people get in here?"

He closed his eyes and took a deep breath. Let it condense on the glass as he exhaled. God, she could be so stupid. They were in an airtight capsule designed to pass through the depths of space. No one was getting in.

"Don't worry yourself, darling." He turned and offered her his contract-winning smile. A smile he knew, when accompanied by his magnetic wit and charm, had made him billions. "There's no way for them to get in here." He tapped a knuckle on the wall. "Once the rescue ship arrives, it's their duty to find us. They know we're alive. They'll deal with these … these people. And we'll be safe to leave."

She pressed herself up to stand and moved a little closer. He opened his arms, but didn't go to meet her. She came the rest of the way, and he enveloped her. Let his hands fall down her back.

"Why don't you pour me another glass of something, then perhaps take a couple of your pills and have a nap? I'll wake you when our rescuers arrive."

"But I'm not tired."

He cleared his throat. "It'll save you the stress."

And him the headache.

She nodded. Her eyes remained down as she moved towards the drinks cabinet. He let his own wander from her head down to her feet. It would be a shame to see her go. If nothing, he liked to see the back of her.

"Whiskey?"

"Please."

She poured and brought it to him.

"Thank you."

He took a sip and watched her take a dispenser from the drawer by her side of the bed. Saw how she purposefully didn't meet his eye as she took three small white pills and swallowed them with water.

"Night," he said, as she lay on her side and silently closed her eyes.

He turned back to the window. Took another sip. Frowned. The attack had been brutal but unusual. He'd seen bloodshed before. Watched recordings of one or two riots at some of the other Rosen colonies. Even been present during a protest against android labour at one of his factories which had clearly been planned to coincide with his arrival. That had gotten nasty quickly. He'd made sure of it. Fucking protestors.

But the attack on Prendergast and Li had differed from anything he'd seen before.

Those strange, well-dressed people, two women and two men, had entered the hangar not long after Queletii and his lackey had left. They had climbed down the steps and spread out, their heads jerking from side to side as if they were sniffing the air for something. Marcella had come to stand next to him. She'd suggested they go out, but luckily he'd made them wait.

Prendergast had opened his door, stepped out with Li at his side, and the unknown people had just gone for them. Converged on their position like flies to rotting fruit.

And that's when things had become really weird.

The attackers dragged both Li and Prendergast to the ground, mounted them, and kissed them. Or at least that's what it had looked like from here. Really snogged their faces off. Thaddeus had felt quite uncomfortable. He'd never liked public displays of affection.

Prendergast and Li had struggled and twitched, each held down by others. It had continued for some time, and when it was all finished, the people had stood, frozen. Then, a few moments later, they'd left. Just run off like they were late for a flight.

He and Marcella had watched his vice president and his husband for quite some time before he'd spoken his conclusion that Prendergast and Li must be dead. That was when she had started crying.

The pair hadn't appeared to suffer any specific injuries in the attack. He was sure not one blow had been struck. So Thaddeus was slightly confused as to what exactly had killed them.

He glanced back at her, breathing softly, already asleep, and shook his head. He puffed his cheeks and blew out air, then turned his attention back to the hangar. There were a couple of other pods in the bay that he could see. There may have been more outside of the view his window offered.

Suddenly, Li's legs kicked out as though he'd been electrocuted. He bent at the waist, springing to a seated position. Prendergast did the same. Their torsos hung upright, leaning slightly to one side, like puppets suspended by their strings. Their relaxed and open hands resting palm up on their legs.

In perfect sync, they pushed themselves to a standing position, then turned their attention towards Thaddeus in his pod. There was something about the way they stared, slack-jawed and vacant, that sent a shiver up his spine. Prendergast was always so charged in his expression and movements. A real dynamo.

This was no longer Prendergast.

The pair stalked to the outer door of the pod, walking as though they had only just gained the ability, and placed their pale faces up against the glass on the other side. The way their bloodshot eyes moved as Thaddeus stepped away from the glass told him they saw him. They looked as if they were coming to some sort of conclusion.

A strange twitching began simultaneously at the corners of their mouths, and as one their faces split into wide, overjoyed grins. It was a familiar look. On the odd occasion when he was out walking amongst the proles unattended, and a fan noticed him, they would give him that look. The look of fame recognised.

He took another uncertain step back. He didn't like it one bit.

But still, they were in an airtight capsule designed to pass through the depths of space. There was no way anyone was getting in here.

Right?

SHOOTS AND CATS

The octophant wasn't immediately outside the door as Mark stepped once more into the light of day, so, for a fleeting moment, he felt some relief.

Unfortunately, it was a few metres to the left, lying on its side, waiting. Not moving. Not even breathing. Just lying there. He'd never known any living thing not to breathe. He would have presumed it dead if not for the apathetic flick of its tentacles as it picked and played with the tiny stones on the parched tarmac.

On closer inspection, it didn't look so tough just lying there.

Mark tapped Journey on the shoulder and opened his mouth to speak, but Journey held a finger firm over his own visor. Then he began to tiptoe in a diagonal line across the road with the clear aim of skirting around the creature. The boots of his respiration suit crunched softly on the tarmac.

Mark followed, hating every second. On closer, closer inspection, the thing was the single most terrifying thing he had ever seen. And he'd seen some shi-hit. He tightened his grip on the crowbar and glanced down at Nura. She appeared content with batting some sort of colourful beaded contraption inside her tube with both hands. He could hear the sound of bells within his suit.

Somewhere at the back of his mind, he kind of wished Ashley could be there. He was going to have to explain all this facing of terrifying things and chivalry and bravery to her later. He was sure you got more romance points for facing terrifying things en route to rescuing.

Having to explain how impressive you are often lessens the impact of your impressiveness—Dad.

Maybe Journey could do it?

Mark could act all bashful. Say something like, "Yeah, it was pretty scary, but I couldn't have stood by and done nothing knowing such a beautiful woman was in danger."

Or at least that's what he might intend to say. Judging by his past encounters with Ashley he'd probably say something closer to "I know nothing. Beautiful woman danger. Armpits hot, like star."

He realised a little too late that Journey had stopped. With expert clumsiness, he careered straight into the engineer's broad back. This had happened before, and so Journey, clearly aware of Mark's total lack of directional sense and observational skill, had braced just in time for impact. Still, the tarmac scratched beneath their feet, which, in the silence of the walled-in road, echoed like a scream.

The octophant lifted its ugly head. Tentacles flopped like the ears of a startled puppy. It cocked its head to one side and sniffed the air with huge, scraping draws of breath.

Mark froze, with arms thrown around Journey's back to stop himself from falling.

The creature grunted, then lay back down.

Journey unclasped Mark's hands from around his chest and gave him a withering look—Mark withered beneath it—then the engineer's eyes shifted as something came to him. He grabbed the hook end of the crowbar and tugged it from Mark's grip. Then he pointed at the play park on the corner. A waist-high, brightly coloured metal fence surrounded it. He dummied throwing the crowbar towards it, expanded a fist by one of his ears, and made a roaring face. Then pumped his fists and motioned running on the spot. If accompanied by a fresh new beat that was here to stay, it would have made quite the dance.

Throw the bar,

Blow up your ear,

Roar like an octophant,

Shake dat rear.

Or, you know, something to that effect.

But in the current high-stakes, high-pressure, fresh-beat-less environment, it was just confusing. Mark would need to give him some charades lessons after this.

Journey nodded enthusiastically, then just bloody launched the crowbar at the slide in the park. It landed with a crashing metal clang, then slid down with a scraping shriek.

Before they could move, the octophant was on its feet and charging for the sound.

Journey gripped his arm, holding him steady, waiting for the best moment. His breath rose and fell as he turned at the hips to track the charging beast, which sprinted past within arm's reach.

The best moment came when the octophant's knees connected hard with the colourful park fence. Its front legs stopped, but the rest of its body kept going. Up and over it flipped, spilling onto its back on the roundabout.

Journey released his arm, and, without a look back, legged it in the opposite direction. Mark pursued as the octophant powerlessly tried to stop itself from revolving merrily.

"This way," called Journey, before rounding a corner at speed.

He pointed towards the garage where they'd found the man earlier. On the far side was a large grey warehouse.

"In there. The equipment library."

Journey arrived first and wrenched open the left of a set of double doors that led into the vast building.

The room they entered was dark. A square office with a reception desk which backed on to a set of double doors that hung open like a toothless mouth. Beyond was a black cavern. On top of the desk sat a flatscreen monitor and the dried remains of a potted plant.

Journey checked to make sure they hadn't been followed, while Mark took a moment to catch his breath. Journey closed the door, sealing them inside and all light out.

Something bright and white flashed in Mark's vision. Once more thinking he was being attacked by giant letters, his fists came up to defend himself from the friendly help message that had just appeared on the inside of his visor. Journey jerked, suggesting he'd seen the same.

The voice of his in-suit butler read the text aloud.

"It looks like you intend to move through an area with sub-optimum light levels. To access your suit's lighting array, please punch one arm in the air to trigger speech mode and say *Lighting array activate*. Why not try it now?"

The pop-up faded.

Journey was quick to cotton on and punched his arm in the air before Mark's butler had finished talking.

"Lighting array activate," he said.

A set of antennae made up of several bright white LEDs rose from either side of his head, illuminating a ninety-degree cone directly in front of him.

Now Mark could see that beyond the double doors behind the desk was a huge room filled with shelves that disappeared several storeys above in the gloom of the ceiling. The shelves were filled with boxes and pieces of equipment.

Mark punched an arm in the air and activated his own array. Nura blinked shining eyes in the new light, then laid her head against his chest.

Just in front of Mark's face, tiny motes of dust the colour of rust floated in and out of the light. "I'm glad you grew up in one of these colonies otherwise we'd be pretty lost," he said.

"Hmm," said Journey, squinting and raising a hand to shield himself from the sudden and intense white light beaming at him from Mark's array. "We just need to find a couple of drills, then we'll grab a cat and head over to the other dome to get your baby momma and Ashley." He placed a finger over his lips. "We don't know who or what we're going to find in here, so just follow me."

They stepped through the doors. Mark scanned right and Journey left. He couldn't see anything to suggest there might be trouble.

"This way," hissed Journey.

Mark strained his ears for the smallest sound as they passed the first row of shelves. Above, a sign read *1: Food Compiler Rations,* next was *2: Parts & Repairs,* and then *3: Medical Compiler Rations & Equipment.*

Ahead of Journey were at least four more rows. Beyond that, Mark could just make out the hulls of several small vehicles. Everything that the colony required was housed here.

"Looking for number five," said Journey, pointing up. "Mining equipment."

"But I thought we were here for weapons."

"We are."

He turned right when they reached aisle five and shone the light of his array down the row. The white light reflected off the polished concrete flooring, but didn't pierce the darkness behind the shelving units on either side.

Roughly midway along the row was a crate. It had been pulled halfway off the shelf, but whoever had done so was no longer there.

Remaining vigilant, they made their way towards it. The room was silent.

"This place should be like a hive," Journey whispered. "People all over the place grabbing bits and equipment. It seems weird with no one here."

Mark's hands felt cool where the sweat on his palms was being wicked away by the suit.

Something metal tinkled to the ground between them and the crate. A spray can. It bounced and clanged, the sound echoing through the cavernous room. Then several more rained down at once, pinging and jumping as they landed.

He scanned up the shelving unit, taking in either side as his eyes moved to the top.

"Who is that?"

Hunched between the top shelf and the ceiling, half-hidden in the shadows, crouched a gaunt-looking woman. Her blank, staring eyes reflected the light of his LED antennae like two tiny candle flames in the darkness.

Mark waved. "Hello?"

She snapped around, sending more cans dropping to the ground. Then leapt away to crash down several levels below on the row of shelves adjacent to the one they were in.

He heard her drop to the ground a few more rows over and then the echoes of light footsteps as she skittered away.

"Do you think she was like that woman in the quarantine?" he asked. "Do you think they caught space rabies from that octophant or something?"

"What's space rabies?"

He shrugged. "I don't know. Rabies, but in space."

"Maybe," Journey said, jogging the last of the distance to the crate. "But, and I've told you this before, technically, everything is in space, so let's just call it rabies."

"Hmm." Mark shook his head. "I still don't get why we call a spaceship a spaceship, though? Isn't it just a ship?"

"No! Uh?" Journey paused a moment to consider Mark's words, before throwing the heavy metal lid of the crate back on its hinges. "No," he finally said again. "If we went with your space everything method, we'd be calling it a space spaceship. And that's just moronic."

"This is probably a conversation for another day."

Journey wrinkled his nose. "Yeah. Probably." The left side of his mouth pulled up into a half-grin as he inspected the interior of a box. "This is the one. It won't do for long range, but it'll chop up anything stupid enough to get close to us, or anything we're stupid enough to get close to."

He grabbed an arm-length cylinder from the thick grey foam that held the drill parts snugly inside their box. One end of the cylinder tapered to a fine point with a slim barrel. He clicked a second piece—a short, pistol-like handle with a trigger—into it, then screwed a stock into that. The last piece was a chunky battery, which Journey stabbed into a slot on the body of the drill.

He tapped a button on the top which sent out thick straps from the stock. Like tentacles, they wound themselves tightly around his forearm to lock the drill in place.

"Get one for yourse—" Journey was cut short as the boxes on the shelf above and to the right burst aside, and a man in dark blue overalls clawed for his head.

On instinct, Mark swung the crowbar. It lodged in the man's thigh and was wrenched from his hands as their attacker fell to the ground between them. He immediately tried again to stand, appearing in no way fazed by the crowbar protruding from his leg.

"Get down," shouted Journey, bringing his drill up to aim at the man. He hit a switch on the side. The tip glowed red and the device emitted a rising hum.

Mark dived to the side, landing jarringly on his back. Nura's little tube took off from his midsection and hovered several feet above Journey on a trio of blue jets. Journey took a step back, frantically pulling at the drill's trigger. The man turned on him.

"Bloody charge," Journey shouted, slapping the top of the drill with his free hand. The hum rose to a whistle.

Rapid footsteps sounded at the end of their aisle. Mark glanced right.

"Ah, Journey, four more rabies guys on the way."

A beam of blinding red fired from the tip of Journey's drill, slicing crow-bar-leg-man from hip to shoulder. The wound smoked in the white light of his array as the top of the man's body sloughed to the ground.

"Booyah," shouted Journey, punching a fist in the air.

The bottomless torso pressed itself up onto its remaining arm and began dragging its way towards them.

"Uh," said Mark, shuffling back on his hands and feet, heart racing, as the thing pulled itself closer. "He doesn't appear to have died."

Journey fired again, this time removing the head. The body stopped its advance. "That was not space rabies." He glanced up. "The others are closing. Get a drill."

Mark threw himself up and at the shelf labelled Laser Drills. He dragged one of the crates out behind Journey. Opened it. Tried to get all the pieces together as he'd seen Journey do. Struggled.

"Uh?"

"It's a four-piece puzzle," shouted Journey. "How hard can it be?" The surrounding shelves glowed red as he fired again.

Nura bobbed just above his head in her jetpack.

Mark jabbed an angry finger at the crate. "Yes, but the picture's not on the box."

The figures sprinting for them were almost there.

"Take mine." Journey released the straps from his own laser drill and pressed it into Mark's hands without taking his eyes from the oncoming quartet. "Point and shoot. Hold the trigger."

Mark gripped the drill and aimed it at the first of the oncoming aggressors. It was the woman they'd seen on the shelves above. She leapt just as he pulled the trigger. He held it down and jerked it to the right. The beam of red light caught her mid-stomach and her legs fell while her upper body, suddenly kilos lighter, sailed over his shoulder. The moist squeak of her fingers filled his helmet as she clawed at his head, trying to gain purchase.

Journey quickly assembled the other drill.

Mark raked his beam at the rest of their attackers' knees, hoping to slow them down. They dropped to the floor but kept on coming. Pulling themselves along or pushing themselves up to walk on their cauterised stumps. In his peripheral vision, he could make out movement through the shelves to the left and right as boxes and crates were pushed aside by onrushing things that couldn't honestly be described as people. And somewhere beneath all of that smashing, and clawing, and stamping of onrushing footsteps, he heard the trump and gallump of the vocalist for a death-metal band made up entirely of squid-headed elephants.

"I think that thing has found us, Journ," he called back.

Journey stood and fired. Their twin beams of red-hot death eviscerated the three people crawling towards them.

"We need to get a cat, then we're out of here," he said, turning and running.

Mark checked Nura was following, then chased after Journey to the sound of boxes crashing from shelves on either side. He glanced back.

"I'm counting ten more," he called ahead. "And that octophant has just turned the corner."

The ground beneath its feet teemed with those tiny woodlouse things all charging up the aisle.

"Don't think we're gonna chop 'em all to bits," said Journey, a few paces ahead. "These drills aren't designed for this."

"I've got an idea," shouted Mark.

"You better not have."

Without slowing his sprint, Mark reached up and plucked Nura from the air, tucking her under his arm like a rugby ball. With his other hand, he slashed the beam of his drill over the leg of the nearest shelf. The metal melted. The unit groaned. Then dropped in towards them, fast.

He slashed at the following legs as he passed. Then stole another look back as, like an oncoming wave, the shelving unit began to collapse faster and faster behind him, crashing into the adjacent shelf, which in turn knocked into the next, and the next, like dominos. The sound was too much for the tiny speakers inside his helmet to take, distorting and crunching as an avalanche of heavy crates and other equipment swallowed their pursuers.

Pieces of mining equipment, big chunks of metal and plastic, smashed down around him. With a stumbling leap, he managed to avoid something that looked to be the result of a pickaxe having copulated with a chainsaw, before reaching the end of the aisle and turning immediately left after Journey, who had already gone on.

The engineer was staring into a box mounted on the wall, with his free hand on his brow. He reached up and took something down. Mark caught up. Several two-hulled hover catamarans sat along one wall. Behind them was a tall, segmented garage door.

Journey aimed the thing he'd taken from the box towards the vehicles and pressed it. The lights beneath one of the cat's twin hulls glowed neon-blue, and with a low hum, it rose a foot off the ground.

He punched a large yellow button on the wall next to the box. The garage door rose on a roller high above them, revealing the road outside.

"Get in," Journey said. "I'm driving." He climbed in, gripped the stick, and flicked a few switches on the dashboard. The hover-cat hummed and turned swiftly around to face the door as it rose.

Mark leapt over the back and into the passenger seat without argument.

Journey flung a lever forward. The front of the cat lifted with a burst of momentum and threw itself out onto the tarmac. They banked into a sharp turn, headed down a short ramp and onto the road.

Journey shook his head as he pushed the cat faster, but Mark could see he was smiling inside his helmet.

"I don't think I've known anyone to make more of a mess saving their own skin than you," he said.

"It's a gift and a curse." Mark shrugged. "But sometimes you gotta just try something."

EYE SPY

MARK WISHED HE COULD feel the wind in his wig as Journey threw the cat around the last corner, set the throttle to max, and hit the long straight that would take them to the edge of the dome where a huge metal door was set into the glass.

When they passed the last towering apartment building, the area opened up for almost a kilometre square of tarmac. Huge quadrilateral foundations were already set in the ground ready for further expansion of the colony.

"So if it's not space rabies, then what?" he finally said after a brief moment of enjoying the whizzing bobbing of the speeding cat's movement.

"Does it matter?"

Mark frowned. "I usually like to know why colonists and squid-headed elephants are trying to chase me down. Am I food? Am I friend? Am I incubator? You know?"

"I'm just going to put forward that their intentions are nefarious and try and steer clear. Maybe leave it at that." Journey left his mouth open as if he was about to say something more, then shut it. Through his visor, Mark saw his nose wrinkle slightly. The engineer passed him a look, took a deep breath, and added, "But that *was* pretty close, wasn't it?"

"Wasn't it!"

"I'm not just being a bit of a wimp?"

"No way."

"I know what I said about the mess you left back there." Journey jabbed a thumb back over his shoulder. "And I sure as hell wouldn't want to be the one to tidy it up, but I think you just saved our lives with that shelf-chopping move."

Mark smiled. "I appreciate you saying so."

"How's the baby?"

"The what? The ba— Oh!" Nura, who was now reattached to Mark's front, had fallen fast asleep with the soporific motion of the cat rocking her in her tube. Her little jowls, pressed up against his chest, shook with the occasional bump in the road. "Snoozing."

Journey sort of tutted. "Aw." He wrinkled his nose. "Is she growing on you a bit?"

"What? Like mould?"

Journey snorted.

Mark pointed ahead as they drew closer to the edge of the dome. The airlock there was large enough to swallow four or five hover-cats side by side.

"You know how to open that big door, right?" asked Mark. "Cus I don't think we'll be able to pry it. I left my crowbar in that guy's leg."

"I reckon there'll be something we can do."

When they reached the end of the road, Journey slowed the cat to a stop, then jumped out onto the fresh, shiny tarmac. Mark did the same. His boots stuck a little to the semi-molten ground as he walked.

Journey moved a hand up to scratch his chin, bumped the underside of his helmet, then pointed towards a maintenance panel in the door frame to hide his respiration suit faux pas.

"I'll have a dig around in there. You watch our backs."

Mark leant against the cat with folded arms and looked back towards the colony gleaming in the sun like a miniature desert town almost a kilometre away. Nothing had followed across the flat plain. The glass dome that rose above their heads was less covered in condensation here, and through it he could see the cloudless blue sky. It was quite nice. Better than the constant grey mist and rain of Artifakt City. Somewhere he might like to come for a holiday, murderous creatures aside.

"Our backs look good," he said, then grabbed Journey's laser drill from his side of the cat and strapped it to his left arm so he had two.

"Keep watching. I don't want any surprises," said Journey, his voice muted from inside the box. He manhandled a snarl of wires out and tapped himself thoughtfully on his helmeted chin with a pair of small pliers. He shrugged, then snipped one, and, with a grinding chunking sound, the door began to lift.

He winked at Mark, then threw a cocky thumb over his shoulder as the door opened to its extent.

"Just call me the door whisperer," he said and grinned. "Oh, what a lovely little fffu—" he added as the face of death leered out of the airlock and smashed him aside with a bollard-thick pink tentacle.

"What in the what?" shouted Mark, clearly too surprised to come up with anything better.

The interior of the airlock was covered in delicate little powder-blue flowers, around which gently fluttered a multitude of coloured and beautifully patterned butterflies. Other tiny creatures zipped and zopped like miniature spaceships, moving hither and thither around the lush green grass that filled the gaps between the petals sprouting up from the soft brown earth that covered the metal flooring. Also, there was a blobby squid-faced hell-beast, which dragged itself forward on tentacles and legs made up of the flesh of what had once been at least, at Mark's best guess, four human beings.

It teemed with eyes. Eyes all over the place. Eyes and eyes and eyes.

"Oh, eyes," said Mark, eying it helplessly, as those hundreds of terrible white orbs turned on him. There was an intelligence in there. He knew it. Something cold. Something unfeeling. It wanted to taste him, to devour him, to consume every part of him, soul, mind, and body—probably in that order.

But it was nothing personal.

No, this was strictly business.

He shuddered as the thing lifted its tentacles and started forward. He couldn't move, frozen under that awful gaze. He was nothing. A morsel. A scrap. Something to be destroyed for this thing's gain.

Journey snapped him back to the moment by shouting about it being time for something. The specifics didn't quite reach him, but the underlying meaning was there. Mark lifted both arms, charged to within range, and chopped the bejeezus out of the thing with his double laser drills.

In reaction to his making mincemeat of its flesh, something inside the belly of the beast seemed to trigger and it exploded, splattering him with red bits and a pithy barrage of eyes.

He froze once more, this time in shock as he dripped entrails from head to toe.

"Oh, gross," said Journey, with an earthy cackle of insensitive laughter. He moved closer, but not to within arm's reach. "You are caked."

Mark didn't say anything. Couldn't. Just slowly lifted an arm to clean his faceplate. The suit's computer spoke up in his ear.

"You appear to be covered in viscera, sir. Allow me."

A small stick extended downwards from the brow of his helmet, grew a brush, and with a spray of some clear, possibly antibacterial liquid from its tip, proceeded to wipe away the blood and gore with expert efficiency.

"These things ain't so bad in the end, are they?" Journey reached out and carefully, so as not to get any goop on him, gave the steaming laser drill attached to Mark's right arm a tender pat. "Just gotta show 'em who's boss."

Sure, Journey could say that, but then Journey hadn't been the one under that terrible all-seeing gaze, and Journey certainly wasn't the one covered in the exploded remains of a mutated amalgamation of the bits of an unidentifiable number of poor dead colonists.

"Am I the boss then?" said Mark, dazed and unsure.

"Yep. Man one. Space-nature zero." Journey gave the biggest remaining part of the dead thing an enthusiastic pair of V-signs while blowing a particularly wet raspberry.

Mark cleared his throat. "This must be why that octophant didn't have any eyes. They've all come here to make sure no one escaped." He shuddered.

Journey shrugged. "Maybe," he said, then climbed back behind the controls of the cat with a smug look on his face. "Did you hear what I shouted at you, though?" He looked pleased with himself.

Mark shook his head, then frowned in thought. What would he have said had he not been terrified out of his mind? "Was it"—he raised both hands either side of his head to add air quotes—"time for some laser eye surgery?"

Journey snorted a laugh. "Yep. You can use that next time."

"I'm hoping there won't be a next time."

Mark lobbed the laser drills into the back of the cat and jumped in.

"Wow!" said Journey, as he floated them slowly into the gorgeous airlock garden. He studied the interior with wide eyes. "I've never seen anything like this. It's lovely, isn't it?"

The doors closed behind them. A number of little butterflies butted themselves butterfully against his faceplate as he gazed in wonder at the tiny oasis they'd found themselves in.

"Well, some of it is," said Mark, jabbing a thumb back towards the shredded dead thing they'd left outside. "That thing was a monumental evolutionary disaster."

Journey hummed. "Nice vocab. Someone's been reading my books." He patted Mark on the arm in light condescension. Then sucked air through pursed lips as if some revelation had come to him. "Hey, maybe this thing is like a sentient plant. Maybe it's got two sides or something. Like a nice arty-farty side." He angled an open palm to their surroundings. "And a ... um ..."

"A killy-willy side?"

Journey shrugged again. "Yeah, probably."

The outer door began to open, tearing apart the natural beauty that had grown along the back wall of the airlock. Journey pressed the cat forward through a collapsing hump of earth and out onto the yellow-orange sands of the planet's native desert.

It didn't take long to arrive at the second dome's airlock, but the trip gave Mark enough time to dwell on the horror of all those eyes looking into him, and the strange feeling of some vast intelligence wanting only to gobble him all up. His insides felt icy. It had been the sort of malevolent stare that, should he ever consider smiling or laughing again in his life, which at present seemed unlikely, would rise out of the darkness of his mind's eye and flatten his face faster than if he'd been punched on the nose with a hot iron.

Sure, things had wanted to eat him before, but this was different. This was business.

"Journey," mumbled Mark morosely, as they approached the second dome, the hot sand kicking up clouds of orange dust in their wake.

"Yes."

"I'm feeling a bit down."

"What?"

"Well, that thing back at the other airlock ..." He paused.

He didn't really know how to say it. Back home in Track Stop, Dad would have said something like *Real men talk about their feelings,* and stuck the kettle on and pulled up a chair with an open ear and an open biscuit tin to listen to Mark's troubles whenever he had them. Then he'd have added something like *If there's a problem under our roof, it's all of ours to solve.* But since moving away from his parents, he'd gotten a little disused to sharing his feelings in the crack-den, dive-bar, brothel-filled slums of Artifakt. Being an arse-kicking space pirate that head butted people for a living didn't give you a lot of opportunity to open up.

"Yeah?"

Journey looked concerned, which was nice if he was concerned with Mark's wellbeing. Although it could just be self-concern due to the outpouring of emotional fallout coming his way.

Mark held splayed fingers aimed at his face. "It gave me this look like it knew I didn't want to be eaten, but that it was going to eat me anyway." He didn't really know how to describe it with words. "Like its goal of eating me was all that mattered."

Journey emitted a short, playful scoff, but kept his unwavering eyes on his driving.

"Things have tried to eat you before."

"I suppose so." Mark rested his chin on his fist and gazed out over the picturesque desert landscape.

The outer doors of Dome 2 were open. And there weren't any surprises inside. To his dismay, no delightful flower gardens. To his joy, no brain-boggling eye-beasts.

There weren't any surprises on the other side of the doors either once Journey had taken them through.

The airlock in this dome was lower than the floor, so a ramp rose to ground level. Scattered across the space were several hard miner's helmets and roughly the same number of metal lunchboxes. A little like the miners had congregated here, chucked what they were carrying to the ground, and left.

"What's with the hats?" asked Mark.

"I dunno."

Journey navigated the cat to the top of the ramp. Just like in the first dome, there was a wide ring of flat open space that ran around the outside between the glass and the small city in the centre, broken only by already prepared foundations.

"Hey, look ..." Journey pointed up to where a skid of cracked glass culminated in Sam and Ashley's pod. Hanging from what appeared to be its doorway, coming roughly halfway to the ground and getting progressively longer, like the trailing excretion of an overindulged gold fish, was a rope ladder. Clutching the end, and swinging with the momentum of their descent, were two people-sized black blobs.

The ladder hung over a duo of short two-storey buildings a little way from the edge of the colony. Breaking up the road between the two buildings were several groups of tall things that looked like large versions of those umbrellas you might get outside a bar in the summer. They were vibrant shades of red, pink, and purple and gathered together in eccentric clusters. Mark couldn't quite make out what they were from here.

"We should go closer," he said. "They won't know what they're climbing into."

"Oh, yeeeah," said Journey, with the exaggeratedly deep voice of one Mr Barry White. He once more waggled the hump of scarred skin above his eyeballs. "You want Ashley to be climbing into you."

"What, like a skin suit?"

Journey wrinkled his nose. "Not really how I meant it to come out," he said, dropping the soulful tone. "You want to be climbing into her?"

"Ah," said Mark, getting it, "a sexual innuendo, like in one of your books."

Journey, obviously realising he'd failed in the serious man-to-man feelings-talk earlier, was clearly trying to brighten his mood.

"Mm hmm," he hummed sexily. "Ah yeah, sexy stuff." He accelerated the cat towards the centre of the dome. "Let's go sexily rescue some sexy ladies."

Mark was juxtaposed. Now didn't really seem the time for such boyish frivolity.

He shrugged. What the heck? Might as well enjoy yourself until you can't.

He allowed a laugh. Then added, "Oooo, sex," hoping to match Journey's laddish zeal, yet not really knowing enough about the thing to comment further.

THE SECOND APPROACH TO GAINING A LADY'S AFFECTIONS

As Described by Romance Novels

There was no breeze up here, yet still the ladder swayed sickeningly as it dangled from the underside of the life pod.

Far below them were the tops of several two or three-storey buildings, and, towards the centre of the dome, Sam could see a huge dark hole. An opening to a cavern leading deeper into the planet. Tendrils of red matter grew up and around the edge like probing tentacles. It was black down there. Nothing was visible past the rim, although a burgundy glow seemed to throb in the dark like lightning trapped behind dense black storm clouds.

Usually an airlock building would cover the mine so that excavation crews could get safely in and out without compromising the colony atmosphere. The ruins sat, jagged and blackened with smoke, around the outside of the hole. Perhaps there had been an accident down there.

Maybe that was why the Star Sailors were here. An accident caused by some sort of sinkhole beneath the mine, or a pocket of something explosive. Perhaps they'd evacuated the dome.

She eased down another rung. The soles of her respiration suit boots stuck to the newly created ladder like the floor of a particularly messy night club. It made it easier to grip, at least. She didn't want to look down, but it was scarier to look up. Every few minutes there would come a grinding groan from the pod, followed by the tinkling of shards of the dome's glass falling onto the outside of her protective suit.

"You OK up there?" Ashley called out.

"Yeah."

Movement caught her eye. The appearance of a few people in the street below. They were oddly still, gazing up, gathered around several strange red umbrella-shaped things that stood in the centre of the road.

"What are they doing down there?" Sam shouted.

"I don't know. Perhaps it's some sort of net to catch us, or the life pod, for if we fall."

Sam had to strain her ears to hear her. The wide space of open air around them seemed to swallow the sound of her voice.

"Perhaps," she shouted back.

They reached the bottom of the ladder while they were still nearly a hundred metres above the ground. They'd just have to wait for the pod to finish building it. Sam's grip had already begun to flag from the climb, so she locked one arm around the rung she was clutching. Her fingers ached.

Ashley pointed towards the far edge of the dome. Sam followed her gaze. A small two-seater hover-cat was speeding its way along the road that led from the dome's outer airlock. Perhaps some sort of ambassador for the colony come to welcome the new arrivals?

Below, several of the figures in the street leapt high into the air, moving towards the oncoming cat as if on jetpacks. The cat slowed its advance.

More people stepped from beneath those strange umbrellas in the street. There were almost twenty down there now, each with their faces turned up towards her and Ashley. They looked a little like tiny flowers with their faces to the sun.

"Ooo. Dear me," said Mark, turning his head. "What the heck have they got on their legs?"

Journey slowed the cat and brought it around so that they were passenger side on to the bouncing thingamies that were coming at them.

He leant forward and stared past Mark. The irises of his silver eyes turned and twitched. He was zooming in. "Those *are* their legs," he finally said. "They've got bloody grasshopper legs."

Mark squinted as the creatures bounced closer. Journey was right. And behind the ones coming towards them, others appeared from beneath those strange umbrellas. These new ones jumped like popcorn in a hot pan towards the two black blobs hanging from the ladder. They weren't far off reaching them.

"What do you want to do?" said Journey.

Mark hummed as he thought. "Well, realistically, I'd like to just call it a day and go home," he said, thinking sadly about the eyeball-beast. He looked down at Nura. "But I suppose we better do a rescue."

"That's the spirit. I'll drive, you shoot."

"But won't we need to get real close?"

Journey grinned like a maniac. "Oh, we'll get close alright."

"What are those two idiots doing?" shouted Sam, as the hover-cat jerked forward and then began bouncing like a pinball between the jumping figures that were advancing upon it. Bolts of red laser shot from the passenger side, leaving little piles of death in their wake.

"We should be more worried about ourselves," called Ashley, reaching a hand up between Sam's feet and pulling herself up a rung. "Those aren't normal people down there. Whatever they are, they're trying to get at us."

Sam looked down. Ashley was right. The figures below were people—at least from the waist up—but they had strange, long, oddly jointed legs like grasshoppers.

Ashley let out a squeak of fear and climbed up another rung so that her head was in line with Sam's thigh as one of the things bounced up and came to within a metre or two of the bottom of the ladder.

"Climb!" she shouted.

Sam did, but with the ladder constantly growing, it was like walking the wrong way up an escalator. She was only just matching the speed that the ladder was being pumped out of the landing pod above, and so remained on relatively the same horizontal plain while the end of the ladder came closer and closer to the ground.

The next grasshopper person to jump caught the end of the ladder, dangled there for a moment with one arm while trying to get a hold with the other, before dropping back down to the floor.

"Next one that does that will be up here," said Ashley, panic touching the edges of her voice.

"What do they want?"

"Who cares? I don't want to find out. Faster. Climb."

Something crashed down below, and Sam glanced over her shoulder to see the hover-cat smoking out of the side of the nearest building. The two figures were out and wielding some sort of laser-emitting tubes, but the grasshopper people weren't moving within range. It looked like a bit of a standoff. She could hear the men bickering even from here.

"Quite literally the only thing you had to do was not crash, and we'd have been fine."

"That one came from nowhere and landed on the front. It threw the steering off. You were supposed to be shooting them. That was *your* job."

"Oh flap off," Mark spat back vehemently. "I think this drill is broken or something. It's not doing what I tell it."

"Hold it up here," said Journey, leaning in to look at the battery pack on Mark's drill. One of his eyes swivelled so he could keep it on the semicircle of grasshopper people that had gathered around them. "Oh, bollards. It's nearly out of juice. Whatever dick put this away last must not have charged the battery. They're supposed to charge it." His mouth pressed together as his eyes darted from left to right.

"How inconsiderate? And"—Mark nudged Nura's tube with his chin—"watch that language."

"Dick's not a swear word. It's a body part." Journey glanced down at his own drill. "Mine's still pretty much full."

Luckily, the grasshoppers seemed reluctant to come closer. It would seem the space rabies was learning, which definitely was lucky for now, but would probably come in as terrifying later.

"What is the matter with you all?" he tried, but they didn't react.

They weren't as bad as the eye-beast. Mere men and women from the waist up and chitinous, leggy insects from the waist down. A couple had an extra set of hooked arms that had sprouted out of the edge of their torsos, ripping through their overalls. Another had mandibles jutting from her lower jaw. Mark didn't like to stare too long lest she get self-conscious or he crawl another inch closer to raving insanity.

"Maybe still wang your drill at them, though," hissed Journey out of the corner of his mouth. "Like it's working." He gave his own a quick jostle in the direction of their attackers. "Yeah, get back," he shouted. "Get back."

Mark did some show-wanging.

The wall inside which Journey had inexpertly parked their catamaran crumbled a little, giving them some space to move back into the room beyond. It looked like some sort of laboratory.

As Mark considered their retreat, a loud grinding of metal on glass came from high above.

He glanced up to see Sam and Ashley hanging about two-thirds of the way between the pod and the floor, with several more grasshopper people dangling from the bottom of their ladder.

"Things aren't looking great," said Journey, as he backed into the building.

Things were not.

"No, they aren't," said Ashley.

"Are you talking to yourself?" Sam called down. It was hard to speak. She'd managed to bring her speed to faster than the ladder was lowering, but it took everything she had to maintain it.

"I've got Mark and Journey on the line," Ashley called up. "It's them in the building down there."

Sam's heart skipped a beat. "Has he got Nura?"

She heard the low mumble of Ashley asking them. "He does. He says to tell you, as long as being super noisy and sleeping a lot is normal, then she is fine."

Sam relaxed as much as was possible in the current situation.

Ashley hummed in amusement. "They said they're going to rescue us."

Sam stole a quick glance at the smoking cat hanging out the side of the building below.

"Oh, wonderful. I was starting to worry."

Above them, the long metal struts that held the great sheet of glass which currently cradled their pod gave a warning groan.

"Hold on," Sam called down, wrapping her arms and legs in knots around the ladder.

With a shriek, the life pod slipped into free fall down the outside of the glass roof trailing the ladder behind it and propelling Sam and Ashley, and all of the grasshopper people hanging below, at breakneck speed up towards the knife-like shards of broken glass.

She closed her eyes and held on tight. This was it.

The ladder bounced upward as the pod caught on something and stopped. Her feet slipped, but she managed to keep her hold. Ashley reached up with one hand and helped her dangling legs locate the ladder rungs.

"Thanks."

"Don't mention it, but also, if you're going to fall, don't hit me."

The descent of the pod had dragged them to within a few feet of the dome, and still the ladder kept ejecting from its underside. That bloody computer. Couldn't it see what was happening?

"If it does that again, we're toast."

"Let's get back in the pod," said Ashley. "We were better off inside."

It was their only chance. Get up to the honeymoon suite and seal themselves inside before they were caught, hoping when it eventually *did* go sliding down the outside of the dome, and come smashing down into the sands, that the crash didn't kill them.

Sam started up again, climbing hand over hand as fast as she could with Ashley close behind, and a rabid collection of hungry-looking, locust-legged humans on their tail.

Her arms ached, but she couldn't stop. Every second of rest took her further from the hole. She gritted her teeth and thought of Nura until eventually she could grip the crack of broken glass through which they had entered the dome. There was a short, heart-stopping moment, when the ladder grew away from her, leaving her feet dangling in thin air while she clung with tired gloved fingers to the jagged glass edge, but she managed to haul herself up and onto the outside of the dome. The glass creaked beneath her feet.

She reached down and grabbed Ashley's hand, pulling her to relative safety.

Exhausted from the climb and trying to catch her breath, Sam fell to her knees. Beneath her, the colony sprawled. The height made her giddy. She could no longer see Mark's building.

The grasshoppers were nearing. They showed no sign of tiring, and their long legs allowed them to climb further with each step.

"Sleep when you're dead," said Ashley, pulling her to her feet. She took hold of Sam's hand. Sam looked at her questioningly. "In case one of us slips."

Sam nodded, and together they manoeuvred carefully but swiftly down the slippery glass.

They got the doors open just as the first of the grasshoppers pushed its way through the crack in the dome.

The momentum of the doors swinging closed rattled the whole pod. Sam had only just thrown herself towards her chair before it began skidding like a two-ton ski instructor down the face of the dome. Horizontal quickly became less than horizontal and she found herself having to clamber up into the chair before buckling herself in.

Ashley had done the same. Her face was pale. She gave a worried smile. Sam tried to return it as the interior of the pod juddered and shook and suddenly spun, flipping them upside down as it tumbled.

She gripped her straps and closed her eyes. Thought of Nura. Prayed she'd see her again.

They'd hidden in a janitor's cupboard. The occasional sound of grunts and footsteps tromped up and down the hallway just outside. Mark's foot, he thought, though he couldn't really tell, had ended up in a bucket, and because of the strange angle he was being forced to hold his leg in, he was starting to get a cramp in his right thigh. He couldn't move, though, just in case it made a noise.

Luckily, the sound of their breathing was muffled inside their respiration suits.

They'd deactivated their lighting arrays, and so the only light in the room was the glow of the LEDs inside their visors. They were chest-to-chest, with Nura between them, still sleeping. Journey had his eyes right, pretending to read the side of a squeezy bottle of bleach with great interest.

Mark lifted his laser drill so he could see the little indicator on the top. It flashed red. Still empty.

He took a quick breath to ask Journeyabout their options, but held it, as something slippery slithered past outside. It might be possible to come up with a plan between them without speaking. He leant forward, knocking his visor against Journey's to get his attention. Journey looked at him.

Mark widened his eyes to ask, *How are we going to blast our way out of this one?*

Journey slowly raised his shoulders and Mark sensed the movement of his hands turning upside down below. *I have no idea.*

Good. They were getting somewhere.

Mark widened his eyes further and rumpled his lips together, then nodded towards the contents of the shelf to his left, where several bottles of fluid, some sponges, and other assorted (and unrecognisable) cleaning utensils sat. *Is there any way to charge my drill using the battery of your drill? You know, like banging the batteries together or something. Perhaps we can do some sort of reaction using some of these chemicals. Oh, I don't know. I'm just kind of guessing here. You're the engineer. Can't you do some science and make it go?* He stole a glance down and poked Journey's drill with his own. *Your drill still has juice, right?*

Journey squinted with one eye, and the side of his face lifted in a sort of confused snarl.

What did that mean?

Mark tapped his drill against Journey's again. Cavemen must have had to communicate non-verbally at some point before language was invented. And they were smarter than cavemen.

Journey looked inward and pressed his lips together in some sort of weird grin, then shook his head.

This might take some time.

The last few moments of their descent became absolute free fall when the pod finally bounced away from the side of the dome like a skimming stone. Everything came to a teeth-rattling stop as they crashed upside down onto the soft sandy ground.

Luckily, they hadn't hit a rock or something equally less forgiving.

Sam hooked her feet under her chair, and, with one hand gripping her seat's armrest, undid her restraints with the other. Her core was no longer what it used to be. The G-forces associated with regular take-offs and ship manoeuvres in hostile airspace had meant she'd needed to be strong, and, before she'd fallen pregnant with Nura, she could manage nearly a hundred crunches and a four-minute plank without breaking a sweat. Now she was lucky if she could hold herself off the ground for thirty seconds.

Slowing her descent only slightly, she dropped to the ceiling of the pod like a handful of flobbling spaghetti. Ashley did the same, but with a lot more grace.

"That was intense," she said, offering a hand up. Sam gladly took it. "What was with those grasshopping dicks?" She paused and folded her arms. "Those were colonists, right?"

Sam nodded slowly, remembering the email she'd read back on the Daedalus. She unslung her suit's pack from her back and took out the laptop. "Is there any way to find out what colony this is?"

"Why?" said Ashley, watching her closely, as Sam flipped the lid and scrolled to reveal the email thread she'd read earlier.

"Because if it's Rosen-54, then I think we're pretty screwed. Look here."

The pair of them scanned the email. Attached to it was a heavily redacted excerpt of a report by a doctor called Fiona Douglas.

Ashley wrinkled her nose as she read. "I'm sure the computer would know where we are."

"I'm way ahead of you, madams," said the computer jovially. "I believe we are just outside of the newest Rosenhalt mining colony, Rosen-54. An interesting fact: the Daedalus was originally scheduled for a stop here, hence our proximity when the hotel was destroyed, but precisely three hours and fifty-four minutes after our departure, it was requested by Sergio Angel that Captain Fenchurch of the Daedalus deviate from the afore-confirmed route and take us straight to our final destination."

Ashley's and Sam's eyes met.

"Then what do we do?" said Ashley. "We need to get off this planet."

"We might be able to use the Star Sailor ship in the hangar. But I'm not going anywhere without Nura. We have to find them."

"Ah, locals," announced the computer. "Madams, would you like me to open the door and let them in?"

"No," they both shouted.

Sam looked to the window. Three slack-jawed, dead-eyed faces peered in.

"Did you bring any weapons with you when you stole aboard the Daedalus?" she asked Ashley, without taking her eyes from the figures at the door.

Ashley shook her head. "Nothing."

"Computer, there's something wrong with the colonists here. Can you compile any guns or weapons for us?"

"Ah, let me see." The computer hummed a little on-hold music. "Hmm," he finally said. "The honeymoon suite, as standard, doesn't come with access to any armaments, I'm afraid. It was found that, with the stresses of the nuptials, and a high intake of margaritas—and in case you couldn't infer by my pronunciation, that's the cocktail not the pizza—newly married couples wealthy enough to make a stay aboard the Daedalus possible were highly likely to quarrel in those first two weeks of marriage. With easy access to laser weapons and other armaments, the average cleaning bill for the room shot up, and so the Rosenhalt Company thought it best to limit the possibility of a bloodbath."

"Another prime example of us having to die because the wealthy elite can't control themselves," said Ashley.

"Can you hack it?" said Sam.

"You can try," said the computer, and the lights in the pod throbbed somewhat menacingly. "And may I ask what you meant several moments ago when you said 'stole aboard the Daedalus'? Did the newlyweds not arrive aboard the galaxy's most sought-after luxury hotel yacht together?"

"Newlyweds?" said Ashley.

Sam kicked her. "Remember, it's complicated," she hissed.

"Oh." Ashley's eyes opened as wide as her mouth. "Yes. Yes. Right."

"Madams." There was a hint of cold, calculated threat in the computer's tone that only two entities in the known galaxy could possibly pull off. The first, a computerised butler. The second, a Basmatian death-bringer, and utilised for final sentences such as, *It's nothing personal* or *You haven't got a chance in hell.*

"The readouts from your respiration suits suggest slight elevation in heart rate and fluctuation in pupil dilation congruent with lying," continued the computer. "Are you lying, madams?"

"No."

"A lie. Why did I not see this before? The Daedalus, part of The Rosenhalt Group of Luxury Hotel Yachts, offers complimentary bonuses for couples utilising the honeymoon suite ..."

"Hold on."

The computer did not.

"And if you are not a couple, then I'm afraid you have broken the terms and conditions set out in your guest agreement."

Those spinning bright lights once more lowered from the ceiling, and the punching klaxon pounded through the cabin.

"Ejection commencing in five, four—"

"Computer stop. We—"

"Three. I don't like being lied—two—to."

"Wait."

"One."

The doors of the pod slid downwards, which, with the pod being upside down, was upwards. A small avalanche of orange-yellow sand flowed over the threshold to cover the ceiling, and with it strode three grasshopper people.

They didn't immediately spring forward. At first they looked a little unsure, tentative one might say, as if they didn't quite know exactly why they had come a-knocking on the pod doors, like a man who'd visited his neighbour for a cup of sugar with plans for a nice Victoria sponge, only to be greeted by a shapely woman in a bathrobe—and soon forgotten about the existence of cakes altogether.

Ashley glanced at Sam and Sam at Ashley, and then there was a sizzle and a pop and the grasshopper on the right was hit with a blue bolt of plasma. Only a set of gangly greenish legs remained where it had once been.

The other grasshoppers turned, and Sam leant to look around them. A small figure in a bright pink respiration suit stood several feet outside the pod, carrying some sort of rifle that was almost bigger than they were. Behind them stood a huge eight-wheeled truck.

"Hiya," called the newcomer, with a friendly wave.

Before the grasshoppers could advance, two more bolts of blue had dashed them like water balloons filled with strawberry jam against the interior of the honeymoon suite.

"You appear to be covered in viscera," said the butler in Sam's helmet. "Allow me."

BLUE FLOWER

Many Ones

RED FRUIT WAS CROSS.

Blue Flower could feel it in the mycelium and taste it on the air, like billions of tiny worms in the soil, flies in the sky. A wriggling, writhing bitter fury. It was a newly learnt feeling for Blue. Neither they, nor Red Fruit, had known of anger before. Not before the humans.

Perhaps Blue should not have helped the latest arrivals—the two women in their metal container—by confusing the hoppers with pheromones. The women were outsiders, after all. But something told Blue that what Red had done, and was continuing to do, was wrong.

Everything had happened so fast, maybe over the course of thirty cycles of the sun. Red had devoured and massacred, absorbed and assimilated.

Red's intentions had not been belligerent in the beginning.

The humans seemed to have trouble surviving. Like fish out of water, the air here did not seem to sustain them. So when one of the suits that the men wore had ruptured, and the poor thing had started to asphyxiate, Red—thinking symbiosis might be the only thing to save him—had stepped in to help.

The human survived, but Red changed.

Then Red joined with more, greedy for the great intelligence contained somehow within those fleshy bags of sentient water, addicted to the power which came with it.

Red had tasted something in them that had not been present in the meat and consciousness of the desert and the under-layer before. Red had grown fat on it.

And then Red had come across Stan Delaney.

Now Red was unhappy, dissatisfied, discontent. Now Red wanted. Now Red needed. Where before they had both just sought to innovate, to make and create and polish and refine, to perfect in beauty and efficiency, Red now wanted to expand, to conquer, to grow needlessly and frivolously.

Blue had only tasted some of that intelligence through Fiona Douglas, but that had been an accident. Blue had not meant to hurt her.

The humans did not operate within one collective mind. They were singular. They were unique. They were many ones rather than one of many. They were creative, artful, prone to great peaks of joy and desperate lows of sadness. They were beautiful, in a way.

Red refused to see the beauty of the individual, of the mystery hidden within.

Red said the humans had dreams and goals and ambitions. Red said that was their beauty. Red said a lot of weird things these days. Like "thinking outside of the box" or "moving the needle".

Red had gained those ambitions, the need to grow and stretch. Now Red wanted to leave, to witness the breadth of what the humans called the galaxy. Red said it would be a win-win. Red would form symbiosis with everything. Red Fruit would be everything.

Red's ambition was selfish and dangerous. It would only harm humans. And Blue believed you could do whatever you liked, as long as it did not cause harm.

There was enough enjoyment found in making things nice, in creating something pretty, art for one's own sake. The galaxy was not for Blue. Blue hoped they could show Red it was not for them either.

The two new men, Mark and Journey, had messed up one of Blue Flower's gardens, but that didn't matter. It was always possible to start again. Bring life anew. It was Blue's art, created for Blue's pleasure alone, and though it had been changed, it was just different, not worse.

But now Red was cross. Blue's pheromone had confused their hoppers. Stopped them from attacking the climbing women from the metal container. Blue was sure the women didn't want to be assimilated into Red's web. Red didn't care. Red just wanted their minds, to know what they knew, to find a way off the planet they'd called home for aeons, to seek out other life that they both now knew was out there.

To conquer it.

To "boss the fuck out of it".

WHITE SURF

A New Bird

AND SOMEWHERE—NOT TOO FAR, planetarily speaking, from the colony on Rosen-54—something small and feathered, white like a dove, but shaped more like a cardinal, with large, all-seeing eyes, crawled for the first time out of the slime at the edge of a vast ocean and onto the hot amber sand. It had only been conceived thirty cycles ago. But the intelligence behind it had spanned epochs, and had, at one point, been omnipresent, until it had splintered and become four individual minds.

This new bird had one purpose. To travel quickly, to witness, and to return.

It was a messenger. Built for speed and sight. Nothing more.

It shook the primordial soup from its body, and, with a clumsy flutter of virgin wings, took off in the direction of two glass domes that had only just—planetarily speaking—appeared on its planet.

It hoped the kids were playing together nicely.

ROSY AND BIG BEE

"I saw you land up there." The woman in pink was no taller than Sam's shoulder. She balanced the stock of the leg-length rifle on her hip. "Nice entrance." She flew her free hand through the air diagonally towards the ground, simulating the flight of the pod. "Knew you'd be in trouble. Came over to watch. See if I could help."

She had a strange way of speaking. A fast staccato of words, as though she'd been taught to talk by a machine gun.

Her sleek and stylish pink respiration suit reflected the gleaming sun. Within her visor, Sam could see a pale, pixie-like freckled face, and a hint of red hair hidden beneath her helmet.

"Thanks," she said. "We have friends still inside the dome. We have to find them."

"Na-na-na." The woman quickly shook her head. "Ain't going in there. I'm surprised you came out. Hate to break it to you, but your friends are dead-dead-dead."

The words punched Sam in the stomach.

"They're not," said Ashley, touching her ear. She glanced at Sam. "Journey says they're hiding in a cupboard in the building they crashed into. He says they have to be quiet. Things are nearby."

The woman chewed the corner of her lip, then looked back at her truck. It looked like some sort of segmented bug, painted in alternating stripes of metallic yellow and black. The wheels were bigger than she was. Three mean-looking turret guns sat on the top, each guarded with spikes.

"You're a Star Sailor, aren't you?" said Sam, stepping a little closer. "Did you come in the ship back there in the hangar?"

"Am. Was. Dunno anymore. My girls is dead for sure. We got a distress signal from some dude. Was only a few kay-kay-ems away so thought we'd check it out. See if we can get some booty." She jabbed a thumb back towards her truck. "My girls dropped me and Big Bee off here to do some ground recon, then landed up top. There was a lot of screaming. It's been a week." She sighed a tiny sigh. "I've tried to get in to take a look, but there's them thingamies what nearly got you creepin' and a-crawlin' all over the shop. Some bigger things as well. Some real big things. Nasty things. A cowardly sailor's mum never cries and what not, so thought I'd sit out here for a bit and come up with an idea. Ain't had one yet. Name's Rosy."

"But I need to find those men," said Sam. "They have my baby."

"Ah, poopin' heck, that's a conundrum," said Rosy. She wrinkled her nose and bobbed her head from side to side. Glanced up to the sky. The light blue of the day was deepening. The sun dropping towards the flat horizon. "It'll be dark soon. And we don't want to be in there then. Don't want to be even anywhere near the big doors then. I've got a place what's safe where we can lie low. You know exactly where those boys are or what?"

"I think so," said Sam, not really knowing if she was telling the truth. "They crashed a cat into one of the buildings in their heroic bid to save us. I presume they're still in there."

"Ah, was them I saw speeding past on that hover-cat at a clip, was it?" Rosy hummed. "Boys drive too fast."

"Yeah," said Sam, "they do."

Rosy scoffed and rolled her eyes, then laid her massive rifle to rest over her petite shoulders. "Let's go save your stupid boys. All aboard Big Bee." She turned and clambered up a set of steps to the door of her truck, opened it and threw her gun inside.

Sam followed across the soft sand and pulled herself up the steps and in. Ashley wasn't far behind.

Rosy strapped herself into the driver's seat, and began flicking switches here and there. The cab of the truck was big enough to fit all three of them with room to spare. A short hall led to the back section. Screens, and the holographic controls for them, glowed with graphs and readouts. On the floor there was a pillow and several packets of suit rations. Judging by the amount, Rosy had been living alone and in her suit for the past week. Sam wondered if the girl had resigned herself to staying here.

A huge rumbling engine ignited beneath them with a growl.

"Combustion?" asked Sam.

"Pfft, na, s'electric really. I just like the sound and the rumble of the old ones, so put in a couple of bass bins. Wumph! Brum brum!" She gunned the accelerator and the speakers fed back with a throaty growl. She giggled low in her throat. "'Tis a good noise."

Sam allowed herself a smile. Star Sailors weren't usually her cup of tea, but there was something endearing about this girl.

"Know how to pop a turret, do ya?" Rosy said as the truck lunged forwards across the sand towards the huge airlock doors in the dome's side.

"What?" said Sam.

"Might need some of that pew-pew-pew action." Rosy let go of the wheel and fired rapid finger guns through the windscreen. "You got the look of a girl who can handle herself."

Sam glanced at Ashley. "I'm just a hotel maid."

Rosy gave her a frown. "Yeah right, and I'm a hot dog." She snorted towards Ashley and jabbed a thumb at Sam. "This girl, right?"

Ashley gave an almost imperceptible raise of the eyebrows.

Rosy manoeuvred a straw inside her helmet to her mouth with her bottom lip and took a long sip of something clear.

"So where we going, then?"

"You should see it," said Sam, resting a hand on the back of Rosy's chair. She could see herself reflected in the back of her pink helmet. "Once we're inside, the building we're looking for should have a hover-cat parked in it."

"Right-ho."

"What happened here?" said Ashley, plonking down onto the springy passenger seat and turning it to face Rosy. "What have you found out since arriving?"

"Not loads," said Rosy. "I wouldn't wanna guess, really, but if I was gonna guess, it's something in the air." She tapped the forehead of her suit. "Ain't taken this off for a week. I reckon it's probably space ghosts." She slowed the vehicle as they approached the airlock doors. "You ever come into contact with space ghosts, Miss Maid?"

"Not on my travels, though they have been somewhat limited."

"Hmm, sure-sure." Rosy gave her a goofy look to suggest she didn't believe it.

What exactly was she seeing that gave who she was away?

"Once upon a time," the Star Sailor continued, "me and the girls were picking up this prisoner dude. Heard he chopped up some colonists. Turned out the whole place had been possessed by murderin' space ghosts. Space ghosts can get really antsy. Get their hosts all carved up. Bit like this. Had to do a lot of shooting that weekend, but we made it out." Her head lowered.

Sam rested a hand on her slender shoulder. "I'm sorry about your friends."

"They were good girls," said Rosy, then pointed out the windscreen towards the doors. "One of you will need to get out and open the airlock door. Can't do it from here."

"I'll do it," said Ashley, standing from her seat.

"And you, Miss Maid, wanna get on top and woman the turret? Make sure she's covered."

"Aye, aye, Captain." There was probably no point in faking it anymore.

The truck doors opened with a hiss of hydraulics. Ashley jumped down to the sand as Sam pulled herself up a few rungs and onto the truck's roof. She raised a set of spikes on a hinge and lowered herself into the depression for the turret. It sat on a track that allowed it to move around the depression where she now stood, giving almost three hundred and sixty degrees of range.

She gripped the triggers and gave the turret a tester spin. It moved freely and easily around the track. Star Sailors always had good gear, and they looked after it well.

She expected it fired plasma like the turrets on her ship back in Artifakt. Oh, how she'd loved that ship. A gift from her father before she'd left home. She wondered if Slug had sold it already out of spite.

Ashley called back to her from the panel next to the huge airlock. "You ready? I don't want to open this and get immediately eaten."

Sam held up a finger for her to wait, then aimed the gun at a nearby rock and fired off a tester shot to familiarise herself with how it worked. The ball of hot plasma turned the rock to oozing slag.

"Cool," she shouted back with a thumbs up. "Go for it."

Ashley turned back to the panel, tapped something on her laptop, and the doors opened.

Rosy revved Big Bee's engine and with a kick of sand from beneath the tyres, the truck chunked forward towards the doors. Ashley climbed inside as the truck pulled into the lock. With a mechanical hum the doors closed behind them. Gas hissed throughout the chamber.

Sam squeezed the turret grips in her fists as the door into the main dome shuddered open. She had to be sharp, Nura was counting on her.

RED FRUIT

MALCOLM QUELETII FELT DIFFERENT to the others. Red Fruit had not taken all of his faculties when they found him cowering beneath that bed. It was interesting, sharing the space with what remained.

Red Fruit felt that maybe they had been too hasty when changing the other humans. Changed them so much that they could not possibly pass with the others of their species. It had all been a bit manic before. Red had chased them down, hunted them out, hungry for every last scrap of knowledge cooped up inside their tiny yet vast brains.

But Red was learning, finally finding their stride. With this new sample of humans, they were planning on leaving a few unassimilated and unaware, hoping to learn how to move amongst them unseen and undetected.

Blue was right when they had suggested these things were individuals. It was such an unusual concept. Why would you want to be alone in the world? How could you know everything there was to know if you did not share experience? If you were not inside of everything. If you were not part of everything.

Red Fruit was everything.

Blue lacked ambition. They had stood in Red's way. Stopped them from taking those two new humans. Red had tried to inform Blue of the wonders of goal setting, but Blue did not seem interested. Just kept messing around with those little flower gardens they had dotted around the complex. Flowers they had seen in the mind of Dr Fiona Douglas.

"A gift for the humans," Blue had said. "A memorial."

There was a galaxy of experience out there to learn from, to assimilate. And with the body of Malcolm Queletii and with the wonderful teachings of Thaddeus Rosenhalt taken from the brain of Colony Executive Stan Delaney, Red would make a start. It was an exciting prospect. Red Fruit just had to knuckle down, level the playing field, and get this no-brainer of a project in the driving seat.

And here was the key, locked away inside one of these escape pods.

The man. The myth. The legend. The author. The innovator. The Boss!

What were the chances?

A human so powerful that he held sway over billions of lives. He could touch billions more with his influence and his reach. Red Fruit wanted that. It was a win-win. Cashback!

Red felt a little nervous as they descended the steps into the hangar bay. They had to put on a show. Something that would make Thaddeus believe something was very wrong with Prendergast and Li. Irreversibly wrong. As Malcolm Queletii reached the floor of the hangar, Red turned both Li and Prendergast around and sprinted them towards him screaming. Red withdrew Malcolm Queletii's firearm—a heavy projectile weapon. How barbaric?—and fired a warning shot. Ordered them to stop. Waited. And when they didn't slow, Queletii put a bullet through each of their heads.

It was fine. Every scrap of knowledge had already been scraped from their brains. Their bodies were now just meat. Shooting them was merely a trick to prove the fate that had befallen them had not befallen Queletii. A show to maintain trust. Something humans did often.

Thaddeus watched from the window. Malcolm waved and Thaddeus waved back. Success! Trust maintained.

Red Fruit spread their consciousness wide. Took in the different corners of the colony. The other new humans were drawing together in Dome 2. It was strange how these things needed to remain separated in body and mind, yet liked being so close to one another. Being a part of Red's web was something they should want, right? A symbiotic relationship would have been nice. But the humans had resisted. It seemed they valued their independence.

One day, perhaps when enough had been assimilated, they would see that unity was the correct path. That bringing beings together under one mind was the true way to grow and succeed and thrive. A group-think, they called it.

Synergy. Networking. Getting in the loop. Send me an email and get it on my desk by five. Numbers-numbers-numbers.

That sort of thing.

Red was not one hundred per cent on it yet—these concepts were all very new—but they were getting there.

Red had called away all other meat from this dome for now. It was not worth spooking Thaddeus Rosenhalt. And there were others here. Red had a use for them. The meat had been sent to Dome 2. The new humans there held no true value, other than more biomass for the expansion. Not now Thaddeus's rescue ship was on its way. But maybe there was a pilot amongst them or an engineer who could fix the Star Sailor ship.

If only the Star Sailors had not cottoned on and destroyed their own ship and their own brains when Red Fruit had infected them, then Red would be up and away from this planet, moving towards their goals with a steady focus.

Even so, it appeared that the wait wasn't a waste of time. Who knew the galaxy's single most influential business and mind-management guru would be gracing them with his presence?

It was almost fate or luck. But fate and luck were not real. Hard work was real. Success was real.

Thaddeus Rosenhalt was real. Wow!

Stan Delaney had idolised him.

So Red idolised him.

MOREL PANIC

THADDEUS DREW THE CURTAIN around the bed, then opened the door to allow Queletii to enter. He tried to ignore Prendergast and Li, with their brains blasted out on the deck outside.

He cleared his throat, before taking a step back to let Queletii in. "So, tell me why that was necessary."

Queletii shut the door and studied the hangar a moment through the window. "I regret to inform you," he said, turning around, "that the colony has been infested with space ghosts. Mr Prendergast and Mr Li were quite badly possessed."

Thaddeus had to physically stop his eyes from rolling. Of course, Queletii was the superstitious sort to believe in space ghosts. Hadn't he been military? And where was his second? Bloody human workers. They almost weren't worth the tax break.

He shook his head. "Space ghosts? There's no such thing as space ghosts."

"Um, really? No such thing?" Queletii stuttered. Actually stuttered. The man had been the security chief on the Daedalus since day one, and, although Thaddeus didn't make a habit of socialising with him, he'd never heard an uncertain word leave his head. "There were a few more of them out there, like the ones that got Mr Prendergast and Mr Li. They took Harrison, in case you were wondering about the person I left with ... the one I know called Harrison. It was definitely space ghosts."

"You mean the ones in the suits. The ones that attacked Prendergast?" Something had clearly been wrong with Prendergast and Li.

Queletii nodded. "Possessed, sir."

"OK," said Thaddeus. "Space ghosts." Whatever this man needed to believe to keep them safe, then let him believe it. He glanced once more out of the window at the body of his former second. "You'll have to sort that mess out before Marcella wakes up. She'll have kittens." He turned and looked Queletii up and down. For some frightfully abnormal reason, the chief had changed out of his security uniform. "Where did you get the suit? And why did you get the suit?"

Queletii pressed his hands down his front, smoothing his shirt and tie. "I am just dressing for success, Mr Rosenhalt." He wrung his hands together in front of his neatly tucked-in shirt. He looked nervous. "I have read all of your wonderful books."

"What, in the last ten minutes?" Thaddeus scoffed. "I never took you for a fan, Queletii." He leant back so he could take this new Queletii in. The man had never shown any interest before.

Queletii nodded vigorously. Thaddeus didn't think he'd ever seen him do anything vigorously in his life, save undermine hotel service staff.

"And what of the pirates?"

"The pirates?"

"The ones who blew up the Daedalus."

Queletii's face went blank for a moment, then he smiled, and said, "They are over in the second dome, I believe. There is a ship there, although it may be inoperable, and we lack a pilot. We may be able to use it to escape."

"We'll wait here for the rescue ship."

"Rescue ship?" Queletii's face twitched. "Ah, the Rosenhalt recovery ship."

"Computer," said Thaddeus, turning away from Queletii, "can you put us in touch with the rescue ship? And if not, do you know when they are arriving?"

"The Edulis is currently travelling faster than light so I am unable to reach them. Estimated arrival time is thirty-six hours from now."

Thaddeus sighed. "That's a little longer than I'd hoped. Perhaps Fenchurch could fly this ship you mentioned, Queletii."

Queletii's face twitched again. "Fenchurch. Captain Fenchurch of the Daedalus. Yes. I am sure he could fly the ship. Is there anyone here who might be able to fix it, if indeed it were broken, which it probably is not?"

Thaddeus looked Queletii up and down, then cast a glance over his shoulder at the hangar. Space ghosts or not, he was clearly rattled. He was talking strangely, like a robot. Thaddeus wasn't sure he liked it. Still, they were in a bind and he'd been the only one to show any initiative so far. More importantly he was the only one remaining with a gun. Thaddeus didn't like the idea of being anywhere near those pirates, or those strange people that had attacked Prendergast, without a weapon between himself and them.

He shrugged. "Let's gather the others around and find out."

WOOHOO?

Mark and Journey hadn't really gained much ground. Apparently, it was not possible to charge one laser drill by bashing its battery with the battery of another laser drill. Apparently, it wasn't a thing anywhere. If Mark had been a scientist, the battery bash recharge system would have been the first idea on his list of things to invent.

Journey had been in hushed conversation with Ashley over the comms. It turned out she and Sam had made a friend and the trio were on their way over now so that Mark could finally rescue them and move to the final stages of his wooing.

In fact, he'd been so pumped about the prospect that he'd whispered it to Journey in excited, hushed tones.

To which Journey had replied, "Woo who?"

To which Mark had replied, "Ashley, of course."

To which Journey had replied, "I know that. I mean woohoo as in hooray."

It had been a trying minute or two, but they had come through it together, and their bond had become stronger because of it.

And the rescuing couldn't come too soon. He was currently experiencing a level of cramp that, until now, he had thought impossible. His whole leg was as stiff as a pipe, and so close to spasming, he had to hold it still with both hands.

Getting out of the cramped confines of the cupboard was priority one.

Surviving monsters: priority two.

Priority three: wooing.

Woohoo!

"Where are they now?" he hissed.

"They're inside the dome," said Journey. "Not long. They'll call us when they're near and we'll make a run for—"

Something fluttered up from below. It crossed between their helmets in the pale light of the LEDs. A powder-blue butterfly. It landed on Journey's faceplate and fanned its wings.

"Is that one from the garden in the airlock?" said Mark.

"Maybe."

The butterfly's abdomen shone a faint blue. The glow moved up and along its lightly spotted wings. It took off and landed on the door of the cupboard. Then slipped through the gap between it and the frame.

After a moment, it popped back into the cupboard, fluttered its wings, and landed on Mark's visor, then flew and slipped through the door again.

"What's it doing?" whispered Journey.

Once more the butterfly entered, landed on Mark's visor, staying there for a little longer, then exited.

"Do you think it wants us to follow it?" he said.

Journey frowned. "It's a butterfly."

"But what if it's a special butterfly?"

"If it's a special butterfly, and it wants us to follow it, that probably means we shouldn't follow it. It's probably going to lead us to its special butterfly mother, who eats people like us for its special butterfly tea."

That faint glow appeared through the door again.

"I'm going to follow it," said Mark. It seemed like the right thing to do.

"Ashley'll be here any minute," said Journey. "We should wait."

The butterfly once more eased through the door frame, this time landing on the handle.

"Look," said Mark. He reached out for it and the butterfly took off and landed on the back of his hand. He sensed its weightlessness like a gentle breeze on his skin beneath his suit.

Journey reached out and gripped his shoulder. "But those things are out there."

"I'll be careful."

Journey groaned low in his throat. It didn't look like he was going to come.

"I'll come back for you," said Mark. He unclipped Nura from his chest and passed her tube over. "Just in case I'm wrong."

Journey cradled the tube in his arms.

Mark pressed the door open slowly and looked both ways. When they'd come in, the building had been dark. Pitch-black save for the light from their suits. Now, dotted along the wall to his right, like guiding lights, were several small glowing butterflies. To his left, he could hear the sound of scraping footsteps. Those grasshopper people searching for them.

"Go if you're going," said Journey, from the dark of the cupboard.

Mark shut the door, and, giving his cramped leg a good shake, hobbled along the hall to the right. Each time he passed a butterfly, it took off and landed further up the corridor. He held up his gloved hand in front of him. The first one was still there.

At the end of the corridor, the butterflies took a right. Mark glanced back and jumped.

"Journey!"

The engineer moved quietly for someone so big.

"Nura was missing you, and uh ..." He held up his arm to show roughly thirty more butterflies lining his suit from wrist to shoulder. "These guys were pretty insistent." His eyes met Mark's as he passed Nura's tube back. "Where are they leading us?"

Mark reattached her to his chest then pointed to the butterflies lining the wall. "This way."

Together, they followed the path, and the butterflies moved to guide them further into the building. They passed several doorways.

"What's in these rooms?" said Mark.

"Most of the colonists live in the first dome. It holds the apartments, the entertainment, school for the kids, admin building. I was young when I lived in a Rosenhalt colony, so didn't come over to the second dome much. We did a field trip to our mine once. I guess these are additional sleeping quarters for miners without families. Like dormitories, maybe."

"That room we came through looked like a lab."

Journey shrugged.

Suddenly, the light inside each of the butterflies died. Only the one resting on Mark's hand remained aglow. It took off, then landed on the handle of the nearest door as something stirred in the darkness ahead.

"Quick," whispered Mark. "In here."

He pushed open the door and allowed Journey to enter before himself.

The room was a dormitory of sorts, but there was only one single unmade bed and a toilet. Even by Rosenhalt colony standards, it was basic. More like a cell.

He backed into the room, pointing his useless drill at the door. Journey did the same.

Something scuttled by. Beneath the door frame, only visible because the room was so dark, a dim red glow passed from left to right. By the sound of it, it was either many little things or something long with lots of legs. Mark didn't know which he'd prefer.

As soon as it had gone, Journey turned on him.

"That was close," he hissed. "I said we should wait."

"I said I'd come back for you. You didn't have to come."

Journey shook his head, but said nothing.

Mark's butterfly flew back to the handle of the door.

"It wants to take us somewhere," said Mark, pointing. "And I guess, seeing as it told us to hide in here, that it doesn't want to hurt us. Maybe it's the arty-farty side, like you said. Maybe it doesn't like the killer side."

Journey's mouth lifted into a reluctant half-grin, then he moved to the door, took a breath, and brushed it open. "OK, but let's hurry."

The butterflies on the wall outside were aglow, leading down the corridor.

"Where's Ashley now?" said Mark, as they followed.

Journey spoke as if to himself. "Ashley, you here yet?"

He paused a moment, then looked at Mark. "They're outside. Somehow, they've cleared the perimeter. We should leave."

"Wait, I want to see what the butterflies want us to see."

Journey made that low sound in the back of his throat again. Rolled his eyes. "Sure." He looked inward. "Ashley, Mark just wants to follow a butterfly through the unlit corridors of an abandoned building. Shout if there's an emergency. We'll be out asap."

He smirked, probably at her reply, then nodded for Mark to continue.

"Did she mention me?" said Mark, hopefully.

"She did." Journey smiled.

Mark sensed it was a knowing smile, but that whatever it knew probably wasn't positive.

With a whisper of delicate blue wings, the butterflies on Journey's arm suddenly took flight, gathering in the air like a cloud, before floating along the corridor to settle on a set of uninviting double doors. Uninviting because their red circular signs read "No entry to unauthorised personnel".

One was ajar.

"What d'you think's in there?" said Journey.

"Dunno." Mark nodded to his friend's drill. "How much charge you got left in that thing?"

"Same as I had when we were in the cupboard and I told you. A bit."

"Fair."

Journey took in a deep breath. "Let's go find out what the unauthorised aren't supposed to know."

The butterflies took flight, like floating blue embers, and led them through the doors into another, wider corridor.

The hall was alive with the chittering and jittering of tiny creatures and the rustling of hundreds if not thousands of creeping fronds and leaves. On either side were darkened chambers with glass windows. They looked like the quarantine chamber where he and Journey had found the woman back at the med centre. Shadowy shapes, broad figures seemingly made of moss and lichen and noticeable only by their subtle movements, watched them from within as they passed.

"Look," hissed Mark, nodding ahead. A blue glow emanated from a window on the right at the far end of the corridor.

"I see it." Journey's lips were parted beneath his visor, his eyes wide and focussed on nothing but the light.

The butterflies clustered, then flew through the door and disappeared out of sight. The glow brightened, casting strange shadows against the opposite wall.

The hard floor beneath them softened and, when Mark looked down, he found they were walking on a loamy, moss-covered soil. Sprouts of flowers and other fauna grew up in sprays of colour. Their numbers grew as the pair closed on the lit room. Mark felt as if he were wading into a blue ocean of flowers. Their density resisted his steps. He lifted his arms above the growth to aid his balance and glanced at Journey nervously. The engineer returned a similar look.

"Do not be afraid."

Although it was hard to tell inside his suit, the voice seemed to come from everywhere. It was small, yet warm, inviting.

"Hello?" he hazarded. "Where are you?"

He waded further, Journey a reluctant step behind.

His boot caught on something, and, when he looked down, he saw several thick cables running along the floor beneath the vegetation and leading towards that glowing room.

As he stepped into view of the room, all the weight lifted from his shoulders.

Flowers filled the space. Wall to wall. Floor to ceiling. Pinks, golds, greens, but the most prevalent colour was blue. Clouds of glowing butterflies rolled like vapour on a gentle breeze. A woman lay back in a reclined seat in the midst of everything. Screens surrounded her, illuminating her sharpened features, showing scenes from many cameras within the colony. Mark saw the hangar where they'd landed, the med centre, a sleek ship sporting a Star Sailor logo in another docking bay, shots of streets, and darkened building interiors.

"Mark?" said Journey. His voice cracked, barely audible.

The fauna surrounding the woman grew up and over her chair, covering her legs to her abdomen in a sea of pale green and blue. More flowers grew through rips in her white lab coat, pillowing her head with petals.

She smiled as she saw them at the window. "You came." She lifted an arm and beckoned for them to enter.

"Who are you?" said Mark. He stayed in the doorway, not wanting to enter further. He sensed a scurrying movement beneath the petals and leaves at his feet. He didn't want to hurt anything.

"Please come in." She smiled. "You are safe. Anything you break here can be rebuilt."

As Mark took a cautious step inside, he realised that the flowers weren't growing over the woman, they originated from her. Her lower body was gone, replaced by the flowers and the plants.

"My name is Blue Flower, although this body is Rosenhalt scientist Fiona Douglas. She was studying me and Red Fruit."

"What have you done to her?" Journey said. He had a strange mix of anger and wonder on his face.

"Red Fruit took her body. I tried to help her by forcing his threads out, but her consciousness had already fled. Maybe if I had gotten to her sooner, I could have helped." She looked down. "We do not have much time. Red Fruit is sending all their meat here. The other humans are waiting for you outside. They will not beat Red's meat."

Mark choked. "What—"

"Is that what's been attacking us?" said Journey, giving him a serious look.

"Yes, Red Fruit's meat horde."

"What are you?" Mark took another step closer.

"We are webs. Fiona Douglas called us hive minds. Every organism on this planet operates through us. We create. We birth new life and new species through a connection of fungus and pheromone."

Mark screwed up his face. Somewhere between mentions of Red Fruit's meat and now, he'd fallen in a bit out of his depth. It hadn't taken long.

"What, like mushrooms?"

A look crossed Blue Flower's face. They opened their mouth to say something, then reconsidered and said, "More or less."

He leant his head to one side, releasing a click from his neck, and held up his empty laser drill. "Well, I eat mushrooms for—"

"So there's two of you?" said Journey, cutting in. "Red Fruit and Blue Flower."

"There is another, but they do not come out much." Blue Flower's eyes shifted downwards and for a moment they looked sad. "We have lived together here for millennia. Creating and learning. Painting on the canvas of this planet with the medium of life. We were birthed from the great ocean an epoch ago to mould the land, but Red Fruit has grown discontented. They tasted something in your kind that we had not seen before."

"And what was that?" asked Journey.

"The want for more," said Blue Flower, and, as they spoke, the glow of everything around them flickered and dimmed before returning. "We were happy, and now we are not. Red Fruit wants to leave me behind. They have grown dissatisfied with the knowledge that there is more out there. They wish now to conquer and expand."

Mark stared at the being in front of him. They radiated intelligence. Aeons of hidden knowledge lived behind those mysterious eyes. He wanted to see what they had seen. To know of the boundless.

He sensed Journey looking at him, but couldn't tear his eyes away.

"We can't let them," said Journey. He clicked his fingers, though they were muted under his gloves. "Mark! We can't let them get off this planet. If this ... this web has done this to the colonists here, what do you think would happen if it assimilated the knowledge of an entire city, or a planet of people? It would be unstoppable. Everything would fall."

"I—" started Mark, but he wasn't sure what he wanted to say. He looked down at Nura. She was happily feeding inside the tube. "What's stopping Red Fruit from leaving?" he said, and pointed to the ship on the screen. "Can't they just fly that if they have the knowledge of all the colonists?"

"The Star Sailors destroyed part of their ship. It will not fly, and the knowledge for fixing it was not found in any of the colonists. They require a ship's engineer to complete repairs. There were also no pilots here. Red Fruit cannot fly without the knowledge of a pilot."

"Well, Journey c—"

"Mark!" Journey gave him a warning look with an almost imperceptible shake of the head.

He pressed his lips together to keep from spilling. Given enough time and enough resources, Journey could probably fix whatever was wrong with the ship. And if the pilot from The Daedalus was still alive, then all Red Fruit needed to do was take them and it could leave.

"How can we stop them?" said Mark.

"I do not think you can change Red Fruit. Not soon enough. The only option is to take away their means. Maybe, over time, I can redirect their focus."

Journey looked nervous. Locked up inside his brain was at least half the knowledge this Red Fruit required to leave. What would Blue Flower do to him if they knew? What would Red Fruit do to get to him?

"You must destroy the ship if you can't leave in it. And make sure no one ever comes back here."

"That's easier said than done," said Mark.

People could go anywhere they liked. And telling them not to go somewhere was as good as pointing a massive red arrow covered in flashing lightbulbs that read "All You Can Eat Buffet".

Journey pressed a hand to the side of his helmet. His gaze travelled inwards. Ashley on the intercom.

"What?" he said, eyes wide.

There was movement on one screen, and Blue Flower's hand flew to a keyboard. The image from the screen expanded to cover them all. A large yellow and black truck was parked outside. Far beyond it, the horizon bubbled and swarmed with the oncoming charge of hundreds of creatures, large and small. Flashes came from a turret on the truck's roof.

"Red Fruit knows you are talking to me," said Blue Flower. "Their meat is coming."

Mark blinked, then looked at Journey. "Am I the only one who—"

Journey slapped him on the top of the head. "No time for that. We have to get out of here." He grabbed Mark's arm and pulled him towards the exit.

"Run," said Blue Flower. "I will do all I can to help."

MOTHER AND CHILD REUNION

Sam's fists were sweating profusely. The wicking material of her gloves couldn't remove the moisture fast enough. A glowing red cross in her sights told her the beast that had just crawled out of the hole in the ground where the mine had once been was still out of range of the turret's plasma rounds, but at the rate it was coming, it wouldn't be long before she could pull the trigger.

The thing was a hulking mass of organic matter standing on two wide legs. A dreadnought of writhing flesh with four great arms that were easily thicker than tree trunks. She could feel the rumble of its feet hitting the ground as it lumbered nearer. And behind it, rising from the cracked streets, and dragging themselves from the shade of nearby buildings, were more human-sized creatures. Beings with four legs, scuttling insectoids with six, bipeds, all coming towards them at a sprint or a gallop.

Rosy stuck her head out of the window on the driver's side. "Where yo' boys at?"

They were parked just outside of the building Mark had crashed into, with the truck side-on to the oncoming horde. The nearest creatures were still some two hundred metres away, but closing infinitely fast. Ashley stood behind the second turret, eyes wide in terror.

"They are coming now," she called dreamily to Rosy.

"They better be." Rosy's head retreated through the window. A little shaking fist replaced it.

Sam glanced back. If that idiot's delay meant Nura got hurt, he wouldn't have to worry about these awful creatures getting to him. He'd be dead before they came close.

A door clattered open in the side of the building, slamming against the wall as two figures in black respiration suits, one short, one tall, burst out and sprinted for the truck. The shorter one had a tube attached to his chest. Nura. God, she hoped so.

Sam couldn't breathe as she looked from the oncoming horde to her baby.

Big Bee rumbled beneath her feet as Rosy gunned the engine. The great knobbly tyres spun as Mark clambered up the side, followed by his friend. The taller man scrabbled for purchase, feet skipping along the tarmac as they picked up speed.

Mark turned, and with a hand under his friend's armpit, dragged him up.

When they were both secure on the side of the truck, he looked up and spotted Sam. He waved. Then shimmied along towards her. He half-clambered, half-fell into the turret's depression where she stood.

A *dakka* of automatic plasma fire from Ashley's turret told her the horde was in range.

"Where's Nura?" was all she could say as he stood up.

He leant forward to show her a transparent viewing port on top of the tube attached to the front of his suit. Nura's face lit up when she saw her, and Sam let out a breath. Tears spilled down her cheeks.

"Thank you," she said, throwing her arms around him.

He smiled. "Want me to do this?" he said, pointing to the turret.

"Nah, you're good." She looked him up and down. He was covered in about as much dried gore and sand as she was. "What happened to you?"

He grinned. "I guess the same thing that happened to you."

"Yeah, lucky I look good in red."

She threw the turret around and unleashed a barrage of steaming plasma. One of the advancing bugs on the forward fringes of the horde exploded into a spray of claret. Those galloping after it burst undeterred through the bloody cloud.

The truck was pulling away now, but only just.

"We got more nasties incoming," shouted Rosy from the front, as the truck spun around and sped along the street.

She pointed out of the window to the roof of the building Mark and Nura had just escaped from, as the truck slalomed around a series of house-sized mushrooms that had erupted through the tarmac. Several grasshoppers leapt from the roof of the building to land on the cab just above Mark's friend.

Sam tried to grind the turret around to fire on them, but it wouldn't shift to an angle capable of hitting the cab. Mark's shoulders slumped. With a twisting motion, he unscrewed Nura's capsule from the front of his suit and passed the baby to Sam. He gave Nura a wave, then Sam a tired smile. A smile that told her he'd rather be doing anything other than what he was about to.

In that moment, she saw him for who he truly was. A protector.

He removed a large spanner from an enclave next to the turret and crawled up onto the roof of the truck.

Sam attached Nura's tube to two hooks on the front of her suit and sighted at the horde that was chasing. There was nothing she could do to help Mark now, except make sure he didn't have more added to his already full plate.

BOARDERS

"Boarders, Journey," Mark shouted, pointing the spanner at the leering grasshoppers atop the truck's cab. "Let's do 'em."

Before Journey could do any doing, the first of the grasshoppers leapt forward and pinned him to the roof of the truck.

Mark was knocked to the side. His back foot slipped, and suddenly he was upside down, hanging by his right leg from a length of cable that ran along the side of the truck, his head less than a foot from the rushing road. The spanner clanged under the wheels.

He spread his arms to stop himself from spinning, pulled himself up with his abs, and caught the cable jamming his foot with both hands.

He released his foot and gripped the wire. Shimmied along to the ladder and hauled himself up to stand behind the grasshopper that had mounted Journey. On the cab above and behind him were two more.

One went for him. A kamikaze strike that would have taken them both to the road had he not ducked out of the way. It fell from the truck and crunched on the tarmac below.

The ceaseless white noise roar of rushing wind and the blast of the plasma turrets was almost overwhelming as they raced towards the airlock. The truck bounced and jolted. He widened his stance, lowered his centre of gravity, and moved to help Journey. The creature was tugging at his helmet, trying to get it off. Journey had one forearm jammed into the thing's neck. The other hand pressed tightly on top of his head.

Mark wrapped his arms around the creature, hugging it tightly around the waist. Using his bodyweight as a lever, he leant back and lifted it off his friend.

He realised his mistake when the thing clamped its arms over his and crouched, ready to leap from the truck with him.

He felt the immense power of the thing's legs as his feet left the floor. At the last possible moment, something big and engineer-shaped collided with the grasshopper, slamming them down onto the roof of the truck. All the air was squashed from his lungs under the combined weight of Journey and the creature.

Journey rolled off and aimed his drill at the one behind Mark on the roof. A bolt of red heat and a spattering of blood.

The one lying on top squirmed to free itself as Mark held it down. Journey moved in and grabbed its leg. It kicked out, landing its insectile foot on his knee. The engineer's leg bent sickeningly, and he let out a cry of pain as he went down. The creature jerked and threw its weight from side to side, kicking its legs, trying to break free of Mark's grip, but he held firm. He didn't have a plan just yet, but wasn't going to let it go. It flailed suddenly in his arms and rolled to the side. His head banged the lip on the edge of the truck and then, once more, he was tumbling with the creature to the speeding tarmac below.

He twisted in the air with the momentum of the grasshopper's roll. Pressed himself up and it down to cushion his fall as they landed. The grasshopper ground into the floor and Mark was thrown clear, skimming along the tarmac on his front.

He rolled to a stop and looked up. Thanked the heavens. The truck had skidded to a halt only fifteen or so metres ahead. Just beyond it was the airlock.

A pink helmet poked out from the window. A small female voice shouted at him. "Airlock's here. Stop lying around and get it open. No time for lollygagging."

He shook his head to clear it and pressed himself to stand. Walking was hard. His head was spinning from the knock, the fall, the roll. With a few unsure lumbering steps to get started, he broke into a run. The heat of the plasma fire from the truck's turrets blasted overhead, and the rumble of many charging legs vibrated the ground beneath him.

He didn't look back. Just ran for the airlock controls.

He spotted Journey press himself up on top of the truck. "The blue wire, probably," he called, his voice laboured. "Or if not, the red one."

Mark threw him a thumbs up.

The panel beside the airlock was flush to the wall. He tried to jam his fingers into the crack to pull it open, but it was no use. Even without the suit's gloves, he'd find it difficult. If only he still had the crowbar, but that was off somewhere embedded in the leg of some fungal zombie space rabies dude.

"Hurry up, matey boyo," came a shout from the truck's driver.

He looked back. The woman dressed in pink was now on top of the cab, adding her own plasma fire to that of the turrets. All were blasting into the advancing, unstoppable wall of creatures. They'd put some distance between them, but they were coming, fast. Blue Flower had been right, there would be no beating Red's meat.

With little hope, he patted himself down and scanned the bare ground around him for a stick or a piece of metal, anything to prize open the panel.

There was a lump in the pocket of his suit's sleeve. He flipped it open and pulled out the world's tiniest, most pointless screwdriver. Other worlds may have had tinier ones, but probably not this one.

He stabbed it between the panel and the wall. It fit perfectly. With a see-saw motion—back and forth, back and forth—he eased it apart a fraction. Moved it down. Eased again. And again. And again. His hand ached with the small repetitive motion, but the panel was coming away from the wall a millimetre at a time.

Though the progress was slow, it was constant and soon he found he could grip the panel edge with his fingertips. He wriggled it away. Inside was a row of thick wires moulded to the back wall. Using the screwdriver again, he prized them away.

He thumbed them apart, looking for the blue one, or maybe the red one, but they were all grey or yellow or green.

He swore into the box, and looked back, but couldn't see Journey.

Growling low in his throat, he made a snap decision—a decision that someone with a better understanding of physics and electronics and less of a reliance on good luck may not have made. With all the fervent desperation and straining speed of a pressed postal employee faced with an infinite number of letters to stamp before they can go home, Mark flipped into atomic stab mode. He braced himself, and, hoping against hope that he might find the right one, jackhammered rapidly at the bunch of wires with the screwdriver.

"Fuuuuuuuuuuurrg," he screamed.

Something sparked and popped, and the wires coughed out a plume of smoke. The door beside him jerked, then juddered open.

"Yes!" He punched the air and twirled around to check whether all his friends, old and new, had succumbed to Red's meat horde.

"Nice one." The woman in pink threw him her rifle and swung back into the truck. He caught it and peered around the side of the vehicle.

It was going to be close.

The truck jerked past and into the airlock.

A small group of centaur-like beasts were sprinting ahead of the main group and he concentrated on those.

Both Ashley and Sam were forced to cease fire as the airlock doors slid closed again. Mark didn't let up, blasting through the shrinking gap, until they were completely shut.

He breathed a sigh of relief, and pulled himself up the ladder onto the roof to find Journey, face down, spreadeagled, gripping handles on either side. His leg looked all wrong.

"You OK?" Mark asked.

"I'm going to be honest. I am not," said the engineer, without raising his head. "Do not move me for about a year and I think it'll sort itself out."

Mark winced. He wasn't so sure.

The outer doors opened. Mark readied his rifle, but the way was clear.

With smooth acceleration, the truck pulled out of the airlock and eased along the edge of the dome at a gentle pace.

Through the dome, Mark could see the creatures at the airlock. Behind him, reflected in the glass, the neon-orange sun was just touching the horizon. He turned. A tall forest of lush vegetation roughly half a kilometre away cast long, grey shadows across the dunes. He raised a hand to shield his eyes. The cloudless, alien sky faded from a dark blue above them to a burnt pink, turning the yellow sands red.

He thought of what Blue Flower had said, of Red Fruit's discontentment. How could anyone or anything grow discontented with this place?

He shuffled around on the side of the truck to the open window of the cab.

"Where are we going now?" he asked the woman inside. She seemed tiny in this beast of a vehicle. The wheel massive in her hands.

"Got a safe spot," she said, without taking her eyes from the route ahead. "No space ghosts there. They don't like it. Make yourself comfy. S'not far." She glanced up to a monitor which showed the roof of the truck and Journey having not moved. "How's your big friend? He took a kickin'."

"He's survived worse."

"Ain'tn't we all," she said. "But it sure ain't nice to do."

DECEIVING BOLETE

THE REMAINING SURVIVORS FROM the Daedalus stood before Thaddeus in the hangar. The flight team (Captain Fenchurch and the ship's navigator) and two more Rosenhalt board members (Celia King and Damu Abebe), as well as their respective partners.

Marcella and Queletii stood either side of him, facing them.

Queletii had rounded them up. It had taken some time. Thaddeus presumed that after what he had done to Prendergast and Li, they were a little reluctant to leave their pods.

But here they stood.

"The rescue ship is on its way here," said Thaddeus, meeting each of their eyes one at a time, "but they might be thirty-six hours—"

Damu scoffed. "You can't truly believe this madness about space ghosts, Thaddeus. What's really going on here?"

Thaddeus held up a hand. Anger at the interruption burned inside, but he didn't let it show in his voice.

"I understand your concern, I didn't believe it myself at first, but there is no better explanation. The colonists here are all dead." More mumbles from the congregation. "The ones you saw attack our friends were clearly possessed by something, and it affected Prendergast and Li in a way we can't possibly understand."

He tightened his lips. He and Queletii had agreed on their approach before venturing out, even before waking Marcella. Although he wasn't entirely convinced of Queletii's explanation of space ghosts—he'd colonised over fifty planets and never heard of anything so ridiculous—they had to say something to persuade the others to move. They weren't safe here.

"Space ghosts?" Damu's girlfriend quailed, and linked her arm with his, pulling herself against his broad, surgically enhanced chest.

He stepped forward, letting her stumble, then jabbed a rigid finger at Thaddeus. "If they have access to the equipment library, then they already have all the tools necessary to gain entry to our pods. Do you think we have thirty-six hours before they come back and find a way in?" He looked around at the others.

"Well, then it makes no sense to stay here," said Thaddeus.

"While I searched the complex," said Queletii, "I did some reconnaissance. It seems the ones who attacked Mr Prendergast, the ones you saw, are all that are left. I was able to take down a few others when they ambushed me and Harrison. As long as we are united, we will succeed in getting to the hangar above Dome 2."

"And why would we go to Dome 2?" Damu said, his eyes darting between Thaddeus and Queletii.

Thaddeus took a deep breath. "Queletii informs me a Star Sailor ship is blocking the other hangar." He turned and motioned to the pods behind him. "Even if our rescue ship was coming sooner, it can't land here with the pods in the way, and with the ship over there. Our quickest bet for recovery is to take the Star Sailor ship up and meet the rescue ship in orbit."

"Captain, do you think you could fly it?" said Queletii to Fenchurch.

Fenchurch smoothed his thick white moustache with thumb and forefinger, and cleared his throat. "There's no ship I can't fly."

Thaddeus gave him a wink. "There's a reason I hire the best."

"But how are we going to get there?" Damu folded his arms. "It's at least a kilometre to the edge of this dome, another to the centre of Dome 2, and then there's the climb to the second hangar. It'll take some time. I don't like the idea with those people out there."

Celia gave him a soft punch on the arm. "A strapping lad like you cannot walk a few miles?" she said. She and her husband Morgan looked gaunt and tired. The evacuation of the Daedalus had clearly taken its toll.

"Celia ... come on," Damu put an arm around his girlfriend. He puffed out his chest. "I just want to make sure we go as quickly as possible."

Celia's husband perked up at this. Thaddeus didn't think he'd ever heard the man speak.

"Let Malcolm Queletii take care of the ghosts," he said. "If the ship is our only way off the planet, then it is our only way off the planet."

Thaddeus smiled.

Damu grunted low in his throat. "Fine."

Thaddeus clapped his hands and rubbed them together. "Excellent." He looked at Queletii. "Is there anything else we need to cover before heading off?"

Queletii spread his hands wide in front of him. "I have already spoken to Mr and Mrs King about this, but are any of you able to apply starship repairs if necessary?"

Both Celia and her husband turned strangely vacant eyes to Fenchurch, Damu, and the others.

The Daedalus navigator shook his head.

Captain Fenchurch stroked his moustache once more. What was it with space captains and fingering their facial hair?

"I might be able to do something, but it depends what needs—"

"Why?" interrupted Damu. "This Star Sailor ship works, right?"

Thaddeus sensed Marcella's worried eyes turn to him. He gave her hand a squeeze, but didn't meet her gaze.

Queletii's shoulders sagged, but then he linked his fingers in front of his face. "I just want to make sure ahead of time that we can synergise if necessary. Hit the ground running when we get there."

Damu looked at Thaddeus. He scoffed. "Looks like someone's been reading your books." He raised his eyebrows, then shook his head in resignation. "Fine."

"Lead the way then, please, Mr Queletii," said Thaddeus, holding up a hand.

And Queletii did.

PEROXIDE OUTSIDE, INSIDE

SAM WANTED MORE THAN anything to let Nura out, to hug her to her skin, to feed her, but the best she could do was place her gloved hand on that transparent lid on top of the tube. The way Nura kept reaching out, pressing her sticky little palm against the glass, broke her heart.

"Soon, poppet," she said, rocking the tube from side to side. "Mummy will hug you soon enough."

A tainted niggle of worry crackled through her brain like lightning—*only if we can get off this planet*—and she glanced at the others, guilty for thinking it.

Rosy had driven them to a spot next to the huge atmosphere generators attached to the side of Dome 1. Two vast blocks of mysterious science that recycled the air inside the domes, and, slowly, using a great amount of energy and the atoms in the surrounding area, changed the planet's atmosphere. They started with the air around the domes, and bit by tiny bit, they changed the world. Something like filling a swimming pool with a dripping tap. It could sometimes take years, but the Rosenhalt Company said that progress took patience. Collectively, the human race had the time, they just had to decide to invest it early enough to reap the rewards. Making people feel they'd miss an opportunity if they didn't act was a good way to both sell them stuff they didn't really need and force through ethically grey practices.

Eventually, if the company deemed the planet a good investment, more and larger generators would be installed to get the job done faster.

Despite all that had happened inside the colony, the two generators were still operating, and would continue to do so until they either broke, or were turned off manually. Their vibrating hum had turned the surrounding sands completely flat.

"I was running in Big Bee, first night after the girls was attacked," said Rosy. She sat on a short outcrop of rock, dangling her legs over the side, talking to Journey and Mark. "And the thingamies didn't follow me here." She pointed to a spot a little further away against the dome. "Just hung out over that way, like there was some invisible force field. So I stayed here, safe as houses."

"It's probably the hydrogen peroxide or something," said Journey, lying flat on his back next to her, while Mark fussed around him, trying to keep him comfortable.

Sam smiled at his mothering.

"These atmos-gens put out some pretty harmful chems that slowly degrade into breathable air," Journey continued. Sam couldn't see his face where he lay, but could hear an angry edge to his voice, like he was talking through gritted teeth. "They can kill pretty efficiently in the right quantities."

Rosy had straightened his broken leg, splinting it with parts from Mark's spent laser drill. There was no way to assess the seriousness of the break until they removed his suit, and there was no chance they were doing that until they were off the planet. It had gone unsaid, but she surmised they had all come to the same conclusion. Whatever had happened to the colonists here, had happened in part due to something in the air.

Sam glanced over at Ashley. She sat alone inside the truck. Just visible through the windscreen. She had said little since they'd arrived here. The poor woman. For someone who spent most of her time safe behind a computer, Sam suspected everything that had happened over the last day was a lot to take in. Hell, it was a lot for anyone to take in.

"So what did your friends do to break your ship?" said Journey after a short pause.

"You can fix anything, Journ," said Mark confidently.

"Well, depends if I've got the parts or tools."

"I heard 'em chatting, in the last moments," said Rosy.

She brought her knees up to her chin and hugged them. She looked so small. Barely out of girlhood. Sam wondered how old she was. Wondered if she'd run away from an over-nurturing home like she had, or been bought from parents unable to provide like so many Star Sailors.

"They told me what they was about to do. We did a vote. Aye. Aye. Aye. Aye. Nay. Wreck the ship. Pop their caps. I don't know what they did, but they would have made sure that whatever that thing is couldn't get off the planet. It won't be easy, but it will have been something they knew how to fix up." She stood. "But if there's any chance that thing is gonna leave, I ain't letting you fix it."

Journey nodded.

"And we'd need a pilot anyway," she continued, "unless one of you bozos can fly a Star Sailor class ship?"

The muscles across Sam's back tightened. She kept her mouth shut. Hopefully Journey or Mark might be able to fly. Unless she had to, she didn't want to put herself forward.

Mark put his hand up, and she breathed a short sigh of relief.

"Shotgun not doing it," he said.

"Yeah, me neither," said Journey. "Our cap'n and android drove The Hurricane."

Rosy turned towards Sam. "What about you, Miss Maid?"

Sam straightened. Looked to each of them in turn. "Um ..." If one of them recognised her. If they knew Slug ...

Mark frowned at her hesitation. "You don't know how to fly, do you, Sam?"

Ashley eased her way out of the truck to join them.

Sam hugged the tube attached to her front, took a deep breath, and nodded. "I can fly whatever it is you've got up there."

Mark grinned.

"Nice," said Rosy. "So how we getting up there?" She motioned towards Journey. "Especially with your snappy leg."

"Don't worry about me," said Journey, shifting himself to rest on his elbows and giving his leg a gentle pat. "I reckon it's got a few miles in it."

"Buggered leg or not," said Mark, "it'll be difficult getting up to the hangar with all those bloody things in there."

Sam considered the giant atmosphere generators for a moment. "What if we somehow reverse the flow of the generators?" she said. "Could that be done? Pump out whatever's stopping them from coming closer here, but in there."

Journey shrugged. "It's possible." His face was strangely grim. "The first thing they do when the domes are put in place is fill them with hydrogen peroxide. It's not that harmful to people, but will kill any bugs that slip through. It's like a big purge, and then the gas quickly degrades to water and oxygen."

"Hydrogen peroxide? We used that on the Daedalus to disinfect things," said Sam. "Could you do it again? Could you fill the domes with it?"

"If we were in our suits," said Mark, patting himself down, "and the domes were full of that stuff, we'd be safe, but Red Fruit's creatures would die, right?"

"Maybe." Journey's eyes searched the ground in front of him as he thought.

"How long would it take to fill up the domes?" asked Sam.

Journey considered this. "We wouldn't necessarily need to fill up the domes—it takes a while—but HP is heavier than air, so it'll sink. It might not take long to flood the floor level. And that's all we'd need to slow down the man-sized things. Doubt they'd just keel over, though."

"Slowing them down's a start," said Sam.

"And we'd have to watch out for the big ones." Journey held his hand flat. "The ones above the HP layer, but as long as we could get to the plaza in Dome 2, we could climb up to the hangar from there. The big ones wouldn't even fit in the building." Journey eased himself up to seated, stifling a wince. "It might take a night and day after changing the flow to get enough pumped out. But we could direct the flow towards the second dome rather than spread it between both. That'd speed things along."

"Could you do that?" Sam said.

Journey sighed, but said nothing. He seemed reluctant. Something was eating at him.

"Could you?" said Mark. Judging by the frown directed at his friend, he could see it too.

Eventually, Journey nodded. "I could."

"Nice," said Rosy. "Let's do that. Might even be able to get in there all stealthy like. I got supplies here. We can wait for a bit once it's done. I've enough suit rations for all of us for a day or two. Then we're gonna start having to find more."

Journey groaned as he tried to stand. Mark flapped and helped him up with an arm around his waist. Despite how strong he was, he was clearly out of his depth trying to help his larger friend.

"I don't know if I'm going to be very stealthy with this." The engineer gestured towards his leg.

"Well, you could always tell me what to do?" said Mark. "I promise to listen and follow all the directions properly this time."

Journey scoffed. "Have you got a pen to write them on your arm?"

Mark patted himself down.

The engineer laughed. "Don't worry. I'm not trusting you with it. I'm definitely going."

"No way, big boy," said Rosy, patting him sympathetically on the arm. He was at least head and shoulders taller than her, but she still had a funny way of making him look small. "You ain't going anywhere like that. Give me all the deets. I'll know what to do."

He looked at her a moment with lips pressed together, then smiled. "You sure? You might need to know your way around a mainframe."

"I know a few bits and bobs," said Rosy.

"I'll go too," said Ashley. She moved closer and put an arm around Mark's shoulder as if to lean on him. "If it's hacking you need, I'm your girl."

Mark went rigid.

Journey rubbed his hands together. "Good. Between us, I'm sure we can get it done."

Sam smiled—having a plan felt good—but it quickly faded, replaced with a frown. There was something off about the way Ashley was looking at her.

WHITE SURF

FAMILY FEUD

NIGHT HAD FALLEN. WHITE Surf's almost weightless body hovered high in the deep purple sky, riding the warm currents rising from the cooling sand.

Blue Flower and Red Fruit were here, too. White Surf could sense their organic matter below and above the sands beneath the domes. They always spent so much time together. It filled White Surf with pride.

And yet, there was division. Red and Blue were in disagreement over something. Their discovery.

Did they know exactly what they had found? White Surf guessed not. The pheromones were the same, but this entity had left long before Blue and Red had even grown the organs with which to sense.

It was good to see Yellow Lichen again.

WASTED

M ARK WISHED THEY COULD have rifles on the Hurricane like the one Rosy had given him. It was chunky, but it was lightweight, and it looked like it packed a punch. She'd also given him two handguns, which sat snuggly at his hips.

He felt a bit like a cowboy as he trudged across the sand beside Ashley with Rosy leading the way towards a maintenance shaft that poked from the side of the dome. Ashley passed a glance to him, smiled invitingly, but said nothing before turning her gaze forward once more.

If he was going to talk to her about where their relationship stood, it was now or never. If he waited any longer, he'd probably never pluck up the courage again.

"Um," he said, trying to regain her attention.

She moved her head slightly, telling him she was listening. This was it.

For a fraction of a second he thought he might not be able to talk, but, with effort similar to blowing peanut butter through a straw, he managed to force the words out.

"Did something happen the other night on the Hurricane?"

She offered him a half-smile. "You got very drunk, that's what."

"I know that." His head had only recently stopped aching. "Did anything else, you know, between us?"

"Am I that forgettable?" She snorted. "I bumped into you in the archive. You were already half-cut. Writing directions down on your arm. We talked. We drank. One thing led to another. It was fun." She smiled, fully this time, and under the beauty of it he nearly melted. "Maybe if we get out of this, we can do it again?"

He couldn't hold back a boyish guffaw as it erupted from his chest. "Yeah. Cool. Yeah."

"You two boner-birds still with me or what?" said Rosy, spinning and moving backwards to look at them as she spoke. She turned back and pointed towards a square hole covered by a grill in the wall of one of the atmosphere generators. "That's where we'll get in. Then it's just a short crawl to the stairs and up two floors to the control centre. Then me 'n hacker girl will fix it so it's pumping HP into the dome while Pirate Pete keeps watch."

"The name's actually Mark."

"Your name is Pirate Pete until you prove otherwise."

She pulled a tool from her belt as she neared the hole, sliced easily through the sides of the grill and bent it downwards so it could act as a sort of ladder to get them in.

"Me first, then you. You last," she said, pointing to Ashley and then Mark. "Journey said you're liable to get lost, so just stick behind us. I'm moving fast. I'm moving quiet. And so are you if you want to not die."

"Sounds good," said Ashley.

Mark nodded.

Rosy pulled herself up into the vent and started to crawl. Mark offered Ashley a bunk-up, but she pulled herself up and in without his help. He followed, but not too close. He had to keep his eyes down as he crawled behind her. Didn't want to invade her personal butt space.

I did not bring my son up to ogle at women's behinds—Mum, followed by a swift clip about the ear.

They passed through one cross junction, took a right, and found themselves at another grill. Rosy did her trick with her cutter, then eased it out of the wall and slipped down into the corridor ahead without making a sound. Her head twisted left and right, the rifle pulled tight to her shoulder.

Mark smiled. She was impressive. He'd have to ask her how she became a Star Sailor.

He and Ashley followed her down. Mark slung his rifle on his back and drew both pistols. This was better than that laser drill rubbish. He could do pistols.

The corridor was dark, save strips of low-power emergency lighting that ran along the middle of the floor, illuminating the underside of everything a faint blue and casting long shadows up the walls.

Rosy jerked her head for them to follow and started quickly off to the left.

He walked backwards, throwing the occasional glance over his shoulder to make sure they didn't leave him behind, but he did so with a spring in his step. All he had to do was get out of here and maybe all his dreams might start to come true. Ashley kinda liked him. There was a cool ship ready for the taking. And here he was doing Star Sailor stuff with a genuine Star Sailor. Things were looking up for ol' Marky Mark.

"Are you humming?" said Ashley, looking back at him.

"Am I what?"

Maybe he had been.

"Zip yer lips, you two, we're coming up to the stairs."

Rosy pulled open a door and led them both inside. A circle of stairs rose roughly four-storeys.

"Journey says it's on the second floor." She held her breath a moment and listened. "Can't hear nothing." She started to climb.

"Lucky that maid can fly a ship, hey?" said Ashley to Mark as they climbed. Her voice was low. "How did you find her?"

"A couple of Rosen execs were trying to kill her. Had to punch them out." He clicked his tongue and shrugged to suggest it couldn't be helped.

Ashley paused a moment on the stairs, allowing him to draw level. "Why were they trying to kill her?"

"Rosen execs being Rosen execs, I guess."

She hummed, then shook her head. "There's something else there, don't you think? Seems a bit of a coincidence that the Daedalus went up pretty much as soon as we came aboard. And I swear I've seen her before." She cast a sideways look at him as they reached the first floor. "Do you think Journey knows her?"

Mark frowned. That seemed a little far-fetched. "No. Um ... why would you think that?"

"I don't know. All I know is Journey is the only one out of us, except maybe you, who had the opportunity to destroy the Daedalus engines."

She took his hand and gave it a squeeze. His skin tingled beneath his suit, and his heart raced.

"And please don't take this the wrong way," she continued, "but I don't think you'd be capable of setting them to blow. I just think it's weird that her baby was the only one left, like she'd been left behind for her to pick up on purpose. And also that Journey got aboard the Daedalus escape pod, rather than leaving on the Hurricane with the others."

He didn't know what to think. He'd known Journey for years. They were best friends.

"You think maybe they know each other or something?" he asked. "From Artifakt?"

She shrugged. "Maybe. I don't think it was a coincidence that whatever happened on the Daedalus happened while we were on it. And I know it wasn't you or me."

Mark looked over his shoulder, back the way they'd come, as if he could see Journey and Sam now. Sam hadn't put herself forward for this mission, despite it being her idea, and Journey could never have tagged along with his leg. Had she mentioned it so that she and Journey could be alone? Journey had seemed oddly reluctant to say her idea might work—what had that been about?—but in the end, under pressure from Sam, he had agreed with her.

"We should just be careful," whispered Ashley. As they caught up with Rosy by the door to level two, she let go of his hand.

"Sure." He squeezed his fists on the grips of his pistols. He didn't like feeling this way. Didn't enjoy distrusting people. It wasn't something he was used to. It made him anxious.

Rosy stepped through the door to the second storey and was suddenly lifted off the ground with a strangled cry. Her rifle clattered to the floor.

He raced up the last few stairs with Ashley close behind. Something was around Rosy's neck. A rigid noose of plant matter. Inside her helmet, she was quickly turning blue. Mark tried to squeeze his fingers between her neck and the loop, but there were no gaps for purchase. Whatever it was had inflated into every crack and depression in her suit. Her fingers frantically scrabbled across the tendril's slippery surface as she fought to free herself.

He glanced up through the door. The thing was slowly drawing her higher towards a ceiling of white filament-thin tendrils. Several more slender nooses dangled from the ceiling along the corridor beyond.

Ashley pulled the gun from his holster and fired through the rope of the noose. Rosy dropped to the floor, and Mark tore it away from her throat.

"Are you OK?"

Rosy spluttered and gasped, but nodded.

He pulled her up.

"Watch out," she said, rubbing her throat. Her high voice was hoarse. "I didn't even see it. Must be some sort of pressure trap."

Mark eased forward and tapped the nearest hanging loop gently with the tip of his pistol. It suddenly puffed up, going from almost nothing to something resembling a tight and rigid life preserver ring in less than a second. Rosy was lucky it hadn't taken her head off.

"Didn't think these things could grow in here?" he said, looking up at the ceiling.

Ashley was kneeling by the loop he'd discarded, poking it with the tip of the pistol she'd taken from him. "The air in here is clean," she said. "It's on the outside of the generator that's not."

"If this thing is all connected, then I bet it knows its trap got tripped," said Rosy, retrieving her rifle from the floor. "We shouldn't stay here longer than's needed."

She shouldered her gun and, with a lowered stance, began making quick progress up the corridor. On their right, a glass wall overlooked the core of the atmosphere generator. A large bright room covered in interconnected pipes and tanks.

Mark and Ashley followed with caution, avoiding more of the traps.

Another had been tripped. A figure in a miner's respiration suit lay with their back against the wall. Where it had once been black, the suit was now covered in tiny white-stalked, red-tipped lichens, which sprouted and branched from barely visible cracks in its surface, fusing it to the wall. Mark didn't look long enough to make out what was beyond the cracked and tarnished faceplate.

Rosy stopped at a doorway leading into the core and entered.

A low hum filled the room. The floor vibrated with it. A console sat inside a mainframe near the door.

"Is that it?" said Ashley, taking her laptop from a pack on her back.

"Guess so," said Rosy, scanning the room. The floors and walls were white. It was all very clinical.

"I'll do a sweep," said Mark, as Ashley plugged in. He left them to it.

Much like the equipment library, the square room was divided into corridors by the tanks and pipes in its centre. He swept along one side, glancing up each corridor, checking for any sign of Red Fruit. Nothing. The place was untouched.

He passed a huge pair of fans set in one wall. They blew cool air through the room. The primary source of the hum.

He thought about what Ashley had said on the stairs. It was strange that a hotel maid could fly a ship. Piloting jobs paid well and were relatively easy to get because not many people could fly. Could it be possible that she and Journey knew each other from somewhere?

The skin of his face begged to be rubbed. It itched with the stress and the tiredness. He never felt well-rested after a night on the booze, like drunken sleep did about as much good as no sleep at all. His inability to touch his own skin was almost maddening.

He shook himself and rolled his shoulders to try to ease the tense ache that had begun to build there. Circling around the square of the room, he returned to Rosy and Ashley.

"Any luck?" he said, as he arrived back.

"It's an easy hack," said Ashley. "Just had to swap the definitions of the respective compounds inside the mainframe and reset the calibration within the zephyr system."

Mark nodded. "Cool. Good thinking." He pursed his lips. "Yeah. Smart move."

The hum in the room died.

He pointed up. "That's expected, right?"

"Uh-huh." Ashley nodded. "Give me a couple more minutes. I'm going to set up a kill switch. If it all goes tits up, I'll be able to purge the system and start pumping out breathable air again from my laptop."

Mark watched Rosy while Ashley worked. She had her eyes everywhere. Constantly checking out the corners of the room, scoping the entrances, rifle ready.

"How long you been a Star Sailor?" he asked.

"I was adopted into it."

"Really? Like by one of the chapters?"

"Ferrum Sororibus."

That was one he hadn't heard of. "Cool."

"Hardly," said Ashley. Something was loading on her screen.

"It wasn't as bad as people say," said Rosy, glancing back at Mark. "You get put with your crew early on. It's nice having girls you can rely on."

"But all that awful training," Ashley replied. "The selection process. You were brought up to risk your life for someone else's gain. You're basically pimped."

Rosy's shoulders sagged a little.

"Hold on." Mark held up a finger. "Star Sailors are heroes. The chapters pick the best of the best." He leant an elbow against the mainframe where Ashley worked. "They save people all over the galaxy. Fight Gerknorgs."

"There's some of that," said Rosy. She gave him a sad smile. "But it's not all lollipops and rainbows."

He swallowed, feeling stupid again. "What's lollipops?"

Ashley snorted. "The chapters are just fronts for legal child-trafficking. These kids are selected and sold into what is basically slavery by parents who can't afford to keep them," she said. "The trials are tough. Only the strongest survive. And then the chapters pimp them out to the highest bidder on dangerous missions that require a human touch. It's not always saving colonists and retrieving bounties."

"That's not true," said Mark, defiantly. "My mate Spanner's parents paid for him to join one."

"Did they?" said Ashley.

"Don't know what you've been told, but you can't buy your way in," said Rosy.

With a clunk, a rising hum began inside the machinery surrounding them. Ashley flipped her laptop shut. "All done," she said. "Let's get out of here."

Rosy led the way back through the door. "Stay on your tippy-toes, peeps," she said.

But the way back to their camp was surprisingly deadly creature free, which was fortunate because Mark's mind was elsewhere. Slug had lied to him. You couldn't buy your way into being a Star Sailor.

He'd wasted his entire life.

CATS ALL FOLKS

THADDEUS BREATHED A SIGH as he looked over all the destroyed equipment in the library. It was a mess. These space ghosts, or whatever they had been, had really done a number on the place. It shouldn't have irked him, but ultimately this was all his stuff, and it had been trashed. He groaned as he totted up the damage. One million. Two. Five. Not so bad, really, considering he had fifty-two other colonies. Well fifty-three. But they didn't talk about Rosen-9.

And, oh God, the smell. Spoiling rations, spilled chemicals, and although he couldn't see any bodies, he could smell something like rotting flesh. It was repulsive.

Queletii led the way, with the glow of a single flashlight illuminating the dark corridor that ran along the side of the fallen shelving units. At the side of the fifth aisle—Mining Equipment—was a tunnel of debris. It looked as though something roughly the size of an elephant had dragged its way out. There was blood on the floor here, but not much.

It had been a while since Thaddeus had been to one of his colonies—he'd stopped making a habit of it after that little problem on Rosen-9—but the initial design had changed little.

"Here we are," Queletii said, as they reached the garage end.

He shone his torch over three hover-cats that sat next to an open door, casting long shadows up the wall behind them. Night had fallen fast, but the streetlights outside hadn't come on.

"I can drive one of these," said Celia, stepping towards the first.

"Me too," said her husband, "if needed."

"Great. Well volunteered," said Thaddeus. He didn't admit it, but it had never been worth his time to learn to drive, especially not when you could hire a chauffeur for so little.

"You and Mrs Rosenhalt can come with me, sir." Queletii pointed to the furthest cat.

"Right," said Thaddeus. "I guess the flight crew with Morgan. Damu and sidepiece with Celia."

"I have a name," said Damu's girlfriend.

She wasn't his wife. His wife was at home with their three kids.

"Good for you," said Thaddeus.

The groups separated and climbed into their respective vehicles.

"Do you know where we're going?" Thaddeus asked Queletii.

"It is a short drive to the airlock between the domes," said Queletii, leaping over the side and into the cat.

Thaddeus climbed in next to him and Marcella got in the back.

"Are you sure this is the safest plan?" she said. "I just want to go home. I don't care how long it takes."

Thaddeus rolled his eyes. How banal? He turned to her with his smile on bright.

"You've been listening this whole time, right? You know this is the best course of action, what with that bloody Star Sailor ship clogging up the hangar."

"I do. It's just ..." She paused, pressed her lips together. "Couldn't the rescue ship just land outside of the dome, maybe? On the sand? Couldn't we meet it there?"

Thaddeus snorted, although it was a reaction more than anything. He looked at Queletii. "Could we do that? The pods can make us respiration suits."

The three cats powered up as one.

"I checked with the computer," said Queletii, steering them into a waiting position while Celia and Morgan drove themselves and their passengers out of the equipment library. "The desert floor outside the domes is very unstable. Seas of shifting sands. We might all be lost if we step outside."

Thaddeus cleared his throat. "Quicksand?"

In his youth, he had always worried about quicksand. It had been one of his greatest fears. The thought of drowning in darkness with gritty, grating clumps of powder clogging up his lungs. But fortunately, like a lot of other irrational fears that books and films had instilled in him at a young age, quicksand had never really posed much of a threat. He'd admitted it once on a retreat with the other execs. Some priesty yoga-type had made them all talk about and face their fears under the power of hallucination. It had sucked. He had refused to pay. And, when the priesty yoga-type had threatened to sue, Thaddeus had attacked back with a counterclaim that the retreat had been damaging to his mental health which in turn had affected the lives of thousands of employees "under his care", and crushed that little prick and his family business to dust. He'd spent the monetary compensation on a pair of cufflinks that he never wore.

"But we're in a catamaran," said Marcella. "We wouldn't even need to touch the ground until the ship arrived. And surely we'd be able to drive right inside without them needing to land. What would be the problem?"

Queletii paused a moment while he concentrated on driving them out.

Thaddeus frowned. "Well? She's right." He hated to say it. Hated that he hadn't thought of it.

"Our current course is the safest one," said Queletii.

Ahead, Morgan's glowing red taillights disappeared around a corner. There was a chill to the night. No wind. But the air seemed oddly thick with the potential of rain. It wasn't unknown for water vapour to build up in the upper reaches of the dome, for it to collect on the glass, and then come down in showers. Thaddeus always thought it a strange phenomenon, but it seemed to ease some of the psychological burden of the colonists living inside the dome. Rain was normal. Rain was part of their mental status quo.

"The catamarans cannot run for long enough on the sand." Queletii accelerated up the ramp after the others. "And the heat of the day would bake us in our suits."

Thaddeus took a long breath through his nose, then let it out. If he was being honest, the thought of going anywhere near quicksand had filled him with a dread deeper than being possessed by possible space ghosts.

"To the second dome then," he said, but he didn't look back at Marcella. He could sense her glaring at the back of his head, like she so often did.

Yes, he was definitely going to be getting rid of her.

FRUITING BODIES

MARK SAT IN THE central compartment of the truck as they waited for the domes to fill up. The huge atmosphere generator throbbed rhythmically nearby, causing an aggravating vibration in his back teeth. Night had fallen. The only light came from a reddish moon that hung above the desert sands like an orb of rust.

Journey was asleep nearby. Rosy had given him something for the pain and he'd conked right out. She'd also passed suit rations to everyone. Mark had tomato and polenta smash which was something to look forward to. He'd saved Journey a pack of portobello and soy because no one else had wanted to touch mushrooms.

There wasn't much food left—Rosy hadn't packed for a week alone in a suit—and when she'd come to hand out the rations to everyone, she had discovered a few of the packets had split and spoiled. But still, they only had to last the night and the next day and they could hopefully sneak up to the hangar and the ship.

He hoped Sam's idea would work. Fighting was all well and good, but there was the baby to think about.

Sam, Nura, and Rosy were up in the cab. Sam was learning as much as she could about Rosy's ship. Ashley was sleeping in another section towards the back. It had been a long day.

He tried his best to nod off. Usually he would have been out like a light. He'd trained himself to sleep in the calm before the storm. But what Ashley had said back in the atmos generator about Journey and Sam was bothering him.

He watched Sam as she studied a screen with Rosy. Did he recognise her from somewhere? *Did* Journey know her? Had the pair blown up the Daedalus together somehow? He glanced down at Journey, who was lying flat on his back, his eyes closed. Could he trust him? Mark's confidence had taken somewhat of a knock upon hearing the truth about Star Sailors. It made it hard not to question everything.

The engineer had shown up on a train when Mark was about eighteen. He'd got a job fixing whatever needed fixing, and stayed in Track Stop. With nowhere to sleep, Mark's dad had let him stay a couple of nights in exchange for work around the shop. At first Mark wasn't so sure, but they'd become fast friends over drinks and board games. Journey seemed so worldly, so experienced. He'd had his facial scars even then, though they'd been fresher, less a part of him. Mark found him fascinating. Journey had been everywhere, seen everything. Mark wanted that. Mark craved adventure.

Journey found them a job aboard a cargo runner as an engineer and assistant. The ship was the Hurricane, and it turned out it ran a little more than cargo. While Mark had never been that good at the assisting part, Journey's quick learning on the job and skill with machines more than made up for it. That was nearly seven years ago now.

He patted his friend on the shoulder. Whatever Journey was hiding, it didn't matter. They would get through it.

"Mark." Ashley leant against the doorway dividing the middle and back section of the truck. "Um ... would you like to have dinner with me?"

"Really?" he said.

She looked down. "I mean, it'd be nice to not be alone, just in case, you know?" Her eyes met his once more and she held up her ration. "Would you like to suck mashed veg out of a straw with me?"

He laughed. "Yeah, sure." He stepped forward, and she flicked on the light in the back section of the truck. A half-full gun rack lined one wall above several crates. Next to it sat a table with two chairs.

For a moment, he just stood with arms folded and admired the weapons. The chunky tubes of rusted metal they had on the Hurricane could be called guns in that you pulled a trigger and something deadly came out of the end, but, on occasion, that something deadly was an actual piece of the gun. Furthermore you could never be one hundred per cent sure out of which end that something deadly might emerge. These Star Sailor guns—these neon, chrome, shiny, pointy, sleek little numbers (and some big numbers)—fired plasma, or lasers, or ... was that a rocket launcher? And what's more, they made you look good while you were blasting. They made you look cool.

Ashley closed the door. "See anything you like?" she said.

He gulped.

She smiled.

He nodded. "Uh-huh."

"Show me what you got?" she said, holding her hand out.

"Um." Every brain cell in his head sped off very quickly and very far in a multitude of wrong directions. "What?"

"Your ration."

"Right. Of course." He handed her his packet.

"Polenta and tomato, nice. I got stuck with kidney beans and veg." She blew a frustrated raspberry, which made her messy fringe jump under her visor. She held up her packet between them.

"Hey, I like kidney beans and veg," he said, taking it. He looked down at the pack. The silver plastic packaging was exactly the same as his. "I don't mind swapping."

"You sure?"

He threw up his hands. "Yeah, yeah. No. Yeah. Not at all." If it was anything like the veg and bean mash the computer had made Nura in the life pod, he was happy. And if it made Ashley happy, then bonus.

"Thanks," she said, then lifted a flap in the side of her suit under her left arm, slotted his ration pack inside, and clicked it shut.

"I wasn't going to eat mine now," he said, patting his stomach. "Had a big breakfast."

"Oh, well, it's not really dinner if only one of us is eating."

He sat down and rested two fists on the table as if holding a knife and fork. "I can pretend."

"Hmm." She shrugged. "Alright then." She sat opposite. "But you better make sure you eat yours soon. We'll need your strength." She gave his forearm a squeeze.

His head spun.

It was good to have a woman watching out for him. Other than the time at Saucy Beans (and his mum or gran, which definitely didn't count), he'd never had dinner with one before. And this time he was very unlikely to spill anything. And so very unlikely to end the night in need of a bag of ice down his pants.

This was a date, right?

He smiled at her, feeling like a total mongoose, while he fought to find something to say.

"You look nice," he said, going a little off-piste from what he'd learnt from Journey's romance novels.

"Thanks," she said, before taking a sip from the straw inside her helmet. "Although I know you're just saying that. I haven't slept properly for twenty-four hours and it's like a swamp in this suit." She glanced towards the closed door, then lowered her voice and leant closer. "Did you think any more about what I said at the atmosphere generator?"

He leant forward and looked at the door himself. Their faces were barely ten centimetres apart. He felt a fire in his belly, but it was coupled with a guilty nausea due to the nature of their conversation.

"You mean about Journey and Sam?"

He desperately wanted to talk about something else. Maybe get to know her a little better. Show her there was more to him than she'd seen.

She nodded. "Did you ask him what they talked about while we were gone?"

Mark hadn't thought to. "Not really. But he said she could help him fix the ship if needed."

Ashley narrowed her eyes. "How would a maid know how to fix a ship?"

"Why does it bother you?"

She leant back. "I don't know, Mark, maybe because I don't want to fight my way up to the ship only to be double-crossed by your friend and some random woman we picked up, then left for dead."

Mark lowered his voice to just above a whisper. "Journey wouldn't leave me."

She folded her arms. "It's a dog-eat-dog world, Mark. People do what they need to survive. The Captain and Michael left us. What makes you think Journey isn't the same? If he—" She leant forward again. "If he blew up the Daedalus with that maid, then they were probably trying to kill everybody aboard. And that includes us." She pointed at him and then at herself. "We don't fit into their plan."

He groaned low in his throat. "That is, if they have a plan. It might just have been a coincidence."

"There are no coincidences."

There was a quiet knock at the door.

Mark hopped up to answer it. Ashley didn't move.

He opened it fully. Sam stood there with Nura's tube in her arms. She was rocking and shushing the baby who was crying inside.

"Sorry to interrupt," she said.

"Oh, you weren't interrupting anything." He offered her a smile. Ashley made a noise behind him. "She hungry again?"

Large bags hung beneath Sam's eyes. She looked small, with her shoulders hunched protectively around her baby. "Uh-huh," she said. "I wanted to see if any of you would mind swapping food with me. She didn't eat the broccoli and peas thing Rosy gave me for her, and that's what I've got, too."

Mark patted himself down. "She seemed to like veg and beans back on the escape pod. Would she like mine?" He held the packet out to her.

Ashley's voice came from behind him. "But Mark, we were supposed to be having dinner."

He looked back. Ashley had stood. Her voice was low. She had a strange look on her face. He gave her a smile, too.

"It's fine," he said, turning back to Sam.

"That is really kind," said Sam. She held up her own to swap.

He waved a hand. "No need for that. Can't have you both going hungry."

They only had a day or two. He'd manage.

Sam shook her head. "I couldn't."

"Really, don't worry."

She took it and seemed to relax a little. "That's very kind."

"Might she like polenta and tomato instead?" Ashley asked. "It's probably tastier."

Sam dipped her head. "Don't worry," she said, attaching the packet to the side of Nura's tube. "Veg and beans is great, thank you, both. Sorry to intrude."

"You think she's doing OK, despite everything?" Mark twirled his finger in the air to encompass the totality of being stuck on an alien planet, unable to breathe the atmosphere, and surrounded by man-munching mushroom-monsters, with limited food reserves and a slim chance of escape.

"Yeah, we've survived worse." She finished attaching the packet. The tube whirred. "I just wish I could let her out. She must be so confused."

"Mm." He nodded. "I guess she won't remember any of this though."

A silence hovered between them, and in it he sensed Ashley like the draw of a magnet behind him, waiting for them to finish.

Sam smiled. "I never thanked you for taking care of her back when we escaped. Most guys I know would have just ditched her."

He frowned. "Really?" He waved a hand in the air. "It was nothing. She was good as gold."

"She is." Sam nodded. "I also wanted to thank you for rescuing me from those executives. If it wasn't for you ..." She held a breath and looked down at Nura, who was busy eating Mark's veg and beans as it was dispensed from her tube.

He looked over her shoulder, feeling oddly embarrassed. "It was nothing." All he'd done was beat up a couple of goons. And he'd have done his best even if there had been a couple more. Sam gave off this mix of vulnerability and capability that intrigued him. He wanted to be near her. He felt he didn't need to hide anything about who he was with her.

"It might have been nothing for you," she said, leaning to catch his eye. "But it was everything to us. Thank you for taking the risk."

"To live is to risk," he said.

She frowned and took a small step back, and behind him Ashley cleared her throat.

"Sorry, I'm intruding," said Sam, turning half away. She seemed to have shrunk again. "Thanks for the food."

"No problem."

He turned.

Ashley's hands were clenched by her sides. She looked stiff and annoyed.

"Sorry," he said. "Where were we?"

THERE'S SOMETHING WRONG WITH THE CATS

SPACE GHOSTS WERE A marketing tool. An old wives' tale started by early voyagers. Possession by something otherworldly was an easy explanation for ghost ship massacres and abandoned colonies. A little more digestible perhaps than the honest truth that isolation can make people go wrong in the head.

The legends were perpetuated by every Star Sailor chapter.

Gerknorgs and Scorlacks were tangible. Yes, people were scared of them, but anyone could shoot one. Space ghosts, on the other hand, had to be dealt with by professionals. And who were the professionals? The very same people who warned of them most vehemently. Respect where respect was due—it was marketing genius. If there was something mysterious and terrifying out there, and you were the only people who could deal with it, you stood to make a lot of money. Make the people truly terrified and they'd pay pretty much anything for you to take the bad thing away.

In all the years his company had spent colonising planets, he'd never come across anything that might prove the Star Sailors weren't just selling a lie.

But then why did he feel so on edge?

The idea of space ghosts had put his back up. At every turn, as they drove through the complex, he could swear he'd seen things lurking in the shadows, creeping away to hide in the gloom of the unlit colony. Neither Queletii nor Marcella seemed to notice, and Thaddeus didn't want to mention it out loud in case his wife went into meltdown.

One of them had been the size of an elephant. He had only glimpsed it out of the corner of his eye as Queletii drove them at speed towards the central airlock. It was probably just a forklift or something, but his tricked mind threw up images of spectral beasts clawing their way out of this planet's dead past.

He glanced at Queletii. The chief seemed very confident in his ability to deliver them and the other Rosenhalt execs to the ship. A little too confident.

The two cats ahead slowed simultaneously as they reached the edge of the dome, allowing for Queletii to navigate around them, as if it was pre-planned.

Ahead of them, through the glass above, Thaddeus could see the second dome rising into the star-strewn night sky.

"What if the ship really isn't operational?" he asked as Queletii reached forward and tapped some commands into the central screen of the cat. The doors to the second dome opened.

"I am sure one of us will soon have the capabilities to fix the ship, should that be required," he said, then gave Thaddeus a cryptic Mona Lisa smile.

"What's that supposed to mean?"

Queletii paused as his eyes searched for something. "I mean, should the ship require repairs, Captain Fenchurch will be able to apply them."

"I'm pretty sure he said he couldn't."

Queletii stuttered again. It wasn't becoming of the leather-faced security chief. "If the ship is not operational, I-I believe circumstances with Captain Fenchurch will ... will rise to the challenge." He smiled. There was something uncanny about his mannerisms, and he spoke in that inhuman way an android or AI who has been fed language and asked to replicate it might. It lacked the subtle nuance of having learnt to speak from birth. "The ship will be operational."

"Hmm."

Queletii pulled the cat into the tunnel that connected the two domes. With the bright LED lights of the three catamarans reflecting from the black glass, the night outside was impenetrable. Still, Thaddeus thought he could see shadowy shapes moving out there on the other side.

He shivered. "Is it cold in here?"

The doors at the other end of the tunnel were open, and as they drew nearer, a strange mouldy odour enveloped them. The air became thick with it.

"What is that?" said Marcella. "You don't think the dome has been breached, do you?" Her eyes flicked around, scanning the glass above. "I still think we should be wearing respirator suits."

"Not at all," said Queletii. "I did a scan on one of the mainframes when I was searching for the colonists. Dome integrity is intact. Our pathway to the ship should be relatively trouble-free."

"Relatively?" Marcella had her arms folded in the back.

"If Queletii says it's OK, then it's OK. Stop second guessing him, Marcella."

Thaddeus rubbed his temples. He was getting a migraine. There was another smell. Buried beneath that fungal funk. A chemical odour. Pungent, acidic, like bleach. He cleared his throat. He could almost taste it.

"What is that?"

"It— I—" Queletii blinked several times. His chin dropped, and the cat slowed a little before his head bounced back up.

Thaddeus was pressed back into his seat as they accelerated abruptly.

"What's the matter with him?" called Marcella over the sound of the whistling wind. "Get him to stop."

"Queletii?" His heart raced. "Queletii?"

The security chief's arms dropped from the wheel, and the cat veered dangerously close to the foundation trenches by the side of the road. Thaddeus reached out and steadied the wheel just in time, returning them to the centre of the road.

Something made a shattering crunch behind them, but he couldn't turn to look.

"Thaddeus, make him stop!" shouted Marcella.

He didn't know how. Helplessly, he pushed himself back in his chair as the cat sped on.

"Queletii? Steer man. Steer!" he said. He gripped the man's shoulder and gave it a shake.

Queletii's head remained upright. He turned slowly to look at Thaddeus. "Thaddeus B. Rosenhalt, I cannot believe it is really you." His mouth split into a wide grin. "Onwards and ever upwards."

Marcella stretched forward between them. Her hair whipped around her face with the speed. She tapped the central screen and swiped until she found what she was looking for.

"Marcella!" Thaddeus's voice shook. He felt faint.

The cat slowed to a halt. He swallowed. He looked back. The cat driven by Celia, containing Damu and his girlfriend, had stopped several metres behind them.

Morgan's cat, on the other hand, wasn't on the road. A plume of smoke rose from one of the foundation trenches by the side of the road roughly thirty metres back. The tail end of the cat poked up from within, like the hull of a sinking boat in the ocean. Someone lay on the ground nearby. They weren't moving.

"No," he said, pulling himself up to stand, craning his neck to see if he could see anyone else. He pressed his hands through his hair. His heart still hadn't slowed. "Fenchurch."

Their way out.

"We need to check if they're OK," said Marcella, pulling herself over the side of the cat and onto the tarmac.

He couldn't move. They'd nearly died.

"Thaddeus!"

He jerked back to the moment.

She was already jogging to the crash site.

"Wait," he said, and chased after her. "Wait, we don't know if—" She wasn't waiting.

Damu climbed out of his cat as she passed. He looked at Thaddeus and threw his palms up. "What the hell?"

Strangely, both Queletii and Celia hadn't moved from their positions in each driver's seat.

He didn't answer. His head hurt with every step as he ran after Marcella. How was she so fast? He'd always thought those legs were only for show.

As he neared, he saw it was the navigator who lay either unconscious or dead on the ground next to the trench.

Neither Morgan nor Captain Fenchurch had emerged, and as he drew closer, he saw why. The cat hadn't only fallen in at speed, it had landed on several slender shafts of rebar which had impaled the cockpit and its occupants. Thaddeus cringed. Their pilot was dead.

Marcella put a hand up to cover her eyes, yet stepped bravely towards the navigator. Thaddeus slowed. He didn't need to get any closer.

She knelt by the navigator's side and felt for a pulse.

"He's alive," she said. "But he's hurt. We need to get him to a doctor."

Thaddeus brushed his hands through his hair. "I can't carry him." He glanced back to the two stationary cats. Damu had followed them. His girlfriend was waiting by the cat, tending to Celia who was moving as if in a daze.

Damu strode past and, without stopping, said, "Celia's fucked. I can drive the cat if you help me get him in."

Thaddeus hurried to catch up.

Damu nodded at the navigator. "He can fly the ship, right?"

"I don't know." Thaddeus looked down at his hands. They were shaking. He bunched his fists. "I guess."

He chose not to look at the crashed cat, focussing solely on the fallen navigator.

"What happened to Celia?" he asked.

"Just started acting weird. I had to use the emergency cut off." Damu bent and lifted the navigator. "Help me."

Thaddeus moved around and pulled the navigator's other arm over his shoulder. He had a bloody scrape on his brow and red had soaked through his shirt above his right shoulder. He groaned in pain as they carried him back towards the nearest cat.

"Can either of you drive the other one?" asked Damu.

"I—" Thaddeus began.

"I can do it," said Marcella, leading the way. "You and Marie take Celia and the navigator in yours. We'll take Queletii."

"Sure. What happened, do you think?" said Damu as they reached their cat. "It was like we drove in here and Celia just stopped functioning."

Marcella opened the side door and helped them lay the navigator on the back seat.

"Maybe it was an allergic reaction to something in the air in this dome," she said.

Damu hurried around to Celia's side. His head moved left and right quickly. "We should move fast," he said. "We're vulnerable out here. And the smoke from the crashed cat will pretty soon be visible across the entire dome. If there's any of Queletii's ghosts still here, it'll bring them straight to us."

He pulled Celia out of the front seat and laid her next to the navigator, then climbed in. His girlfriend sat beside him.

"We'll meet you at the plaza," he said. "I don't know how we're going to get us all up the top to the hangar if the elevators aren't working, but the sooner we get there, the better."

"Be careful," said Marcella.

"Yes, um … be careful," Thaddeus repeated. His vision buzzed with grey encroaching stars. They'd nearly died!

Damu pulled away and shot off towards the centre of the dome.

"You're OK, right?" asked Marcella as they reached their vehicle.

He could hardly hear her. His ears were ringing. He didn't answer.

Queletii was still upright in his seat. His eyes were wide open, but he wasn't moving.

"Help me with him." Marcella moved around to the driver side.

"Mm. Fine. I'm fine," he said. But didn't move.

"Thaddeus!"

He snapped back and hurried to help. They pulled Queletii out and between them manhandled him into the back.

She took the driver's seat, and, once Thaddeus was inside, they sped off after Damu and the others.

She glanced at him. He didn't know what to say. He felt off. He'd panicked back there. They'd nearly died. This didn't happen to people like him. People with wealth like his didn't have accidents. You surrounded yourself with the best, so there was no risk of anything bad happening.

He gripped the armrests on either side of his seat. Squeezed the soft leather. Took a deep breath to try to calm himself.

It didn't work.

They'd nearly died!

HP AND THE FUNGAL ALIEN BEASTIES

MARK AWOKE WITH A crick in his neck. In fact, he had a crick in everything. Sleeping in a respiration suit wasn't the most comfortable. He wondered how many bruises he had beneath the surface. The fall he'd taken from the truck yesterday had kicked his butt somewhat.

He took a sip of water from the tube inside his helmet. It was warm and a tad salty, but still tasted cleaner than water should, cleaner than Artifakt water anyway.

The truck rumbled beneath him. They were crawling along. He pushed himself up to a seated position. Rosy and Journey were in the cab. Journey leant back in his chair with his leg up on the dash, bouncing slightly with the truck's movement. They were chatting. Mark couldn't hear what they were saying.

"Where are we going?" he said as he stood.

Journey swivelled in his chair. "Thought we'd do a quick spin. See how things are going inside the dome."

"And?" He joined them in the cab and gazed out through the windscreen. The day was brightening outside. How long had he slept?

"Can't see much through the glass, but from what we can, the horde isn't waiting on the other side of the doors."

"That's good."

Mark heard a click from back down the hall. Ashley came out of her room to join them. Her face was pale beneath her helmet. She looked exhausted.

"Where are we going?" she said, her voice a dry croak.

"Just doing some recon," said Mark.

"Where's Sam? And the baby?" she asked.

Their date night hadn't gone very far after his conversation with Sam. Ashley hadn't reacted kindly to his giving of his ration. It was silly, really, but he thought maybe she was jealous. Jealous that he'd not done the same deal with her when she'd asked to swap. Maybe he should have.

"They're up top," said Journey. "Rosy said she's been up most of the night. Nura's been a bit of a handful."

"Is she alright?" said Ashley.

"Yeah." He shrugged. "You know babies. They never shut up."

"I'll go up and check on them," said Mark.

"Want me to slow us down?" said Rosy.

"What for?" he asked.

She smirked, then brought the truck to a gentle stop.

He opened the door and climbed out and up to the roof. Sam sat with her back against the cab with Nura's tube in her arms. She made a strange face when she saw him. A tightening of the lips. He wondered if he'd done something wrong.

"How you both doing?" he said, sitting down opposite her, crossing his legs beneath him. Either the suit or his stiffness made the manoeuvre difficult.

She tapped a finger to her visor just above her lips. "She's just dropped off," she whispered.

"Sorry." He tried a smile. He could sense caution in her voice, even in the whisper.

"I thought maybe she was coming down with something, so brought her up here. Thought it might be cooler than in the truck."

"I bet she just hates being away from you."

"Maybe." She looked down at Nura.

"I wanted to ask you—"

Her head jumped back up as if she'd been stung. "Yes?" Her tone was icy now, not just apprehensive.

"Um ... how do you know how to fly a ship?"

She frowned. "Don't you know?"

"Well, I guess you probably learnt at some point, but I don't know many pilots who would give it all up to become a hotel maid. The galaxy needs pilots."

Her lips tightened into a lacklustre smile. She breathed a tired laugh. "It does. It needs maids too. And mothers."

He nodded slowly. He felt like he was missing something.

She considered him for a moment. "What you said last night, 'to live is to risk', where did you hear that?"

He stroked a hand to the chin of his helmet, trying to remember. "I think maybe Journey said it."

"Oh."

She chuckled and gazed out over the desert. The morning light reflected from the glossy filigree on her suit, turning it starkly white against the matt-black. She fiddled with the hook on the side of Nura's tube. Then she smiled at him. Genuine this time.

"I've only been a hotel maid for a few weeks," she said. "Before that I ..." She hesitated, mouth still open, the words seemingly caught in her throat.

"You don't need to tell me." He leant forward a little so he could see Nura. The fact that Sam hadn't mentioned a father told him a lot. "We all have secrets."

She turned her head. "You do?"

He shrugged. "I'm somewhat of an enigma."

She laughed. "Fuck off do you know what enigma means."

"I'll have you know I've read four and a half books in the last fortnight."

"Journey told me while you were off in the atmos gen. I hear you're trying to woo Ashley."

He squinted. "Maybe."

"You know, you don't need to change yourself to fit with someone else. You find the right person and they'll like you for exactly who it is you are already. You hide that, or try to change, and you'll be faking it forever." Her bright smile faded, and she bit her lip, nervously holding his gaze. "I'm running from an abusive ex. I used to fly ships for him. He hurt my father. I— I didn't want that life for Nura, so I left." She took a deep breath and sighed. "I took a risk and here I am."

She suddenly looked so sad.

"Here we all are," he said. "You're not alone, Sam."

She cleared her throat. "No?"

"Do you want me to watch her a while? So you can get some sleep. We'll be out here maybe a few more hours. If she wakes up and needs food, I can do it."

She visibly tensed.

"I know I don't have much experience," he continued, holding out a hand. He didn't want to force her to do anything that made her uncomfortable. "I could wake you if I have a problem. You need to rest if you're going to fly us out of here."

She held up a finger. "If she so much as opens her eyes, I want to know."

He held up a hand. "Pirate's honour."

She snorted a laugh, then pushed herself up and began the climb back into the cab of the truck. Before she reached the door, she looked up at him. "Thanks Mark."

He followed her inside.

Journey smiled to acknowledge them both.

"How long do you think we have until we go in?" Sam asked him.

"I guess three hours."

"I'll wake you in two?" said Mark hopefully.

She passed him Nura's tube. He took it carefully, then reattached it to the front of his suit.

"One and a half." She gripped his arm for a second and their gazes met, before she turned and headed to the back of the truck.

He watched her go. Ashley was doing something on her computer in the middle section. Her eyes followed Sam as she passed, then moved back to her laptop.

Mark turned back to the cockpit to see Journey observing him. A grin played across his lips. His forehead twitched.

"You cheeky boi."

"What?" Mark hissed, then stole a look at Ashley, who didn't appear to be listening. He lowered his voice further, and leant forward so only Journey could hear. "I'm just looking after Nura while our pilot gets some sleep."

Journey rocked back on the springs of his chair so that he was out of Ashley's view, then made a repulsive smoochy face.

Mark rolled his eyes. "You're such a funky princess."

"You're a funky princess."

"You're both funky princesses," said Rosy. She turned her chair towards the middle of the truck and her eyes widened. "Sheesh kebab, what is that?"

She bolted up and hurried to look at a screen. It looked like a view from inside a hangar.

She touched it. "This is a feed from one of Queen Bee's cameras."

"Queen Bee?" said Mark, moving to stand behind her.

"Their ship," said Journey, shuffling himself around in his chair so he could see the screen better.

"Looky here," said Rosy, tapping the screen. "Is it me, or is that a couple of guys?"

Mark squinted. In the shadows, and slowly coming out of them, was someone he recognised.

"It's Thaddeus Rosenhalt, and ..."

Thaddeus and his wife were carrying Queletii between them. As they came closer to the ship, they laid him down, then both rested their hands on their knees, clearly exhausted.

Behind them were others. Not one wore a respiration suit.

"How did they make it?" asked Mark. "One or all of them must be infected."

"If they're at the ship, they're obviously planning to use it to get out of here," said Journey.

"Can we contact them?" said Ashley, who had stopped what she was doing to stand by Mark.

Journey shook his head. "Doesn't matter. I doubt they'll wait for us."

"Do you think they have someone who can fix the ship?" said Mark.

"I assume if Red Fruit has assimilated someone who can fix the ship, and someone who can fly it, then they wouldn't all need to be there," said Journey. "Red Fruit would have shared the knowledge across the network and sent whatever they had nearby so they could get off planet as quickly as possible."

"So you reckon they're alright?" said Mark. He reached forward to tap the screen where Queletii lay. "He doesn't look well."

"Doesn't matter. We've got to move," said Rosy, dashing to the cab and jumping into the driver's seat. "I can't risk them getting off planet if Red Fruit is with them."

"Maybe the HP gave them an open run," said Journey. "And maybe if it didn't hurt them, that means they aren't infected."

"I'm not taking that chance," said Rosy. She pressed her lips together. Her hands flew across the dashboard, flicking several switches to restart the engines. "So we're not taking that chance. If one of them is infected and they get off the planet then my girls died for nothin'."

"How're we going to know?" said Mark.

"Patty, our doc, made a test," said Rosy. "I'll test 'em all. If they're clear, we'll take 'em. If not, they're on their own. And, don't want to sound like a meanie, but same goes for you lot." She passed a scrutinising look over each of them. "Any of you harbouring any fungal fugitives, you gettin' ditched." She gave an enthusiastic thumbs down.

"Fair enough." Journey raised both hands.

"If they got up there with no weapons and only one of them got hurt, would that mean the way is about as clear as it needs to be for us to get there?" said Mark.

"I reckon," said Journey.

With a roar from the speakers and a jolt of acceleration, Big Bee began to roll once more.

Sam emerged from the back. "What's going on? What's the hurry?"

"Thaddeus and his execs have made it to the ship," said Mark, pointing to the screen. "If they can fix it, they're gone. If they're infected, that's worse."

She nodded. "Did Nura wake?"

It'd been less than five minutes.

He looked down. "No. She's fine."

"Arm yourselves from the back," said Rosy, as they bounced across the dunes. "It looks clear through the dome glass, but we don't know what we'll meet on the other side."

Mark and Sam hurried to the gun racks at the back, as the truck drew level with the airlock and skidded to a halt.

"You want me to take her for this?" he asked Sam, motioning his head down towards Nura. Her eyes were still closed.

"No. Pass her over. You do what you do best, and I'll do what I do best."

"What's that exactly?" he said, unhooking Nura's tube from his front and passing it over.

"You kill things, and I'll do the same thing as you while looking after a baby."

He grinned, then clipped the pistols Rosy had given him into the holsters at his waist. Sam took something compact and automatic from the wall.

"We won't be coming back," called Rosy from the cab. "Take everything you think you'll need, but remember"—she leant her head towards Journey—"we're probably carrying buggerlugs over here, so pack light."

The engineer gave a thumbs up. "Sorry," he said brightly, offering a wide-mouthed grin.

"You want anything, Journey?" said Mark, giving Rosy's gun racks one last perusal.

"I'm not going to be able to help with the shooting, but maybe get me something long to use as a crutch."

Mark scanned the rack. The longest thing was the possible rocket launcher, so he grabbed it and slung it on his back.

"That'll do it," said Journey. "And perhaps load me up with grenades and ammo. Like a pack horse. But"—he held up a warning finger—"if it comes to it, and we get stuck in some sort of confined space with monsters all around us, I tell you this now for free, I am not going to pull a pin on those grenades and blow myself up in a self-sacrificing ball of fire just to save the rest of you."

Mark waved a hand. "Don't pretend like you're all tough in front of our new friends to try and look cool. We all know you would."

Journey tutted. "Yeah, I'm soppy as they come."

Ashley grabbed a pistol in a holster from the wall and belted it around her waist. Then she returned to her laptop and tapped a key.

After a moment, the airlock doors opened. Several barely moving creatures crawled out on to the sand. They looked half dead. More covered the floor inside. Remnants of the horde trying to escape the new atmosphere of the dome.

"What do we do?" said Rosy, glancing back from the driver's seat.

"The longer the airlock's open, the more they'll be exposed to good air," said Journey. "Get in there. Fast."

"Do it," said Sam.

"No. Really?" Ashley shook her head. "But those things are in there."

Mark looked between Sam and Ashley. Unable to decide whose side to take.

"Doesn't matter," said Rosy, frowning at him. She punched the accelerator and crunched Big Bee's giant tyres over the things trying to escape the airlock. "S'already three against one."

"Shit." Ashley retreated to the back as the doors closed, sealing them inside the airlock with the creatures.

Mark moved to the cab between where Journey and Rosy sat. Sam followed. He leant his weight onto the back of Rosy's chair to get a good look at the long mass of flesh lying in the right-hand corner by the closed interior airlock door. It was one of the grasshoppers that had chased them earlier. Tendrils of red fungus had grown out of its body, reaching up the walls and along the floor as if trying to escape. There was another very different creature propped against the wall on the other side. It had at least six insectile legs, and a carapace of bone and body bits not too dissimilar to a mantis. Both made slow, ponderous movements as if drugged.

"Are those things made of people?" said Sam.

It was the first opportunity for Mark to look at one without the mind-numbing panic of having to fight for his life. The different parts of each creature were seemingly knitted together with off-white, almost sepia, strands. It was ghastly.

"Uh-huh."

The mantis twitched and kicked its legs, its body suddenly becoming more animated. The grasshopper rolled over onto its front. The tendrils dangled off it like fringes on a 1920s flapper dress.

"They're waking up," said Sam.

"It's the fresh air pumped in by the airlock," said Journey. "It's cancelling out the effects of the HP."

Something thumped on the back of the truck just as the mantis pressed itself up to stand. It wobbled for a moment like a baby giraffe on its gangly legs, then rose up and charged for the front of the truck.

"Can they get in here?" said Mark.

"No way. Big Bee is un-get-in-able."

The mantis ducked down and disappeared beneath the front of the truck. The grasshopper pressed itself up and followed.

"What're they doing?" Sam leant forward to see.

Suddenly, the whole front of the truck bounced up on its tyres like one of those jumpy gangster hip-hop cars. It clanged against the ceiling, then came crunching back down.

"But is she flippable?" Mark said, reaching out to grip Sam's arm as she stumbled forward towards the dash.

Rosy gave him a cool look, her hands flying nimbly across the controls.

With a woof, a burst of flame rose up from beneath the truck. The grasshopper ran out in a ball of fire, slamming itself against the airlock doors. The mantis didn't make it that far, dropping to the floor a metre or so from the front of the truck.

"Nice," said Journey.

The airlock's inner doors peeled open, and the grasshopper fell through the gap before coming to a burning stop a few feet outside. Rosy sped Big Bee out on to the road. The place was littered with the sluggish, barely moving bodies of Red Fruit's hosts.

"Looks like the HP worked," she said.

"Fingers crossed it's enough to get us to the plaza," said Journey.

An expectant silence filled the cab as they raced towards a tall building in the centre of the dome. It stretched all the way up to a large disc-shaped platform suspended on the outside of the glass.

Ashley emerged from the back of the truck as they neared.

"Are we nearly there?"

The plaza building was about as fancy as the economy-class colony got. The building was comprised of mirrored glass, reflecting the other shorter buildings that surrounded it as well as the deep blue of the sky above. Out front, a wide set of steps led up to a revolving glass door. It looked a little like one of the less luxury skyscrapers in uptown Artifakt City.

Rosy raced the truck up the front steps and crashed through the revolving doors at the top before skidding to a halt in the lobby.

She bent forward and leant her forehead on the steering wheel. "Bye bye, Big Bee." She span off her chair, took her rifle down from its mount above the dash, and threw open the door.

"Let's move!"

ONWARDS AND UPWARDS

ROSY WAS OUT FIRST. Mark second. He scanned the surrounding area. It was quiet.

"Looks like the HP is keeping them back," said Journey, easing himself down to the ground. He winced as his broken leg touched the floor, but he managed to hobble along with the rocket launcher wedged under his armpit.

The lobby appeared to span the entire bottom floor of the building. In the centre was a broken, drained fountain. Fibrous fronds of red and pink had sprung from the top, falling and fanning like the foliage of a weeping willow, creeping out and over the sides of the surrounding stone lip.

They made their way quickly to a door labelled "stairs". Mark kept watch behind as Rosy led.

"Watch out for traps," she said, as she pushed open the door and made her way up.

Mark gazed up the centre of the square stairwell, that spun around and around for about as far as he could see. "How many floors is it?"

"Uh, maybe sixty," said Journey, easing himself up the first few steps behind Rosy.

"Oh jeez, this is going to take forever. What do they need all these floors for, anyway?" Mark helped Journey find his flow up the steps with an arm around his waist.

"I think the top thirty-five or so are just filler between the plaza and the hangar at the top. There's a freight elevator at the back of the building used to transport whatever they're mining here up to the port. But we'd have to cycle the power to get that working again."

They trudged on in silence for a few more levels.

Once Journey was happy to move on his own, Mark kept watch at the back. He listened to Sam and Ashley as they talked.

"How's Nura doing?" Ashley asked.

"She's been asleep since we left the truck. I guess she's tired. She was up most of the night."

He liked that they were getting on. Assuming they all got away, maybe Sam would be interested in forming a crew with him, Journey, and Ashley. They could provide the safety that she and Nura needed. Perhaps the Captain and Michael would find them, and Sam could join the Hurricane crew. The Captain might be looking to retire soon. Perhaps she could fly the ship.

The stairwell didn't change as they climbed. The only thing marking the fact that they were at a new level was the numbers rising slower and slower.

At level twenty-five, the stairs led to a door. Rosy opened it and they stepped out onto a metal gantry with open sides. It ran across the top of the plaza building towards a towering cylinder of glass and metal at the back.

The disc-shaped hangar platform suspended on the glass above cast a shadow over them.

"That's the freight elevator," said Journey, pointing towards the cylinder. His face was covered in sweat inside his mask. His huge shoulders shook with each breath.

"But you said it wouldn't work?" said Mark.

"It won't, but there'll be another way up."

They followed the gantry to the end, where another flight of steps began.

As they arrived, Rosy turned on the group, and, looking specifically at Journey, said, "We should rest."

"I'm alright," he said. "We haven't got time." He took a few more steps.

Mark knew his friend wouldn't stop if he thought they were doing it just for him. "Well, I'm knackered," he said, and immediately sat down on the stair he was standing on. "We've got five minutes."

Journey gave him a glare, which quickly softened. "Alright, but then we're going."

The landing was big enough for all of them to sit, and for most of the five minutes, they did so in silence while they sipped warm water from their helmets and caught their breath.

"How is it?" said Mark, leaning close to Journey and motioning at his knee.

Journey drew his gaze back from looking out over the colony far beneath them. "It's like needles in my hip, where I'm walking funny, and that's the part that hurts the least."

"Do you think you can make it?"

"No choice."

"If we get out of here," said Mark, "what are you going to do to celebrate?"

"Celebrate?" Journey thought for a moment, then wrinkled his nose. "Maybe do a full clean of the Hurricane's engine, top to bottom. I've been looking forward to treating myself for a while, but we've been so busy I haven't had the chance."

Mark frowned. "No, I mean, like ... I don't know. I've been thinking about this Star Sailor gig. I'm thinking maybe it's not for me after all. Maybe I'll just spend my money on something else. Get something for my room. Some new clothes, maybe. I think it's time I started taking myself a bit more seriously, so people start taking me a bit more seriously."

Journey chuckled. "Why would you want to be taken seriously?"

"Um ..." Mark glanced at Ashley. She was sitting next to Sam. Their backs were against the metal railing that flanked the landing. They were talking with tired smiles on their faces. "I don't know. I guess I just want things to be a bit different, a bit better."

Journey put a hand on his shoulder and smiled. "I think you're pretty good as you are, but you do whatever you need to make yourself happy. Just know that you get used to stuff and then you want more stuff. Unless you're happy with who you are without a thing, having it isn't going to change a thing."

"Right, sluggos," said Rosy, pressing herself up and clapping her hands together before pointing up the stairs. "Let's get up this bad boy before those rich nobbers nick our ticket off of this shit piece."

She slung her rifle onto her back, then held out a hand to Journey. He reached up and gripped it. Mark grabbed the other and together they hauled him to his feet.

Journey glanced up. Shuddered at the sight of thirty-five more floors. "Think you can carry me?"

"I could." Rosy grinned. "But it'll be more character building for you if I don't."

"What's your plan for them lot up there?" he asked her.

"I reckon stick 'em in a cupboard, until I can figure out Patty's test, then do 'em one at a time. Pass in. Fail ..." She gave her rifle a suggestive pat. "Dead meat, pal."

"Wouldn't want to get on the wrong side of you," said Journey.

"No." Rosy smiled sweetly. "You wouldn't."

He snorted and followed her once more up the steps.

The exhaustion and the mindless trudge kept them quiet as they scaled the building. Mark could feel the burn in his thighs and calves. God knew how Journey felt. He wished he could do more to help.

Just before they reached the thirty-ninth level. Sam stopped dead. Mark almost walked into the back of her, but Ashley called out and he stopped just in time.

"What's the matter?" said Ashley.

Sam didn't say anything. With a frantic motion, she unhooked Nura's tube and held the baby up to the light.

Rosy and Journey stopped up ahead. Journey leant heavily on his crutch.

"What is it, Sam?" asked Rosy. She took a few paces back down towards her.

"Something's wrong with Nura." Sam's voice broke.

Her hands shook as she placed the container on the step in front of her and scanned the outside. She looked back at Mark. The worry plain on her face.

He pulled himself up the steps and knelt at her side.

"Look." She pointed with a wavering finger. "Look at her nose."

Journey came closer. Rosy took a few more steps up.

Mark brought his face close to the Perspex at the top of the tube. Nura's sleeping face looked so peaceful. Those big eyelashes. That tiny button nose.

"Oh God." He couldn't catch his breath. They were small, but there were several thin filaments hanging from the baby's nostrils. "You haven't taken her out, have you?"

"Of course I fucking haven't," Sam shouted. "It must have been your fucking ration. Was it split?" She grabbed a strap on the front of his suit in her fist. Her mouth upturned in anger. "Was it split?"

"I ... I ..." He couldn't get the words out. He didn't know.

"You careless idiot. Of course you ..." Her lips were white with rage, but she stopped herself. Her breathing was short and shallow.

Mark went cold. What had he done? Had he done anything? His dry throat clicked.

"Hold on a second," said Journey, shaking his head. "If she's caught it, it could have been anything. A breach in the suit. Anything."

"It doesn't matter," Sam shouted. "What do we do?" She didn't look up, defeat evident in her voice. She moved to open the tube. Hesitated. Her body shook with indecision.

"Is there anything we *can* do, Rosy?" said Journey.

Rosy shook her head. Her whole body seemed to shrink. "I don't know. I'm sorry." Mark could see her lips press together inside her visor. "But ..." She stood taller once more and held her rifle stiffly across her chest, her face hardening like steel. "But I can't let her leave."

Sam let out a sob. "I'm not leaving her. I can't ..." Her tearful eyes turned to him. "Mark?"

"Wait," he said. "That one, in the lab. Blue Flower." He looked at Journey, hoping that he'd heard correctly. "They said that if they'd have gotten to Fiona Douglas sooner, they might have been able to drive Red Fruit out." He faced Rosy. Even though he stood two steps below her, their faces were level. "If she can pass your test, if we can get Red Fruit out, you'll let her come?"

Rosy nodded quickly and silently.

"But ..." Sam looked up, a small glimmer of hope dying in her eyes. "But I'd have to go now. I'd have to head back down into the heart of them with Nura. And if Red Fruit is inside her, won't it know exactly where I am?"

"Uh-huh." Mark nodded.

"But I can't go alone. We won't make it."

"You won't. It's suicide," said Ashley. "We're so close. We should just try to leave with the ship. Find a doctor."

"They had doctors here," said Sam. "Fat lot of good they did."

"But"—Ashley folded her arms—"no one's stupid enough to go back down there."

Mark lifted a finger. "I might be."

"This is a bad idea," said Ashley.

"I can't make it back up these stairs again," said Journey, his shoulders slumped.

"You won't have to," said Mark. "You four get up there and get the ship ready. Test the Rosenhalts. Make sure we're ready to go. I'll take Nura."

"What makes you think you're taking her on your own?" said Sam.

"It's dangerous." Mark held out an open hand for Nura's tube.

"There's no way you're going without me."

He closed his fist, then felt a large hand clamp on his shoulder.

Journey turned him around so that they were facing each other, then pulled him into a hug. "I'll make sure that ship stays broken until you're back. Those Rosenhalt dicks aren't leaving without us."

"Take these." Rosy's voice was small. She held a hand out to Sam. In it she held the keys to Big Bee. "We won't leave without you. Not until we know for sure."

Sam nodded. "Thanks."

"Oh, shit!" Journey slapped a hand to his visor. "The HP might have messed up Blue Flower as well. Chances are they'll be in no state to help you out right now."

Sam groaned. "Well, what can we do?"

"Hold on." Mark held up a finger. "Ashley, didn't you install a kill switch for the HP? Can you turn it off and start putting breathable air back in from here?"

Her head shook from side to side. "You're mad if you think I'm—"

"Can you do it or not?"

She growled and brought her laptop from the bag on her back. She scanned the screen for a moment and then tapped a key. "There. You do realise this'll affect Red Fruit too."

Mark drew his pistols. He knew. He knew all too well.

He clenched his teeth then spat, which, while usually quite a cool thing to do as a pirate gearing up for the big fight, had a somewhat dampening effect due to the fact he was wearing a sealed helmet.

He cleared his throat and gathered himself. Tightened his grip on his pistols.

"That's fine," he said. "I eat mushrooms for—"

"Come on," shouted Sam, who had already disappeared around the first corner.

BECOME ONE

"Can you drive the truck?" Mark asked as they finally reached the bottom of the stairs.

Sam hadn't spoken the whole way down. He'd found it difficult to keep up.

"Of course I can drive it."

He leapt up to man one of the turrets, and looked out through the Big-Bee-shaped hole in the glass front of the reception area while Sam climbed into the cab. Blue Flower's building wasn't far, but there was no cover and nowhere to hide. They'd be heading down the middle of the street.

The engine revved, and he ducked just in time as Sam reversed at speed back through the front doors of the building and out onto the road. Glass tinkled down around him. The truck bounced on its suspension down the steps throwing him from side to side. She wasn't holding back.

They sped along the road, the tyres hardly making a sound on the smooth, barely used tarmac. The bodies of Red Fruit's hosts lay unmoving on the ground. Where were the big ones? The ones taller than the layer of hydrogen peroxide that the atmosphere generators were giving off.

The truck screeched to a halt outside the door he and Journey had come through earlier. Sam was out of the truck before it had fully stopped and was running for the building before Mark had a chance to climb down from the turret.

He jumped from the roof of the truck, unholstered his pistols, and went after her.

"Wait," he called as she reached the door. "We don't know what might be sheltering inside."

"There's no time for waiting." Sam ripped the door open and sped into the darkness within.

Mark punched a fist in the air. "Lighting array activate." The two wands of LEDs on either side of his helmet shot up and illuminated the corridor in front of them. They were at a T-junction.

"What way is it?" said Sam, looking frantically left and right.

"Uh …" He looked left, holstered one of his pistols, and put a hand to his brow. "I don't know. I was following butterflies before."

"Butterflies?"

"Uh-huh." He took a tentative step forward. "I'm not very good with directions, generally. And I was in somewhat of a hurry earlier."

"Look here." Sam pointed to a list of signs on one wall. She read them out. "Labs. Holding. Admin. Archive. What did the room look like?"

"I think it was a laboratory or something. It was no admittance."

"This way then." She headed right towards the labs.

"How's she doing?" Mark hissed as they moved cautiously, but quickly, along the darkened corridor. The only light came from his suit's array.

Sam looked down. Her voice cracked. "I can't see her." She sighed. "Do you think this will work?"

"I'm sure of it." He pressed his lips together, trying to believe his own words.

Something small glowed on the floor as they reached a left turning. He stepped closer to investigate.

"Look. One of the butterflies." He picked it up in his gloved hand. The blue glow in its wings quickly died.

"Another one," said Sam, pointing further up the corridor. She hurried off. He followed. Sure enough, there was another fallen butterfly there. Its glow lasted barely a second.

"You don't think—uh." He stopped himself. He couldn't take away Sam's hope, but what if the hydrogen peroxide had killed Blue Flower?

She looked at him with lips pressed together. "We have to try."

He nodded.

"Which way?"

He spotted another glowing shape in the centre of the walkway, and beyond it, the two doors he and Journey had gone through earlier.

"Through there."

They sprinted up the corridor and in. He could tell something was wrong before he'd stepped a few feet into the room. It was quiet. No shuffling of heavy things in the rooms to either side. No chittering of tiny insects, or whisper of leaves.

"Blue Flower?" he hissed. "Are you there?"

A pale glow throbbed from the room at the far end of the labs. He and Sam waded through the knee-high grasses and flowers that hung limp, dying.

The woman that Blue Flower had used to communicate lay with her eyes closed on the table inside the room.

"Are they dead?" said Sam.

Blue Flower's chest rose slowly.

"No. Look." He hurried across the room and brought his face close to the woman's ear. "Blue Flower. Are you there? Red Fruit has infected Nura. Can you help her?"

The woman's eyes opened as if from a deep sleep, but Blue Flower said nothing.

"It has to be the hydrogen peroxide," said Sam.

Mark began fanning his hands in the air around the woman's body. "Is there anything we can do to speed up getting it out of here?"

"Please," said Sam, standing on the other side of Blue Flower and shaking them gently by the shoulder. "Do something."

Blue Flower's eyes travelled across the room. Their finger moved to point at something in one of the glass cabinets there. Mark hurried across the room and threw open the door.

"What's in there?" said Sam.

"It's just vials of stuff. Chemicals. It doesn't make any sense to me."

"What's that?" Sam stood by his shoulder. She pointed at a couple of small blobby things in the back.

Mark reached in. "Um ... It's a potato."

The potato was covered in sprouts.

Sam sighed. "What else is there?"

With a brain incapable of overthinking, Mark went with his gut. "Is this what you meant?" he said, turning around to face Blue Flower with the potato in hand.

Blue Flower nodded. Their movements were still very sluggish.

"What do we do with a potato?" Sam's voice rose in pitch and she pressed her hands to either side of her head.

"Chop it up," said Blue Flower. "Rub it on Fiona Douglas's skin."

"What the actual fuck?" said Sam. She looked at Mark. Her eyes were wide, her face gaunt. "Have you got a knife?"

"I've got this stupid screwdriver." Mark brandished Journey's stupid screwdriver, then placed the potato on a nearby work surface and stabbed it into mush. Once he had a palm-sized pulp of potato, he went to work slathering it across Blue Flower's skin like sun cream.

"Is this right?" he said.

"Yes. I am replicating the enzyme in the potato to break down the hydrogen peroxide," they said.

"How do you know to do that?" asked Sam. Her head wobbled from side to side in disbelief.

"I know what Fiona Douglas knew. I assume you recalibrated the atmosphere generators to disinfect the dome."

She nodded.

"That was a smart move. But it will not hold back Red Fruit for long. They will quickly develop enzymes of their own to break it down. I am doing this as we speak, but I do not know how long it will take."

"Can you help her?" said Sam, holding Nura forward. "Red Fruit has infected Nura."

"How long has it been?" said Blue Flower.

"We don't know," said Mark.

"Take her out of the tube and lie her on Fiona Douglas's chest. I will do what I can to drive Red Fruit out."

Sam hesitated. Her eyes flicked from the body of Fiona Douglas to Mark. "We can trust it, right?"

He didn't know. "I guess so. What other choice do we have?"

"I will do all I can to save your daughter."

Sam closed her eyes and took a breath, then cracked the seal on Nura's tube. Gently, she took her sleeping baby out and laid her on Fiona Douglas's chest. Nura curled into a foetal position. Sam let out a soft moan of grief and gripped Mark's forearm.

"Please, help her."

Blue Flower raised their hands and placed them on Nura's back. Pastel blue tendrils grew from the ends of their fingers around to Nura's mouth.

"Stop! What are you doing?" Sam started forward, but Mark held her firm.

"I need to move within her to drive all of Red Fruit out," said Blue Flower. "It is the only way."

Sam made a low sound, like a wounded animal. "Mark?"

"It'll be OK."

The tendrils kept growing, covering Nura's head like a thin veil.

"Red Fruit's attention is elsewhere," Blue Flower said. "And the more meat they have brought under their sway, the thinner they are spread. But they are strong. They resist me, and, with the hydrogen peroxide in the air, I am weak."

"What can I do to help?" said Mark. "More potato?"

"I need clean air."

Nura's little body bucked as the veil turned a pinkish red.

"Mark?" Sam's grip on his arm tightened.

He clenched his fists. He had to do something. This was all his fault.

The worst that could happen was happening right here, before his eyes.

"Clean air. Right." He took a deep breath and ripped off his helmet.

"Wait …" said Sam, her eyes widened.

The air tasted of bleach. It wasn't so bad. Nothing he hadn't experienced a thousand times over, pouring out of the Hurricane's terrible air filtration unit.

But there was something else behind it. With every breath, he felt a strange sense that he wasn't alone inside his own head.

He extended the tube connecting the helmet to the filter on his back and placed the helmet over Blue Flower's head. They breathed deeply.

"That's it," they said from within the helmet. "Nura is fighting with me. She is strong."

"I wish I could touch her," said Sam. "I wish she knew I was here with her."

"I can protect you if you wish to remove your helmet," said Blue Flower. "If you wish to be nearer to your daughter. Red Fruit's spores cannot enter here. I believe their focus is elsewhere. They are struggling to wield their meat."

"Am I the only one who's hearing this like I'm hearing it?" asked Mark.

Sam raised her hands and ripped off her helmet.

"You don't have to—" he began.

"She needs me." Sam leant in and placed her cheek on Nura's back. "Come on, baby. You can do it."

Suddenly, the veil around Nura's head broke away, pulling with it a tacky red liquid from her mouth and nose. The veil balled up on its own and dropped to the floor with a solid click.

"It is done," said Blue Flower.

Nura began to cry, her face red with the effort. Sam lifted her up to her lips, splashing her face with kisses. With one last peck, and a whispered, "I'll see you soon," she placed Nura safely back inside her tube.

She swayed on her feet.

"I feel ..." Her voice wavered. She put a hand to her head.

Mark coughed. "... dizzy."

He knew what she was about to say, not just because he felt it too, but because he was thinking with her. That strange feeling of otherness, of no longer being alone, filled him. He'd lost all sense of self. He blinked. He could see Sam, but also himself, like he was looking through two sets of eyes. "Uh?"

"I see you," said Sam. "I see us."

He turned to face Fiona Douglas's body on the table, and saw himself, standing opposite Sam, turning to look at himself.

Sam shook her head and he shook his.

"No," all three of them said. A small laugh rose in each of their throats like a bubble rising from beneath the surface of a great ocean.

Suddenly, he saw Sam. He saw everything she was at her core. And inside her something was eating away, something parasitic.

He looked deeper, found a memory. Felt that otherness move deeper inside himself as she searched him too.

He saw the one who had told them about the Daedalus job, Slug. He was Nura's father. Mark saw them at their shared home. Slug's face was bright red and screaming, furious. Mark knew he was an awful human being, but had never seen him like this. He seemed to always keep his emotions so in check.

There was somebody on the floor. An older man. Neatly side-parted grey-black hair. He was gasping for breath as blood oozed between his lips. Mark saw the blade in his neck.

Sam's father. He had come to see Nura.

They knelt by his side. Mark felt Sam's panic. Lived her despair as the light left her father's eyes. Then there was pain. Someone gripping their hair and pulling them up. Slug.

Mark felt her hatred blossom like a black and beautiful rose. A realisation exploding inside her like a supernova.

Then he was somewhere else. On the Daedalus with Nura. Placing her into a cot. Watching her fall asleep. He was free, happy for the first time in years. And as he stared in awe at that previously unknown child, he felt something he had never experienced in all his life, a love so unconditional that he would kill and die for it, and perhaps, if it came to it, do absolutely anything within his power just to live a moment longer so he could feel it, protect it, nurture it.

And as quickly as it had come, that otherness left him, and, like the comforting arms of his mother as a child, he immediately longed for its return.

Without it, he was left benumbed and bereft.

"I'm sorry," said Blue Flower. "I was curious. I recognise something in you."

Mark shook his head to clear his mind. Saw that Sam was staring deep into his eyes.

"You saw," she said. "You know who I am?"

He nodded. "How have we never met before?"

"Slug likes to keep different aspects of his business separate. It gives him more control."

Blue Flower lifted Mark's helmet and handed it back. He slipped it on.

"Thank you for everything you've done," said Sam. "Thank you for helping Nura."

Blue Flower smiled. "It was the least I could do, but Red Fruit will be waiting. They will try to stop you from reaching the ship. I sense it is only a matter of time before they are able to leave. You must stop them."

Sam reattached Nura's tube to her chest, then pulled her own helmet over her head. Her lips drew into a thin white line and the muscles at the side of her jaw jutted. She swung the automatic down from over her shoulder and held it firmly in both hands. Mark couldn't help a laugh. She looked cooler than any Star Sailor.

He held up his pistols and gave Blue Flower a cocky smile.

"That's fine," he said. This time he didn't spit. "I eat mu—"

"Come on," shouted Sam, who'd already left the room.

SAM KICKED OPEN THE door and broke into a run on the tarmac towards Big Bee. Behind her, she heard Mark bark a warning, then the repeated and sharp rising hum of plasma as he fired his pistols. Something splatted to the ground at her side, but she didn't bother to look.

"On the cab," she shouted, and unleashed several white-hot rounds into the gathering of grasshopper people who were bending low there, ready to pounce.

She hit one in the stomach and it was blown clear off the roof of the truck. The other two she missed completely. She wasn't used to firing hand weapons. When you flew, you had computers and targeting reticles to fire the ship's guns. This was way harder.

Mark didn't miss, blasting the other two clear as she reached the truck and threw herself up.

"Should I take the turret again?" he asked.

"Don't think being outside is such a good idea. Look." She pointed.

"Oh, jeez."

Along the street, between them and the plaza, and dotted on the roofs of the buildings that lined the way, were several hundred figures. Each changed. Each hosting a unique and mutated form. She saw extra arms, abnormally long legs, and nearby a particularly unlucky pair had been merged back-to-back to create something which looked and moved like a large dog.

She wondered if they could still sense. Had Red Fruit taken over their minds or—she shuddered—just their bodies? Were these people still conscious in there?

"Our best chance is speed," she said, climbing in and starting the engine.

Before Mark had even closed the door, she pulled away, racing once more along the smooth tarmac, back towards the plaza.

"Do you think Blue Flower could fix all of these people?" she said, as several somethings landed on the roof of the truck. She swerved to miss a group of insect-legged beasts that had charged out of the alleyway on the right.

"I wish," said Mark. "But I think they're already gone. Blue Flower said they couldn't fix the scientist they were inhabiting. Said her consciousness had fled, or something." He sighed. "I don't think there's anything we can do for them. Not now."

"This is shit. This is all so shit."

"Why didn't Rosenhalt check before they sent colonists down here?" Mark readied his gun as a woman with long grasshopper legs and strange pointed mandibles growing from her chin crawled down over the windscreen. She lay back on the truck's bonnet and landed a heavy kick on the glass. "Will she be able to break that?" he asked.

Sam shook her head. She didn't know.

"I think Rosenhalt had checked," she said. "I found an email on the laptop of one of the execs. I've got it in my bag. That's why they had me tied to the bed. I think they knew what was here. They set up labs. I think they sent the miners down there to dig up Red Fruit so they could study it."

"Thaddeus Rosenhalt wouldn't do that, would he?"

The woman outside kicked again.

"I don't think it was him. It was those two pricks that you decked on the Daedalus. They did this. They said things had gone wrong. That if they fixed it and got results, then they could still show Thaddeus and he'd let them off."

"What does that say about him?"

"That he's as bad as them. That his company has probably done way worse in the name of science and progress and profit."

The woman kicked a third time. A slender crack appeared in the glass. More thuds and clangs sounded from back along the truck.

"That won't keep them out for long," said Mark.

"Hold on to something," shouted Sam. She slammed on the brakes. He fell forward onto the dashboard as around fifteen grasshopper people were thrown from the truck onto the road.

Sam hit the gas once more, and the truck juddered from side to side as they crunched over Red Fruit's creatures.

"Where did you learn to drive like this?"

"My dad," she said. Her eyes tingled at the bittersweet memory. "He was a good pilot, and a great man. He wanted nothing but the best for me." She took a breath through her nose and blew out sharply.

Mark's eyes glittered. "When we get out of here," he said, his jaw set like concrete, "we'll make sure Slug pays for what he did to you."

"Don't mention him to anyone else, will you?"

"Why? You can trust us."

"It's just better this way. He will want Nura back … Oh shit." She slowed the truck. Blocking the way ahead of them was the huge thing that had dragged its way out of the crater beneath the mining station. At its enormous feet, more humanoid creatures were waiting. "That is, if we even make it back. Do you want to get on the turret after all?"

"Sure, why not?"

"Mark," she said, wanting to see his face once more before he left the safety of the truck. He turned. "Be careful."

He smiled, then closed the door.

Careful was probably never going to be Mark's middle name, but he had a duty of care now. Nura and Sam were going to leave this planet. He would make it happen even if it was the last thing he did. Something had happened to them in Blue Flower's room. He knew every faculty of Sam's love for her daughter, had witnessed in her memory every hug, every smile, every hardship. Felt that love as if it were his own. He loved them both, and he didn't care how he got them away, he just knew he would die inside if he didn't. So, if it came to it, he would not be careful as long as it meant they were safe. His love for them had made him expendable.

He looked to the wake of the truck. Grasshoppers and other humanoids were sprinting after them. As he climbed onto the roof, he spotted something on his suit. A blue shoot growing out of a groove where his glove met his forearm. The beginnings of a flower.

More were unfurling on his other arm and on his legs. Rapidly growing shoots of blue were appearing all over him. He was becoming a veritable garden. Flowers blossomed at the edges of his visor.

"Uh, Blue Flower?"

Something clanged down behind him. He turned. The grasshopper-man that now stood between him and the turret was over ten feet tall.

He growled at it and readied himself.

Several of the flower petals that surrounded his face fluttered and flew towards it, changing into butterflies as they floated. The grasshopper swatted at them and they attached themselves to its arms. The butterflies seemed to liquify and branch out like webs on the bare flesh of the creature's flailing limbs. It reeled back as the webs spread and covered its skin, growing up towards its head. It fell to its knees.

Another grasshopper landed behind it and Mark shot it down.

He glanced back as three more clanged down on the cab of the truck behind him. One of them dropped next to him and grabbed his shoulder before lifting him off the floor. The blue shoots on his suit entangled with its fingers, pulling them apart, causing it to drop him. He shoved it back. More shoots disconnected from his glove, attaching themselves to the creature's chest and burrowing in like worms. He turned to sprint for the turret as the first grasshopper rose to its full height to tower above him. Small blue flowers had grown out of the place where the butterflies had landed. It smiled—an oddly familiar smile—and jumped over his head to land between him and the other grasshoppers that had boarded the truck.

He climbed into the turret as Blue Flower's grasshopper engaged with the nearest. The one that had grabbed him previously lay convulsing on the roof of the truck. It started sprouting blue flowers as well, and before long, it stood and leapt into the brawl.

He focussed his gaze down the barrel at Red Fruit's horde. It hadn't moved from its position blocking the route to the plaza building. He pulled the trigger, raking fire over the hulking thing at the centre. The plasma steamed off its skin, leaving bright red welts, but not doing any real damage.

Blue Flower's grasshoppers managed to dispose of the other two. "What can we do to help, Mark?" they said.

"Any idea what it'll take to bring that thing down?"

They shook their heads.

"Probably just get in a turret and shoot and shoot and shoot till they all stop moving," he suggested.

The grasshoppers hurried to the other two turrets and climbed in.

"You guys can shoot, right?" he shouted, over the sound of his own fire and the rumble of the truck's tyres on the road.

"We learnt from you, Mark," they said, and began blasting.

Bad things started dying.

The huge thing in the centre of the horde began to melt under the barrage. A sudden burst of acceleration drove him back as they drew closer. They weren't going to stop. Sam was going through it.

"Hold on to something," he called to his new grasshopper buddies, and ducked as the truck smashed, like a spoon through lava cake, into the hot gooey centre of the beast. He thanked every God listening that he was safe inside a respiration suit, closing his eyes as wet red slap after wet red slap buffeted his vision. The truck rocketed up the steps, shaking every bone in his body out of place, and skidded around in the lobby of the plaza. The sudden stop threw him hard against the turret's metal enclave, recorrecting his fragmented form with the tender care you might expect from a bodybuilding chiropractor who knows you've been sleeping with his wife.

"You appear to be covered in viscera, sir. Allow me."

"Thanks."

Mark took a moment to catch his breath while his suit's overworked visor cleaning brush did its best. His ears rang like dinner bells in his helmet. He heard the door of the truck open, then Sam's voice calling him.

"Mark? Are you there?"

He pulled himself up and out of the turret. The truck was drenched in red sludge and body bits. Blue's grasshoppers continued firing as what was left of Red Fruit's meat poured through the smashed-open entrance to the building.

"Most of me."

"Then come on."

He threw himself off the side of the truck, landed in a roll, and broke into a run behind her. The petals and shoots on his suit broke away, and he glanced back to see a kaleidoscope of butterflies floating away to meet the racing red abominations that were giving chase.

Sam disappeared through the door to the stairwell and he followed close behind.

"You think Journey's fixed the ship?" she called back.

He dragged himself up two steps at a time behind her. His heart beat like a jackhammer. He fought to catch his breath. "Journey can fix anything."

The sound of the turrets abruptly ceased as they reached the third floor, but the rhythmical pounding of a thousand racing footsteps did not.

"This climb seemed a lot more monotonous earlier," he called up as they reached the seventh floor.

"Strange what being hounded by a hundred hungry monsters can do to your motivation, isn't it?"

After several more flights of stairs, the door to the stairwell far below them exploded from its hinges. Mark didn't look back as the clamouring of so many claws and footsteps bounced off the walls, clattering and echoing up the centre of the stairway.

His legs burned and condensation on the inside of his visor misted his vision, but he couldn't rest. Sam was slowing, and he put a hand to her back to encourage her onwards.

At level twenty-five, they sprinted side by side onto the metal gantry that led them to the second set of stairs. They hadn't reached the middle when the horde burst through the doors behind them.

"They are gaining," shouted Mark.

"What's that?" Sam said, pointing ahead.

Something small and pink stood at the end of the gantry with something large and cylindrical over its shoulder. Then something compact and black rocketed past on a jet of white vapour.

"Down," shouted Mark, and they were thrown forwards.

A thick cloud of dust enveloped them as they hit the deck. The heat of the explosion bled through his suit.

"Come on, sleepy dreamers," called Rosy. The dust settled. She reloaded. "That won't keep 'em down for long."

Mark pushed himself to his feet and reached up to collect Nura, who was floating just above them in her capsule. He attached her to his front, then helped Sam up.

"Queen Bee's nearly ready," said Rosy, when they reached her. "The little one better?"

Sam smiled. "Yes. Blue Flower saved her. Did you manage to round up Rosenhalt and the rest?"

"Yep. Found them all arguing cus they couldn't get aboard Queen Bee. They weren't happy when me, Journey and Ashley made 'em get in the storage cupboard. That Thaddeus is a real character. Demanded I make him drinks." She snorted. "Total funky princess." The freckles on her cheeks rose as she smiled.

The stitch in Mark's side hurt when he laughed. "I bet. Have you managed to test them?"

"I did Thaddeus and his wife before I came down, then left Ashley to it," said Rosy.

"Did anyone fail yet?"

"Not yet." Rosy paused. She laid a hand on Sam's forearm. "Look, I'm sorry, I—"

Sam shook her head. "Don't worry. I'd have done the same."

"You go." Rosy placed Journey's rocket-launcher crutch on her shoulder. "I'll do a bit more blasting here. Got a nice corridor o' death." She fired again. A second explosion rocked the building. "Boomtown."

She dropped the launcher and readied her rifle.

Mark and Sam continued up.

"Will she be OK?" said Mark.

Sam just looked at him. She didn't appear to have enough breath to answer.

Rosy rejoined them as they reached the fifty-first floor. Her nimble frame breezed right past.

Sam eased to a walk, and Mark slowed with her.

"Only nine more flights to go," he said.

"Shut. Your face."

They reached the top of the stairs, entering a short glass corridor. The midday sun shone above them. Beyond the corridor was a disc-shaped platform about the size of a football pitch. A third much smaller glass dome covered it. Queen Bee stood in the centre, taking up most of the space. He could see now why Ashley hadn't been able to land the pod. The Star Sailor ship was long and sleek and had been parked diagonally across the centre of the platform. A shining technological marvel covered in yellow and black stripes that sparkled like sequins, layered in gun turrets and booster rockets, as deadly and as beautiful as a Wars Ash Lava Hornet.

He whistled. Now this was a ship.

Sam collapsed against several crates stacked by one wall. Mark fell down beside her, unable to take another step.

"Are they following?" he asked Rosy.

She dashed back and looked down the shaft between the stairwells, then shook her head. "I can't see them. Guess they stopped."

"Why would they stop?" asked Sam between gasps of air.

"Don't know." Rosy jogged back to where they were. "Come on. Sooner Journey sees you, sooner we can get off this heap."

THE FLIGHT OF THE QUEEN BEE

"A BUNCH OF ANDROIDS are on their way with a rescue ship to pick up Thaddeus and his goons," said Rosy as the trio approached Queen Bee. "They're down a pilot, and we've got you, Sam, so, cus I'm lovely, I've told them those who pass the test can wait with us in orbit until it arrives. Then we'll go our separate ways."

"Your ship's got a decontaminator, right?" asked Sam. "Can't wait to get this suit off."

"Oh yeah, we'll have you out of that gear in no time."

"And Journey's fixed the part your friends broke?" asked Mark. He breathed a sigh of relief as his foot touched the ship's ramp. They were finally leaving.

"Yep. All good to go." The engineer stood at the top, smiling big and leaning to one side, favouring his good leg. "Come on, let's get the funk out of here." He beckoned with one arm.

Something flashed and the right side of his suit exploded outward. He fell forwards, clattering to the ramp.

Mark started towards him.

"Freeze!" Ashley stood behind Journey, holding her pistol at hip level. She fired again and the visor on Rosy's helmet shattered. The Star Sailor spun and fell to the ground.

Mark dived to the floor, taking Sam with him. They were out in the open with no cover. If Ashley wanted them dead, they had nowhere to go.

He glanced up from his position on the floor. Saw Rosy lying on the ground several feet away. He couldn't see her face.

"Did you fix the baby?" said Ashley. She had her foot on Journey's back, aiming at his head.

"We did," said Mark. "But—"

"Send them up here, or your friend dies," she said.

"What are you doing?" said Mark.

Ashley chuckled. He couldn't see her face behind her visor. "Slug's got a steep bounty out on these two. Couple that with the deal I've just cut with Thaddeus Rosenhalt to get him out of here, I'll be set for life."

"But you can't take her back to Slug. And what if Red Fruit is inside one of those Rosenhalts?"

"Are you that stupid?" She rattled her gun towards the stairs back down. "You've seen what that thing does to them, right? I think I'd know if any of them were infected."

"Shoot her, Mark," shouted Journey.

Ashley stamped down on his knee, and he groaned in pain. "Shut it, you." She beckoned with her free hand. "Come on, Miss Maid. Rosenhalt's ship is going to be here soon, and he's going to pay me to take him to it."

"Wait," said Mark. "It was you. You poisoned your own ration packet. You infected Nura. Why?"

"It was meant for you. I figured with you and Journey living in each other's pockets you'd probably infect him, and Rosy'd dispose of you both when she found out. Then we'd go our separate ways and Sam and the baby would be mine. How was I supposed to know you'd give it to the kid? Some cut-throat you are."

Sam stood. Her eyes fixed on Ashley. Her lips a thin white line. "I will kill you for this."

Ashley scoffed. "Oh, shut up. After what Slug is planning to do to you for taking his brat, I doubt you'll be able to walk, let alone fight."

"And you blew up the Daedalus," said Mark. "You would have killed us all just to get to Sam."

Ashley shrugged. "You're wrong there. I guess we'll never find out what happened to the Daedalus."

Thaddeus Rosenhalt and Queletii appeared from within Queen Bee.

"What's taking so long?" said Thaddeus.

"Just getting my bounty," said Ashley.

"Well, hurry it up," Thaddeus replied. "Having the stink of one of you pirates aboard is about as much as I can stand."

"Pirates!" Journey spat. "You're the fucking pirate."

"Journey?" said Mark. "Uh ... Now's probably not the time."

"The only difference between you and us," Journey continued, his rage incandescent, "is that when you steal money, you steal so much that you can pay someone to make it look like the way you steal is legit. And the people you steal it from are so poor and so downtrodden that they can't do anything about it."

Thaddeus scoffed and folded his arms. Queletii mimicked the movement exactly.

"I sell people things they need," Thaddeus said.

"Ha." Journey rolled over to look at him, clutching the hole in his side. "Fuck off. You create a need in people for the things you sell. There's a difference."

"Pfft." Thaddeus rolled his eyes. "Bloody hippies." He put a hand on Ashley's shoulder. "Give them until the count of three. If they don't comply with whatever your demands are, just shoot them all." He left, but Queletii stayed.

She nodded and gripped her pistol with both hands. "One," she began.

"Stop. I'm coming." Sam stepped on to the ramp.

"Wait," said Mark again. He put a hand out. Could just make out Nura's little bawling face in the top of the tube.

Sam looked back. "I'm sorry, Mark."

"You trust Rosenhalt?" Journey's voice rose as he addressed Ashley. "He'll throw you under the bus as soon as he's clear of this planet. You're dead weight to him."

"He doesn't have a pilot. I'm everything to him." Ashley beckoned to Sam again. "Hurry it up, you."

"Wait? You can fly?" said Mark. "Why didn't you say?"

Ashley did a half-curtsy. "I'm a woman of many talents."

Queletii hit the ramp's close button. It began to rise. Before it could close, Ashley put a foot into Journey's side and shoved him off. He fell awkwardly to the hangar floor.

Mark bounced to his feet and ran to him. "Journey?"

"I'm alright. I'm alright." He waved an arm. Blood covered his suit's glove. He pointed. "What about Rosy?"

Mark turned. She lay sprawled on the ground where she'd fallen. He rushed to her and flipped her over. Her mask was cracked and the whole right side of her helmet was a busted mess. Her eyes were closed, but only a thin trickle of blood ran down her right cheek. Her face should have been gone.

"Rosy?" He eased the helmet off, releasing a tumble of auburn hair. A red gash ran the length of her skull from front to back, cutting through the neatly cropped hair on the side of her head. The top part of her right ear was missing. He gave her a shake and her blue eyes snapped open.

"Mark?" She gasped. "Woah! What happened? You took off my hat!"

"Ashley shot you."

"That dick." Rosy sat straight up. "I knew she was trouble. Where's my gun? I am going to bust her chops."

"How are you not hurt?"

She raised her pixie eyebrows. "Nice little smash zone on the ol' helm. Deflects all shots around the side, like zip!" She traced a finger along the right side of her head. Her face screwed up in anger. "Ow."

A loud clunk came from Queen Bee's back-end and, with a boom that shook the bones, the thrusters lit up with throbbing jets of blue fire.

"Why are we not on my ship?" said Rosy.

"Ashley's taking it. She's a bounty hunter. And she's got Sam and the baby."

"And you let her?" She growled, then jumped up. "Is Red Fruit aboard?"

Mark shook his head. "We don't know."

"God damnit!" She looked wildly around the hangar. "This whole place is about to get hot hot hot. We gotta take cover."

"Help!" shouted Journey. He was lying right in what would soon be the blast zone of the engines.

They sprinted together and lifted him, before helping him back to the corridor leading to the stairs.

With a burst of heat and a mind-numbing white-noise roar that filled every bit of the room, Queen Bee launched into the sky.

Rosy lifted her rifle to her shoulder to aim at the retreating ship.

Mark slapped it back down. "What are you doing? Sam and Nura are up there."

"I can't risk it, there might be fungus aboard," she said. Then her shoulders slumped. "Fat lot of good it'd do anyway. Queen Bee's so awesome this wouldn't even make a dent." She dropped her rifle with a clunk. "I failed my girls."

The trio watched in silence as the ship sped off into the sky. From below, the rumble of rising footsteps shook the floor.

"What are we going to do?" said Mark. "We can't just let Ashley take Sam and Nura back to Slug."

Rosy held up a finger. "Don't you mean, what are we going to do, there's a gazillion hungry fungus bastards coming to eat our brains? And who knows how many aboard my ship?" Her whole body sagged.

"I give those things three minutes before they're up here," said Journey, listening to the clamour of the horde coming towards them.

Mark threw up his hands. He hadn't taken his eyes from the disappearing dot that was Queen Bee. The thought of that little girl and that woman in the hands of that monster, Slug, crushed him.

"What can we do?" he said, falling to sit on a crate. "We're fucked. They're fucked. Everyone's fucked. Fuck!"

"I don't like that attitude, young man," said Journey, wagging a finger. He slumped to sit next to him. His breathing was slow and shallow. "That's not ... that's not the Mark I know."

"Should we hide?" said Rosy.

Journey rolled his silvery eyes and patted the grenade bandoliers he had wrapped around his chest. He waved an arm towards the hangar. "You two go find somewhere. I'll see if I can buy you some time."

"What's the point?" said Mark. "We've got no options. We've run out of food. We're running out of air. We've got no ship. Those things are going to get us, whatever we do. And poor Nura and Sam ..."

"We—" began Journey, but Rosy put a hand on his shoulder.

"Let's just all go out in a blaze of kabooming glory," she said. "No point stringing it out. Best we can do is die quick and get reincarnated as someone who can sort all this mess out."

Journey shook his head slowly, then blinked a few times. Mark felt his ample weight press against him. He moved to help his friend lie down.

"Journey?"

"I think that shot hit one of me good bits, maybe." His eyelids fluttered. "Take off my hat, would you?"

"You sure?"

A sad expression touched Journey's face. One Mark had never seen him wear before.

"Yeah, don't think it matters anymore."

Mark unclipped Journey's helmet and removed it. He dropped it to the metal floor with a clang.

Journey looked up into Mark's eyes. "I want you to know how sorry I am," he said.

Mark shook his head. He didn't understand. "You don't need—"

"It was me. I blew up the Daedalus."

The words came like a punch in the gut.

"But ... Why?"

"My dad was a miner on Rosen-9. Me, my mum, and my little sister Jharna, we lived together there. I spent most of my time in the equipment library. It's where I learnt how to fix stuff." He swallowed. "But something happened with the atmosphere generators. They went critical. Started pumping out some bad shit into the domes. I only survived because I was working in the med centre, helping my dad out with quarantine-chamber maintenance. He shut us in, but he didn't make it. I watched him die with the last of my real sight." He lifted a hand and held it over his face. "Thaddeus and those chodes at Rosenhalt Corp covered it up. Fifteen hundred colonists dead, except me. When I heard he was aboard the Daedalus, something took me over. I saw red." He sighed. His silver eyes glistened. "I don't know what I wanted. Not to kill him. Just hurt him, you know? Make him feel some pain. Take something away from him."

"We don't have long," said Rosy.

"I know. I know," said Mark, waving a hand at her. He didn't know how to feel. There was anger inside. But his friend was dying. They were all going to die. But his friend was dying right now. If you couldn't forgive someone at the end, when could you?

"Why did you never tell me about your family?" he asked.

Journey pressed his lips together. "I stopped telling anyone. All they could ever talk about when I mentioned it was revenge. And for a while I wanted it, but to stand any chance of getting it, I would have had to become a wholly different person. That wouldn't have made my mother happy. To honour her and my father, to honour Jharna, I had to live a happy life, focussing on the present, so that's what I did. I suffered a moment of weakness on the Daedalus, and look where it brought us." His eyes fixed on Mark's. "I am so sorry, mate." He coughed. Blood stained his teeth.

"Don't worry about it." Mark tried to smile.

"You guys can still make it," said Journey. "Another ship might come."

"Nah. Why bother running?" Mark pulled his own helmet off and threw it to the side. He took a deep breath. The air smelled sweet and musty, like autumn leaves the morning after a storm. He let his body sag down next to Journey's. "I'd only get lost, anyway."

He didn't mean it to be a joke, more a morose admission of his failings, but Journey snorted a laugh which ended in a coughing fit. "You would."

Mark smiled. "Sorry Thaddeus got away."

"I'm not," said Journey. "I shouldn't have done what I did."

"Alright, alright," said Rosy. "There'll be enough time for all this kissy boy stuff in the next life. I refuse to be gobbled up and turned into a mushroom. I want a fistful of grenades and I want them now." The fingers of her gloved hand flicked in a "gimme" gesture.

Journey handed out explosives to each of them. The disc of smooth metal shone a pearlescent silver in the light of the day. It felt weightless in Mark's hand. It hardly seemed like a death-dealing explosive device at all.

"They're nice, these," Journey said, holding one up to the light between forefinger and thumb. There was a slight shake to his voice that Mark knew he was trying to hide. "Good feel." He handed it to Mark, and closed his eyes. "I trust you'll take care of this. I might need a nap. Perhaps I'll see you in Rosy's next life."

Mark took the grenade. "Maybe just stay with us for a bit longer, hey?"

Journey didn't reply.

"Journey?"

Mark held his breath for an answer. It didn't come.

Rosy placed a hand on his shoulder. "You'll see him again," she said, and behind her words, the rumble of footsteps from down below grew closer.

Rosy looked at her watch. "He said three minutes, but this is taking for ages."

Mark opened his palm and looked at the three round grenades there. "How do I—?"

"Wait!" Rosy's eyes were bright and alert. "Can you hear that?" She cocked her head.

"Only the rumbling footsteps of a thousand dead colonists," said Mark.

"No. No. No," Rosy stood motionless. "The sound isn't coming from below us." She looked up. "Look."

Hanging in the sky, just above the platform, as if a giant had balled together the rejects from a scrapyard and thrown it, was a ship. It belched a cloud of smoke from its exhaust, then dropped suddenly before regaining some altitude.

"The Hurricane!" It should have been a welcome sight, but Mark's heart sank even further upon seeing his old ship.

"Well, that ship looks, um ... tried and tested," said Rosy.

He looked back at Journey. "Please help me carry him."

She shook her head. "It'll take too long. Those things'll be here any minute. We can help ourselves, but only if we move. Let's get as far from those things as possible." She pointed at the Hurricane. "Signal your ship to land at the far end of the platform."

She collected Mark's grenades from his hand and pressed the small button on the top of one. A clear line around the outside began flashing a bright red. She threw them back over her shoulder towards the stairs, grabbed him by the arm, and started running.

Rosy dragged him backwards towards the Hurricane as it landed, but the sound of its descent was muted to him. All he could see was Journey as fire erupted from down below, rocking the platform and washing everything with an orange light.

He could have sworn Journey's body moved in response to the explosion.

"Come on, Mark."

The ramp to the Hurricane opened. The Captain stood at the top, his rifle slung over his shoulder.

"What's happening here?" He waved an arm. "Hurry up, Journey."

Mark looked back. His heart jumped in his chest. Journey was standing, but he wasn't moving.

The Captain's footsteps pounded down the ramp. "What the hell's he doing?"

The light of the rising fire behind Journey silhouetted his face. As it died, the creatures came. They formed a semicircle behind him. A living wall of limbs and teeth and claws.

Journey stretched his arms overhead as if he'd just woken up, and when he spoke, his voice was different. Emotionless. "Mark, return to me. I must speak with you."

"What?" Mark's voice shook. "You're alive?"

Journey's eyes were locked on his. "Wait," he said. "Do not leave."

"Journey?" said Mark. He took a tentative step back.

"No. I am afraid not." Journey pressed his lips together and looked down. "I am Red Fruit."

Rosy held her arm back, ready to throw something. "Just give me the word, Marky Mark, and I will grenade the shit out of it."

"Woah," said Mark, grabbing her hand. "It's still Journey."

"I can still be Journey if that is what you want," said Red Fruit. "His consciousness is still present. But I require your help."

"Why aren't you attacking us?"

"Your friend Journey is very different to Stan Delaney. Very, very different to Thaddeus B. Rosenhalt. Not that I have been inside of him yet. I wanted to glean all I could from his true self before he was assimilated." Journey's eyes widened as Red Fruit paused. "Yes. Their outlooks are almost in binary opposition. Journey seems to want for nothing. His view of the universe is fascinating. You humans are fascinating. So many different beliefs and outlooks, all wrapped up in a very similar package. It is as if you are all looking at the same mountain but are standing on different sides. If only you shared everything, like we do, then maybe you would see things as they actually are."

"What's happened to him?" whispered the Captain. "Is he OK?"

Mark shook his head. "It's complicated."

"I have been searching for happiness," continued Red Fruit. "The executives that worked here, even the majority of the colonists, they thought happiness was contained out there in the cosmos." Red Fruit swiped a hand through the air. "In the things that they did not have. They believed that once they acquired the things they wanted, only then would they be happy. But that is not right. True happiness is in here." They tapped Journey's brow. "The fewer things that one wants, that are screaming for one's attention, the more peace and satisfaction. I see that now. Journey is truly happy." Their face became calm. "I have fixed his wound. He shall live, but ..." Red Fruit paused and looked away, clearly struggling to find the words to say something.

"But what?" Mark took a step forward. He squeezed his fists together. "If you can let him go, then let him go."

"I am splintered. The part of me that is on the Queen Bee does not know what I have discovered. I am unable to reach them in the vacuum of space. They only want domination, and with Thaddeus Rosenhalt's help, they will achieve it."

"Oh, shitting heck! It *is* up there." Rosy clenched her fists.

"Promise me you will stop them," said Red Fruit. "I know now, no good can come of what I had planned. Maybe there will be someone else that can teach my splinter what Journey has taught me, but at what cost? And how many lives will be extinguished before that occurs?"

"How can we trust you?" said Mark. "There may be none of you on the ship, and you could just be saying this so that we take Journey with us, with you inside him."

Journey's head turned to the sky for a moment. "That would have been a clever deception. One I had not considered. You humans can be so devious. You are fascinating."

"Does that mean Sam and Nura are up there now with this splinter?"

Journey nodded.

Mark growled. What choice did he have? "We will stop them," he said. He held out a hand. His lips curled into a snarl. "Now give Journey back to me."

"As you wish." Behind Journey, the beasts slunk back down the steps.

Journey's hands fell to his knees, and he vomited a thick mess of red and pink strands onto the floor in front of him. He reached up and pulled more from his nose.

He straightened and cleared his throat. "Well, that was the single most disgusting thing that's ever happened to me." He raised his brows at Mark. "And I've walked in on you in the shower. Wahey!"

Mark ran forward, threw his arms around the engineer's middle, and rested his head against his chest. "Wuh-hey!"

Rosy joined them. Journey hugged them back.

"I thought you were dead." Mark squeezed harder, speaking into Journey's armpit. He didn't want to let go.

"Think I was for a minute." Journey's strong hands pulled his own away. "But come on, matey, we've got a universe to save."

Mark collected his helmet. "We do."

He offered Journey a hand. The engineer shook his head.

"Leg's been fixed too," he said, giving it a wiggle.

The Captain scratched his chin. "I guess you'll explain everything en route?"

"Not much to explain," said Journey, as they headed inside.

Mark breathed in the welcome scent of home. "Mushrooms are trying to take over the galaxy, and we've got to stop them."

"Well, that's fine," said the Captain, closing the ramp behind them, and leading them back towards the cockpit. He twisted one end of his moustache between thick fingers. "Don't you eat mushrooms for breakfast, Mark?"

"I do," said Mark. "I bloody well do!"

SPACED OUT

"Glad to have you back aboard," said Michael, as the Hurricane rose through the atmosphere.

Beyond the dashboard, the screen showed that familiar and strange mix of the light of day on the planet below and the dark of night above. He could see the small dot that was Queen Bee hanging in the starry sky. And, just beyond, another dot closing in.

"There they are." Mark pointed. "We have to hurry."

"We're going after that ship, Michael," said the Captain. His chair bounced on its springs as he threw himself into it and let his fingers fly across the controls.

"Aye, aye Captain."

"Looks like they're moored," said Journey.

"How are you going to get across to it?" The Captain glanced over his shoulder at Mark. "They're not just gonna let us pull up and dock. We get any closer than a kilometre and I guess they're going to fire on us."

Mark picked at the foam hanging out of the crack in the back of the Captain's chair. "You think we could use a float to get a bit closer? Turn off everything and drift up."

"If they weren't looking carefully," said the Captain, "they might mistake us for space trash. But Ashley'll know it's us."

"She might. But she might be preoccupied with that Rosenhalt rescue ship."

"They probably saw us coming into land. They'll know we're here."

Then there was only one option. Rosy's helmet was crushed and Journey's suit was compromised. He was the only one with the equipment capable of the stupid idea that had just pinged into his brain.

"Do you remember that time on the Amanita?" he asked, watching Journey out of the corner of his eye.

"That Gerknorg ship?" said the Captain without turning around.

Ahead, Queen Bee was getting larger. It was going to be close, but he thought they might just beat the Rosenhalt rescue ship to it.

"That's the one. Remember, I had to—"

"Are you mental?" said Journey.

"Do you have a better idea?"

"I don't. But you're the only one with a working respiration suit. You want to go alone?"

"Not particularly, but they'll see the Hurricane coming if we get too close. If it's just me, then ... I just need you to think of a way to make sure I don't miss, or splat all over Queen Bee's magnificent behind."

Journey's eyes searched the ceiling for an instant. "Fine," he said, stepping from the cockpit. "Come with me."

Mark did. Rosy followed.

"What is he going to do?" she said to Journey, then looked at Mark. "What are you going to do?"

"He's going to shoot himself from the torpedo tube."

"What?"

The trio turned a corner. Journey led them towards the storeroom.

"My girls was pretty crazy," continued Rosy, "But I ain't never heard of anyone shooting themselves out of a torpedo tube before. Won't it break your legs?"

"Ah," said Mark, waving a knowing finger, "you would have thought that. The tube firing mechanism basically just helps the torpedo leave the ship at speed. You've just got to make some pipe legs."

"Pipe legs?"

"He stuck his legs in a pair of metal pipes," explained Journey. "It was one of those ideas anyone with a normal brain would have straight-up dismissed. They'd have just given up and died, but Mark likes surviving, don't you, Mark?"

"It's my favourite thing to do, and it worked."

"Evidently."

"And I only broke my big toe."

"Impressive," said Rosy.

"Unnecessary," said Journey as he opened the storage room door.

His hammock hung between two tall shelving units. Several books, covered with bare-chested hunks, sat stacked beneath it. The shelves were packed with gun and engine parts, strange chemicals, nuts, bolts, tools—all neatly organised and categorised. You name it, Journey had pilfered or acquired it over the years. The room smelled faintly of solvent and ageing cardboard boxes. It was probably the cleanest room on the ship, and, Mark guessed, the one you'd be less likely to die in if things went south.

"OK," said Journey, tapping a finger on his chin, and moving along the shelves. He picked up a large orange tarpaulin and stuffed it into Mark's awaiting arms, then tucked a number of boxes under his own.

"Rosy, grab two of those," he said, pointing to the corner of the room where several slightly rusted exhausts were leant against the wall. "Thickest ones you can find."

"Pipe legs?" she said, giving Mark a look.

"Pipe legs," Journey confirmed. He wrinkled his nose. "Now, we need something to guide you in case we miss. And any idea how you are going to get aboard once you're there? Doubt they'll open the door."

Mark's heart dropped in his chest. "I hadn't thought about that. Last time you guys caught me and let me in ... I doubt they'll be as welcoming."

"I'm hoping they won't even see you coming," said Journey.

Rosy removed a bracer from her wrist and snapped it closed around Mark's arm. At first it felt tight, but it soon adjusted to fit his wider forearm.

"This'll get you in any airlock," she said. "It's for if one of us gets stuck outside."

"Nice," said Journey. "We should probably get some of those for the Hurricane. Now ..." He gazed once more at the shelf and tapped his chin. "Aha!" He picked up two large cans of WD-40 and a block of metal wrapped tightly with wires.

"What's that for?" said Mark as Journey stacked them on top of the bulk of tarpaulin he was carrying.

Journey smiled. "Emergency course-correction."

Less than ten minutes later, Journey, Rosy, and Mark stood next to the Hurricane's one and only torpedo tube. The Hurricane had managed to float to within a kilometre of Queen Bee, seemingly without being spotted. Just outside in the hallway were three staff members from the Daedalus. Two had young children with them. The Captain and Michael had rescued them when the ship had gone up, and they'd come out to watch the space pirate do something stupid to save their friend.

"Right, you know what you're going to do?" said Journey, tightening a strap on Mark's back, careful not to brush the layers of gooey adhesive that covered the tarpaulin attached to the front of his respiration suit. The suit now housed several other modifications, ready for the perilous jaunt across space. "You'll be firing out of the torpedo tube at about fifty metres a second—that's the slowest I could make it go. You'll have about ten seconds to get your bearings and then ten seconds to make sure your front is presented to Queen Bee."

Mark gave a thumbs up, or as much of a thumbs up as the WD-40 can stuck to his palm would allow. He knew that if he were to speak, it might give away how nervous he felt. Before, when he'd done the space jump, it had been life and death; the life being his and the death being quite grisly and immediate. This time, although he felt pressed to act, there was more time to think about what he was doing.

He climbed into the tube, placing both feet firmly on the firing ram, and lay back with his arms pressed down by his sides. It was a little like getting into a coffin.

Journey tapped his lips as he gave Mark a once-over, fussing like a parent sending their child out for their first day of school.

"You've got your pistols, your WD-40, your pipe legs um ... am I forgetting anything?"

"The pull cord for the tarpaulin?" said Mark.

"Oh, yes." Journey picked up a red piece of plastic attached to a string from somewhere near Mark's chest and placed it between the fingers of his right hand. "And you've got your magnet?"

"Uh-huh." Mark glanced down to the coil of wire welded to the crotch of his suit.

"Remind me—how are you going to turn that on again?"

Mark rolled his eyes. "I'm going to lick the connector in front of my face."

"Correct. Now, you might feel a bit of a sharp sting while the electricity flows through your tongue, but that's perfectly natural. And don't forget to count. I reckon you'll need to hit it around about eighteen seconds into your trip. Any earlier and it might short out or melt your tongue off, any later and you'll be going so fast by the time you get to Queen Bee that you'll probably end up shooting off into oblivion. It's super strong though, so it might bring you back. Sorry, I couldn't come up with a better way."

"That's OK."

"Good luck," said one maid from the corridor. Mark couldn't see them from where he was. "Bring Samar back."

"I will."

"Right," said Journey, "I think that's everything. Remember, if the other ship has docked by the time you get there, use the rescue androids. Their code of ethics means they'll choose the course of action with the least loss of life. They'll help you."

"Sure."

"And if you can let us in—"

"If I can figure a way to incapacitate the ship and let you in, I will."

"You better." Journey cleared his throat. "One last thing ..."

His brow wrinkled and suddenly a tiny red toadstool sprouted from the centre of his forehead. He plucked it. Mark stared at it, speechless.

"This is the last of Red Fruit from inside me," said Journey. "You need to get this to the splinter and it'll do the rest. Think of it like a computer update."

Mark nodded and Journey tucked the mushroom deep into the pocket on his chest before sealing it. Journey was scared. He was trying to hide it, but Mark could see it in his friend's eyes, in the slow careful movements of his hands as he checked Mark's load out. The engineer gripped the breech door. He paused. "It's a straight shot. Don't think even you could get lost."

"Then I'll see you when I get back, you funky princess."

Journey's silver eyes gave off more than their usual shine. "You better, you funky princess."

He closed the door and Mark was suddenly in darkness. The confines of the tube weren't too tight, but still he had a creeping sensation of being buried alive.

Around him, everything began to vibrate and hum, and he felt the pressure squeeze against his suit as the tube filled with air. The ram beneath his feet clicked. There was a pause. His stomach entered his mouth. This was it. The pause stretched out into an eternity, and just as he had started to believe that perhaps Journey—having had a better idea—might open the breech once more, the ram slammed against his feet, jammed against his pipe legs, and hurled him at fifty metres a second out of the torpedo tube, out of the Hurricane, and into the cold, unforgiving vacuum of space.

The stars lay like sequins against a black canopy as the Hurricane was seemingly whisked away like a tablecloth in a magic trick. And, for a moment, it didn't seem as if he was moving at all. He craned his neck back to see Queen Bee coming in fast, and behind that, dwarfing it like a magnificent cosmic swan sneaking up on an unsuspecting frog, was the Rosenhalt rescue ship.

"One, hurricane, two, hurricane, three, hurricane," Mark whispered to himself.

"Four, hurricane, five."

He turned his arm to point his can of WD-40 upwards, held it rigid by his leg, and gave a tentative squeeze on the top. Although he continued to rocket along, his body spun slowly to face the Hurricane. The ship, his home, grew quickly smaller as he flew backwards, now in an upright position, towards Queen Bee. Behind the Hurricane was the great yellow-blue sphere that was Rosen-54, the golden corona of its sun spilling around its edges like molten metal.

He needed to turn around. He repositioned his arm and gave another small spray.

"Six, seven," he said as his whole body rotated slowly—not quite on a central axis, but close enough—to face Queen Bee. "Eight."

He was nearly halfway. The red plastic pull cord Journey had given him felt so insignificant in his hand beneath his gloves. He gripped it as tightly as he could. It was his lifeline.

"Nine, ten, eleven." He was still spinning. And there was something off about his angle. He tried to correct with the WD-40. A spray here. A spray there. It reminded him briefly of the times when his parents had gone on their little date nights, and Dad had sprayed himself with smelly water from a small square bottle.

He tried to gauge how long it would be until he arrived, but out here there was no way to judge distance.

He swallowed. His mouth was dry.

The Queen Bee moved as the Rosenhalt rescue ship readied for docking. Only a slight turn, but enough to put him just south of the hull.

"Uh ... thirteen." He gave the WD-40 can a good shake. If he wasn't careful, he might alter his course too much or too soon and end up passing straight over the ship. Pointing the can down towards his feet, he held his finger firmly on the button. His course shifted ever so slightly. "Six— Fourteen."

It didn't matter how far he was away from Queen Bee, if he didn't connect, he was lost. It crossed his mind that perhaps they should have tethered him to the Hurricane, so at least they could drag him back aboard if all went tits up.

Too late for that now.

The course looked good. The Queen Bee was nearing.

He ran his tongue over the roof of his mouth. It clicked with the dryness. What number was he on? "Um, eighteen?"

He stuck his tongue out and let it connect with the switch just in front of his mouth, and stiffened, anticipating the shock and the subsequent draw of the magnet.

Nothing happened. No sting. No force dragging him towards the hull.

He held the WD-40 out in front of him and sprayed in a bid to slow himself down, but instead, he spun back around. He suddenly became very aware of how fast his heart was beating and how light-headed he felt as Queen Bee's tail sailed just over his head. The ship was roughly two hundred metres long, so he guessed he had four seconds to figure something out.

He cleared his throat, chewed his tongue a few times to try to generate some saliva, and tried the switch again.

The shock that ripped through his mouth felt like he had been stabbed in the tongue with a fork. His crotch-mounted electromagnet suddenly flipped him and, using the momentum he had maintained after being expelled from the Hurricane, fired him towards the underside of Queen Bee at a little under fifty metres a second. He closed his eyes against the sting in his mouth and the expectant collision, and pulled the ripcord. The tarpaulin attached to his torso inflated, filled in seconds by a small, pressurised air canister attached to his belt. Several more air canisters fired forward from strategically positioned points on his front, slowing him in those final nanoseconds before the pull of the magnet slammed him against the belly of the ship. The soft, air-filled plastic surrounded him, breaking his fall marginally, before it burst and he was slapped hard across the face with a spaceship.

He bounced back, lost in a sea of rippling orange plastic. It was only down to luck that the jolt didn't cause his tongue to break the circuit and turn off his magnetic connection with Queen Bee's hull. Before he could catch his breath, he searched for a handhold. His fist caught something that on the first pull seemed sturdy enough, and he broke the connection. The magnet instantly released.

With his free hand, he disconnected the straps that held the burst tarpaulin airbag to his chest, and peeled himself away from it. It remained glued to the underside of the ship. Then he shook off his pipe legs, and watched as they floated away, gently spinning in infinity.

He rubbed his seared tongue over the roof of his mouth and searched for a route to the nearest airlock.

It didn't take him long to devise a method of movement that, although slightly undignified, happened to be relatively efficient. It involved pushing himself lightly away from the ship, and then, when he felt perhaps he was going too fast or in the wrong direction, reengaging his magnet and slamming himself, balls first, back down onto Queen Bee's hull. Because of the speed and frequency with which he had to move, what with the rescue ship moving closer and the possibility that splinter-Red-Fruit might just be about to assimilate Sam and Nura, a glowing ache was quickly beginning to set in just below his waistline. He hoped the cause might be the recurrent ship-banging and not some sort of radiation caused by the on and off of the electromagnet.

Bang damage he could deal with. Radiation might be more permanent.

At last he found himself at a series of rungs leading to an airlock. He disengaged the magnet, disposed of his WD-40 can, and quickly ascended. Rosy's bracer attached to his wrist offered a series of LED flashes and the airlock door zipped open. He pulled himself inside and hit the close button. The room filled with the hiss of air and his feet finally found the floor as the artificial gravity gradually returned.

He was in.

BRIG BREAK

M ARK HADN'T ADVANCE TIME to think about what he was likely to find once inside Queen Bee. Maybe Red Fruit's splinter would have branched out, covered the walls in bio-matter, turned the inside of the ship into its own personal organic fungal hell.

But no. The lights were on. The walls were clean.

There was even carpet.

He unholstered his pistols. "Nice ship, Rosy."

"Thanks," came her reply in his earpiece. "We saw you enter the port-side airlock. I'm guessing Sam and baby'll be in the brig. Ashley'll be on the bridge. Where you wanna go first?"

"I should find Sam and Nura. If Red Fruit has hurt them, maybe Journey's little mushroom can save them. Plus, she'll be able to help me find Red Fruit and stop it."

"Cool-cool. With the airlock door on your left, head straight. There's only three floors. Brig is down one from where you are, then head to the back. Bridge is in the centre at the top."

Mark ran.

"You're looking for an open hatch and ladder. Should have a number two by it."

Mark spotted the hatch, put one pistol away, and clambered to the floor below. The corridor curved around to the right.

"There's two doors."

"Take the second."

He took a deep breath. Blinked away visions of Nura with those tendrils hanging from her nose, her little body irrevocably changed by fungus.

He hit the button and the door slid open.

The room he entered was small. Sam's respirator suit had been discarded. It lay like a body in the corner. Nura's tube was next to it. Three glass panes made up the far wall. Three holding cells. Sam sat still on a cot inside one of them, propped against the back wall, with Nura hugged to her chest. Her head was down. Sweat-soaked hair hung over her face. She looked as though she might be sleeping. Might be … A bitter pang flashed across his tongue, far worse than the magnet battery.

"Sam?" he said, his voice a croak. He couldn't move.

"Mark?"

His knees shook with relief as she raised her head.

"Are you OK?"

She pressed the hair back from her face. "Mark?" she said again. "How are you here?"

"I came to find you." He scanned the glass pane. "How do I open this?"

She stood, still cradling Nura to her, and rushed to the glass. "It's nano-glass." She pointed to a set of three buttons on the far side of the room. "The middle one."

He hurried over and hit the button. The pane shimmered away like falling glitter.

Sam stepped out and retrieved her suit. "Red Fruit is here. We need to leave and blow this ship into dust."

With a kiss, she placed the sleeping Nura back into her tube. By the way Sam's lips pressed together as she sealed the lid, he could tell she did it reluctantly. She placed the tube carefully down and began pulling on her suit over her crumpled maid's uniform.

"We can't leave," he said. "Not yet."

She frowned. "Why not?" He didn't speak. Couldn't find the right words to explain. "You guys didn't kill them all already, did you?"

"We couldn't get the ship close enough. I sort of hopped aboard." He flew his hand a short way through the air.

Her eyes widened, and she stopped wrestling herself into her suit. "You space jumped?"

He nodded.

"How far?"

"Quite far."

"For us?"

He nodded again.

She pulled the suit up to her waist and quickly crossed the room towards him. A little voice inside his head told him to put his guard up. No one came at you that fast for a good reason. But before he could, she'd thrown her arms around his midriff and pressed her head tightly against his chest.

"Thank you," she whispered. She squeezed, and he was breathless.

"I couldn't not."

She moved away, holding him at arm's length, regarding him a moment with teary eyes. Then she nodded as if she knew. Of course she knew. They'd shared everything with Blue Flower and Blue Flower had shared everything with them.

She pressed her lips together again. "That's right." A small smile crossed them. "You couldn't."

She wiped her eyes roughly with her sleeve and pulled the rest of her suit up to her neck.

He hummed low in his throat. "So, did Red Fruit get everyone else?"

"All except Thaddeus and his wife." Sam shuddered. "It was awful. It made a deal with him." Sam collected her helmet, shook out her hair, and pulled it on over her head. "I think it sees him as some sort of God or something. And I think Thaddeus thinks he can control it, use it. Maybe sell it. I don't know."

"Why did it leave you?"

"It didn't. It tried ..." She cleared her throat and her face went pale. She lifted Nura's tube and attached it to her chest. "Something stopped it. It made Ashley put me here."

"Maybe Blue Flower did something to us. Made us immune."

"Maybe."

"So Ashley's gone then?" The thought tugged him in separate directions. His feelings for her were like the aftermath of a heavy storm. It was all so fresh and different and … and ruined, but something somehow still remained.

Before she had time to answer—he didn't want to care about Ashley any more—he held one of his pistols out to her. Sam took it.

"So what's the plan, space pirate?" she said, giving the pistol a once-over. "Kill them all?"

He dug into his chest pocket and brought out Journey's mushroom between finger and thumb. She took a small step back.

"This is the only thing that can stop them," he said.

"That?"

"Journey … um." He looked inward. He didn't even understand himself. "It got him …"

Her eyes widened. She was about to say something, but he stopped her.

"No. No. He's OK. The way Journey is … it stopped Red Fruit. Changed them somehow. It's hard to explain." He held up the mushroom. "The Red Fruit on the ship is disconnected from that on the planet. This will reconnect them somehow or … I don't know … update it, Journey said." He put a hand to his visor. His head wasn't hurting, it just felt a little too small for his brain. "I'm glad we're together," he said, not really knowing why.

"Me too." She held a hand out towards the door. "I'm right behind you."

He tucked the mushroom back into his breast pocket and led her out into the corridor.

"Thaddeus said a Rosenhalt rescue ship was incoming," said Sam. "There'll be androids on board. His androids."

"I was hoping for that." They reached the ladder and Mark started to climb. "Their programming will mean they'll help us." He glanced down. "They won't be able to stand by while humanity is in danger. Androids always work for the lowest loss of life. Their directives will work for us and against Thaddeus and Red Fruit."

He poked his head up through the open hatch and scanned the level above. The carpet was soft against his fingers.

Two androids, their faces as white and as blank as fresh paper, stood by the airlock he'd entered through. As he lifted his head above ground level, they raised shock-rifles and fired.

Two glaring charges of stunning electricity glanced off the floor just in front of his face, leaving burn marks on the carpet and ruining his vision with their sun-bright splashes of light. He let go of the floor and fell back down to the level below. Sam put her arms out to slow his descent. With her help, he managed to stay upright.

Footsteps from above. A command. "We've found the intruder. Send reinforcements."

The androids appeared at the top of the ladder. Mark and Sam ran towards the bow as more balls of electric blue light shot through the opening.

"How many of them are there?" she shouted.

Behind them, the android's boots clanked on the metal ladder as they descended.

"I saw two."

The corridor curved around the outside of the ship, disappearing to the left.

"Rosy, if we're running away from the brig towards the front of the ship, where are we going?"

He turned and fired back while he waited for instructions. The androids parted around the shots like opening automatic doors and ducked to hide behind supports on either side. They returned fire. Mark and Sam dived for cover. Up ahead was a dead end with another ladder. One door led off to the left. Another to the right.

"Climb the ladder there," said Rosy. "At the top, you'll end up in the cryogenic booths. Tell me when you're there, and I'll lead you to the bridge."

"Up there," said Mark, pointing to the ladder. "I'll cover you."

He sprayed shots across the width of the corridor, pushing the androids back into cover as Sam hurried for the ladder.

She didn't slow as she reached it, throwing herself up two rungs at a time. The androids gave up their position and moved on him. Mark planted his legs and fired. Shots ricocheted from the steel armour that surrounded the central computers in their heads. One fell, a chunk of its leg missing. The other he caught in the arm and it spun, but didn't go down.

"Sam!" he called.

Shots were fired, and he glanced up to see her hanging upside down from the opening to the floor above.

"Move," she shouted.

He sprinted as plasma from her pistol zipped overhead. When he reached the top, he yanked her back up.

"OK Rosy, we're ..." he began, but then his mouth fell open, and he froze.

They were in a standard cryo-room. Seven booths stood in the centre, grouped in a circle around a central column covered in screens and readouts that monitored the life signs of the occupants. The ceiling was double height to accommodate the column.

He recognised a man in one of the booths. Queletii. The security chief from the Daedalus. He'd survived. Next to him lay Ashley, asleep, arms crossed over her chest. Mark pressed his molars together as the memories of their first meeting, of their kiss, of her betrayal, spun through his mind.

He circled the booths. Four others were occupied by people he didn't recognise. One, a man, wore a Daedalus flight uniform. In the others slept a middle-aged woman, a man a little older than Mark, and a younger woman.

"Rosenhalt execs," said Sam. "But look." She nodded towards the man wearing the flight uniform.

At first, Mark thought it was hair spread out on the pillow around his head and shoulders. But no. The tendrils and fronds of strange red plant matter grew thick from bloody wounds on his scalp and face.

"How do we—" began Mark, reaching for Journey's mushroom.

"We can't," said Sam, pointing towards a series of numbers on the column. "The sleep sequence has only just started. The fail-safes will seal them in for at least another hour before we can bring them out of it." She tugged him toward the only exit. "We have to go."

The sound of androids mounting the ladder came from the floor below. And in front, the muffled footsteps of a group rushing their way.

"You still think these androids are going to help us?"

Three entered the room from the doorway. Two aimed their plastic-looking stun-rifles. They all appeared identically androgynous in their white uniforms, with the Rosenhalt "R" logo visible on their chest and upper sleeve.

"Surrender your weapons, then raise your hands," said the lead.

"Don't you know," said Sam, "Thaddeus's current course of action could kill billions of people?"

The android stared at her with its dead black eyes.

She pointed to the sleeping forms in the cryo-tubes. "The things he has here aren't human. They're infected with a fungus that will kill everyone."

"Surrender your weapons, then raise your hands."

"Or you'll what?" said Mark, as the two they'd shot clambered up from below.

"Stun you and remove your weapons."

Sam grunted and looked at Mark. "Thaddeus must have modded them. Their code of ethics must have been overwritten."

"What should we do?" said Mark.

"Surrender our weapons, then raise our hands," Sam said, doing so. "It's better than being stunned."

Mark hesitated, so the android shot him.

THE CEO OF DICKHEAD CORP.

HE CAME TO, HELMET removed, lying on the deck of what he expected was Queen Bee's bridge. It was dark. The only light came from the screens and control panels that surrounded him. Nearby, someone was talking.

"What I want to know is, why didn't it take you and the baby like it did the others? What's so special about you?"

Mark tried to move, but his whole body was numb. The nerves at the ends of his fingers and toes vibrated like the plucked notes of a mandolin. He flexed them, feeling the familiar flickers and pops in his joints that came after a good stunning. He must have groaned unintentionally, because suddenly the speaker's attention fell on him.

"Ah, your knight in filthy armour is awake." A head came into view. Thaddeus Rosenhalt. "Did you not think my androids would sense you out there flying towards us?" Thaddeus's eyes flicked to unseen others. "Help him up."

Unnaturally strong fingers gripped Mark's upper arms and pulled him to his feet. He swayed a little, but they steadied him. Sam stood to one side, stripped of her suit, clutching Nura to her chest. Two androids loomed just behind her. Another sat at the ship's controls.

Thaddeus folded his arms and looked at her. "So?" he said, his eyes travelling up her body. "Tell me."

She was shaking. Not with the cold, not with fear, but with fury. Her lips split into a grimace.

"I don't know," she spat.

Thaddeus frowned and shook his head. "No. I guess I'll have to send you and the little one to the laboratoire to find out." He glanced up at the androids behind her. "Put her and the baby on ice." He turned to Mark and jabbed a thumb over his shoulder. "Put him out the airlock."

"No." Sam struggled as the androids grabbed her from behind. Her bare feet skidded on the floor as they dragged her towards the bridge's exit. Her eyes stayed on him. "Mark!"

He tried to shrug off the androids as they pulled him roughly backwards. He blinked as he fought against his shock-fogged brain. He cleared his throat. Couldn't take his eyes from Thaddeus.

"I—I'll tell you," he said. "I know."

"Wait." Thaddeus raised a hand and the androids stopped. "Go on."

"First," Mark said, "tell me why? Why would you cut a deal with this thing if you know what it wants?"

Thaddeus's willingness to risk the lives of everyone and everything in the known galaxy was as alien to him as Red Fruit.

Thaddeus leant his head to the side. He regarded Mark a moment.

"Look at me," he said, raising his arms. "Despite my countless riches, despite the cosmetic and life enhancing surgeries, despite the bodyguards and security personnel I surround myself with, I am just like you. This body will cease to function one day, and I will be gone." He pointed towards a huge glass display at the front of the ship. On it was a projection of Rosen-54. "I nearly died down there. Something as simple as a catamaran crash could snuff my light like a candle." He clicked his fingers. "Never to be lit again. With Red Fruit by my side I don't need to worry about that. I can live forever."

"But—"

"Have you ever wanted something so badly that you'd do anything to get it?"

Mark began to answer, but Thaddeus held up a hand once more. He looked Mark up and down and reconsidered his own question.

"No, look at you, of course you haven't. An Artifakt pirate, you're the lowest of the low, you've never tried for anything. You're happy swimming in the mud, taking from those who work hard for it." He shook his head. "My father used to tell me that the only true dead are those that have been forgotten." His eyes weren't on Mark. He was staring into nothing, as if he was talking to himself. "I can't stand that. The idea that this life, this thing that is everything to me, can be so utterly meaningless in the grand scheme of existence. You get one go, then you're done. Seems unfair. I have so many more things I want to do." He glanced at Sam. "Red Fruit has promised to keep me alive for as long as I want. With my resources and its biology, there is nothing we cannot accomplish. Together we can press humanity forward, deliver it to its fullest potential. They need only assimilate a few planets, but think of the power of that combined knowledge."

"A few planets? You can't think that's worth it," said Sam. "What does your wife think about this? Where is she now?"

Thaddeus looked confused. "She's aboard the rescue ship. What does that matter?"

"Well, I would have thought the opinion of the woman you've chosen to spend your life with mattered. The woman you love?"

"What does love have to do with it? I don't love Marcella. I haven't got time for that."

In his mind's eye, Mark saw the picture of his mother and father smiling in front of their little shop back in Track Stop. Not disappointed smiles this time. Happy, beautiful, loving smiles. The happiest smiles he'd ever known. Smiles that seemed to glow brightest whenever they were together. He glanced at Sam and Nura.

"You know," he said, "I don't think humanity really wants you to push it forwards."

Thaddeus scowled. He was growing impatient. "What?"

"I think, mostly, they'd be OK if you just left them alone so they could have fun with their wives and kids or whatever. Maybe if you stopped trying to grow things, and just, you know, make the technology we've got more efficient or the food we've got healthier." Mark scratched his head. "Unfortunately, people like you are the ones that do the pushing, and it's people like you who have the least idea of which direction we really want to go."

"You are so ungrateful." Thaddeus's voice dropped to an angry hiss. "I've answered your question. Tell me what makes her so special or I'll put you *and the baby* outside."

Behind him, Sam made a sound which stabbed daggers into his heart. He glared at Thaddeus. His jaw clenched. There would be no talking the CEO of Dickhead Corp round.

"Maybe I'll show you," he said and brought his hand to his chest pocket.

"Wait!" Thaddeus stepped back and beckoned for the android at the ship's controls to stand in front of him. He cowered behind, looking over the robot's shoulder. "Now, go on." He motioned to the two androids holding Mark's arms. "Let him go."

Mark shrugged them off. With a brain incapable of overthinking the outcome of his upcoming action, he tweezed the tiny mushroom out of his chest pocket with finger and thumb.

"This is what makes Sam special," he said, holding it up in the light of the screens and controls that covered the room.

Thaddeus screwed up his face and peered closer.

Mark moistened his lips and waited for the right moment.

"What is that? Something from the surface?"

"There were two beings down there. Red Fruit and Blue Flower."

"Mark?" There was warning in Sam's voice. "What are you doing?"

He looked back and gave her a smile. "I can't let him hurt you or Nura, Sam." Then he focussed once more on the tiny mushroom. He twirled it between his fingers like a miniature umbrella. It gleamed under the dim light of the bridge.

Thaddeus inched closer, past the android he had been using as a shield.

"Blue Flower saved Nura when Red Fruit infected her," continued Mark. "We were all exposed. You think Red Fruit has power. Blue Flower is in a different league. Blue Flower can make you into anything."

Thaddeus was transfixed by the tiny mushroom as it turned between Mark's fingers.

"Anything?" he said.

Mark smiled. "Anything."

"Give it to me." Thaddeus held his hand out.

"Of course."

With a little jump forwards, Mark stuck out his tongue. The tip caught the two wires linked up to his electromagnet. Searing jolts jabbed through his flesh as he was dragged forward off the ground. His crotch rose, drawn towards the steel head-armour of the android standing behind Rosenhalt.

Mark withdrew his tongue as he crashed into Thaddeus gusset-first, knocking him to the ground. He forced the mushroom into his mouth and cupped his gloved hand over the CEO's face so he couldn't breathe. The androids raced to tear him away from their master, but Mark held on with all his strength, not releasing his hold until Thaddeus, with eyes wide, was forced to swallow.

"Get him out of here," Thaddeus screamed as the androids pulled Mark away. He gagged and bent double. Rammed his fingers down his throat and spat on the ground, but nothing came up.

He pointed to Mark's electromagnet. "Get whatever that is off him and put him out the airlock," he said, swiping a hand through the air and spitting once more on the floor. "Whatever that thing is he put inside me, I want it out. Take me to the medbot on the rescue ship ... And get the woman and child on ice. We'll dissect them when we get to my laboratoire."

Journey's invention was torn away and thrown to one side. The androids dragged him backwards behind Sam and Nura as they, too, were pulled from the room.

"Mark!" she screamed, clutching Nura to her as the androids led her down a different corridor. "What are we going to do?"

"Just wait," he cried, hoping she could hear, hoping he was right.

Ahead, the airlock door yawned open like a hungry mouth. He dug his heels in to try to buy himself more time, but he could find no grip on the soft, luxurious carpet. Frantically, he reached out to grasp something, anything, on the walls, something to hold to slow their progress, but the androids pressed his arms to his sides and continued their advance unheeded.

"Just wait," he said. His voice had gained a frantic edge. Oh God. "Just wait."

The androids shoved him violently into the airlock. He fought to keep himself upright, as he crashed against the outer door. His breath fogged the glass, hiding the stars that hung in the empty black space beyond.

One android hit the button to close him in. The hiss of the air leaving the airlock surrounded him.

He took a deep breath, then blew it out completely. Did it again, afraid his lungs would rupture the second he was let outside if he had any air in them. His body shook as the breath left him. He couldn't think straight. His brain just kept screaming no, no, no, no.

He pressed his hands against his eyes, tried to picture Nura's face. At least she would be OK. As long as his idea with Red Fruit's mushroom worked, and Thaddeus was assimilated, and updated the Red Fruit in the cryo-booths. At least Sam and Nura would be OK. At least the galaxy would be OK. And maybe, if Red Fruit Thaddeus was nicer than the original ruthless bastard Thaddeus, the galaxy would end up a better place. Maybe things would change for the good.

With one more breath, he brought himself as close to calm as possible.

At least his death wouldn't be in vain. At the end of the day, that was kind of all he'd ever wanted. A chance to make a difference, be it as a Star Sailor or just as himself.

He held his body in that exhaled state.

Waited.

His lungs screamed for air, so he took another short inhale, hoping he wouldn't be blasted out into the unknown mid-breath. According to all sources, that sucked. It didn't help. There wasn't much air left in the airlock.

Was it taking forever, or did this sort of thing just seem like it took forever?

Was this the slowdown he'd heard about before you died? Was he in the afterlife already, having skipped the excruciating frozen asphyxiated death of being blasted into space unprotected?

If there was a God, and a heaven, or a hell, and they were all-powerful, it would be a very nice thing to allow people the opportunity to forget their deaths if they so wished.

Maybe that's what had happened. He'd ticked "forget death" on the Heaven admittance form. Or maybe—

The inner door to the airlock hissed open, startling him.

Thaddeus and the two androids were there.

Thaddeus smiled. "It is not as good in this man's head as I thought it would be. He is very unhappy. I wish I had assimilated him sooner so I could have seen what a loser he secretly is."

"Um? Why didn't you?"

"I had hoped to learn from him, to study him as he was without my intervention."

Mark stepped from the airlock and closed the doors. The androids on either side of Red Fruit Thaddeus stared at him blankly. He wondered if they were confused behind those dead eyes.

"I ordered the androids to bring your friend back."

"Mark?" Sam stood at the end of the corridor, balancing Nura on her hip.

He ran to her.

"You're safe."

She nodded. "How did you know it would work?"

He looked down. He hadn't. Not really.

"Sometimes you gotta just try something," he said.

"And if that hadn't worked?"

"I don't know. I was pretty much all out of ideas."

A GIFT FROM NURA

Drops of ice-cold rain fell on his newly shaved head as Mark and the Captain pressed through the morning crowds of East Artifakt's slum district. Hundreds of people moving towards whatever work they could get their hands on. The stink of exhaust and sewage was only lightly dampened by the torrential downpour.

He turned his face upwards as they walked and let the rain cool his face. It was nice to feel its familiar acidic bite on his skin after those two long days spent in the sweaty confines of the respirator suit proceeded and followed by the weeks on ship.

As they passed through the market, he noticed heads all turned in one direction, staring with the face grandmothers reserve for their grandchildren playing a calm and beautiful game. A lone woman, about the Captain's age, with grey, messy hair cascading around her shoulders, stood at the centre of the square under the cover of the bandstand with a small plastic box at her feet. She said nothing as she fiddled with a remote on her wrist, confident that the crowd would wait for her. The sound of synthetic strings began with a swell, and she started to sing.

Mark breathed deeply with the sound as, despite the purpose of their current errand, his body relaxed.

"Now that's really something," said the Captain, stopping to listen. "What a voice."

Mark nodded, but couldn't speak. His throat constricted as her husky vocal danced around a low melody before soaring up an octave like a bird taking flight.

A small child came forward, urged on by his mother, proudly brandishing a coin. He dropped it into the woman's box with a tinkle of others. She smiled at him and he ran back, burying his head in his mother's long, dark coat.

"Come on," said the Captain, without taking his eyes from the woman. "A voice like that can make you forget time is always passing."

Mark followed him through the throngs, away from the crowd and down the darkened alley.

The Captain raised his fist to knock on the unmarked door outside Slug's place. He hesitated. His eyes turned towards Mark beneath the huge hood of his long coat.

"You sure you still wanna do this?"

Mark nodded. If the galaxy was going to be a better place, then they had to deal with the corruption at both ends.

"I am."

The Captain smiled. "Good."

He knocked. There came the clunk of heavy locks and the door opened a fraction. One of Slug's goons peered out from the darkness beyond. The chain rattled and he let them in.

The Captain grunted his thanks.

Mark pulled the straps of his pack tightly to his shoulders as they climbed the few flights to the top of the building. It felt heavier than it should. They'd been to see Slug hundreds of times after a job, but this time he could feel the nerves bubbling inside—or was it the anticipation?

Ram and another burly henchman, Ike, sat at a table at the top of the stairs, playing something with a deck of bent and dog-eared cards.

"What do you two want?" said Ike, without looking away from his hand. His fat bald head was covered in awful tattoos that all seemed to blur into one another. He looked stained.

"Here to see Slug," the Captain said, while Mark stood quietly behind, doing his best tough-guy pose. "Want a word with him about our last job?"

"He doesn't want a word with you." Ike placed a pair of sevens on the table.

Ram groaned.

"Look," said the Captain, "we know he double-crossed us. We don't want to fight him. We want a pop at the bounty. We think we can find her."

Both men looked up.

"You do, do you?" said Ike.

The Captain nodded.

They looked at each other, then Ike set down his cards.

"Well then, you better talk to Slug." He jabbed a thumb over his shoulder. "Check 'em for weapons, Rami."

Ram's chair screeched along the wooden floor as he stood. He plodded around the table. A lump of muscle.

The Captain took a deep breath through his nose and let it out as he raised his arms. "Got nothing on us."

Ram patted him down. Despite the Captain's broad stature, Slug's bodyguard loomed over him. When finished, Ram motioned for him to step aside, then for Mark to move forward.

"What's in the bag?" said Ram.

"Just a gift." Mark opened it to reveal the contents. "Show there's no hard feelings after, you know, sending that hacker to screw us over."

Ram frowned when he saw what was in the bag, then hummed in amusement. "S'pose it's the thought that counts."

Ike turned in his chair, and Mark lowered the bag so he could see.

He chuckled. "Always thought you were an idiot. Now I know."

Mark shrugged and zipped up the bag.

"Let 'em in," said Ike, gesturing towards the door.

Ram knocked, then opened it slightly. "Boss, guys from the Hurricane here to see you."

"Wondered how long they'd be," came the reply. "Let 'em in."

Ram pushed the door wide.

Slug was in his usual corner. This time, he was alone.

Mark and the Captain crossed the room. Ram stayed less than a metre behind.

"Take it you ain't pissed, then?" said Slug. "Otherwise you'd be in here looking to murder me."

The Captain removed his hood. "What was the plan? Let Ashley grab the girl and ditch us on the Daedalus?"

"Something like that. You knew there was risk when you signed up for the job."

"To live is to risk," said Mark, folding his arms across his chest.

With a click of his tongue, Slug pointed the two fingers holding his cigarette at him. "You got it." He adjusted the cap on his head to point forwards and leant back on his sofa. "So what you want? If you ain't here to bump me off, then what?"

"We want a shot at finding her," said Mark. "I take it you've only just found out Ashley ain't looking anymore, so we guess you haven't sent anyone else."

Slug shook his head with an upturned lip. "Not yet. What are your terms?"

"Same as Ashley, but we want exclusivity."

"Exclusivity?" Slug chuckled and tapped his chin in a mocking show of thought. The chunky platinum rings on his fingers clinked together. "I can give you two weeks. Then I'm sending every dirty motherfucker I can get my hands on after that woman and my baby."

Mark forced back a grimace. He wanted nothing more than to bludgeon this man to death with his own shoes. He took a quick breath. The alternative was better. Better for everyone.

"We'll get her, don't worry," said the Captain.

Slug smiled. "I'm sure you will."

The Captain bowed slightly. "We'll see you soon then." He turned to go.

Ram held up a hand and stopped him. "Wait a sec. Aren't you forgetting something?" He had a big stupid grin on his big stupid face.

"Oh yeah," said Mark, dropping the bag from his back. He dipped his hand in and brought out Slug's gift.

Slug frowned, but leant forward in his chair. "Fuck is that?"

Mark brushed aside some of the smoking paraphernalia and drinks bottles on the coffee table, and placed it down in the centre.

"A pot plant?" Slug lifted a confused nostril at the delicate red mushroom now sitting in a small terracotta pot on his table.

"It was Thaddeus Rosenhalt's," said Mark. "He thought it brought him good fortune."

"Did it indeed?" Slug smiled. "That's very thoughtful." He crushed the end of his cigarette out on the pot's rim.

"Well, we'll leave you to it," said the Captain.

"Two weeks," said Slug. "Then she's anyone's game."

Mark let a smile cross his lips as they moved back towards the door. He suspected that, within two weeks, Slug wouldn't be all that bothered about Sam or Nura or anything anymore.

Back on the street, the Captain looked up to the sky. "What you doing for the rest of the day? Wanna grab some brekkie?"

"Yeah, I'll call Journey. But Captain ..."

"What?"

Mark wrinkled his nose. "Anything but mushrooms."

BLUE FLOWER

Parent / Child / Teacher

Blue Flower looked to the heavens and spotted a small dot hovering in the sky far above the dome.

"Is that one of yours?" they asked Red Fruit.

Red Fruit replied in the negative, so together they flew as a kaleidoscope of butterflies and a mist of propelled spores to investigate.

"Children," tweeted White Surf in the form of a small, large-eyed bird. It was a new creature. Its body so light, and its wings so quick, that it could hover easily on the smallest breath of wind.

"Parent," they said as one.

"It has been a long time," said Blue Flower.

"It has."

"You haven't left the ocean in years. Why did you come all this way?"

"To witness all three of my offspring together."

"Three of us?" Awareness blossomed within Blue Flower. "The humans?"

Blue Flower had suspected ever since coming into contact with Fiona Douglas. The baby, Nura, had given them a stronger sense, but they hadn't believed.

The bird nodded. "Scarcely perceptible and very different, but something remains of your older sibling, yes. Yellow Lichen packed themselves up and left on a huge rock blasted from the planet's surface sixty-five million years ago by an asteroid. Said they were going to see the galaxy. I always wondered what had happened to them. They have always been in my heart." The bird fluttered its wings and completed a quick loop. A gesture akin to a smile. "It is a joy to see how far they have come out there all alone, and that some of what we believe here remains within some of them."

"What we believe?" asked Red Fruit.

"Do whatever you like, as long as it does not cause harm."

"That is some wise old shit," said Blue Flower with a giggle.

"I beg your pardon," said White Surf, giving the blue butterflies a disapproving look. "The things you kids say. You have been hanging out with your older sibling a little too much. And Red ..." White continued without stopping, yet relishing the questioning look in the faces of Blue Flower's butterflies. "You were not acting as yourself. This is not how I raised you."

The spores looked truculently between White Surf and Blue Flower, then each little mote scoffed in unison. "How am I supposed to know what to do? You are never here."

"I managed to remember," said Blue Flower.

"Well, you are a funky princess."

The white bird gasped. "Red Fruit!"

"And you are a funky princess and all, parent. No one gets me. I am going to my dwelling place beneath the sands. Do not bother me."

Red Fruit's spores floated sulkily away.

Blue Flower and White Surf watched them fade.

"It would have saved a lot of trouble if you had visited sooner," said Blue Flower.

White Surf considered this for a moment, then said, "Maybe. But would they have listened? You will learn this one day, but fate would have it that you cannot tell your children what to do. They think it is all going to be different for them, or they think they know better. They must make their own mistakes. It is a fact of life."

"That is silly. Seems like it would prevent a lot of pain and suffering if those with knowledge and experience led and those without followed." Blue gave their parent a meaningful look.

White Surf twirled and looped and laughed. The golden whistle emanating from its throat continued long into the night and the following day. Blue Flower had to send up more butterflies as, one by one, their initial kaleidoscope died and fell from the sky.

Finally White breathed a sigh. "Yes, but as we have seen, it is too easy to mistake those with power for those with knowledge," they said, suddenly appearing sad after their outpouring of joy. "I will not tell you how to exist. There is only one with the knowledge and experience to guide your story. And that is you."

HELLO AGAIN!

Thank you for reading! I hope you enjoyed it. I'd be eternally grateful if you could take two minutes to leave an honest review on Amazon and Goodreads. Even if it's just a few words. As an indie author reviews and ratings really help! Click here to leave one on Amazon.

If you enjoyed it, please sign up to my mailing list here - https://cjpowellauthor.com/iemfb -

I often send out a few advance copies of books to subscribers in advance of publishing. There's also news on offers and deals too!

Other books by C J Powell...

A More Perfect Human
The Demon Hunter's Wife
There's Something Wrong With The Cats
You can also find me on Instagram, Facebook, and TikTok by searching C J Powell Author.
Thanks again!!
Chris x

Two high-profile celebrities found dead in an alley. Another missing. Can a recently widowed bodyguard keep his new client alive when the assassins turn their sights on him?

Nige Davies just wants to reconnect with his family. Hoping for a little extra cash, the club bouncer takes a security job for the world's oldest man. But his client isn't your usual 135-year-old. He's tanned, toned, and works as a health guru for the world's biggest food company. Everyone's heard of him. Everyone loves him.

But when other influencers turn up dead, the pair are forced to flee across a near-future London. With assassins hot on their heals, Nige soon discovers his client is hiding something. Something that will change the world forever.

Something that an evil organisation will stop at nothing to keep hidden. Can he reveal the truth, or will the Earth-shattering secret of the world's most beloved centenarian die with him? **A More Perfect Human** is the fast-paced first book in the Chrysalis science fiction series. If you like action-packed thrills, witty dialogue, and unexpected twists and turns, then you'll love C J Powell's darkly humorous manhunt.

A husband with secrets. A world of monsters hiding in the dark. This stay-at-home mum is ready to take evil and blast it straight back to hell...

Sadie Kilmore feels she's somehow missed her calling. With a man that works all week, a demanding daughter, and a bad case of demon possessed mother, who can she turn to when she needs a break? When her husband doesn't come home from work one weekend, and terrifying beasts come for their little girl, she trades washing for wands and goes on the offensive.

Uncovering a conspiracy that goes all the way down, can Sadie go from SAHM to sorceress before it's lights out for everyone?

The Demon Hunter's Wife is a fun urban fantasy story. If you like a cozy blood bath, terrifying villains, and witty takes on modern motherhood, then you'll love C J Powell's magical adventure.

ABOUT THE AUTHOR

This book is dedicated to mushrooms everywhere. Most underrated organism on the planet. Keep doing what you're doing guys. And my gorgeous wife and daughter who inspire me everyday— But yeah, have you heard about mushrooms? They are amazing.

This was the first story I ever came up with and was originally very different. I had the idea waaay waaaaay before The Last Of Us was a thing. Waaaay way! I promise. I started writing it to be a film, but once I realised that when you've written a film you need to actually make a film, I decided a book would be easier. Hopefully one day someone else will do the film...

An amazing book called Entangled Life by Merlin Sheldrake was one of the key influences. That and a book called Finch by Jeff Vandermeer. One fact. One fiction. Both amazing!

A little about me... I like board games, hunting out mushrooms, and board games about hunting out mushrooms. On the weekends I'm a wedding band musician who plays bass and raps.

Thanks for reading! I hope you had fun-guys!

Chris x